W9-BON-081

More praise for
ASHANA

"The rape of innocence was never more hauntingly portrayed than in this story of Aleksandr Baranov, the embodiment of Russian imperial adventuring, and Ashana, his unwilling concubine and a fierce protector of the ancient lores of her people."

JAMES A. MICHENER

"A formidable task of viewing North America's settlement through the eyes of the vanquished rather than the victor is vividly achieved in ASHANA."

Seattle Post-Intelligencer

"The broad, sweeping tale enlightens and astonishes. This is a strong rendering of the exploitation of native Alaskan culture by foreigners."

Publishers Weekly

ASHANA

E.P. Roesch

BALLANTINE BOOKS • NEW YORK

Grateful acknowledgement is made to the following for permission to reprint previously published material.

ALASKA NATIVE LANGUAGE CENTER: Adaptations of the "Raven Story" and the "Foggy Woman Story" from *Dena'ina Sukdu'a III Dghiliq, Sukdu'a* by Joan Tenenbaum. Reprinted by permission of the Alaska Native Language Center. University of Alaska, Fairbanks. ALASKA PACIFIC UNIVERSITY PRESS: Adaptation of "Spider Woman and her Two Sisters" from *Athabaskan Stories* by Alice Brean. Published by Alaska Pacific University Press (formerly Alaska Methodist University). Reprinted by permission. HARPER AND ROW, PUBLISHERS, INC.: Excerpt from *Eurasian Folk and Fairy Tales* by I. F. Bulatkin. Copyright © 1965 by Criterion. Reprinted by permission of Harper and Row, Publishers, Inc. UNIVERSITY OF OKLAHOMA PRESS: Adaptation of the "Second Beaver Story" from *Tanaina Tales from Alaska* by Bill Vaudrin. New edition copyright © 1969 by University of Oklahoma Press. Reprinted by permission.

Library of Congress Catalog Card Number: 89-42776

ISBN 0-345-37298-0

This edition published by arrangement with Random House, Inc.

Manufactured in the United States of America

First Ballantine Books Edition: November 1991

12 11 10 9 8 7 6 5 4 3

I have for a long time now been keeping a girl, the daughter of Raskashikov. I taught her to sew and be a good housekeeper. She can be trusted in business matters, but I found that during my absence she showed weakness. . . . I sin too sometimes from weakness, and sometimes because it is necessary. . . .

—Letter dated May 20, 1795, from Aleksandr Baranov, manager of a Siberian trading company in Kadyak, Aláyeksa, to Grigorii Shelekhov, owner of a Siberian trading company in Irkutsk, Siberia.

ACKNOWLEDGMENTS

We extend our appreciation and thanks to the many individuals who have lent us their support during our research and writing of *Ashana*. Particular thanks go the following:

Robert and Maria Ackerman, Lydia T. Black, Kate Duncan, Peter Kalifornsky, James Kari, Richard A. Pierce, Joan M. Tenenbaum and her Dena'ina storytellers, and to curators and librarians throughout the United States and elsewhere, including the staffs of the Washington State Library and Timberland Regional Library System, Olympia, Washington; the Bancroft Library, University of California, Berkeley, California; Alaska State and University Library systems, Juneau and Fairbanks, Alaska; the National Museum of Man, Canadian Ethnology Service, Ottawa, Canada; and the University of Washington Libraries, Seattle, Washington.

Thanks go to Gloria and Seth Milliken of New York for years of continuing hospitality, and to Mary Mackey of Olympia, Washington, our word-processing expert.

We are grateful to Jean-Isabel McNutt for her craftsmanship and insight.

The unstinting support, sustaining trust, and peerless advice of Samuel S. Vaughan and Olga Tarnowski, our editors at Random House, will always be remembered.

The storytellers, legend bearers, folklorists of many clans and races, from ancient times to the present, must have special recognition, for without their wisdom stories such as *Ashana* could not be written.

PRONUNCIATION GUIDE

The Athabaskan alphabet of Ashana's people has four vowels and thirty-six consonants.

The Athabaskan vowels are pronounced as follows:

Full vowel sounds: a   i   u
Reduced vowel sound: e
Suggested pronunciations:

> "a" as in art
> "e" as in ebb
> "i" as in ice
> "u" as in up

As to consonants, note the following:

> "*l*" is voiceless
> "y" is a fricative, glide

For study of the Athabaskan alphabet and pronunciation of sounds, please refer to: James Kari. *Dena'ina Noun Dictionary*. Fairbanks, Alaska: Alaska Native Language Center, University of Alaska, 1977, First Printing.

ASHANA

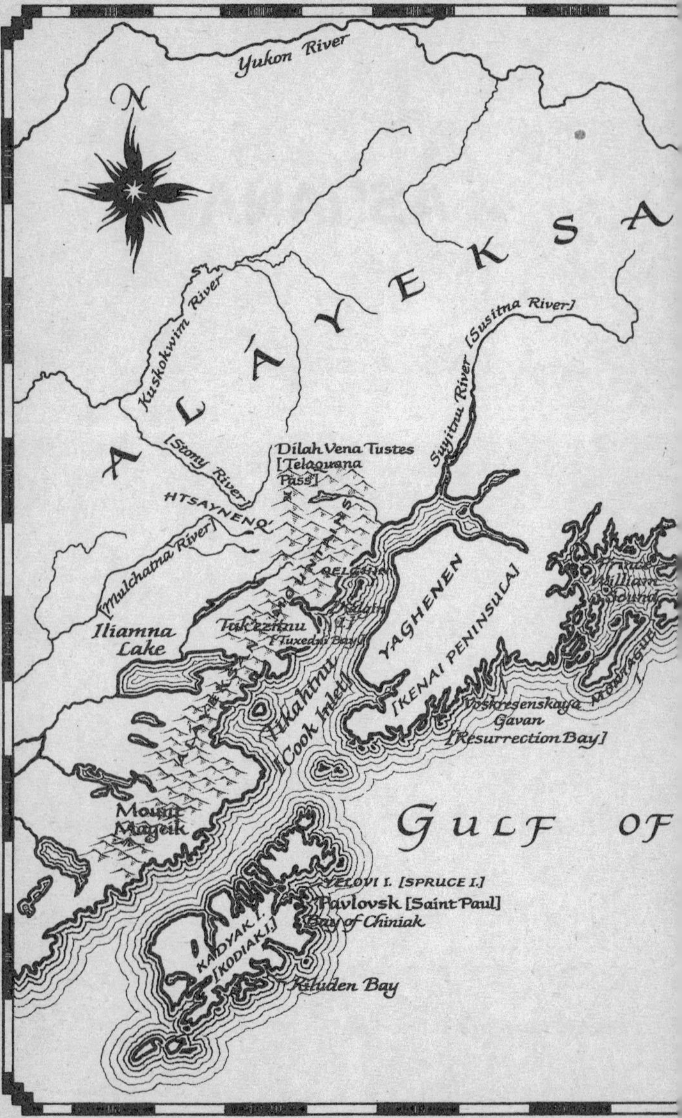
Yukon River
N
ALÁYEKSA
Kuskokwim River
[Susitna River]
Suyitnu River
Dilah Vena Tustes
[Telaquana
Pass]
[Stony River]
HTSAYNENQ'
[Mulchatna River]
Iliamna
Lake
[Tuxedni Bay]
YAGHENEN
[KENAI PENINSULA]
MONTAGUE
I.
Tikahtnu
[Cook Inlet]
Voskresenskaya
Gavan
[Resurrection Bay]
GULF OF
Mount
Mageik
YELOVI I. [SPRUCE I.]
Pavlovsk [Saint Paul]
Bay of Chiniak
KADYAK I.
[KODIAK I.]
Kiluden Bay

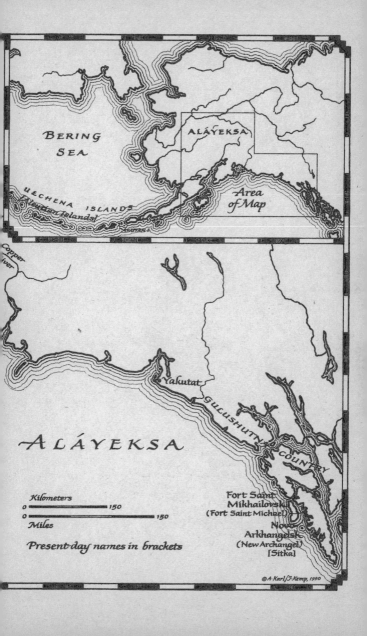

BERING
SEA

ALÁYEKSA

UECHENA ISLANDS
(Aleutian Islands)

AKUTAN I.

Area
of Map

Copper
River

Yakutat

GULUSHUTN COUNTRY

ALÁYEKSA

Kilometers
0 _____ 150
0 _____ 150
Miles

Present-day names in brackets

Fort Saint
Mikhailovskii
(Fort Saint Michael)

Novo
Arkhangelsk
(New Archangel)
[Sitka]

© A. Karl / J. Kemp, 1990

○ ○ ○

Eight young monks, sponsored by a Siberian trading company, set out in 1793 on a mission to Christianize the native peoples in a region known as Aláyeksa.

The monks left Valaam Monastery—their sanctuary and their home, their place of study and meditation—on its island in Lake Ladoga, not far from St. Petersburg. An honored place of religion and wealth, the ancient monastery instilled in its inhabitants a faith that stood as firm as its own monolithic granite walls, which loomed through the dark mists rising from the surrounding lake.

Much of Valaam's wealth lay in the fertile islands dotting this vast and ancient lake, where the monastery owned numberless hectares of lush meadow and forest land. The worship and meeting rooms bespoke the riches lavished on the monastery, both by believers who lived secular lives on the outside but who made their donations, and by men who could no longer abide the wickedness of the secular world and came to live in Valaam permanently, giving their holdings to the church.

The monks on their way to Aláyeksa were leaving behind an ideal retreat. The isolation, the harsh climate, the monks' own wishes allowed no traffic for most of the year. For those inclined to solitary communion, the dense forests provided satisfaction for mind and soul—a virginal, peaceful setting, the untouched beauty of which lay in the relationship of the monastery to the land itself, not in the handiwork of men. No builder alone could have created the total majesty of Valaam.

Red leather bindings, their spines lettered in gold, still preserve the writings of a few of those monks who served that first mission to Aláyeksa. These manuscripts rest in the archives at Valaam, where the dust of the past almost overwhelms the senses, but where the spirits of history open the mind; they seem to wait for a distant archangel to read them and to judge the courageous, dedicated, but sometimes exceedingly foolish, arrogant, and cruel men who gave their lives in the service of their church.

One manuscript at Valaam is bound into a covering so out of character that it seizes the eye. It is of deerskin burnished with age, the whole stitched and tied with deer sinews as fine as embroiderer's thread. The design on the front and back cover is created from a mixture of dentalium shells, small bird claws, and tiny seeds, which give the binding a look in singular contrast to both the adjacent red leather tomes and the dignified atmosphere of the monastery itself.

The manuscript carries the attestation of the Monk Kristofor; it is written on parchment so fragile the edges crumble at a touch.

I, Monk Kristofor, who have taken the vows of loyalty for service to the Almighty God, to the Tzar, and to the Russian Orthodox Church, and have sworn to uphold the truth, leave this document to be read by those who have an open mind and a compassionate heart.

When I wrote down the story contained in these pages, I was tempted to change it, to make corrections according to the light that has blessed those of us who serve the Holy Church. I confess even to thinking I should soften certain portions of the manuscript, to make more palatable the record of the men of the church and of trade and business who went from the culture and civilization of Russia to live and work in the wilderness of Aláyeksa, for some of the statements set down could be deemed critical of the men of the church, blasphemous, others slanderous to the men of trade and commerce, if it were not that truth be its own defense.

I further attest that I have not changed a word. I could not. I could not plant my hand over that of Ashana, Qaniłch'ey Ashana of Yaghenen, who told me: "Do not change one word because every word I speak to you is truth." She threatened a curse if I disobeyed. I hesitate to confess to my Brothers that I would heed a warning from one outside our faith, for she was no Christian. "The šdónályášna, the monsters of Aláyeksa's mountains, will be upon you if you change one word, one meaning, one idea," she said. "They will stay your hand from the writing."

I have seen the mountains of Aláyeksa. They are fierce-some.

"Write what I say," Ashana directed. "The batterings, the abuses, the griefs of Aláyeksa will never pass from generation to generation in the stories and tales of Aláyeksans unless I, Qaniłch'ey Ashana of Yaghenen, tell of them. Sufferings such as ours do not offer the strands storytellers weave into their imaginings. Their recitals sing of strong men, great hunters, war heroes, valiant deeds, uncommon adventures. No one sings of the hostage, the slave, the victim. The sharp ulu slashes the whale's flesh. We see the deep wound. No one asks the whale how the cruel cut feels.

"Tell our story to the four winds. From the days of the ts'itsatna, our ancestors. *Nanutset*, history. *Lach'u*, truth."

I have done as Qaniłch'ey Ashana of Yaghenen ordered, and have reposed this manuscript in the archives in the month of December in the Year of Our Lord 1843.

(s) Monk Kristofor
*Valaam Monastery, Lake Ladoga
St. Petersburg, Russia*

BOOK ONE
◈ ◈ ◈

○ ○ ○

1

*Many generations before Dena'ina came to live on this earth,
humans moved about in their bird or animal forms. It was the
time of no daylight. People could not go from one house to another without getting lost. Chulyin, the raven, lived with his
grandmother. One day he said to her, "I will go and find the
Light." Then he flew and flew for a long time until he came to
a faraway chulyin village. There it was bright daylight.*

*In that place lived a rich man who had a daughter. One morn-
ing chulyin saw her going to the stream for water. He followed
her. He flew into the tree above her. He dropped spruce needles
into the water. She took them home in her basket. She drank the
water with the spruce needles in it. Then she began to swell.
Soon she had a baby. The child was intelligent and grew fast
and always wanted things to play with.*

*One day the child asked for the sun and the moon. The grand-
father could not say "No," for he had always given the child
everything. First, Grandfather stopped up the cracks in the door,
then the smoke hole in the roof. He made everything tight. Then
he gave the sun and the moon to his grandchild. At once the
child turned into a chulyin, for that was who he was, a small
chulyin. He flew out of the crack in the corner of the house that
Grandfather had not sealed. Little chulyin flew and flew. Then
he dropped the sun and the moon into the sky. He told them
which way to go, which seasons to make hot and which cold.
Soon daylight came to Aláyeksa. And that is how chulyin went
out and got the Light for our Dena'ina, our people.*

But then, after generations on generations of Light in Aláyeksa,
chulyin turned and showed his evil side. Darkness descended
again upon my homeland, Yaghenen.

7

* * *

"Hostages! I demand hostages! Young people from your village, Chief Ni'i. From every Yaghenen village." The words of the alien slashed into me as I cringed beside my mother, Sem, heard her whisper, "Stand still, Ashana, stand still."

"No. No hostages from my village." Ni'i, my father, hurled the words back at him.

Ni'i, the leader, the qeshqa, of several Kahtnuht'ana villages beside the coves and along the rivers of Yaghenen, had been arguing with Aleksandr Andreevich Baranov, the leader of the band of invaders. "Russians," they called themselves, but in our tongue we said *Tahtna*. Our men knew what the aliens wanted: They came to steal our furs, as they had already been doing for a long time across the length of the Ułchena Island chain in the waters of western Aláyeksa. Now they came to seize our men for the seat hunts, just as they had enslaved the Ułchena seagoing hunters, leaving their bereft families to starve. The Tahtna could not reach many of our people as yet, but winter was coming and our summer camps high in the mountains would soon be snowed in. Our people always moved back to the villages along the shores of Yaghenen when the cranes began to fly south.

The cords in my father's neck tightened. He jammed his raven-headed speaking staff into the ground as if to draw strength from it. The women around me shrank back against the wall of our house, their children huddled behind them. The leaders of the clan pressed close to Ni'i.

I pushed myself hard against my mother, and there was fear in her voice as she murmured, "Quiet, Qaniłch'ey, Ashana. Do not call his attention to you." Her hand clutched mine, and her fingers dug into my skin.

Throughout my fifteen years, my mother's strength had comforted me whenever I was frightened, but during those days the evil facing us seemed stronger than she was. The alien leaders of the band of *promyshlenniki*, the fur hunters from the Siberian *taiga*, first matched wits, then broke into open argument with my father; this lasted until late on the third day, when the fog drifting into our village began to dim the waning light, making the aliens seem grotesque and menacing.

Baranov bragged again, his demands growing harsher. "Vitus Bering discovered Aláyeksa for my country more than fifty years ago. He sailed here in 1741, as my people count time. And now Tzarina Catherine the Great, Empress of all the Russias, has ordered me to take possession of your land for her glory.''

"Discovered our land? How can you say *discovered*?'' My father's voice was filled with scorn. He added proudly, "Yaghenen is our home here on the shores of Tikahtnu, the great ocean river. You call our land *Kenai*. That is not its right name. I remind you: Its name is Yaghenen. We Kahtnuht'ana Athabaskans have lived in Aláyeksa for many generations; we go back into the dim past of all human beings, and we know what our land is named.''

"Ni'i, you don't understand. Listen. Always, after Russians discover a country, we give our protection to the new people. And I will give you good Russian names. Chief Ni'i, I will call you Raskashikov. My Tzarina has granted me authority over this land. I give you proof of her benevolence.'' Baranov motioned to one of his men, who rummaged in a pack and drew out a copper plate. The alien leader handed the shiny metal object to my father. "See the imperial mark of Tzarina Catherine the Great. It is the emblem of power, respected by people everywhere.'' He pointed to the grooves on the metal surface.

My father traced the incised lines with his finger, then silently passed the piece to our shaman.

While our leaders handled the metal plate, Baranov pressed on. "Keep my gift as a bond of friendship between us. Display it. The entire world will know that the Tzarina has claimed your people for her subjects.''

Ni'i, tall, muscular, proud in the rich tradition of our forefathers, towered above the intruder; Baranov, paunchy, alien in his baggy dress, hair the color of the mottled seaweed along our shores, gripped his whip as he stared at my father: two bull caribou, each the leader of his herd, their horns locked in struggle.

Through the minds of us Kahtnuht'ana people, voices echoed from across Aláyeksa: cries born of suffering, cries that recalled how the Tahtna had first tramped from boats many times larger than ours onto the shores of the Ulchena Island of Attu far to the west, and had then stayed to steal furs, to plunder land and people, sweeping eastward along the Ulchena chain, coming unbidden to Kadyak Island and then to Yaghenen. I knew those voices echoed heavily in the words our leaders and my father exchanged that evening.

Mothers belonging to the clans on the Ulchena Islands to our west quietened their children with threats of the Tahtna: *Hush,*

my child, Ivan Soloviev will get you. They told how Ulchena
hunters had been roped and bound back to front, twelve deep,
on the shores of their island home; how the fur hunter Ivan
Soloviev fired straight into the line of men to show off the power
of his gun. A single shot tore through the bodies of eight hunters.

Be good, or the men from Siberia will steal you away.

Ulchena homes had been stripped of their men; daughters
and wives had been raped and left for dead or dragged off as
hostages.

Sssssh, my little one.

In 1784, only eight years before Baranov threatened Yaghenen, Grigorii Shelekhov had settled his Siberian trading company on Kadyak Island, striking terror as far as his hands
reached. He levied Ulchena men for his sea hunts, but some
deserted the alien camps and returned home for the hunting and
fishing season, so that their families would be fed. As a warning
to those who did remain with Shelekhov, his hunters forced the
escaped Ulchenas at gunpoint from their villages and marched
them far into the tundra, where they were beaten and speared,
then booted into heaps and left to die.

My father and the other qeshqa of our clans knew it was that
same Grigorii Shelekhov who had sent Aleksandr Baranov to
our shores to manage his fur trade. That long-ago day Baranov
must have sensed resistance building among us, for he changed
the direction of his argument.

"Let us not talk of injustice." His eyes were fixed on my
father, his voice remained cold. "As I told you, I bring you the
protection of Russia. And Tzarina Catherine will show you how
to be civilized."

A murmuring stirred my people. There was much shuffling
of feet as the elders pressed around my father, urging him to
send the aliens away.

More words. Like the tides of Tikahtnu that lap the shores of
Yaghenen, the parley between Baranov and my father pushed
out, pulled back. Each leader, crafty in language, wary in the
way he expressed himself, spurned concessions and covered up
any signs of weakness. The tension in Ni'i's face and neck told
me of his rising stubbornness, but the flicker in his eyes dis-
closed a fear I had not seen before.

"I have told you, Baranov, we have never needed your protection in the past. I repeat, we do not need it now." My father
handed back the metal plate, the mark of Imperial Russia.

"You dare spurn Tzarina Catherine the Great and my country?"

I have no clear memory of what happened next. Movement . . . shouts . . . the loud noise of guns. Three of our hunters lay dead, and throughout our village people stood as if rooted to the ground, their only sounds the low moans of despair. There was no time to learn what had happened; I heard steps racing away behind me and turned to see two of our boys dash up the ladder toward the openings on the roof of the house. Again the sound of gunfire stabbed in my ears, a violent crack like that made when the limb of a tree, whipped by winter winds, is torn loose from its trunk. One of the boys, Shila, halted as the blast rang out, poised a moment in midair, then half turned and fell backward with a shriek that haunts me to this day. Blood gushed from his back.

My senses warned me to flee, but I could not move; my mother held me firmly by the hand. The cries of the fallen boy dwindled to low moans, and then there was silence.

Wailing filled the air of Yaghenen. Baranov's voice cut through the cries: "Ni'i, we shot those men because they threatened us with their bows. I warn you, tell your fighters there must be no more of that." He spoke quickly in his alien tongue, and the strangers again pointed their guns at us. My mother pushed me behind her, and I sank to the ground. I thought we were all going to be killed, but the guns fired over our heads. The smoke and thunder stilled the wailing. Unable to hold herself rigid any longer, Shila's mother threw herself onto his lifeless body, her grief pouring out as her son's blood had done. But the women whose husbands lay dead stood silent, motionless.

As the Uľchena had learned before us, so we Kahtnuht'ana learned that day the truth of the Russians in Aláyeksa.

My father shook his raven-headed staff at Aleksandr Baranov. "Murderer! You lie! You do not come in peace!"

As if nothing had happened, Baranov said, "The time for talk has passed. I *will* take hostages to Pavlovsk on Kadyak, Aláyeksan hunters *will* do work for my company. And you Kahtnuht'ana *will* provide meat and fish for my camps. If the men I levy fail to do their work, hostages will be killed. You leave me no choice, Raskashikov. Your people must obey me." He snapped his whip.

Women threw themselves onto the earth. Men gripped their bows, and a rumble as of distant thunder rolled through them.

I stared into the holes of the aliens' guns. Our shaman alone dared a gesture of defiance; arms arched skyward, his silent lips implored the help of spirits greater than the leaders of our clans.

Again, Baranov commanded, "Order your men to lay all their bows and spears on the ground. Over here."

Voice low, eyes down, the Uĺchena interpreter passed on the demand. When my father hesitated, Baranov ordered his men to prepare to fire. As Ni'i repeated the command, some of our men began to protest, but more shots fired low overhead forced them to stack their spears, arrows, and bows under Baranov's watchful eye. A few men hung back, clustered, and tried to hide weapons behind them. More alien shots. My father's stern voice spoke again, and the last of our men stamped furiously to the pile, glaring first at Ni'i, then at Baranov. Anger seethed within every Kahtnuht'ana as he shed his arms, most of them crafted by the owner himself.

Shifting his stance, Aleksandr Baranov turned toward me; his eyes bore into mine, cold as the blue ice of Aláyeksa's glaciers. "From your house, Chief Raskashikov, I demand your daughter. Her royal rank shall serve me."

"No! I pledged Ashana to Jabila, a man from a clan north of this village." My father's words sounded strong, then his voice broke. "He has paid the bride-price. She is his wife."

"Your bride-prices mean nothing. Such couplings do not have the blessing of the Holy Russian Church. Only priests may unite a man and a woman in marriage."

I thought of my husband, Shani Jabila, named for the summer rainbow. Jabila! Safe on the hunt far from the evil men. Jabila with the strength of a bounding caribou, the heavy grace of a wary grizzly, the eyes of the eagle. But most of all the quick mind, the spirit, of tiqun, the wolf, an intelligence that had sustained Jabila's clan from that ancient time when the tiqun first changed from animals to people. *Jabila, hear me now! Stay far away from these men.*

Our clan elders pressed close around my father, trying to piece together a way to resist. Several hunters knelt to pick up the bodies of the murdered men and the boy and to bear them to a ceremonial place deep in the forest. My friend Shila, lightning, killed by the lightning of alien guns; his life ended in storm as it had begun in storm. Shila was well named, for Kahtnuht'ana custom directs that the baby be called by the first image the mother sees after its birth.

"Stop! None of you will leave. Pledge me the hostages." Baranov's words chilled like the winds that howl across our land in the time of cold.

Qil'i, evil, settled a blanket of silence over everyone. As I huddled on the ground, I asked the secret animal being within me, my joncha, to bear me away to join Jabila. I struggled to blot out the murders, the word "hostage." In the face of guns he could not best, my father conceded to the intruders young men of our villages as hostages, and an ongoing supply of fish and game.

We had lost control.

"QaniÍch'ey Ashana." My father motioned to the shaman to help me to my feet. "Windflower." His staff tilted downward, no longer borne high with a leader's pride.

"Ashana, this day chulyin, bird of our clan, turns the evil side of his spirit upon us and takes back the Light. The man Baranov demands that you go"—Ni'i's face turned from me and his voice fell—"as hostage from my house. I would say no, and die. But if I refuse, many in this village will be killed . . . the men and the boy . . ." He choked as he pointed to the dead bodies in the dirt, the hunters still kneeling around them.

I thought of a fragrant flower picked in the morning, torn from its meadow with drops of dew still clinging to its petals, that by afternoon wilts and loses its delicate freshness.

"I cannot. I will not go. I belong to Jabila!" Agony shook me, and my cry mingled with the wails of our women.

"My daughter, I offer to go in your place, but he refuses me. He demands you for his woman." My father's spirit crumbled as if a pestilence fevered his body and sapped his will.

"No! No! No! Jabila, Jabila!" But he was hunting far from home and could not hear me.

From the time I became aware of boys as creatures different from girls, my heart had always called to Jabila. Sitting near our fire pit with my brother Seltan when his friend Jabila came to visit, I wanted to take part in their talk, but custom more than shyness held me back. Whenever Jabila stayed in my home, I watched, caring little to run outdoors and play with the children as I would otherwise do. My brother's friend came often to our village during my growing years, ate many meals with us. He and Seltan drew close as blood brothers long before the slocin pledge that made them life partners. I wanted little attention from Jabila, but he gave me almost none—there would be a greeting for the small sister, a mimicking of some action of mine, a teasing like that of my brother. Dreams brought Jabila alive in my mind: we walked the hills dotted with groves of slender birches, or I sat close to him as we listened to the warblers in the trees. Throughout the time of my growing up, as my small childish braids changed to the heavy braids decorated with shells worn by girls entering womanhood, much of my shyness melted away, but never enough to allow me to break custom and talk with Jabila. I often hoped that he would take me out in one of our enclosed, two-hatch skin kayaks, teach me to handle the paddle as Seltan sometimes did. But by Kahtnuht'na tradition only young men had the right to learn that skill.

I remember the summer when Jabila stopped his teasing, grew elusive. It was the season before Baranov invaded us. As the time neared for Jabila's manhood rites, he spent most of his days alone in the forest, days that in the past he had shared with Seltan—talking together in our house, competing in games with other young men, setting trap lines along the mountain streams with my brother. When he did come to the house, he would not speak to me.

Then, as qeliq', the spring season, melted the snows, the songbirds began to return from the far south, and Jabila stepped into our home. He carried fine pelts, fresh meat, and agates for my mother and father. I hid behind a post and watched him. Lithe as a young bird, handsome in new deerskin, he seemed to me as mighty and as far away as the eagle whose feathers fringed his garments.

"Ni'i and Sem, I come with . . ." Jabila's voice faltered.

Silence. My father said nothing. My mother watched, biting her lip, holding back a smile. All work and play in the big room stopped. Everyone waited. Jabila glanced from person to person, his shyness that day in great contrast to his usually confident, outspoken self.

"Sem. Ni'i . . ." My mother's name came first as if the young man begged her help, "I . . . I . . ."

My parents still said nothing.

At the opening to her japoon, her private sleeping room, my father's second wife, K'enteh, beckoned to me. I did not want to miss what my parents and Jabila said, but she kept motioning. When I was inside the japoon, she whispered, "Here, take off that old deerskin. Your mother and I made this one for you."

K'enteh stood on tiptoe, pushed my hair back from my fore-head, and began braiding it. "Ashana, your raven-black hair shines like no other girl's in the village. Stand still, you move so quickly, so lightly—like the raven."

She held up the new garment—a white fringed deerskin, qen-ich'eni, embroidered with porcupine quills, small shells, and eagle down. It was the most beautiful dress I had ever seen.

My mother pulled aside the covering to the japoon and grasped me in her arms. "Come, Qanilch'ey Ashana, Jabila has brought his bride-price for you. Your father and I have ac-cepted."

That day Jabila became my husband, and in keeping with Kahtnuht'ana custom moved himself and his possessions into my parents' house, where he would live for the first year of our marriage.

Throughout the spring and into the summer, lying in my hus-band's arms, tucked against his long body, I knew at last why my parents had assigned me companions, women carefully cho-sen to guard me during my growing-up years, attendants so strict that no mischievous boy or lustful man could spoil me for my husband; in our clans no highborn man would take to wife a woman used in a careless manner. I knew Jabila treasured me; we lay awake in wonder during the nights, yielding to sleep for only a few hours. In the daytime we climbed the trails hand in hand, walked in meadows spread with red and yellow poppies and blue gentians. Jabila knelt among patches of flowers rimmed with evergreens, his long fingers searching; then he picked a perfect windflower—Qanilch'ey Ashana—as white as the snowy mantle that covered our mountains in the winter season.

"Lovely like you, Qanilch'ey Ashana," he whispered, and held me close; his black eyes smoldered with love.

In the heat of that summer we swam in the small lakes that reflected the blue of the sky and the crest of a peak towering above us, our brown arms stroking in rhythm. The caress of the cool water on our skins whispered of our desire for each other. We laughed. We chased through thickets, ran over fields of blos-soms where hummingbirds fed. One day I stayed so motionless that a small winged creature dipped its long beak into an open bud right beside me; as it sipped the sweet nectar, I slowly reached out to grasp the beautiful bird, but when I opened my hand, my palm held only a few crushed petals. Who can hold a hummingbird in her hand?

That tragic day when the Tahtna came, my mother's arms
drew me close, tried to protect me from the evil that shattered
my new life with Jabila, a life begun, it seemed, only yesterday.
My mother—Sem, star. Always, I had turned to her for help.
As if speaking from the midst of tushe*I*, the dense fog that hangs
over our coastal waters in cold weather, she said softly,
"Naq'eltani, the Forever Spirit of Kahtnuht'ana, watch over
Ashana. We are the children of the raven, but today he has
turned his capricious side upon us. The forest darkens. I cannot
see through the fog that crawls in from the sea and covers us.
Naq'eltani, you must save Ashana."

When I was a small child I did not understand the chants and
entreaties the older folks made to Naq'eltani. I questioned my
mother about their meaning, and she explained, "We give homage to Naq'eltani, who is the source of all our bounty—the beautiful flowers, the success of the hunts, the birds of summer, the
fires that warm us in the cold season—everything that makes life
on Yaghenen good."

Another day, many seasons ago, one never to be forgotten, I
had asked, "Where does Eltani live?"—for "Eltani" is what
we call the Spirit in our everyday talk—and my mother's answer
puzzled me.

"Eltani lives everywhere, child. In the sky. In the sea. In the
animals. In the trees and birds. Here among us. He lives in the
fire that cooks our food. And he watches over us."

I remember crying out to her angrily, "But, Mother, where
was he when I needed him? Why wasn't he with me?"

"Ashana, my daughter, you have known only nine summers.
You are too young to understand what your father and I know
of such things. Naq'eltani . . ."

But I had screamed, "Why didn't he save my little brother?"

When, crying, I tried to run, she had caught me in her arms
and led me to sit with her on a driftwood log not far from our
house. Our thoughts were filled with memories of that terrible
summer day. My father had told me to watch my baby brother
while the men fished and my mother and the other women
searched the nearby slopes for squirrels. I sat with him for a
long time, humming him to sleep with the tunes I knew he
loved. Several bow lengths from me, a berry patch, its bushes
laden with tempting red fruit, caught my eye. The baby was
quiet, no one was around. I could not resist skipping the short
distance to the closest bushes. A few berries . . . a few more;

moving deeper and deeper into the thicket, I forgot my responsibility and gorged on the sweet ripe fruit.

"Ashana! Ashana!" My father's call brought me back to the creekside. "Where is the baby?"

Hours of search. Along the stream bank. In the woods. Back to the water. There was no trace of my missing brother. The search went on through the short night and into the next day and the next. Sternly, my father stared at me, his words sharp, demanding to know why I had left the baby alone; the grieving woman's mask spread over my mother's face.

A couple of days later, my Uncle Minya, my mother's brother, told of tracking a huge brown bear from along the stream to a warm spot under an overhanging ledge. It was then that my village knew the fate of our small one, for animal hunger knows no difference between a Kahtnuht'ana baby and a salmon threading its way upstream from the sea.

In her quiet way Sem had talked with me; stubbornly, I had broken in, "Why didn't Eltani save my brother?"

"For whatever reason, Naq'eltani needed our little one, and he chose the bear to bring the child to him." I had fought against her arms, but she held me. "Be still, my child. Listen." All around us the breeze had spoken gently among the leaves. Below, I had heard the faint lapping of the waters of Tikahtnu on the rocky shoreline.

The agony of losing my baby brother walked with me that dreadful day as I faced the man from Imperial Russia. Impossible for me to submit as his hostage. In my fright I screamed at the pair who had brought me into this world, "Naq'eltani! Naq'eltani! Why doesn't he save me now?"

And overhead chulyin flew, cawing his evil laughter.

From our hunters, our traders, our storytellers, my people learned that Vitus Bering's sailors had borne home to Baranov's country stories of our seas and islands teeming with fur-bearing animals.

The sea hunts demand skill and the courage to search the ocean at water level. In my Yaghenen home, visiting Ulchena traders told of island men seized for Tahtna sea hunts. I remember the meeting of our leaders, before the coming of Baranov to Yaghenen, when Jabila had asked, "Why do the Tahtna force Aláyeksans to hunt sea otters and whales?"

Around the evening fire, Minya, who had returned only a short time ago from a sea hunt with the Ulchena, had answered

Jabila's question and explained Baranov's ways to our leaders. "The aliens are afraid of our seas. They will not risk rowing themselves across the open sea in Ulchena kayaks from one otter breeding place to another. They are clumsy with the paddles, scared to sit right down at water level." Bitterness echoed through Minya's words. "They have guns, so they seize men and kayaks from many villages of the Ulchena and drive them out to sea to hunt in packs of hundreds or more.

"That man Baranov is behind it all. I have learned from the Ulchena how he schemed to steal furs. Baranov sailed from Okhotsk in Siberia on his ship *Three Saints*, but wrecked his boat on an Ulchena island. The islanders saw the sorry plight of the starving men, and shared food and offered shelter.

"The Tahtna lived with the Ulchenas that entire winter. And while Baranov waited for his crew to repair his ship and for the seas to calm, he used his time to gain favor with the islanders. He learned their language, watched and listened, all the time spying on the sea hunts. Baranov saw that the Ulchena planned their hunts, as we Kahtnuht'ana do, by watching the signs nature gives them."

Aláyeksan men knew the seas well, and they knew, too, that success depended on always preparing for their hunts carefully: using what they saw in the clouds and the state of the weather, and what they read from the flight of birds. When hunters agreed that the signs told them the time was right, they rowed out before dawn in two-hatch kayaks—small crews, large crews—six kayaks, twenty kayaks.

In the forward hatches sit the men known as the most skilled in the sea hunts—those who most often have brought back to the village the largest catch, the greatest numbers of otters. All crewmen scan the surface with vigilance, and the keenest-eyed in spotting action in the water raises his paddle in signal. Quickly, all kayaks are drawn into a circle enclosing the area where bubbles are rising to the surface, indicating the presence of the animal. The instant an otter's nose and jaws push up for air, the men in the forward hatches hurl their spears or harpoons or shoot their arrows. If they miss, everyone waits; but however long the hunt may take, the sea otter loses. No quarrels mar the hunts, for the men follow strict rules: Always, first right to the kill belongs to the hunter who first strikes the otter. Even if the creature has been struck several times, credit for the catch goes to the hunter who hurls his weapon closest to the head. If all seem to hold an equal claim, the crewman who first called out as he took aim and made his shot holds the right to claim the catch. Each weapon bears the owner's mark, a symbol different from all others, and the means of avoiding doubt and argument.

"Baranov pretended just to watch the hunt and enjoy the sport. But it is plain to me that it was then he decided to use the islanders, for he knew he had found skilled sea hunters." Minya's voice turned sharper.

"So, his very first winter in Aláyeksa, Baranov formed his plan: Seize Aláyeksan hunters. Enslave them. Force native kayakmen to the sea hunts. Grab women and children for hostages. If the men run, kill hostages. Strip the seas and islands of their rich furs. Take hold of Aláyeksa and its hunters for the glory of Mother Russia."

Over the years, I have often pictured Baranov shipwrecked on that faraway Uĺchena island. Talking. Listening. Watching. Scheming. I knew his hands itched as he stroked the lustrous, silky furs, each pelt so large that when laid out it covers over half the height of a person, each pelt worth hundreds of Russian rubles at the trading center far south of Irkutsk, where Siberia, they said, bordered on China.

We had listened that long-ago evening to Minya talk of the truth of the Russians. When they hunted far out on the Uĺchena Islands, the aliens had seemed distant from us on Yaghenen. But our qeshqa spent many evenings around the fire talking, working out the best plan for us: A group of skilled hunters said we should flee into the interior, while a number of fighters, quick and adept with bow and arrows, said, "Stay and fight." The more knowing, my father Ni'i among them, won out with their reasoning: "Once we run, there will be no end. Our people cannot run forever. Stay and fight? We cannot. The aliens have the gun power. But Yaghenen is our homeland, and we will not give it up. Let us bargain with the aliens. Let us use our trading skills."

Plans too many times have a way of failing. Our people stayed on Yaghenen. But oh, the darkness that spread over Aláyeksa and covered our villages!

I had been staring at Aleksandr Baranov while he bargained with my father, but soon my eyes wandered over my people. Women with sons who could be taken drew their faces into masks, sketches of the horror that ate at them as the evil took hold of us. The men huddled in groups, their weapons lying in piles beside the Tahtna. A net of silence wrapped around us; not even a child's cry or whimper broke the hush.

Mothers of girls my age eyed me with sympathy, but their faces showed something more. They wondered, I am certain, if Ni'i would hold me back at the cost of one of their own. They could not be blamed if fear for their daughters was stronger than sympathy for me, but loyalty to the clan forbade them to give voice to their worries.

In my despair, as if lost far out on the muskeg, I seemed to sink down, down . . . I struggled against the wet quagmire of soil and moss and half-decayed shrubs and bark clutching at me, I felt the bog tightening around my legs. The pounding in my head clubbed first one side of my skull, then the other. Slivers of pain jabbed my eyes, and I seemed to sink deeper into that grasping clutch as the distant line where the muskeg met the sky blurred.

"Chief Raskashikov, I must claim other villages for Tzarina Catherine the Great. I have months of work ahead. I order you to hold your daughter and the other hostages for me. They must never leave your village. When I send for them, they will be taken to Kadyak. My men will guard you, and you will provide them food and shelter. Remember what I say, Raskashikov."

A jerk of the alien leader's hand, and his men fired final warning shots low above our houses. My father's harsh breathing sounded through the darkness that crawled over us. I sensed that in his anguish he, too, sank into the muskeg.

All work ceased in our village. Fear bred fear, draining us of strength and reason. Efforts centered on the burial rites for the murdered men and for Shila. They deserved ceremonies, the cremation rituals that Kahtnuht'ana custom bade us perform when a human being departs this earth. We had the will, but the alien guards denied us the right. We were allowed to cremate the bodies; that was all. During the evening and far into the night, while the pall of smoke and the smell of burning flesh hung over the village, I heard the cries of the bereaved families mingle with the mourning voices of the rest of our clan.

My own fear for Seltan and Jabila, who had gone hunting with Minya, lay heavy. Before first light on the day the hunters would return, I slipped out of my japoon, managed to evade the Tahtna guards, and spent the morning hidden in the sheltering spruce. The hours dragged, my only companions an osprey family in the branches overhead, a few gulls flying in from the sea, a couple of rabbits that pushed their way through the underbrush. Then, hearing the hunters, I ran to warn them. When I told them of the tragedy in our villages, Minya at once decided Seltan and Jabila would stay with him. The four of us would wait until it grew dark and then slip home under cover of night.

The next day arguments rose around our fire pit. My husband Jabila's furious voice. My brother Seltan's clipped words to my father.

"I tell you, Ni'i, Ashana will stay with me." Jabila strode angrily between my brother and my father. "You accepted my bride-price. You pledged her to me. Qaniłch'ey Ashana is my wife. She is not property for you to bargain off as you wish."

For the first time that I could remember, Seltan, too, raised his voice against my father. "I will not let my sister be a slave. What happened to the leaders' plan to bargain and trade?"

"Seltan, there was no bargaining with the aliens. Their guns overpowered our bows. They killed four of our people."

My husband's black eyes stared down my father. His long-fingered hands clasped, unclasped, fists pounding. "We should have moved north. That is what I wanted to do." Jabila's tone was harsh; I knew he questioned Ni'i's leadership.

"Remember, our qeshqa decided to stay. We believed we could carry on honest trade with the Russians. Trade between Aláyeksan clans has gone on for generations, and we are the best of all the clans. We made a choice we thought good for all of us, but Baranov did not come to trade honestly. His guns did the bargaining." My father's voice bore the despair we had all come to know.

"Taking Ashana hostage will not make Yaghenen safe. The aliens do not stand by their word." Jabila choked with anger.

"Father, you should have listened to warnings the Ułchena brought us. But you did nothing. You did not even post guards. I must tell you, Ni'i, you qeshqa *allowed* our people to get caught."

And I remember more of what Jabila had to say, as the servant laid more logs on the fire to keep the flames high. "The Tahtna take thousands of Aláyeksa's furs. Pay nothing. Share none with the hunters. The Tahtna are greedy. They can get all the furs they want. So, why hostages?"

"You must understand," Minya had answered. "As I told our leaders, the Tahtna take hostages and use them in work camps. People who are family and friends of the hunters. Our hunters dare not disobey orders. It is the only way hostages can be saved from being shot. If any Aláyeksan man escapes or refuses to hunt, the Tahtna drag out hostages and kill them.''

I knew that my brother did not dare ask what Minya was thinking: Why had Ni'i and the elders not planned ahead? Did they not understand what had gone on for so many summer and winter seasons across all of Aláyeksa? Did they not know that the Tahtna with guns would raid Yaghenen? How could our leaders dare dream that their skills in bargaining among Aláyeksa's clans could gain them riches in trade with the aliens? Had Ni'i stupidly closed his eyes to the lach'u, the truth, of what tangling with the invaders would mean?

The argument raged for days, deadlocked. My father and the leaders defended their actions, contending that Russian guns left them with no choice but the one they had made. Others, led by Seltan and Jabila, charged that our leaders should have foreseen the tragedy and moved deep into the mountains, far beyond our summer camps, before the Tahtna ever set foot on our peninsula.

Outside our houses, alien eyes and guns watched our every move.

2

Terror stalked my wait for Aleksandr Baranov's return. At night I lay awake, rigid with fear, or sobbing, till Jabila calmed me, stroking me and holding me close. I could not force myself to think ahead to the time when I would not feel his tall slenderness against me, when I would not be able to reach out and touch him.

"Thrown to an alien to use and rape," Jabila raged. "Not my wife."

Every day, K'i'un, Seltan's chosen bride, and I worked hard—patching a kayak, cleaning a skin, stocking the fish racks. But on the days when Seltan and Jabila had time from the hunts, one by one we slipped away to talk in a secluded spot known only to the four of us; and we pledged ourselves to secrecy so that villagers, our own families included, would not drop an unguarded word and the Tahtna learn of my will to defy them. I could not see myself as hostage. Our talk sounded brave, but words did not make action; they only mingled with my anguish.

Late in the winter season, before qeliq' would begin breathing strongly and warming the days, ideas began to shape in the minds of Jabila and me, and in those of Seltan and K'i'un.

Our plans settled, one morning before first light crept over the crest of the mountains, K'i'un and Seltan in one open-hatch skin boat and Jabila and I in another paddled west from Yaghenen, over the waters of Tikahtnu. Only the four of us knew our flight would take us across Qelghin Island and beyond the Aláyeksan mountain range to Sem's people.

"Qelghin is a stopping point when crossing Tikahtnu. A break needed when the ocean river runs heavy," Seltan had said as we planned our escape.

Physically fresh and strong, elated at our slipping away unseen, the men drove hard with their two-bladed paddles. Awkward at first, stroking too fast or too slow to match Jabila's rhythm, I kept adjusting my stroke until my arms moved in cadence with his. The dense red tinge of early dawn lightened the sky, but soon both sky and water became gray-green, a sameness blending both halves into one world. Swiftly as a sea gull in low flight, we skimmed Tikahtnu. In less time than Seltan had figured, one of the cliffs of Qelghin broke the horizon and we entered a cove on the southeastern shore of the island.

Borne by a surging wave, Seltan's kayak scraped against a rock, tearing a small rip in the skin covering. We beached and hid ourselves behind low-growing bushes along the shore.

"I'll mend it," K'i'un said. She stitched the rent closed, using deer sinews and a bone needle from Seltan's walrus-hide bag. K'i'un was not yet wife to my brother, but she came with us because he had paid most of his bride-price for her, had planned to pay her parents before another season had passed and would not risk her being taken as hostage. I glanced at the two of them. K'i'un had liquid brown eyes, long black hair, delicate limbs—she was a beautiful fourteen-year-old Kahtnuht'ana. K'i'un had eyes only for Seltan. I knew. It was the kind of love I felt for Jabila.

Wary and watchful, we took only a few moments to eat some dried salmon from our packs. Our hopes lay in gaining the mainland and from there climbing the Aláyeksan coastal range and following the ancient trails through the mountains to the high plateau country, Htsaynenq', then escaping down into the distant valley where my mother's Athabaskan clan lived. If we survived to complete the journey, the people of Sem's homeland might accept us as family or they might treat us as strangers: We did not know. Resting in the sun's warmth, I heard the fresh breeze speaking from the western mountains we would soon climb to safety, but before I could understand if it promised freedom, the direction of the wind changed and whatever message it may have borne disappeared.

When Seltan's torn boat had been patched and waterproofed with a coating of the grease Jabila carried with him in his pouch, we crossed open water to search the coastline for a river that would lead us inland toward a pass heading west to Htsaynenq'. As we neared the western shore, we headed for an irregular line, a place where the waves crashed against the cliffs and rocky bluffs. Ahead and to our left, a massive chunk of ice sheared off with a terrible splintering crash, thundering into the water, tilting, turning, and then vanishing. Our boats shuddered as huge waves thrust our prows skyward, then dropped us heavily back on the heaving surface. Stroking frantically, we changed course, speeding toward waters that looked free of floating ice. But from behind us came a monstrous roar, as of many bears joining in a single snarl, and as we turned to look, another overhang of ice cracked and tumbled toward us. For a moment our lives stood still, the raw power of the ice, frightening yet majestic, holding us in wonder, our paddles motionless.

Freezing water spired high above us, blotting K'i'un and Seltan from sight as more shards broke off and spread stabbing, swirling circles across the water. Jabila and I fought to keep on course, but the boat scraped against an ice face hidden by the lashing sea, jerked, and flipped upside down.

The icy waters embraced me; I clamped my mouth shut and held my breath. With all the skill of an Ulchena islander, Jabila's powerful thrusts righted us. Our waterproof gut shirts, laced into the lips around our kayak's hatches, had saved us from falling out. Terror sped my paddling; then, gulping air, I realized the paddle had been wrenched from my hands—my motions were futile nervous reactions.

"Bend low, Ashana!" my husband shouted, his shoulder muscles straining as he tried desperately to keep us on a straight course, swinging his paddle rhythmically from side to side at a driving pace to prevent us from tipping over again.

As my exhausted body sagged against my knees, I let out a wild cry and twisted around to look for Seltan and K'i'un, but I could not see them. Frightened that they had not come through the ordeal, I almost panicked. Naq'eltani! Had I been the cause of their deaths? My body grew as cold as the icy spray that pounded us, drawing away more of my fading strength.

When we had pushed off from Yaghenen, our spirits and our courage ran high; I believed we would escape. But now, worn out by the hours of rowing and my cramped position in the boat, the menace of the threatening ocean river, my courage was ebbing fast. How would we endure? Could we stay alive until we reached the mountains, refuge, safety?

I feared the devil side of chulyin; if he had indeed turned against us, we could fail. I was not certain which I feared more: the devil side of raven or the dread that our Forever Spirit, Naq'eltani, had deserted us. Either way, the nutin'at dnayi, the people who lived far below the surface of the sea, might snatch us into the depths. *I beseech you, Eltani . . .*

I finally dared to look back, then laughed aloud: Seltan rowed a short distance behind us, his hair a wet, tangled mass, his face shining; and I knew raven's good side flew with us. We entered an estuary and followed a river that fed its mountain waters into Tikahtnu. When we could paddle no farther upstream, we pulled our two boats up from the shore and hid them in the dense underbrush, where they could not be seen from the river.

We scrambled over boulders and fallen trees. For long stretches a scarcely visible trail opened to the west; deep ravines forced us into a crooked course, weaving in and out along the mountainside and past sharply pitched crags. Far below, the cascading river tumbled along its rock-strewn bed. I heard Jabila calling: "This way. A deer trail." We walked silently for a long distance, later pausing in a opening between the trees to gaze across a timbered valley to the peaks that glistened sharp and dazzlingly white in the midafternoon sun, rivers of ice wedged between their high promontories.

The sun was not yet a half disk when we rounded an outcrop and sought a cave that would shelter us for the night. We let down our packs and tried as best we could to make ourselves comfortable. I was farther from home than I had ever been before. Exhaustion soon claimed my companions, but the horror that had torn us from our village drove sleep far from me.

A streak of light from the waning day played across the cave wall opposite me. Lines and figures took shape, and for the first time since crawling into the shelter, I noticed the drawings. My heart skipped a beat, for the nanutset of a long-ago generation of my people spread across that wall. With my fingers I traced out pictures, nearly all of them faded; but I could still see some of the red pigment the painter had used. Was that a man? A woman in deerskin garments? A little fox? A walrus? An umiak with several people in it? A hunter with arrow and bow? Sea lions? Picture messages by an artist long dead, maybe by more than one, from the time when our clans first came to this land.

I tried to imagine the artist, life among his people. A presence in the cave reached out to me, perhaps an ancestor. If these drawings could speak, they would bring to life more of the ancient stories that make up the lach'u and nanutset, the truth and history of my clan. These pictured the tales my father and grandfather had told me about the beginnings of human beings, from the far-back time when birds and animals changed into creatures like us. Our ancient ones had undertaken the long walks of life that weave through the nanutset of our people, from West to

East, into a vast inland country laced with rivers, plains, forests, huge land-bound seas. In time—none of our clans know exactly when—our Athabaskan ancestors had commenced another great walk: East to West. Pushing toward Aláyeksa, they had begun to retrace the ancient routes of those who had etched trails toward the distant line where the earth meets the morning sun. Then, ages later, Athabaskans had first walked onto the high plateau country, Htsaynenq', and into the valleys west of Tikahtnu—claimed it for home. Some of them must have trod the same path we four followed as we tried to escape, more unknowing of what lay ahead of them than we were that day. From that region, our more immediate ancestors had turned east to the land of rugged mountains, eternal snowfields, glaciers, pounding tides—the land my clan had held ever since for its own.

Yaghenen.

An arm slipped around my shoulders.

"Ashana, why aren't you asleep?" Jabila drew me toward him.

"I'm afraid. I can't sleep. I hear the Tahtna guns. The keening of our women."

Not wanting to disturb K'i'un and Seltan, we walked from the cave, arm in arm, upward off the trail among the trees of the mountainside. As it grew dark, I reached up and traced my fingers across Jabila's face, down his neck to his shoulder. A need burned within me to memorize every feature of my lover's body. One eyebrow had grown into a funny little peak, as if it had a question to ask. Long arms and legs were muscled by years of hunting and climbing our mountains. Eyes I had often seen flash with anger were that night gentle, drawing me to him. He had earned respect in his clan to the north of ours as a fearless young man, one born to become a qeshqa.

My husband.

Leaning down, I pulled Jabila with me under a sheltering willow. Easily, warmly, we touched and touched again. A head shorter than he, I stretched out beside him. My body, too, had grown slim and firm from climbing trails, caring for a line of squirrel snares, and searching our mountains for berry patches. I had kept my face free of blemish, for my parents chose not to pierce my lip or cheek to insert any of the labrets or ornamental stone decorations many girls wore. Night covered us; Jabila could not see my eyes, which, he told me many times, looked into his and reached out for him as no other woman's eyes had ever done.

As often happens on Aláyeksan nights, yuyqush, the northern lights, displayed its curtains of colored streamers across the sky, streamers of greens and reds and yellows bathing us in a glow not of this world.

"Dear one. Now I know." Jabila's whispers breathed through my hair. "The light in your eyes. From yuyqush." His lips touched my eyes lightly, skipped down my cheek, lingered. I could barely hear his words. "My love of the northern lights."

Even with the love we had known, that night became a special time, far from danger; as with our first lovemaking, I felt Jabila's body tremble. I tightened my arms around him; he pressed against me. Passionately we merged into the one being that dwells at the core of each of us, and for those moments knew freedom. His drive began and grew, creating a powerful pulse inside me, then rose and rose, cresting and crashing and receding like a tide that has spent its energy, its soft rolling waves caressing us. We lay together until morning, fulfilled.

With daylight, as we walked along trying to match the fast pace Seltan was setting, I forced myself to play a game to keep from sinking deep into the bog of my despair, trying to recall happier times: the evergreen forests that hid trails to shining waterfalls . . . my mother teaching me how to weave . . . storytelling around the fire pit in the long nights of winter. And I wondered: Would the Tahtna allow my father and mother ever again to wander through Yaghenen's trees in the stillness of morning, listening for songs as Kahtnuht'ana have always done from the time of our ancient beginnings, listening to hear their lucky song come to them from a rock or a small animal or a tree, the song that would be theirs to sing so that their children's lives might be saved?

Tears wet my face as I relived the time when my father had taken me to watch Seltan and Jabila pledge loyalty to each other, becoming slocin, lifetime partners, according to the traditions of Kahtnuht'ana men. They had stood with their feet in the waters of Tikahtnu some distance from our village and exchanged new arrows. My father's pride echoed in every word when he talked to my brother and Jabila, telling these young men from different clans that they would become future leaders among our people. Then he surprised them with the gift of a new kayak he had made and hidden until that day. My father had held me close, his good humor spilling over, as from the shore we watched the new partners speed through the waves that rolled across the surface of the ocean river.

What lay ahead for my people? Would traders from other clans—Tutl'uht'ana, U*l*chena, Utnuth'ana—ever again bring us their shells and copper and baskets? The Gulushutna their Chilkat blankets and carvings and masks? Or had the Russian guns leached away the life essence of their clans, too? I grieved that our rich life of Yaghenen, of all the clans of Aláyeksa, had been shattered.

Qeliq' on Yaghenen: The season I loved best. Sunny days would rid the air of its bite, and I always knew that by summer's end we could pick and eat fresh berries. Some summer tasks I loathed; when the meat of the sea otter or small whale had been cut up and laid out to dry, we had to take the guts down to the shore, scrape and wash them clean. With sharp clamshell knives our mothers would cut them into long strips, making certain they were thoroughly dry; then, they were rubbed in whale oil to keep them soft. The tedious scraping, the stinking odor of oil clinging to my hands, would make me wish I were a boy: Boys could race their kayaks or roam far into the mountains for game, but girls had to help with women's work—skinning, cutting and sewing clothes or waterproof pouches and floats, cooking, snaring squirrels.

To train me in these skills, my mother had taught me to sew with a bone awl and thread from the tendons of deer. "Next to preparing our food, sewing serves us best," she would remind me when my fingers lagged. From walrus hides, fox furs, sealskin, and caribou and deer hides we fashioned clothing for our family. The seams had to be firmly and finely stitched if the garments were to keep out the driving wind and rain. Gradually, as I grew older, my stitches improved under my mother's watchful eyes, but she let me know that they must be even finer, more closely set, before she would permit me to stitch a cover for a kayak. A woman had to apply the greatest skill she possessed to sew a safe, waterproof covering for the boat's framework. If fingers turned slovenly, leaving stitches weak or loose, the seams would rip apart in the thrashing waves and doom the sea hunter; a careless mistake with the awl could ruin a precious skin.

That day of our escape across Tikahtnu the seams of our boats had held; the only damage had been in the small tear in the skin of Seltan's craft, caused by the sharp edge of a rock. I understood then why my mother had been so insistent.

* * *

Farther along those western slopes the trees and shrubs began to change, became spiny and weathered. Low evergreen bushes, black and white spruce, balsam and poplar mingled in the more open forest land with tamarack and willows. None of them matched the towering evergreens on the slopes of Yaghenen. No longer burdened by the kayak, and with our few possessions and what remained of our food supply slung over our shoulders in pouches, we followed a trail that clung to the face of the cliffs, at times becoming a barely visible path on which we could sometimes see the faint tracks of animals.

"How do you know exactly where we are going, Seltan?" I asked my brother that second evening. We had reached Dilah Vena Tustes, a pass through the mountains, and had stopped to rest. Seltan had been sitting by the fire talking with Jabila about the trail. The air breathed foreboding. It was as if the dghili dnayi, the mountain spirits, were closing in to bar our flight.

"Remember, Little Sister, our grandfather told us that Dena'ina live in the country west of the mountains rising beyond the coast. He spent several seasons among them, trapped and hunted with their men." Seltan squinted skyward, and in the waning light watched a chulyin flying overhead. "You have heard Father tell us. It was in one of those villages he found Sem. The time he first walked into that country with Grandfather." He laughed, "And they both said a man can tell when he gets there by the smell of sagebrush."

I persisted. "Maybe Grandfather followed a different trail." I was worried. My brother did not seem to have a sure way of leading us through.

I wondered how we could find out where we were, what trail we followed. At home on Yaghenen, we had a system: From ancient times, the Kahtnuht'ana had been able to tell exactly where they were and where they would go; their sense of direction was related to the flow of rivers. A person fixes on the nearest big river and, from the way it flows, can easily figure out directions: up at a higher elevation . . . downriver . . . this way, dach', . . . that way, yach'. But there in the mountains, far from the river, we lost the means to guide us; I feared that neither my brother nor my husband could set us on our true course west. Neither had we found moss hung on trees by hunters, which was one of the means by which Kahtnuht'ana used to mark trails. No blazes showed on trees. No piles of stones pointed the way.

Torrents of rain, driven by gusting winds, blinded us; the sky was dark, and we could not take our bearings from the stars. One night, huddling together in a cave, we kindled a fire from fragments of wood we found scattered on the floor. Half the night had passed before we began to dry out in the comforting warmth. We had intended to move on at the first sign of daylight, but another slashing storm forced us to stay in shelter. When the rain slackened, Seltan left us to look for game and Jabila to scout for a better trail. K'i'un and I kept the fire burning. It was past midday when Seltan returned with a ground squirrel he'd killed. Then Jabila came back. "We'd better stay on the path we are following," he reported. "It's the only trail there is." We threw more branches on the fire, wrapped the squirrel in leaves, and buried it in the ashes; when it was ready, we all hunched around the flames, enjoying the succulent fresh meat.

Always, Jabila's was the lightest voice among us. "At least, we're better off than the wolf hunter from the starving village. Remember him? Looking for caribou?"

I laughed at my husband. "Hah! But the foggy woman saved him."

"Follow me tomorrow. I will be that old foggy woman," K'i'un challenged all of us.

Seltan kept a straight face, "You women, always taking credit."

I felt a need to keep our minds bright, to lift the low mood the weather had settled over us that morning. "Jabila, tell us about the foggy woman." I took his hand, waiting to hear his rich, sonorous voice, the voice I so loved.

"In one of the villages of my clan, long ago, it was the time of want. That season hunger had stalked among the people longer than anyone could remember. The mighty wolf hunter—for that was the distant times before human beings, the time far back when my ancestors were wolves—roamed the mountains day after day, but he could not find even one caribou. And his wolf people grew hungrier. One day, he sat on a log at the edge of a huge forest, his head sagging between his shoulders. Below, where the caribou should have been, he could see nothing. Many in his village would soon starve to death. Then a strange wolf woman came and sat down beside him."

" 'Stay with me,' the hunter said.

" 'No, I shouldn't,' the stranger replied.

"Rain began to fall, and tushe*l* draped around the hunter and the woman. Quickly, they scraped together a brush shelter and crawled in. They stayed inside a very long time. When the great hunter looked outside, he saw only rain and dense fog. He could not hear any caribou.

"Finally, the woman said, 'I told you I should not stay here with you. I will go.' She picked up the new baby that had come to her while she lived in the shelter and slung him on her back in a skin bag.

"It was raining hard, and the fog was thick. The hunter said, 'I do not want you to leave.'

"But she went anyway.

"The hunter followed her a long distance. Then he sat down on a log and watched her climb up the mountainside. She walked straight ahead. She did not look back. Something strange happened. No rain fell around the wolf hunter. The fog thinned out. As he stared after the woman, the sheets of rain and clouds of fog circled her, followed her. They were so thick that soon he could not see her. The wolf woman disappeared, taking all the fog and rain with her.

"The mighty hunter looked down into the valley. No fog. No rain. Below him fed a big herd of caribou. He picked up his arrows and bow and raced down the mountain. He shot many of them. Then, he made a huge pack and dragged it home. The village ate again. The hunter's wolf people were happy. And that is the way the foggy woman saved the village of my people in that long-ago time."

We told more stories, talked of happiness we four had known, laughed over the day Seltan and Jabila became slocin and raced their new boat across Tikahtnu.

My brother had never answered my question, and I faced him again. "Could Grandfather have taken the trail up from Tuk'ezitnu Bay? That was some distance south of here."

Seltan poked the fire with a stick. "It was not only Grandfather and Father. Other hunters from our villages walked this trail." He looked at me, then at Jabila and back to the fire.

"How do you know if this trail leads to Htsaynenq'?"

"Ashana, we must be near the pass. We will find a river on the other side and follow it to where we want to go."

"We should have made certain of directions before—"

"That was not possible." My brother stared me down. "You know we dared not ask questions about such things."

I could have bitten my tongue for complaining to Seltan, who strove only to bring me to safety.

Seltan.

My brother, whom I trust to this day. Heir to generations of those who had made long walks over Aláyeksa's mountains and valleys, he had loved the sea near which he was born. He possessed a special kind of instinct, a certain knowledge, deeper, as Minya had often said, than that of any other man. He *knew* if an animal was near—a dear at the edge of a pond a few paces from the trail, a caribou beyond his arrow's range or a bear deep in hibernation. He was a great hunter among our people.

Raven-colored hair—thick, black, and straight. I could spot Seltan in any gathering by that hair. His rich dark eyes set deep above high cheekbones matched mine. When he hoisted a slain deer over his broad shoulders, the sinews of his arms and back knurled with ridges and knots. Taller than Jabila. Heavy arm muscles like an Ulchena's, for he had trained on the sea in their kayaks.

During our growing-up seasons, Seltan had always known when I was not truthful. He corrected me, led me to straight thinking, never allowed me to be less than a proud Kahtnuht-'ana. I always looked to my brother for protection, and he allowed no one to harm me.

Seltan always chose the finest pelts for his venqel'a, his clothing. He insisted that his moccasins be decorated with certain shells he found in a hidden cove along the coast and with quills from the strongest, healthiest porcupines. "A young man particular in his tastes. Almost a fussy one," my mother said. She assigned only the best seamstress to help her sew Seltan's shirts, trousers, boots, fur capes. Mother always embroidered his arrow quivers, his knife sheaths, his wristbands, his headbands. She may have called him fussy, but, eyu! she took great pride in her son!

Seltan. The most loyal of Kahtnuht'ana.

K'i'un, the slightest of us, stumbled across a log early one morning and fell against a boulder, bruising her leg and hip. Uncomplaining, but often lagging, she pushed on until nightfall. When we stopped to make camp, Seltan unrolled his pack, took out his fur cape, and spread it on branches and leaves to serve as K'i'un's bed for the night. I eased her onto her good side and said, "Seltan, get me ferns from under those trees."

I bound a moist, cool pad of leafy green ferns over the ugly red and blue bruises, tying it on with deer sinews from Jabila's pouch. K'i'un relaxed, the taut lines of her face smoothing; light flashed from the polished agate labret inserted in a small hole in her lower lip. Curling toward the warmth as a child does, she looked less than her fourteen years. Another season, and Seltan would have finished paying his bride-price to her parents, then she would become my true sister.

We moved slowly for the next couple of days, giving K'i'un time to work off some of the soreness and adjust to the climb. Our path disappeared in puddles of water; our feet tangled in the brush and half-decayed moss. Much as we needed to move west as fast as possible, the beating rains forced us to seek shelter once more.

Fog. Rain. Through the mist, framed by a ray of light that played momentarily upon a gnarled trunk, I saw the face of my mother and sensed that she walked with me, wishing that both of us could join the Athabaskans in the village of her childhood. At times, I reached out as if she walked close enough for me to take her hand. Sem had eased my bewilderment at the changes in me from child to woman, calmed my uncertainty and fear over what I would face when Jabila would take me to his home and people after our first year in my father's house. She would sit with me in her japoon or on a log beside the stream near our village and talk of the joy as well as the work I would come to know with a home and a family of my own. Many girls my age seemed more shaken than I about the events of growing to young womanhood and the life ahead; but when they talked with Sem, she listened and answered questions with the same care and warmth she devoted to me; each girl walked away with more cheer, more spirit, than when she had come.

The fire of life burned in Sem's eyes. Her fair judgment toward my father's other wives and the women of our villages set examples for many to follow. But let her hear of slovenly work— a poorly sewn qenich'eni, a basket of berries allowed to ferment, a snare set and forgotten—or of malicious words or sly, furtive deeds, and her anger was swift, her punishment certain.

My mother, Sem, star, named for the bright light in the sky the night she was born.

Through the rain and fog I heard her pleading voice: "Naq'eltani, the Forever Spirit of Kahtnuht'ana, watch over Ashana. The raven has turned his capricious side upon us. The forest dims. I cannot see through the fog that crawls in from the sea to cover the earth."

At night, huddled close to our small fire, we drew comfort from the thought that we were putting distance between us and the Tahtna. We dreamed of meeting Sem's clans and of what our life could be among them. Even while our hopes built, we worried about the welcome we would receive, for her people might fear the Tahtna had pursued us.

The days passed in our journey westward, days when we dared not pause to snare game or dig roots; we chewed on the dried salmon we had brought from Yaghenen, holding a little back against starvation. Our food nearly gone, we could no longer ward off the heaviness that haunted us, thick as the fog that shuts out the sky.

We spoke of chulyin, of our sorrow because he had turned his evil side to us. In the darkness, nightmares preyed on me. I stood in a clearing, my qenich'eni shredded from dragging my body over the rocky terrain, snow and ice everywhere. Nowhere could I see any of my family. I screamed for Jabila, but my voice froze, no words came. A circle of huge beasts surrounded me; they held torches that flickered through the black of the night. Their tails curled and lashed and whipped toward me. Terror held me rigid. But most frightening were the savage eyes that stared at me, strangely blue for the eyes of wild beasts. I tried to shrink away from them, sink into the ground. A bear rose on its haunches to full height, snarling, "We have put your people to death and burned your village. Some escaped, but we will track down everyone." In my half sleep I tried to call out, but again no sound came. "Baranov waits for you on Kadyak. We must take you to him." The ring of bears danced around me. The torches blinded my eyes as the beasts squeezed toward me, each snapping a whip of walrus hide near my feet. The circle broke, and two monsters strode close. One huge beast held my arms while the other looped his whip around my throat. . . .

Struggling to sit up, I crawled away from Jabila and out of our shelter. Frozen with fright, I could not cry out to warn my sleeping companions of what I saw: a figure not more than seven or eight arrow lengths from me. Half asleep, I shook my head, blinked. Not a beast. Quiet, seated on a rock, was Uncle Minya, who served my father as a special messenger or to bear warnings when danger threatened.

"Ashana." His voice was soft like my mother's. "You had a bad dream. I have been watching you."

"Why are you here, Minya?" The images of the nightmare rose in my mind. I was seized by fear that the Tahtna had trapped us. My face drained of color, my heart pounded, and I sank onto a rock in front of him.

"We must talk. I have things to tell you," my uncle said, as he rose to his feet.

Our voices roused the others. Seltan and Jabila rushed out of the shelter. K'i'un held back, frightened.

"Uncle! How did you find us?" Seltan stared, shocked that after our long walk anyone could have tracked us to that distant place.

"Why are you here?"

"Why did you follow us?"

"Who is with you?"

Jabila, then Seltan, pelted Minya with questions.

"Sit down." Minya wasted no words. "Things at the villages are bad. Very bad."

K'i'un crept to Seltan's side, grasped his arm. "What has happened?"

"The Tahtna came for Baranov's hostages. Three or four of our young men tried to run from them. They shot one, the eldest son of the shaman. That is five Kahtnuht'ana the aliens have murdered. Baranov's men have surrounded our village. They hold guns on Ni'i and Sem and our leaders. They demand you, Qanilch'ey Ashana." The soft voice hardened; and if I had not known my uncle well, the face staring at me could have been that of another man, its narrowed eyes those of a stranger. His genial friendliness had been strained through torment, his features lined with bitterness. Minya had slipped an invisible mask on his face; it was the carved driftwood mask that hung in my Yaghenen home, a sea-lion mask that showed the onlooker only its wooden face, slits for eyes, a tight mouth. No emotion, no feeling, no reaction for the stranger to read.

Like thunder in the far distance, my uncle's words pressed against us. "The guards said, 'We give you six days. Find the girl and bring her back. If you do not, every third day we will shoot one of your people till she is here.' "

K'i'un screamed. Jabila held me tightly against his body. I wanted only to flee, to take my husband far into the mountains of Aláyeksa and hide forever. Chills raked me as I saw again the murdered Shila, his hands grasping the soil of Yaghenen, his life blood draining away.

"How did you find us?" Seltan asked, pushing aside the tragic messages.

"I could not sleep for many nights after the Tahtna forced us to pledge hostages. When you fled in the early mist, I stood on the headland and watched your kayak." There was sorrow in

his voice, and his words dragged. "I willed . . . that you four
. . . would escape."

"Why are you here?" Jabila demanded. "Did you tell them
you saw us leave?"

"No, I did not. I grieve for what is happening." Despair
sounded in my uncle's voice. "I told them only that I believed
I could find Ashana."

"Why didn't you let the Tahtna look for us? They could never
track us into these mountains." I had not wanted to challenge
Minya, but the words spilled out. Then, through the slits of the
mask, his eyes showed his anguish. He had always been a favorite with me, and in my heart I knew he had not betrayed us.

"Ashana, the Tahtna leave us no choice. I have been gone
nine days. Today, someone dies. It could be Ni'i. Your mother."
As far back as I can remember, my uncle had always held responsibility to our clans above any personal wants. "If you do
not return, my niece, many will be shot. And the aliens will not
spare children."

Seltan started to speak, but Minya silenced him.

"Let me finish. We have no weapons to resist the Tahtna
guns. I fear for our people. We are forced to give hostages.
Hunters. Food. They will make slaves of us, and many will die,
as the U*l*chena have. I see only grief ahead." The sorrow deepened on Minya's face. But he said it: "Ashana, you must go
back with me. You have no choice."

His words echoed, hollow. "They know nothing of you other
three. Go on to the Htsaynenq' country. Stay away until . . ."
His voice broke. "At least you will survive."

Almost shouting, Jabila protested, "We will not let my wife
go to Baranov alone. The four of us mean to live our lives together. Far from Yaghenen, if we must." My husband strode
past the shelter and back again, pounding fist into hand. "If
Ashana goes back, all of us go back."

"Jabila is right. Minya, you know the life of the hostage
women. Slaves, they are." Seltan snapped a branch across his
leg. "I will not let my sister go."

Minya paced beside a fallen evergreen, scarred and blackened by lightning. Morning sun splintered against the trees. The
four of us drew close together, stared at my uncle. He studied
us, his face hardening. The silence was stifling.

"Listen to me. What will happen if the four of you go back?
Jabila, you will be shot on sight." Minya spoke firmly, his voice
echoing with the pain of his thoughts. "Seltan, you will be taken

captive and put out to the sea hunts. K'i'un, they will drag you off and make you a hostage for the rest of your life.''

K'i'un turned her face away, her sob choked against Seltan's body.

"Know this: None of that will help Ashana. She is already marked as a hostage to be taken to Kadyak or people will be shot.''

But Jabila did not intend to yield. "That is my choice—to go with her! Ashana and I belong together. She is my wife.''

"I just said, Baranov will separate you,'' Minya insisted, "and it will all end. Jabila, you will be shot for taking her from our village. You know the Tahtna guns force us to do what the aliens demand. There is no choice for any of us.''

"Are you sure the aliens have not tracked you here?'' Seltan asked.

"Yes. I volunteered to find Ashana. The Tahtna guards saw me row away from Yaghenen. It was foggy. Tushel covered me, and I turned north for a distance before heading west. No one could see me. No one knew where I went. So I did not lead them here.''

We four listened, silent. Minya's words had sealed my fate. Escape could not be my choice, so I was torn between what must be done and what I wanted to do. I would not let my husband go back to be shot; but the thought of leaving him stabbed at me, even though my return would keep him free.

"Jabila,'' I said, "we have had time together. Nothing can blot out our memories. . . .'' I held my husband close as my voice faded. I tried again, forced back tears. "Our uncle speaks the truth. We know it. Your freedom means life for me. Go free; I . . .'' Oh, how hard I found saying what I had to say! "Eltani needs you to be free, not dead. Go. The three of you. To Sem's people. Far from the Tahtna.'' Seltan began to protest; but I continued, stumbling over words, weeping. "I will return with Minya. You lose me, but our people need you to help resist the aliens. I will have none of us blamed for the blood of our men and women, for children, for Ni'i and Sem.''

Jabila's hands played through my hair, down over my face. I heard his whispered words, his breaking voice: "Ashana, one day we will make a way to kill the Tahtna. Then we will come for you.'' I stored his lingering kiss in my memory, to be relived during the days when the black water would follow me.

Silence bound us until Minya said, "I agreed with our clan leaders to bring back Ashana. That will save the rest of you, and you can do more if you are alive and unknown to the Tahtna. I cannot put into words the despair I have suffered coming to you."

My three loved ones and Minya walked slowly with me to a granite cliff jutting from the mountainside, and we stared westward. My uncle's mask cracked; he wept with the four of us. Through tear-filled eyes, I searched the distance, looking toward the hills and streams of Htsaynenq', Sem's homeland, a country for which my heart poured out its loss. I would never hear the voices of our distant relatives, who would welcome word from Sem, nor would I ever smell the fresh sage of which my grandfather had spoken.

Driving rains blinded Minya and me as we forced our way eastward toward Yaghenen, back along the trail we had struggled over only a few days before. I stumbled behind my uncle, hanging on to the long leather strip tied around his waist. The cold crept inward, more than weather chilling me. A frozen mummy, wandering abroad from an Ulchena burial cave, would have had more mettle for the journey than I.

Scream to the heavens, to Naq'eltani, to the raven! But the rain pelted us, and wind and cold dug into our faces. I tore at my hair and pulled it over my face, blackened my skin with ashes from our campfires: the ancient Kahtnuht'ana way for a people in mourning to show sorrow and despair. I was dead in spirit.

When we reached Tikahtnu, the storm had abated, the waters of the ocean river had calmed. The fog still followed us, masking Qelghin Island, but Minya needed no sunlight: The currents and the winds spoke to him, and from them he always knew his way on the water. He beached our kayak on the shore of Yaghenen, at the lower end of the trail to our village. My heart walked with Jabila as my body dragged up the winding path to what had once been home.

○ ○ ○

3

Against the green trees and the gray mountain rock, my father and mother, parents of other hostages, and our villagers huddled in groups—bereft, staring toward us, silent as if carved from stone. Back along the length of the trail and up above, on an outcropping, more of our clan stood in mute, anxious knots, their rain-drenched clothing whipped by the icy wind.

"Take us, not our children."

My father planted his legs firmly in the center of the trail winding down the slope to the shore, but the Tahtna guards roughly pushed him aside and forced us toward their Ulchena umiaks, beached at water's edge, some distance from our Kaht-nuht'ana boats. Desperate to save us, many of the crowd pressed alongside the aliens and pulled at their arms, grabbing at us as we stumbled in a straggling line, prodded by the Tahtna guns and stung by their whips.

My mother gripped my hand, pleaded, her voice harsh with sobs, "Free Ashana. Take me."

A keening rose from many strained throats. "Leave the children. Take us."

A respected war leader threatened, "No Tahtna will be safe on Yaghenen if you do not take elders for hostages."

The alien fur traders ignored every plea, shoved aside anyone who dared push toward us.

We lunged, tried to break away, but our feeble revolt quieted at a shot fired over the heads of parents and elders. Another lunge. A lone shot. A Kahtunht'ana grasped his chest, spun around screaming, and slumped to the ground, his arm and shoulder bloody.

Our alien captors shoved us into the waiting boats and tied

us hand and foot; the grim Ulchena oarsmen pushed off, dipping their paddles into the gray waters of Tikahtnu.

No sea lion lazed on the shore.

No seal broke the surface.

Our animals knew.

I struggled to turn around for a backward look at my people. The nearest *promyshlennik* slapped me hard across the face, but I stared shoreward long enough to etch into memory the scene of the Kahtnuht'ana men and women I was leaving.

The shaman, known among our Yaghenen families as a healing, jovial man with his mystic rattles and dolls, stood empty-handed, arms rigid, fists clenched, lifting his face to the sky as if making a final plea to Naq'eltani. He grieved at his failure to drive away the force that bound us hostage, grieved for his eldest son, murdered while the village had waited for Minya to bring me home, and for his second son, who had been seized as captive in place of his slain brother.

Standing beside my father, the war leader spread his arms wide in final argument, anger and terror creasing his face. He had seen Shila, his youngest son, murdered by the aliens at the bargaining over trade that became a demand for hostages. His middle son sat in front of me in the umiak, sobbing.

An elder from Jabila's clan, wise in the councils of my father, was standing half turned toward my mother, his face aged and haggard. He knew that his words would never ease her fear and grief.

And Sem: proud headwoman of our village, her braids nearly waist length, she stood with her hands clasped and stretched downward before her, a desolate, weeping figure.

Ni'i, his head lowered, his shoulders sagging, reached out his raised, open hand, palm upward. His mouth formed a last entreaty, unheard and useless, to call us back. A final supplication to our captors for mercy? A plea to me for understanding?

The light of day waned. The shoreline receded as distance pulled us apart. Shadows played eerily across the scene, lines stretching from one troubled face to another. Like rough-hewn sculptures, the figures merged into one another, then separated. Great veils of fog drifted across the sea between the umiak and the land I was leaving behind. A heavy curtain of cloud unfolded, mingling with the sea-fog to blot out my last glimpse of home.

I bowed my head to avoid seeing those harsh-featured aliens, and snapped and bit at them whenever a grimy hand reached out to touch me. At the bottom of the umiak, rotting fish heads and guts swirled in the stinking water around my feet. A Tahtna called Igor opened his pants and relieved himself over the side, his urine spraying back against our faces.

Turning away, I saw that the land where my people stood was shrouded in a dense gray blanket like the fur of tiqun. And on that misty pall I saw the wolf, a powerful spirit of Aláyeksa, its face contorted in anger and grief. The specter hung for a moment above the water, then disappeared, leaving only the memory of my lost Jabila.

4

When we beached on Kadyak Island, rough hands, fingernails split and black with filth, untied me. A second rope was fastened around my middle and I was yanked from the umiak. With less care than hunters dragging otters from the sea, I was pushed past half-eaten, vermin-covered carcasses into the settlement the Tahtna call Pavlovsk. The stink of rotten meat and of pelts soaking in urine vats was my first introduction to the head village of Shelekhov's Siberian trading company, the band of traders managed by Aleksandr Baranov.

I shrank back, but the Tahtna kept pulling on the rope. I was aware of curious eyes peering through cracks in gut-covered windows and from behind fish-drying racks, but no one called to me.

The door of the largest building was flung open and a voice roared, "Who is there?"

Aleksandr Andreevich Baranov, a squat figure with broad shoulders, wide-set eyes, and a nose that seemed to dominate his whiskered face, strode out through the mud and halted in front of me, switch in hand. "Untie her."

Roughly the Tahtna hunter slipped the ropes from around my waist and fumbled with the knots that bound my hands.

Baranov ran his eyes over me and frowned. "This ragged slattern? She is not the wench I picked out at Ni'i's village. The one the chief gave me was his daughter. A princess she was, a beauty."

"We brought—"

"What the hell is this wretch doing here, Igor? Get me the princess."

"Princess, you say?" Igor snorted. "A bitch, that's what she is. Kicks, scratches, bites. Snarled at everything we said. Princess, hah!'' I was shoved forward.

"Get back to work, Igor.'' Baranov flicked his switch across the back of the hunter. As I rubbed my aching wrists, the Tahtna leader motioned me inside the house. His eyes questioning, his face scowling, he stamped off down the path without another word.

Alone, I paced the room like a fox in a cage. To keep fear from sliding into madness, I forced myself to take note of this place: a building entirely above ground, its floor of logs cut flat on one side and laid together. A smaller house than many on Yaghenen, for some of ours extend five tree lengths from one end to the other, the floors of bare earth. Here, no smoke hole in the roof provided an exit for the spirits of the dead to escape this world. I looked for the japoon where I could withdraw to myself, but saw none. In the corner was a walled-off space, a pile of furs lying on the floor. An alien, strange house. Forbidding.

No fire pit commanded the center of the main room, but against the side wall a stone structure showed signs of fire; I ran my hand along the stones above the opening, rubbed off the soft black deposit—it was soot, the same stuff we used to blacken our faces in times of mourning and grief. I coated my face with it and tore at my hair.

All feeling had left me; my body sagged. My spirit had lost its bright flame; I hoped before the alien assault on my body took place that spirit would flicker and go out forever.

How long I lay huddled on the floor I do not know, but from somewhere I heard women's voices, Aláyeksan accents. The smell of cooking drifted into the room, spreading odors that bore no likeness to anything I knew. Still numbed by thoughts of my murdered people, I did not know what I would do when Baranov returned. I struggled to hold back the dread of alien hands touching me, roaming my body. I hated the man, and I would hate him till I died.

"Stand up, woman,'' Baranov ordered, puffing on his pipe as he turned to his Uĺchena interpreter. "Attu, ask her. Is she Chief Ni'i's daughter? The one I picked out in his village on the Kenai?''

I looked carefully at the interpreter called Attu; he was the same man who had translated Kahtnuht'ana to Tahtna when my father and Baranov bargained outside my home. Attu did not face me, but lowered his eyes and repeated the question in my tongue.

"Yes," I whispered.

"She can't be. Chief Ni'i's daughter wore a white deerskin. And I remember how the metal and shell on it sparkled when she walked. Her hair shone." Baranov growled to his interpreter, "But this, this one . . . !" His face wrinkled with disgust. "She is dirty. Her hair is matted and snarled." He walked around, inspected me from all sides. "That ragged old parka is no good for any woman in my house."

Baranov sat on a bench for several moments, smoke curling from his pipe. Then, giving his head a shake, he strode toward me, leaned close, touched me with the toe of his boot. "You smell. Look at your face, smeared with soot. You are no chief's girl. That savage has switched the princess with one of his slaves, but he will pay. Princess, bah!"

I sickened as the Ulchena interpreted the alien's crude insults. In the back of my mind flashed the thought: If he thinks I look so bad, and believes I am not the hostage he demanded, he will send me back to Yaghenen.

Quick words passed between the two men.

"Baranov wants to know where your good deerskin dress is. The one you wore when he saw you. Do you have it?" For the first time the man called Attu looked straight at me.

Scared of what lay ahead, I mumbled, "In the bottom of the umiak. In my basket."

I had brought with me the qenich'eni I was wearing the day Baranov claimed me hostage: a soft deerskin, porcupine-quill embroidery on the yoke and hem, made for me by K'enteh. She had helped my mother sew my bride dress; it was now with Sem, and I wondered if I would ever see it again.

Another exchange between my captor and Attu, then he repeated Aleksandr Baranov's instructions to me. "A woman, Watnaw, will bring you a basin. She can speak Kahtnuht'ana. She will show you how to clean yourself the way he expects you to. Then he will decide if you look like the right woman."

Baranov's voice boomed out at me again. "You are forbidden to go to the women's sweathouse."

Show *me* how to get clean? Another insult. All my life I have taken pride in keeping my body and my clothes clean, rubbing my hair with candlefish oil to make it shine. Most Kahtnuht'ana swim in the sea or river nearly every day, summer and winter. Teach *me* to be clean!

"Baranov orders you to wipe the black off your face. Tidy your hair—wash and braid it. Your basket will be brought to you. You must put on the dress Baranov saw you wear. He wants to make sure you are Chief Ni'i's daughter, the one he understood was the princess."

"Princess!" I spat back at him. "We don't know such a word on Yaghenen. What does it mean? Whore? Slave?"

"Careful, Ashana." For the second time Attu—strange name for a man, I thought—met my eyes; and in them I read sorrow, suffering, the same suffering I had seen in Minya's eyes when he had found me on the trail. He spoke slowly, carefully. "Let me help you understand. 'Princess,' in the words of the Tahtna, means a woman of high rank. One born with special privileges. 'Royal,' the strangers say, 'noble.' " He glanced at Baranov, who nodded approval as if he knew some of my language. "The aliens hold people of royalty as a class above all others. And they use royalty any way it will serve them to get what they want.

"Back on Yaghenen you are a leader's daughter. In your village you have special rank. And here, being a princess puts you above all of us. You are not a common hostage. Aleksandr Baranov has need of your royal rank. He will use it to help him get what he wants. You will see, and . . ."

Hearing his name again, the hard-eyed master of the house interrupted. "I am going to the men's sweathouse. Order her to get clean." Once again his eyes raked my body. "Princess? I'll see. I will have to see."

He dismissed Attu and motioned to a young man who had stood listening in the shadow beside the fire—a dark-faced man, thin, small-boned, wavy black hair hanging almost to his shoulders. "Hurry, Richard, get Watnaw. I cannot waste more time here." By Baranov's manner I sensed Richard must be a servant or another hostage. I could not place his clan—his features, his stance, the shape of his face, did not look Aláyeksan.

We spoke little. Watnaw's manner toward me was remote rather than quiet; deliberate, I thought. But her touch did reassure, the first kindness since the aliens had wrested me away from Yaghenen. The water refreshed my body, scratched and bruised as I was from the days of running toward Htsaynenq'; but my spirit still suffered. My body was washed, dried with a piece of material Watnaw explained was a "cloth towel"; then she started to pull my soft white deerskin dress over my head, but I pushed her back. "No. I will not wear this dress for Baranov."

"He ordered you to be clean. To put on your good dress."

"I said, I will not wear it. Watnaw, we need to talk." I held out my hands to her, but she drew back.

"No time now. I must tell you, Baranov ordered me to help you get settled. Only that. No talking. No making friends."

I stood there, the truth of my hostage state becoming clear as she insisted, "You must wear this dress. No one disobeys Aleksandr Baranov's orders. If we do, a hostage will be killed. It could be me or you."

In the face of the threat of death, not wearing my dress lost meaning. As I got into my trousers and put on the dress, I watched Watnaw closely. Her looks, the shape of her face, her accent, marked her Gulushutna from a land south and east far across the ocean. I wondered if Watnaw's remoteness stemmed in part from the age-old rivalry between her people and most other Aláyeksan clans. I had expected her, another Aláyeksan woman, to be warm toward me, but Baranov's orders forced her to stand apart. As Watnaw tidied the cluttered room, my joncha warned me to listen and be wary.

When Baranov stamped in, Watnaw turned toward the kitchen, but before she left she slipped a sharp clamshell into my hand and whispered, "Watch out. You will need this. Tahtna men expect to share their host's woman. It is the way here." Not talk to me? What Watnaw had just done had been friendly. I did not understand, and had not yet decided how to deal with Baranov.

Clean and dressed as I had been ordered, filth still drowned my spirit as Baranov turned me around, inspecting me. "Well, I must say you look much the same as you did back in the Kenai village. Princess Qan . . . Ash . . ." He stumbled over my Kahtnuht'ana name, his curse sharp. "Hell, I will call you Anna. You will be Princess Anna. A good Russian name. Easy to say."

Chuckling, Aleksandr Baranov sprinkled liquid—the stuff had an odor I had never smelled before—from his mug onto my hair. As he patted my head, he mumbled, "I christen thee Anna." Then, he lifted me up, tossed me in his arms.

My skin tightened, and I tried to draw away from his rough hands. I was afraid. He was going to use my body. Dread mixed with disgust at the way he tossed me around with less thought than Aláyeksans give to their game of throwing a seal's shoulder bone and laying bets on the way it falls. *Run, escape*—the words pounded in my head; I drew away from him, my eyes darting around the room like those of a captured ermine. Captive, I could not run.

"Richard," Baranov called to his small, unusual-looking servant, "tell all the men to come for a celebration. And tell them to call my woman *Anna. Princess Anna.*"

Old Half-Man, a rich and powerful hunter known from our long-ago ancient wisdom, lives high in Yaghenen's mountains. Crafty and very wise, he has only one arm and one leg and dances on the mountaintop using a stick carved from a tree limb. When ceremonies in our village required spirits of great power, my father's Old Half-Man masks (used together, two masks had the strength and power of that old hunter, who could see two ways) would be taken down from the shelf and dusted, the feathers and string lashings renewed, and the paint refreshed. One Half-Man mask would be worn by a dancer who faced one way with a message, the other Half-Man mask was worn by a second dancer who faced the other way with another message—two halves of the same spirit, divided, able to see two different ways, to speak two different messages.

I was too young, then, to know what the masks meant. But that day, facing Baranov, I began to understand. The spirits of Yaghenen had sped down Tikahtnu, across the sea, over the mountains; I knew this because, for a moment, it was as if a raven paused above the fire pit, his eyes looking deeply into me. *Courage*, *Ashana* passed from him; and down over my face he slipped the Old Half-Man masks. And then the raven was gone. Like the two dancers in my father's house, my mind divided and became two halves of the same spirit: One part watched every move, uncertain, waiting, wary, hating Baranov; the other part escaped into the Yaghenen mountains where Old Half-Man danced.

My masks, invisible, were unseen by the Tahtna who filled the room. They had come, I knew, to view the prize their leader had seized.

"Men! This is Princess Anna." Baranov motioned toward me with his mug.

The faces of the aliens lit up with anticipation. Richard filled their mugs. I noticed he poured from the same jug Baranov had used when he sprinkled my head. As the men drank, their voices grew louder, their laughter more coarse; and the warning Watnaw had whispered pulled me to the sharp edge of caution.

Waiting, shaking, I struggled to hold back terror. (*Control yourself, Ashana. Watch and be ready.* The voice of my joncha.) I slipped the clamshell Watnaw had given me into my hand. She had told me I might need one, and I had hidden it in the folds of my deerskin.

I faced the men, my masks intact.

Beasts from my nightmares ringed about me, closing in. But they were no nightmare. These beasts, smelly aliens, waited to snare me.

"Tame her, men," Baranov's harsh laugh echoed throughout the room.

"Come here." First one ruffian, then another, grabbed at me.

"Aha! Now I've got you." Igor, the man from the umiak, lunged at me.

"K'usht'a! No! K'usht'a!" From behind the wary and powerful masks, I slashed a deep gash into the alien's hairy arm. Blood trickled along the skin and off the man's fingers.

"Princess, hah! Bitch!" Igor wiped his bloody arm as the men drew back.

"You tame her yourself, Aleksandr. We got broken-in women."

There was silence. The men glared, but, whether backing away from me in surprise or yielding to their rising need to couple with their hostage women in the shacks, they stopped grabbing at me. For the moment the threat had passed, but in their eyes I saw a barely disguised hunger; my joncha warned that it could devour me.

"Drink up, men. Go back to the women you have already broken in." Baranov chuckled, emptied his mug, refilled it. "I will tame her. Hah! I'm a better man than any of you. I'll bed her myself." His eyes raked me.

I shrank into a corner, but alien stares lingered and from the loud laughter and ogling eyes, I knew the men spun nasty tales about me. Baranov circled among his workmen, constantly pouring liquid into mugs until first one Tahtna, then another, faces red, limbs unsteady, stumbled out of the house. As the door opened and closed, sounds of revelry drifted up to me from the workshacks below. Laughs. Oaths. Screeches. Women's screams. Those *promyshlenniki* were abusing the women. As the last man staggered out, Aleksandr Andreevich Baranov picked up a jug and stamped after him.

* * *

Beluga blubber and cabbage boiled together; salted pig meat and smoked fish; the lingering odors of sweaty aliens, their foul breaths, sodden footwear, stale vodka—the smells of Baranov's house were as sickening as the feeling that churned my stomach while I waited in dread. "The finest house in all Aláyeksa," the alien leader had bragged to my father. Head man of the Tahtna in Aláyeksa, manager of a trading company with boats many times larger than any my people knew about, and he lived in such small, ill-smelling quarters? Some of the odors rose from food dropped on the floor, and I wondered how the intruders cleaned their habitations. We Kahtnuht'ana always stored moss and fresh sand at the side of our rooms to spread over spilled grease and freshen our earthen floors. Here, the cooking smells must have hung in the room for days.

My captor reveled with his men in the hovels at the lower end of the village. Hoping that he would stay away for the night, wild thoughts poured through my head. Escape! Run. Run now, Ashana. High into the Kadyak hills. Hide. Find a boat. Row to Yaghenen. Escape. Escape. I knew if I ran, hostages would die; but nothing could stop me from pulling open the door and looking toward freedom.

"*Nyet!*" An alien on guard outside—I had not known he was there—pushed me back and slammed the door.

Nyet? No? *K'usht'a* in my tongue. I had learned my first Tahtna word.

Another guard paced the length of the house, marching from one end of the porch bordering the side of the building to the other. I was cut off. I could not run, I could not row away, I had no chance of escaping. My despair deepened.

The cooks from the kitchen were gone. Attu had left. That strange servant, Richard—Attu had told me he was from Bengal, wherever that was—had also disappeared. Watnaw, too. I was alone. No sound but the pacing of alien feet—unnoticed at first, they pounded loudly when I realized they barred my way to freedom. I closed my eyes, buried my nose in my deerskin, but it could not shut out the stench that hung in the air as I settled onto a bench at the side of the fire pit.

I finally lay down on a bearskin stretched on the floor and drifted into a half sleep. The blaze flickered; in my weaving in and out, fighting against the horror of sinking into the quagmire, I wakened, calling for Jabila. I knew the alien beast would soon come to claim my body.

As I drew the bearskin close, the raven appeared again in the smoke from the fire pit. *Stay close to the spirits,* he said. I tried, but the power and strength of the Old Half-Man masks eluded me. I caught the barest glimpse of the divided mind, then it was gone. *Try harder, Ashana. You must learn the way of the spirits. Then the aliens will never understand you . . .*

Lifted free of the bog into which I had sunk, I fled high into the mountains of Yaghenen. Jabila's voice . . . Seltan's . . . I lay among the giant evergreens . . . heard the cries of the forest people . . . watched those monsters of our forested mountains—the šdónályášna—as they leaped and twisted in their angry dances.

Sometime during the night I sensed that Aleksandr Baranov stood over me. I blotted from my mind what would come. He lifted me. I made no response, lay in his arms as limp as a strip of blubber. I heard him kick open a door and felt him stretch me onto his pile of furs.

Our eyes clashed a moment. I saw the working of his lips and wondered when he would drop down to use me. I stayed limp, slowed my breathing. He must have sensed my rejection. He did not touch me.

Without a word, he turned, walked slowly to the door, and eased it shut behind him.

5

For a long time that first season on Kadyak I lived alone. I remained untouched. Guards stopped pacing in front of my door, but as the days dragged I saw them stalking the waterfront, their Tahtna eyes on the island and its hostage herd. The servants in the kitchen provided food, but remained distant, hostile if I attempted to draw them into talk; I gained no warmth from them, Aláyeksan though they were. Something more than language and tradition separated us, I knew.

Watnaw came regularly, but kept a barrier between us. From her bearing, her few words, I sensed an inborn authority. When she tossed her head and threw her braids from over her shoulders, even the cooks listened. But she bore no warmth toward me, either. Taller and more muscular than I, she fit the Gulushutna pattern. We had little difficulty speaking with each other because our languages bear a common kinship. And by that link, formed long ago during our trade fairs when we had met peaceably, our two peoples had reached an ease of understanding. There were times in those early days when I sensed Watnaw had difficulty keeping the chasm between us; the basic kindness of one human being toward another sometimes broke through, and we seemed on the edge of friendship. Then the gap between us would widen again and we would drift further out of touch than we had been before, when she must have seen me as a terrified child far from home and half out of my mind.

On the days when I could not reach Watnaw, when her Gulushutna spirit could not meet in understanding with my Kahtnuht'ana one, life was bad. Watnaw had nothing to say to me, and it was as if the Aláyeksan mountain range divided us. But I needed a friend, and I kept trying to find one.

Heartbreak for Jabila and my people had become my only

companion. But perhaps in the future there would be escape, and in that hope burned the only light for me on Kadyak. When the guards no longer blocked my door and I was permitted to walk outside, I ventured first around the house, then several steps along a path toward the shore, always looking for escape. I *would* escape; Jabila had told me so that day on the trail west to Htsaynenq': "Ashana, one day we will find a way to kill the Tahtna, and then we will come for you." But even with the power of hope, I knew that killings would stalk me for the rest of my life.

Although no eyes met mine with friendship, they still watched me closely. No friendly hand reached out. That first season, I did not want to believe the silence of other hostages toward me, but I began to realize that a ring of isolation circled me, and I knew my captor was the cause. It was part of his scheme to break me. I seemed more devoid of human contact than the tusked Siberian pigs—ugly, fierce, covered with coarse brown-black hair—that climbed the low roofs and fed on the grass and lichens, tore at the packed sod almost as soon as the workmen replaced it. As angry in captivity on Kadyak as I was, they belonged back in Siberia.

In my despair I asked myself, Was being hostage the same as being criminal in Aleksandr Baranov's mind? On Yaghenen, our clans considered murder the most blameworthy of offenses. The penalty: banishment for many years, if not for life. On Kadyak, though they knew I was not a criminal, the aliens framed me with a silence as final as that banishment.

I longed to reach out, beg some person to talk to me, ease my loneliness. One day Attu and Richard worked at the table and I screamed at them, demanded that they tell me why, why the isolation thrown around me on Kadyak.

Silently, they looked at me. When I kept insisting, Attu finally answered me in his heavily accented Kahtnuht'ana. "Baranov ordered no one should talk to you, Anna." Richard said nothing, but his eyes met mine, and in them I saw the glacier-cold look of his Russian master. Attu finished his explanation. "He threatened anyone caught talking to you."

"Why?" I demanded. "A little talk will not hurt . . ."

"It is simple enough. Baranov ordered it."

The day came when Attu told me, "I have to take a boat of supplies to Baranov. He must be gone many weeks, inspecting his artels. Richard has orders to teach you Baranov's language.

You will be expected to know how to speak a few Russian words when he gets back to Kadyak.''

Richard walked into the big room of the house carrying a salmon, its scales still glistening with water, and dropped it onto the table. "Fish." Jabbing it with his fingers, he repeated, "Fish. Fish."

My mind jolted. What? Was he trying to tell me what a fish is? From the ancient beginnings of our people, we have known fish. My people were hungry then.

As the Kahtnuht'ana wisdom teaches, chulyin, the raven, said, "I will save you." He took his boat and paddled out to fish. He drifted with the tide. He watched a run of sea herring. He caught a salmon. He ate it to give him strength. Then he caught herring and killed them. He rubbed skin and entrails on every part of his boat. Then he rowed home. He said, "I did not catch anything. I am tired. I am going to sleep." The people cried that they were hungry. Then one said, "I am going to look at his boat." Everyone ran to the shore. They saw the bits of herring. A woman said, "Chulyin is joking. He caught fish." Then the salmon began to run. They had followed the herring smeared on chulyin's boat. The salmon filled the stream. They flowed into the villages. They filled the houses. They filled the pits.

Ever after, every spring at ts'iluq'a, the salmon run far up the same streams. They spawn, lay their eggs in the waters, and the people of Aláyeksa have plenty to eat. It is in this way that we have salmon, the gift of food from raven.

I knew Baranov intended to destroy my Kahtnuht'ana being. But I am of the raven clan. The raven is my people, my culture. Baranov and Richard did not understand how we Kahtnuht'ana think, and they did not know a way to find out. Never would I tell them. Never would I let them know why I do not need to learn their word "fish."

I said nothing.

Richard looked at me, his round eyes questioning. "Fish," he insisted.

I said nothing.

"Table," he tapped on it, trying another word.

I said nothing.

Richard shook his head; drawing in his breath, he said, "Bowl."

I read anger on his face as his eyes narrowed; then he turned and stamped out of the room.

The next morning, Richard was waiting for me by what he said was the "fireplace"—what we called the fire pit in Yaghe-nen—in the big room. "Man." "Woman."

So, he was keeping at it. I did not reply.

"Ashana, learn. Baranov said obey . . . or hostages die. Attu said to tell you."

I heard the words. I looked at the man, but he was no longer Richard. He was the killing hand of Baranov; the hand was forcing me to a choice, the awful choice my father had made when he said, "I would say no and die . . ."

Watching Richard, holding back from rash words, I felt strength because my joncha spoke to me: *The raven has helped your people endure since their ancient beginnings. You are of the raven clan. The aliens cannot destroy you. They cannot control your spirit or your mind. They cannot even know them. Learn their words, but do not take them for your own. In this way, you trick the Tahtna. You will save hostages from being killed.*

So, it began. I mumbled, "man," "woman." Richard banged his hands together. "Good. Now try again: table."

Then, walking across the room, touching every object we passed, Richard let me know Baranov expected me to learn the name of each one. He pointed to things, shaping the sounds by which meanings could be tied to words. Even though I knew my joncha must be heeded and the words learned, dragging out the sounds was a way to resist.

I remember days when he started his teaching earlier than usual. "We have to speed up your learning. Look. Black leaves. Tea." He grabbed a mug, mimicked drinking. Slowly, I repeated the word "tea" after him, my tongue and mouth detesting the alien sounds; but after I tried a few times, he accepted the frame into which my Kahtnuht'ana fitted the word.

One morning, Richard shook his head. "Weeks have gone by. I have tried to teach you Baranov's words, but you do not take to the Russian sounds. Ashana, you will never . . ." Richard surprised me, calling me by my Kahtnuht'ana name.

Through it all, Richard's own speech made my learning hard: his words rolled out with a rhythm so different from any Aláy-eksan and did not even match that of this Tahtna master. Some days, seated across the table from each other, seeing his efforts to handle Baranov's difficult language, I sensed Richard was at times as uncomfortable as I with the speech alien to both of us. But he persisted: He dared not neglect his orders to teach me Tahtna.

I wondered during those times, What *is* Richard? Slave? Servant? Hostage?

The leaves turned yellow. Autumn closed in. Only at night could I dream of home. The relentless substitution of harsh Russian words for my musical Kahtnuht'ana tongue made my head ache with alien sounds.

Long ago, before the time when animals and birds turned into people, a family of chickadees lived on the shores of Yaghenen. One day, a whale washed up from the sea onto the beach. A chickadee saw the whale and landed on its back. The chickadee people said, "He is so little. He can't eat it all." But the chickadee kept pecking away. A peck at a time. Peck. Peck. Peck. Soon the whale was only a skeleton. Backbone and ribs. The chickadee ate the whole whale.

Word by word by word, destroy my language. Uproot me from home, from the familiar. Isolate me from people. Breed in me a captive mind. Feed me alien food. Peck. Peck. Peck. Leave me a Kahtnuht'ana skeleton on Kadyak's beach.

A pair of goat horns lay in the corner of the kitchen—curved horns taken from majestic creatures that lived high in the mountains of Yaghenen. Men in my village polished and carved horns like those, sometimes into large, beautiful spoons. My first idea had been to sneak into the kitchen at night and take the horns, hide them under my sleeping furs. No, Ashana, I thought, you are no sneak thief. Head up, I walked into the kitchen, picked up the horns, and carried them to my room.

The cooks stared.

Richard blinked.

No one stopped me.

It is said my people are not the great carvers of Aláyeksa: that fame traditionally belongs to the Gulushutna; but I can still see our Kahtnuht'ana carver's strong fingers holding a horn in one hand, a sharp-pointed stone in the other.

"How do you know what animal you will carve?" I had once asked him.

He had turned the horn, held it up to the light, studied it, put it down for a time, picked it up, searched it again, and finally said, "I wait. I wait until I see what creatures live in that horn.

Then, I chip around them . . . scrape away . . . dig out . . .
Aha, see, Ashana, see a little rabbit at the point . . . a deer at
the curve. The animal is not carved on the horn, it lives there.
I just help it to get out.''

The horns brought me a little bit of home, for as children
Seltan and I climbed the rocks in our summer camps and watched
the sure-footed creatures scamper easily from one steep ledge
to the next. As I closed my eyes and dreamed of happier times,
another thought wandered through my head. ''Ashana, why not
carve a large spoon like one we had at home on Yaghenen?''
Yes, I know—tradition holds that men do the carving. Men find
the elusive creatures in the horn. But I would . . .

When Attu's duties kept him on the island, he and Richard talked
often of Baranov's obsession with ships and sailing them, and
awe and respect colored Richard's words. ''Understand, Ashana, Baranov is a man who gets what he wants. He cannot
depend on his company to send ships from home, so he is set
on building a big ship right here in Aláyeksa. Baranov drew the
plans himself, and he put in charge an Englishman sent over
here by his company. So, that is what goes on at *Voskresenskaya
Gavan*.'' He laughed. ''The Englishman says he cannot handle
that hard Russian name, and he calls the place *Resurrection
Bay*.''

Attu joined Richard in this house many evenings. I listened
to their talks, as, stretched out by the fireplace, they recalled the
building of the *Phoenix*, the first alien ship made in Aláyeksa.

''Baranov spent a lot of time drawing plans. Every one a huge
ship: three masts, two decks, eighty feet long,'' Richard said.

''Yes, I saw the drawings on his desk, listened to him boast
about what a grand ship he would build,'' Attu agreed. ''He
said no one in Russia cared enough to send him iron and lumber.
But he would show them. He would find the materials in Aláyeksa to build his ship.''

''Baranov had a hard time finding the things he needed, but
he discovered a way to make what he had to have. Made caulk-
ing. Mixed paint. Sent men to Montague Island to cut trees.
Had them dig coal from the mountains on Yaghenen. And he
made iron—''

Attu broke in, his tone hard. ''Iron! Baranov stole most of
the iron from my people. Iron from shipwrecks they spent many
seasons pulling out of the sea and off the rocks in the U*l*chena
Islands. He stole it, like everything else, at gunpoint.''

Those talks gave me my first inkling that Attu had his own mind and wanted to speak it. He was more than just an echo of Baranov.

"But Baranov has what he started out to build. His ship, even if it is not finished. The cabins and deck—all need a lot of work, more paint." Richard sounded awed.

According to the two friends, for many months Baranov's thoughts and work and energy had focused on the shipbuilding; and it appeared that my captor was planning at least two more ships.

One night I asked them, "Why so many big boats?"

"Trade, Anna. Baranov needs them for trade. He cannot trust Shelekhov to send enough ships from Russia for all the furs he stacks up." Attu's voice deepened, he paced the room. "Aláyeksa's finest furs rot and are lost while Baranov waits for ships. So he intends to build his own fleet."

During that talk about boats, the Bengalese said to me, "You must stop saying 'Tahtna.' Here in Pavlovsk village you must say 'Russian.' " A frown trailed across his face. "The manager is *Russian*. Aláyeksa belongs to *Russia*. You must become *Russian*."

Ashana, a whisper in my ear. No breeze stirred the nearby trees, no grass rustled around my feet as I stood on the rocky shore watching the *promyshlenniki* herding captive Aláyeksans into boats for the hunting fleet that was putting out to sea.

The whisper again, *Ashana*. A presence unseen. And for an instant I seemed back in the cave during the escape toward Htsaynenq'; I had wondered, then, if a long-ago ancestor had painted the pictures on its wall. That day on Kadyak, I knew. *Watch the scene carefully. Paint it in your mind,* the whisper, stronger, insisted. *Remember it well, for the time will come when you must record it on caribou hide for our people to read and learn what happened here.*

Caribou hide? The only one I owned was folded into the bottom of my basket. It was large, well tanned, without gouges; but I had thought to use it for practical purposes.

Practical? the whisper asked. *What can be more practical than recording the crime you see before you?* The whisper sounded impatient. *Watch!*

Rowers settled into two-hatch Uĺchena kayaks or "baidarkas"—Richard insisted they be called by the Tahtna name. The shore teemed with hunters: five hundred kayaks, one thousand

men, the larger number of them Uĺchena Islanders. Some Gulushutna and Koniags. Kahtnuht'ana, too, for I saw Tema, one
of the men taken from Yaghenen the same day I was.

Old men and young boys struggled with heavy packs, loading
the larger boats, "baidaras," some carrying forty people or
more like our Kahtnuht'ana badi did. At first the scene was
muddled in my mind: the men, the boats, the sea. Then, I began
to see details: ivory carvings on hunting hats, gutskin rain garments, lines in weathered faces, harpoons and other gear lashed
to the skin-covered kayaks, the mountains in the distance.

Watch, Ashana. Never forget what you see. Paint it. Paint it.
A whisper, an approving pat on my shoulder, and a brisk touch
flitting through the air left me with the feeling that I had a purpose to carry out.

Levy was what the Tahtna called the seizure of our men for
the sea hunts.

Slavery was what we Aláyeksans knew it to be.

Far out on the sea, whitecaps beckoned the hunters; only a
few minutes before, no breeze had stirred; then, quickly, a fitful
wind began rattling the thatch on the roofs of Kadyak's buildings.

From the set of each hunter's face, I knew he screened his
inside self from the Tahtna; but I could read the rage in Aláyeksan eyes. When a man lagged, an alien gun butt and curses
forced him forward. A sullen mood hung over the village and
harbor, and I wondered what strength our hunters could pass on
to one another with the few furtive words they managed to slip
between them.

As the fleet moved outward into the pitching waves, I watched
until their shapes dimmed in the distance and they became black
humps low on the water, like a pod of whales scudding across
our seas.

Back from the shore, women stood in silent knots, unwilling
that their men be taken, helpless to stop it. They knew the aliens
would drive the hunters into dangerous seas, and scores would
not return. I understood their pain and my heart reached out to
each of them.

Spirit who whispered to me, you set me a great task. Will I
be able to paint the lach'u, the truth of Aláyeksa, on my caribou
hide?

◎ ◎ ◎

6

"I am busy this morning. I cannot teach you." Richard sounded rushed.

We had practiced hard on the Tahtna words for a long time after the fleet had left. I was frightened when he told me, "Baranov is sailing his new ship to Pavlovsk. And he has ordered a *praznik*, a celebration, to honor the first alien ship built in Aláyeksa. I have to see that everything is ready."

For that day, relieved of teaching me, Richard skipped around, fussed at the cooks to speed preparations. Workmen dragged kegs onto our porch and opened them; the liquid—*kvass* seemed to be the word—gave off an evil smell, but the men smacked their lips. Under Richard's direction, servants poured the waterlike vodka into the *kvass*. "That will sweeten the stuff," he explained, "and stretch out the vodka so they will not swill it down."

No image had yet formed in my head picturing the clan of Baranov's Bengal slave. (From Richard's actions and the rights Baranov exercised over him, the word "slave" best described his status.) "I come from far away across the ocean, south and west of here," he had told me one afternoon when I had questioned him.

Some days his thoughts had seemed to take him back to another time and place; his prodding at me became less commanding. When I had asked about his home, he had stopped briefly in his pecking.

"My father had eleven children. We were starving to death. Most families in Bengal never had enough to eat. Always too many mouths to feed."

He had sunk down on the bench, sadness lining his face. "I remember a Captain Moore from England. He came in his big

60

ship to trade in my country. This Captain Moore, he had bags and bags of rice. My mother had another baby coming. Moore said he needed a cabin boy. My father said he would take a bag of rice for me"—Richard's voice cracked—"a small one. The captain saw how terribly hungry my brothers and sisters were. So he gave my father a big bag of rice."

Richard had sat very still a few moments. "I can hear to this day what Captain Moore told my father: 'Eat only half of this rice; plant the rest. And when the crop comes in, do the same— eat half of what you have. Always plant half. Do it that way every year, and you will never starve.'

"I had no way then of knowing what it meant—leaving home. But I had plenty to eat and a place of my own to sleep on the ship." His voice had lightened. "I stayed on the ship for years. Till we came to Aláyeksa. I did not know such a place existed."

"Why did you come here, Richard?"

"Well, Captain Moore did his trading at many different ports. I do not remember the names of most of them. He would buy a lot of goods—silk and dishes, beads and brass pieces, muskets, tools, spices, tea. You know, Ashana"—Richard laughed— "Captain Moore liked to have me dress in clothes from different ports. A few fitted me fine. Others did not. I looked so strange in some of the outfits, he'd point at me and roar.

"One day he says to his first mate—that's a longtime sailor on the ship who helps the captain with his sailing—'We will take this stuff north to Aláyeksa. I hear tell the Russian Baranov has stacks of fur he will trade for what I have.' And then the captain said he would sell the furs for big money at Canton—that's a town in China. It seems he could do this because the Chinese trade with the English, but not with any other foreigners.

"We had to stay in Pavlovsk several days. Our ship got into a bad storm on the way north. The mast broke. And the weather here put on a hard blow. Baranov agreed with my master to fix up our ship. While the work was being done, the captain had him eat on board. As the cabin boy, I served the food and drink. Five days Baranov stayed on the ship, and during that time I listened hard and learned several Russian words. The same words got said many times in five days. Repeat things, and you learn." The strain in Richard's voice had eased as he talked to me.

"Baranov traded furs for everything Captain Moore had. And when the captain got ready to sail out to China, Baranov brought him a few of his best furs as a gift. The finest pelts Captain

Moore said he had ever seen. Said he would never sell them. And other gifts—several baskets you Aláyeksans make, and a few driftwood carvings. Masks. Copper pieces. I would like to find some for myself.''

And then Richard's face sobered again. ''You know what Captain Moore gave Baranov?''

''No.''

''Me.''

''What!''

''Me. For those skins and baskets and other things.'' A wry smile matched the irony of his words. ''Anna, I gained value along the way with all that sailing around like I did. The day Captain Moore traded for me with my father I was worth only a bag of rice. But here in Aláyeksa, I became quite valuable.''

For the first time since I had come to this house, Richard allowed me to glimpse into his human self; and I saw a great deal more than a doll in the hands of a shaman. But the door closed quickly as he pulled his own mask over his face.

Abruptly, he broke off his rememberings. ''I must get to my work. Baranov and his navigator will sail in here soon.'' Then he asked, ''*Voskresenskaya Gavan* is on Yaghenen peninsula, isn't it?'' And he answered his own question, ''I remember now, you said it was across the mountains from your village.''

''Yes, I lived on the west side of Yaghenen before Baranov took me for hostage.''

Richard's eyes narrowed a moment. The muscles in his neck stiffened. I had seen the same reaction in my father when he and Baranov had confronted each other that day in our village. ''We are all hostages or slaves of one kind or another.'' Richard's usually high-pitched voice lowered; bitterness laced his words. ''But I intend one day to unyoke myself and go back to my family.''

Once again the teacher, he shook his fingers at me. ''Now, remember what I have told you. When Baranov comes, everything in this house will be ready. But you are the one to greet him. You are his woman.''

He stood up, faced me. ''Let's go over the words again. *S priezdom*, welcome home. *S priezdom*.''

''*S priezdom*,'' I repeated, my voice dull, the tone flat. ''*S priezdom*.''

Richard gritted his teeth. ''Anna, your face. You look as if you swallowed rotten cabbage. Say it again, and smile. *S priezdom*.''

My heart beat no welcome for my captor. Let him never return to claim me. But to avoid conflict with Richard, I forced a smile and repeated the greeting several times.

"Good enough." He grinned at me, slapped his hand against his leg.

Richard strode into the kitchen, and I heard him ordering the cooks to work faster. For some moments I stood frozen, thinking of the hated *S priezdom* and of Richard's loss of family and home. He might appear to have adjusted to his slave role; but some of his words, certain actions and looks showed struggle. I wondered if a Bengalese had a joncha that would help separate the front self from the deep inside person.

Servants had dug pits in the open space between buildings and made fires in them; all day they tended bear and whole pigs roasting in the coals. A *praznik*. A big potlatch, just for a ship? On Yaghenen we held our big potlatches—our special ceremonial festivals—for important reasons. Often to honor a man of heroic deeds, but, more usually, when one family had an obligation to another: When someone died, a family different from that of the dead person would take care of the burial, the cremation, the food for the mourners, everything that must be done at the time of the death; then, later, sometimes as long as a year afterward, the dead person's family paid back the kindness. The father of the family gathered his furs, his carvings, his box of prized shells, his agates and copper, all his wealth. Then he would send out word of a big potlatch—a lavish celebration, nothing spared. Everyone came. The family debt would be repaid, and usually all the wealth given to the guests. As a result, the host family had to begin its wealth-gathering all over again.

A Kahtnuht'ana potlatch always had to do with people, but here on Kadyak, the Tahtna talked of giving a huge feast for a ship. I did not understand why, and no one broke the isolation thrown around me to explain.

A pause settled suddenly over Pavlovsk. Men flowed toward the beach. Only the servants tending meat at the pits stayed where they were. The first Tahtna ship built in Aláyeksa sailed into sight. When it dropped anchor, kayaks and umiaks paddled by Ulchena rowers brought men and supplies to shore.

"See her? That is the ship, Baranov's *Phoenix*." Richard stopped beside me, watching the excitement. "Fine masts those tall trees make. But those sails! Ashana, I should have taught you about boats. Sails."

Richard, I thought, do not start pecking at me. He did not. He just talked on.

"Sails are made of canvas. But no one has canvas in Aláyeska, so the women sewed together every bit of old material they could find—deer hides, old trousers, jackets, blankets, anything." The Bengalese eyed me with a wry grimace. "We'll just have to hope the patchwork does not split apart before the *Phoenix* gets across the ocean to Okhotsk for new riggings. And the boat needs decent finishing work inside . . . the carpenters had to use . . ."

But I did not want to hear any more of Baranov's accomplishments. Richard had other duties, and ran to take a hand in moving Baranov's packs off the *Phoenix*. Workmen made way as their leader headed along the path to the house. Baranov stopped several times, talked and laughed. I realized that in a breath he would walk through the door. Sweat broke out on my palms; my heart was pounding. All through Richard's pecking, I had tried to force Baranov's face from my mind, but now it clamped onto me as deadly as the hawk's talons sinking into small prey. The hawk was swooping in, and his prey had no place to run. I turned away from the window and crouched at the side of the fireplace.

Baranov ignored me as he walked across the room and hung his gray coat on the peg, took a jacket off another.

I waited, teeth clenched. Anger, fear, hate, and uncertainty drew my face taut. No smile, although Richard warned me to put one on. No *S priezdom*, not yet; but I would say the greeting if it meant saving hostages.

"The *praznik*. The *praznik* has begun, and we must join the men. Come." Baranov waved his arm and signaled me to follow him.

I stared at the whiskered face, the eyes.

"Come. Hurry."

My limbs had no power. My head failed to heed the order. The prickles of a thousand tiny claws attacked me as they did every time the man came near.

Outside, music and singing had begun, and above the shouts and curses sounded the screams of a woman.

"Come!" His tone of voice changed from invitation to command. Still I could not move.

"Don't you hear me, Anna? Get out the door!"

"Nyet!" Impulsively, I spat out the first Tahtna word I had

learned from the guards who had penned me in this house when the aliens dragged me onto Kadyak.

The whip gripped in his hand lashed at my legs below my qenich'eni. The sharp sting made me jump toward the door. He caught my arm, his face close to mine. "Behave yourself today," he said, flicking the switch at my legs again.

An impulse to hide, to escape. But, pulled along by his grip on my arm, a grip so tight each finger dug into my flesh, I had no escape; drawing over my face the invisible sea-lion mask Minya had worn that day on the trail toward Htsaynenq', I watched my captor through its eye slits.

Near the fire pit in the yard, the servants handed us bowls of chunked pork, pieces of bear, and boiled cabbage, mixed with a few plants from Kadyak. I took a little fruit from a long bench spread with the last of the summer berries and small apples. Between huge portions of food, drinking mug after mug of vodka and *kvass*, the men bragged to one another about the new ship, their voices a guttural racket. They ignored me; only Igor leered the few times he passed close by.

The music became wilder. A number of *promyshlenniki* formed a circle and danced in a way I had never seen before, squatting down suddenly, knees wide apart, heads and bodies straight as pine trees. Rapidly kicking out first one leg, then the other, jumping, shouting, rising, dropping down again, slapping boots, stamping heels, the men moved their circle around, first in one direction, then the other, always keeping time to music I could not understand.

"A Cossack dance. The *prisiadka*," Richard said at my side.

He must have orders to watch me, for he hung close; Baranov was off circulating "to swing a mug" with his men—the alien practice, Richard told me, of toasting one another. I noticed that Richard had dressed differently for the *praznik*: white cloth wound high around his head, and through the bright-colored belt shone his kris, one of a couple of heavy daggers he had told me Captain Moore took in a Pacific trading stop.

I almost laughed out loud, remembering that he had said, "Anna, I figured I had earned at least one small token for all those years I had sailed with the captain. So, when I left the ship, I decided to borrow the kris."

Richard handed me a mug of *kvass* and vodka. I tried it. The liquid bit my tongue, but it did not smell as bad as the odor from the kegs on the porch. Legs stinging and red, heart pounding, I watched and listened. Strange music was plucked from Tahtna balalaikas and gusli, musical instruments the Tahtna said they had played for several hundred years.

In midafternoon, shouts boomed from the shore, mixing with the noise of the celebration. Stretching across the bay, kayaks followed by umiaks loaded with furs moved into sight. Men at the food and dancing, women who had waited in dread in the huts, rushed to the waterfront to welcome the return of the hunting fleet. Over the shouts of men I heard the anguished sobs of women mourning for the many hunters whose kayaks did not draw up on the beach. My pain for them seared deeply, but my mask cloaked it.

That time, no spirit whispered and no unseen presence touched my shoulder, but I watched and recorded every face, every boat; the painting on my caribou hide had begun to live in my mind, and it would not be complete unless it showed the return of the fleet.

"A fine catch. More otter skins than we have ever taken before." I heard Tema tell Baranov through an interpreter as the *promyshlenniki* crowded around him and Kuskov. The sight of the man from Yaghenen and the sound of his voice pulled at me. Longing to run to him, I stepped toward the beach without thought or fear of punishment, but then I stopped, knowing I would not be permitted to talk to any Kahtnuht'ana hunter. I would not create unnecessary risk for one of my people.

All afternoon I had sipped vodka and *kvass*, eaten my fill, peered at the *praznik* through the slits in my mask. Whenever Richard passed me to direct the servants and hostages, he refilled my mug. Time slipped by. The bite of the drink softened my feelings. The sting eased. A lazy feeling crept through me, later deepened into numbness. I stood up to say a few words to Richard as he filled my mug yet again, and he grabbed my arm to keep me from falling.

Dimness of first light crept into the room. Dizziness seized me when I rose, and a dull ache lived behind my eyes. As I propped myself up on my elbows, my leg grazed a warm body. I started to pull away. An arm across my stomach pinned me down; the body beside me turned, and the usually hard eyes, softened with a night's sleep, stared at me. I tried again to slide away, but Baranov bent my head toward his and covered my face with kisses. He moved closer; I tried to cry out, but my dulled senses failed me.

"At last," I heard him whisper as he slid himself onto me.

While his private revelry spilled out, a vague, clouded state slowed my entire being and subdued any feeble efforts to resist. The few shreds of sanity, the ragged hold on time and place, dissolved, and I welcomed the blackness that curled around me and blotted out his rape.

Later, sunlight pried open my eyelids. As I awakened, words drifted on the still air. "Anna. Anna. Princess Anna."

Slipping from under my captor's arm, I groped for my old dress, shivered at the sight of Aleksandr Baranov as he rose and followed me in a loose-fitting, long white nightshirt, his penis pushing the fabric out in front of him. Grabbing me, he pulled me back to the furs where we had slept.

By early afternoon my mind cleared. Blame my submission on the vodka and *kvass*. Blame it on the *praznik*. Blame it on letting down my hate. Blame it on . . . A vile taste in my mouth, I buried my head in the furs and sobbed for having yielded, realizing that I had lain stupefied in the cold room, dulled by a vodka haze. Hysteria surged through me—blame for betraying Jabila, blame that the use I had detested marked me, revulsion at Qanilch'ey Ashana, Baranov's "broken-in woman."

Clutching my goat horn, staring at it, I tried to find the creatures of home hidden there, but could not see a single one. It was as if all Yaghenen had withdrawn and closed itself to me.

Tushel rolled its dense cover over my mind; and leaving untouched the food someone had placed in the room, I sank into a bog deeper than any since the *promyshlenniki* had first dragged me ashore onto Kadyak. Betrayal of Jabila knifed at me. I sought my joncha. It did not hear me. *"Nyet! Nyet!"* I screamed at Richard from my bog, when he insisted on starting the din of his Russian teaching, and he fled before my anger.

More *praznik*, and Aleksandr Baranov joined his men, renewing the celebration. The house stood silent. Slowly, I walked to the fire pit, blackened my face with soot, pulled my braids apart to let my hair hang in disarray, in mourning. Dead to my people. Dead to Jabila. Dead to myself. Back in the sleeping room, remorse made me sink in a heap onto the furs. Sobs racked me, and I stifled them against my fists.

"Anna, get your clothes on. I'm back to talk to you." Baranov held out a mug for me. The stink of vodka and *kvass*. I retched; without a thought, I struck at his hand and hit the mug, spilling the stuff onto the floor.

"You need food. Richard says you have not—" My captor

grabbed my arm. I slashed at him with the clamshell that I still kept hidden in a fold of my old garment for just such a time. He avoided the blow, warded off another and grasped my wrist, squeezed my hand until he forced me to drop the shell.

"Don't be the bitch Igor says you are." Baranov forced me down onto the pile of furs. "You've had months to get used to my house while I've been gone."

I stared at him, said nothing.

"Last night you were a pleasure. What is wrong now?"

Still no answer.

The burning liquid had blotted me out the night before. What could I tell the man of that night and that morning? What had happened to me in my stupor did not lessen my loathing for every hour spent on Kadyak or my hatred for everything alien in Aláyeksa.

"Richard says you are learning your words. Good. Good. But you must change your manner." He stamped to the window, stood there some moments picking at his teeth with a little stick.

"I will tell you this, Anna: I have given you time enough to adjust. Now, I *order* you to change. I am told you walk around my house naked. This is not a Kenai house, and I will not allow it. Throw away your ragged old skins. Dress like a Russian woman." He strode close, grasped my shoulders. "You will change. Today. Now." His eyes hardened, his grip tightened. "Obey me, or I will send you back to your father. I will take twenty of your people for you, and order half of them shot. You can answer to your village for that."

I knew Aleksandr Andreevich Baranov did not make idle threats. I tried to hide my fear and swallowed a sob. He stepped back. The parting from my parents and the elders on the shores of Yaghenen flashed into my mind. I dared not drive the man to killing people of my village because I disobeyed his orders.

My captor stared at my soot-covered face, my torn hair, my dirty dress.

In a gentler tone, he cajoled, "Behave yourself, Anna. You have a place in my house. I need you to be the first woman of Pavlovsk. And your rank makes it possible. I do not want you to be one of the work crew." His tone hardened. "But do not cross me. Do not force me to put you down in the shacks.

"There is no need for trouble between us, Princess Anna. Your life here in Pavlovsk can be a good one. You can have almost anything you want." His hard tone began to soften.

"Anything I want? Then tell me, Why am I here? What am I?" I knew the answers, but I had been stolen from Yaghenen, from all that I cared about, and I must force the murderer to face me and answer with his own words.

His mood shifted, he snarled, "There is only one thing for you to remember. You have a duty to your father and to me. Keep the bargain your father made with me."

No, Baranov. Never lay that on my father. Anger flashed through me. Your guns fixed the bargain.

Then, as if I had no feelings, meant nothing more to him than an otter pelt, he changed his tack again. "Strip off those skins. I have something better you will like."

Lifting the lid of an old wooden chest and rummaging for some moments, he pulled out a cloth garment. Green-gray like our seas on a misty day, much longer than our qenich'eni, it lacked the luster of deerskin.

"You will look like a noblewoman in this dress, a Russian lady."

If Aleksandr Baranov thought the wrinkled, musty-smelling old cloth would transform me into a Russian, he was mistaken. Covering does not change the heart.

"When Grigorii Shelekhov and his wife Natalia sailed home from Kadyak back in 1786, they left behind this chest of clothes. And there are other nice things you can have."

While he bent over the box, pulled at its contents, the Old Half-Man masks slipped over my face, my mind divided, and the masks hid my revulsion at the same time they seemed to offer submission.

Before he left, Baranov put his hand under my chin, tilted my head up, traced his fingers down my cheek. "Princess Anna, your tears have streaked the soot on your lovely face. I will have the Aleut woman bring warm water. Akoota is her name. She will help you learn how things are here. Clean up and put this dress on."

Tough and harsh one moment, almost amiable the next, called by his men "the master at bargaining," Baranov bargained with my life at will.

Fear had walked with me every day since Aleksandr Baranov's eyes first fixed on me, for I loathed the man. His presence had stalked me as I fled across Tikahtnu and into the coast range with Jabila and Seltan and K'i'un. Since that day my mind had not known a moment of freedom. Fright had dogged countless of my waking hours. Unable to weave together the reeds of Kadyak life, shattered, I paced the room in his Russian house. During the weeks of isolation before my captor returned and took me, I tried to convince myself: No. No. No. It did not happen. I repeated the denials until I was exhausted. Restless sleep bred endless nightmares and I awoke screaming, starting up from the furs to run away. But I could not run from Pavlovsk and Baranov.

One escape, perhaps a defeating one I thought at first, was to bury myself in learning the Russian words from Richard. Days on end I closed my mind to what was happening around me, blotted out thought of my place in this alien house, masked my grief at the horror that looped around all Aláyeksans and for the many men who died at sea with the hunting fleets. Then, as the days wore on and my joncha spoke clearly to me again, I began realizing that the more Tahtna language I knew, the better I could understand my enemy and fend him off.

I loathed the way the Tahtna drank to the success of the hunt, ignoring the human loss. Why, then, did I dull myself with the *kvass*? For that little time I was able to blot out loss and grief. Terrible, the price.

My body stripped of physical respect, forced to discard my civilized Kahtnuht'ana possessions—my deerskin garments, dentalium-shell beadwork, feather hair decorations, porcupine-quill wristbands—I watched Akoota shake out the old dress. My skin crawled as she slipped it over my head and let it brush against my body.

Akoota. Captured—stolen—by Shelekhov years ago, dragged from her people as I had been from mine. A captive, a hostage Ulchena. Nearly as broad as she was long. Eyes narrow in a face round like a full moon marred with small lines. Skimpy braids, and hair so thin it seemed much had been pulled out. Teeth, broken stumps or missing. Short legs. Shoulders like a man. And I wondered, What part did she play here on Kadyak? Had she come to me, crafty like Baranov, with orders to change me?

"I do not like the smell of this old dress." I began to pull it off.

"Anna. Leave the dress on." Akoota spoke in Ulchena-accented Kahtnuht'ana.

My mind still numb with horror at the coupling with Baranov, I stared at her with my Athabaskan eyes and bit back my words. I did not want to risk making her angry and having her complain about me to Baranov.

As she washed my face with warm water, her tone changed. "Don't fight so hard against the Russians. It will be easier that way for you." Her hand gripped my arm, pulled it toward the basin. "I know you want to survive, and—"

"I do not want to survive on Kadyak. I will kill myself." I decided to let her know from the start the direction of my feelings.

"Anna, you must—" she began.

"Do not call me Anna!" I snapped at her. "I am Ashana."

"Baranov orders 'Anna,' " was her only response.

Without a pause the U*lchena* went on washing my face and neck and arms. "You are young, Anna. It is hard here. I know how hard." She splashed her hand into the water basin. "But you must think of what you will do to your people. Kill yourself, and your village will pay. You could cause more people to be killed. And, for sure, Baranov will take another hostage."

Her words tore into me. "I could not stand it when they first dragged me here. I tried to kill myself. Jumped off the cliff. It only made things worse. At first I served only one man. But after I threw myself onto the rocks, they put me in the work huts. Every *promyshlennik* who wanted a woman used me."

For the first time I looked her straight in the face, long enough to see sorrow and misery and fright.

"When I tried to kill myself, the aliens took three more hostages from my village"—she choked, looked away—"but worse, Anna . . . seven of our men . . . the Russians shot them."

Akoota pushed the basin aside, took a strand of my hair, untangled it with a long-toothed ivory comb, and began to braid it. "I came here as a new hostage, the same as you are now. The Russians ordered me to accept everything. I had to. I wanted my father and mother to survive."

"How could you accept the Russians?"

Her face sombered, her words coming slowly. "The hardest part is to put the past behind. Every hostage has to. Bury it deep in the back of your mind. Forget everything and everyone. Any way you can."

"No! No! I will not forget Jabila."

"You must, Anna. Your past. Your Kahtnuht'ana man. Put them far from you. Live one day at a time. You cannot survive if you don't."

"Bury memories of loved ones? My life on Yaghenen? How can I bury them?"

She knelt down, took my hands. "If you want to keep sane,

you have to. No other choice. I cannot tell you just how I did it. But you will find your way, the same as I found mine.''

For a long time we sat, studied each other, let our thoughts weigh the terrible choices the aliens forced upon us.

"You are their hostage. You cannot escape. Make yourself see what you face. Try to think the way the Russians think.''

Not wanting to hear about getting along with the aliens, I changed the subject. "Akoota, tell me. In all the weeks that I have been here, why hasn't anyone, any Aláyeksan, been friendly? You. Watnaw. You help me, but you are not friends. Richard said there had been orders, but he has never told me why.''

"That is the way the Russians deal with new hostages. Order everyone to stay away. Guard you close some of the time. Isolate you. Force you to feel alone. Abandoned. You will try to talk to people. But when the Russians have given orders, nobody dares talk to you. If they risk it, well, they'll probably get beaten or shot.'' Akoota's voice lowered. "And it does not take long to wear down most hostages. They seldom can resist from one full moon to the next. And so the Russians get their way. The first steps to making you submit.''

"I will never accept them.''

"None of us like it.'' She stood up, stepped back, then turned and looked at me. "But if you understand how they think, it helps you survive. Now, try with this dress. I know you do not want to wear it. But pretend. Baranov ordered you to dress like a Russian. So do it. That will be your first step to survival. What difference, the dress you wear?''

I lifted the sleeve to my nose and sniffed. "It smells musty, like old furs stacked and damp.'' As I moved my arms, I felt a tearing along the side; the cloth was coming apart.

Akoota laughed. "You will not have to wear it long. It is older than you are. The cloth is rotting.'' She turned serious again. "Do not try to make your lot worse. Let Baranov see the rotten dress. He will have to let you wear your own clothes. There is nothing else.''

I thought how fresh and sleek I looked in my deerskin. It had been cut to fit my figure, show me off, not cover me up in layers of smelly cloth. I felt like running outdoors, into the mountains or along the beach, any place where fresh air would blow away the stench that hung around my body—stale tobacco smoke and nose-turning odors of kitchen leavings and long-stored sweaty cloth. When the drenching rains at home on Yaghenen soaked our clothes, we hung them on pegs to dry while we warmed ourselves, sitting or standing naked beside the fire pit. Our skin garments had the smell of the open air, a fresh clean scent. The Tahtna material filled the air around me with an alien odor, decayed and captive.

"Hide that rebellious look, Ashana. Remember, you are Princess Anna. Baranov is a crafty one. He can read from your face what is going on in your head. Do not make trouble for yourself. For others. Think only of what you do now, today. Let him believe you accept things."

Akoota paused, a question in her eyes. I did not respond, for I did not believe her, did not like what I heard, and did not want to become a second Akoota; but I listened as she finished.

"As I told you: Put all the past behind you, Anna. You are hostage. The rest of us know your life is better than what we have with the aliens. Do not lose the advantage of living in Baranov's house."

From my window, to the left and in front of me, I could see the barracks and two-story warehouses of the Shelekhov Company. Here in Pavlovsk the shacks of the Tahtna workmen and the hovels for the Aláyeksans clustered near the waterfront—dismal, sagging structures, evil-smelling and drab. In the bay, a three-hatch kayak slid toward shore, powered by an Ulchena in the bow and one in the stern. The man in the middle hatch squatted without an oar; he had to be a Tahtna, for he did not row; Baranov was returning from Yelovi Island, where his workmen were laying down the ways for building his second ship. At the sight of him, my skin prickled.

From the flat headlands of Pavlovsk, cliffs and mountains rose sharply. The deep bay provided a safe harbor for the sailing ships that stopped to trade. The beach lay flat along part of the cove, but to the south and east steep rocks jutted into the sea. A stream rushed down a small ravine, pouring its waters into the bay. After winter, Richard told me, the birches and alders along its banks put out bright green leaves, and the island comes alive with birds. But beauty cannot hide the slaughter of our animals.

"This year's fur catch numbers far less than what we took when I first came," Baranov complained to Kuskov as they sat at our table eating their meal. The next day he ordered new sea-hunting ranges to be found and began levying more Aláyeksan hunters. The slaughter went on.

Off to one side of our house grew crooked rows of cabbage in a plot Richard called "the garden." A couple of aged and crippled Koniags, unfit for the sea hunts, scratched with hooked sticks among the cabbages and other plants brought by the aliens. The only excitement for the Koniags occurred one morning when several pigs and scrawny cows broke out of their pens and lumbered toward the garden. Cursing, whipping their sticks through the air, the ancient Koniags had to chase after the animals. It was an odd sight, and I stood at the window pitying the men.

Cows. There was not a creature that I knew of like them in all Aláyeksa. A cross, it seemed to me, between a bear and a moose, but ill-fed and bony, hipbones poking out of coarse, dull-looking skin. I wondered at the foreigners' need to bring plants and animals from Siberia when The Great Country had such an abundance. Those foreign creatures looked as out of place as the Tahtna themselves. If the aliens had respected what Aláyeksa offered—edible roots, all kinds of berries, fish, sea animals, game in the mountains—they would have had far less difficulty feeding themselves. But they saw none of these things, except what they forced Aláyeksans to supply them at gunpoint. Instead they saw furs. Always furs. The subject of most talk. The goal of most activity. All to meet Aleksandr Baranov's need to grab the rich fur treasures of Aláyeksa for his "Mother Russia."

A basket of fresh berries was on the kitchen table between hunks of blubber and salmon. I took a few, crushed them in my hand; it had been a long time since the red berries of the Yaghenen mountains had stained my fingers . . . Oh, to be a child again in our camps, with other children, filling baskets with fresh, clean-smelling, ripe fruit. To run with the other girls and hide when the boys chased us, careful not to upset a basket and face scolding, for our parents had taught us not to be wasteful of nature's bounty. But they did not often chide us for eating handfuls of the fat berries, as a reward for the work. Each evening we dumped onto long split logs the baskets of fruit, to be mixed with candlefish oil, patted into cakes, and dried in the sun for winter food. The red juice and grease discolored my skin, stained my fingernails, ran between my fingers and up my arms to my elbows, even stained my deerskins—but, oh, the sweet, fresh smell of those berries! Naq'eltani, how I long . . .

Akoota had told me that the way of sanity in this place demanded that a person not look back. "Forget your Kenai life," she had said. She seemed to have accepted all the Russian words for things and people Aláyeksan—even Kenai instead of Yagh-enen. "Think only what you must do each day to survive." But my survival lay in my divided mind, in Naq'eltani, in the spirits that lived deep within me, not one of whom the Tahtna could ever know.

And when Baranov came into the room, Richard had said, "Smile and welcome him home. *S priezdom.*"

How could I look at my captor and say, *"S priezdom?"* "Welcome home" should come from the heart, but my heart did not welcome Aleksandr Baranov that day he had whipped my legs, nor could it any other time.

"I am frightened. Stay until he comes, Akoota."

"I will stay, if you need me."

Both of us listened carefully as the Bengalese explained again how I must perform at the table, for Aleksandr Baranov did not like to eat alone. Usually a man from the company would sit with him; but that night, Richard told me, I would be Baranov's eating companion. He sat me down on the bench at one end of the table and explained that Baranov would sit at the other, then went over how I was to behave.

"Now, Anna, the bowl and the spoon. You must—"

"Do not peck at me, Richard. We have bowls and spoons in my home. The ones on this table have been made by us. Carved out of our wood. Painted by one of our people." I flared at Baranov's servant for putting me down, but felt Akoota's cautioning hand on my shoulder.

"Well, you have never sat at Baranov's table with him. I only want to teach you the right way," Richard spat back.

I kept my eyes fixed on the slab of wood supported by four short posts. "A table," he had told me before. Did he not know the object had also been made in Aláyeksa? To calm my fury, I counted the rings in the section of wood from the tree that had been cut down to provide this "table," ran my fingers over the rough-hewn surface. Some of the furnishings of our Yaghenen homes, the polished wooden benches and storage boxes—creations far superior to the crude objects in this house—glowed in my memory.

There was a thumping on the porch. Baranov strode through the door, and Akoota retreated to the kitchen. Richard, no long-er the creature who spat Russian words at me, faced his master and turned back into his compliant self, taking Baranov's coat and hanging it up. Pulling out the bench at the other end of the table, he seated our master and poured him a mug of vodka. At my end of the table, an unseen mask covering my face, I painted on a smile and, as I had done the other night, forced out the necessary *"S priezdom."*

"I am glad to be here," Aleksandr answered in Russian; his eyes flickered over me, seeming to approve the sight of Natalia Shelekhov's dress. "You look splendid."

It was a quiet meal; few words passed between us, Baranov's Kahtnuht'ana more sparse than my Tahtna. Richard moved between the table and the kitchen, bringing food and clearing away dishes. The salmon I liked, but neither the small, white, partly soft stuff called "potatoes" nor the turnips had flavor. The boiled cabbage tasted as bad to the mouth as it smelled to the nose.

Then, to end the meal, Richard brought in a large bowl filled with some of the fresh berries I had noticed in the kitchen earlier. He spooned the fruit into smaller bowls. I watched, puzzled, as he poured onto Baranov's berries a strange white liquid; it was like the milk that comes from the breast of a mother as she feeds her baby.

Richard noticed my questioning look and tried, in Kahtnuht'ana, to explain: "Cow's milk," he said.

"We have nothing like it in Aláyeksa."

"That is one of the reasons the Russians brought cows with them." Then quickly, in a lower voice and still in Kahtnuht'ana, he added, "But I will not touch it. Cows are sacred in Bengal."

His last words created an even bigger puzzle for me, but he busied himself and said no more; I was left to wonder about the rank of the animals in his native land. Richard had kept an eye on his master, but Baranov seemed preoccupied, uninterested in such a trivial subject and probably unable to understand much of what we said to each other in my language. A few more Russian words between the two men sent Richard scurrying out to the kitchen, soon to return with the brass samovar and a pot.

"Tea. Remember when I showed you the dried leaves?" He repeated to me the word familiar from his pecking.

He poured brown liquid from the pot into two mugs, then added steaming water from the samovar. A quizzical smile swept across Baranov's face as he watched the quick slender fingers of the Bengalese; and I thought our captor must sometimes wonder about his servant's cleverness, often be as mystified about him as I was.

Outside, the early dusk signaled shorter days and the coming of the cold season. The rain had started to beat on the roof and drum at our gut-covered windows. The flames from the stone grease lamps on the table and the blazing logs in the fireplace spread light, then shadow, across Baranov's face, his features hardening in the brightness, softening in the dimness. I did not know how I looked, and wondered if he could read the fright in my eyes.

At a motion of his master's hand, Richard again poured tea for us, cleared the other dishes, and left us alone. What could I say to Baranov? Should I let him know my progress in his tongue? Recite the pecking of "table," "bench," "fire," "cabbage," "kitchen," and the rest? Would talking with him ease my people's fate? Hold off his guns? No, for there was only *his bargain* with my father. I mistrusted the man, hated him, so I held my tongue.

Breaking the silence between us, my captor stabbed his finger several times at the table and asked, "Tell me your Kahtnuht'ana word for table. I want to know."

"No word." Why should I tell him everything?

"Fire?" He pointed to the flames in the fireplace. "Fire?"

Not wanting to give him any feeling for my cherished language, I slurred the word. "Daz'i. Daz'i."

"Ummm. And how do you say 'light' and 'sun'?"

My mind jolted. Why those words? A trap? *Sun, Ni'i,* my father's name. *Light?* Should I tell him how the Dena'ina first got the Light from raven? My thoughts flew back to the day on Yaghenen when Baranov demanded me for hostage. I recalled my father's words: "Ashana, this day chulyin, bird of our clan, turns the evil side of his spirit upon us and takes back the Light. The man Baranov demands that you go."

And my world had crashed.

"What are you dreaming of, Princess Anna?" Baranov looked suspicious. "I asked you how to say 'dress.' "

Quickly, I regained the present, ignored his questioning look. "Dahbak," I said flatly.

He said "dahbak," his sounds heavy.

My captor wanting to know Kahtnuht'ana?

He forced talk from these few words, no doubt seeking to ease the strain between us; but I did not open my feelings to him. As we shuffled words back and forth, I considered asking him again what my place on Kadyak was supposed to be. But I did not.

Motioning me to stand, he cut into my thoughts. "Let me see how you look in your new dahbak, Princess Anna."

I gathered up the folds of the dress and slid toward the end of the bench. The garment caught on the rough edge of the wood, and the back of the dress tore, exposing my thighs and legs, every part of me from the waist down. As I tried to free the cloth, it ripped again and I tripped and fell flat on the floor at Baranov's feet, as bare as a *beluga* (as the Tahtna named our small whales) washed up on the shore. My body and face burned with shame.

Roars of laughter filled the room, laughter that I had heard others say belonged to Aleksandr Andreevich Baranov when he was truly amused. "That old dress is no good. Let's get rid of it."

He leaned over and tore the rest of the garment from my body. His strong, rough hands turned me over onto the bear rug.

I no longer had to wonder about my place in Pavlovsk village.

⊛ ⊛ ⊛

7

As the season drifted from one full moon to the next, the days shortened and the nights stretched into the long dark of deepening winter, Baranov stayed close to the Kadyak artels, and Attu had free days. So, between Richard and Attu, I began to understand more of the alien ways, the patterns of life and the beliefs of the intruders.

On Yaghenen, winter brought us time to rest, to relax and enjoy food stored during the summer and fall, to draw families closer together by storytelling, singing, dancing, and games. But the Tahtna kept the pace of life much the same from one season to the next. The *peredovshchik*, the bosses, drove the workmen hard all year round, rushed them from days of laboring to nights of carousing. During the short daylight hours, they built storage sheds, cut timbers for huts and logs for the shipbuilding on Yelovi Island, cleared and leveled a piece of ground for a *church*.

"Church? Is that a kashim? A place for the men to meet in?" I asked Richard.

"Yes. No. Not exactly." For a change, Richard seemed puzzled. "A *tserkva*, church, is a place where the monks say their religious thoughts. Pay their respects to the being they believe creates them. And they call the people to come and watch and listen." He stopped a moment, frowned. "If I catch the right meaning from the churchmen, the church is good for the spirit."

Shortly after I had been dragged onto Kadyak, the monks had sailed into Pavlovsk harbor on the Tahtna ship *Three Saints*. Monks, a breed of people beyond my knowing. With the black capes and hoods, they looked to me like ravens—part bird, part human. Perhaps they, too, harked back to earth's beginnings, to the days before human beings, when ravens had lived in villages like people do. As time went on, the ravens became our ancestors and for long ages changed in and out, out and in—ravens to people, people to ravens. But I would not want monks for ancestors. They looked at me as if they had been caught between changes; I would not have been surprised if the flapping capes they wore turned into wings, and if one day they flew away. When I told Richard and Attu, they hooted at me.

Attu said, "I will never be able to look at them again with a straight face. I will expect to see one of them fly up over the island flapping his wings and cawing."

"It certainly could happen." Laughing, I shook my fingers at both of them; but I also knew of the raven's capricious side, described in the words of my father that beat like wings in the back of my mind: *Chulyin turns the evil side of his spirit upon us.* Whenever I saw the monks I worried whether or not those men, too, had their trickster side and, like chulyin, could steal the Light.

"Why do the monks sound so strange?" I asked. "The one that comes to talk to Baranov has a different tone to his voice."

Richard sat down, ran a hand through his hair. "Monks are . . . it is hard to explain, Anna." He paused, thinking. "Early in life something in their heads sets them off distinct from other men. And the life they lead . . . it is entirely apart from that of anyone else. They live in houses kept just for monks. They study and think and write. They keep separate from other people. Isolate themselves." He stopped, his face puzzled. "I could say they are not part of the world that the rest of us live in."

"I do not understand. They shut themselves off, but do they still hunt and fish and pick berries like other people?"

"No, I do not think so. The monks live by themselves, behind fences and walls that protect them. This is how they keep their minds free from outside beliefs. They live by strict routine. Every day, the same. Inside their walls, the monks grow animals for meat and raise food in gardens like the one here on Kadyak, only much bigger. They say blessings for anyone who gives them food and land and rubles. They believe very strongly that only they know the way to live. None of them leaves the place where they live unless they are ordered out to tell people in other parts of the world what they believe—like these, coming to Aláyeksa from the Valaam Monastery to teach you people. Yes, they sound different, with their chanting and reading and special kind of talk, because they *are* different."

"Is that why they did not want to live with anyone when they came to Pavlovsk?"

"Yes, Anna. Remember when they got off the *Three Saints?* Right away they demanded a place to live by themselves. Baranov had no space to give them, and they were forced to move in with the *promyshlenniki*. That led to lots of trouble."

"Yes. I have heard Baranov tell Kuskov the monks here have always been a problem."

"They do not think Baranov manages right. They are against everything. The dancing and drinking and carousing. The workmen's filthy oaths. Women in the shacks all night. Disrespect, they say, for the Holy Church. It is all contrary to what they believe." Richard shook his head. "I don't know how it will work out, but I do know the monks make Baranov a bad problem."

As he talked, I recalled the raven men as they had filed off the ship and onto Kadyak. First the head monk Ioasaf, straight and tall in his black cape. Behind him trailed the other monks. All of the Tahtna in Pavlovsk, Baranov at their head, put on a strange performance. At a motion from Ioasaf there on the beach, everyone knelt down, even Aleksandr Baranov. They bowed their heads as if afraid to look at the churchmen. Ioasaf moved his hand back and forth in front of his chest, his fingers clutching a shiny object made of two crossed sticks, and chanted strange words. Then everyone stood up and greeted the newcomers.

Since that day, Kadyak has known no peace.

In this room, the head monk Ioasaf had challenged Baranov. "Relieve us monks from the burden of daily labor. We must devote ourselves to meditation and study. We must have time to chant the monastic rituals. It is God's will for us," the stern-faced monk had informed the manager.

"I wrote Grigorii Shelekhov for a village priest. I needed a man used to working with his hands and mixing with people at the common level. A man willing to face severe conditions. Sometimes privation. Aláyeksa has no place for scholars, not yet."

In blunt words Baranov had told Ioasaf that survival on Kadyak allowed no wasted time—every adult had to cut wood, fish, hunt game, do any work the day demanded or he could have neither heat nor food. Work or starve: The monks were no exception, for he had warned, "I expect every monk to share in the labor."

The head monk had argued, "The Mother Church will be horrified to know you have put its scholars to hard labor in Aláyeksa, ordered us to work like serfs. I know this company belongs to Grigorii Shelekhov. I will report the rotten state of affairs to him."

Unawed by the finely dressed holy man with his unscarred hands and superior attitude, Baranov had roared back, "Archimandrite Ioasaf, do that! Shelekhov lived here. He knows Aláyeksa is severe. I will write him again that I cannot support more than a village clergy. You men belong in monasteries. You see we have none in this country. I have no place fit for any of you. We would both be better off if you go back to Valaam Monastery."

But Ioasaf had not finished. He leveled another charge against the manager. "Grigorii Shelekhov told me when we went on board at Okhotsk"—the black-robed figure shook his fist in Baranov's face—"that he had put enough food and supplies on the ship to provision us for three years. His letter tells you the same. I demand that you deprive us no longer of what is ours. Give us our food now."

This was an attack on his integrity, Baranov had raged, banging his fist on the table. "Food, you say? The fact is, Your Eminence, Grigorii Shelekhov did not send so much as a crust of bread for you monks. Look in my warehouses. Search the *Three Saints*. Go through this house, if you will. I speak truth: He did not ship one kopek's worth of supplies to Aláyeksa for you. You will find life harsh in this wilderness. You will have to manage the way all men do. This land favors no one, man or beast."

Or woman, I thought.

Baranov and the head monk had argued for hours, and resolved nothing between them.

Although Baranov seldom talked to me about company business, in my presence late at night relaxed by vodka, he often fretted about the men in black garb, muttered complaints about their unreasonable demands; I understood enough to learn that he had been dissatisfied with them from the day they walked off the *Three Saints*.

Later, during the short winter days, when the burden of work had slacked off, Baranov did assign men to cutting timber and building a bunkhouse for the monks, in part to relieve the crowding on the *promyshlenniki*, but more to eliminate the wrangling between workmen and monks that could get a man killed.

I remember when the Ulchena and the Bengalese sat at a table explaining to me something of what went on at the church, trying to figure out why Baranov complained about the monks even while building a church for them.

"You see, it is this way, Ashana," Attu smiled. "The monks preach that they are important, that the only worthwhile people in this world are Christians. And that the monks have the magic power to change people into Christians."

Richard laughed. "That is right. They will change you from a savage into a civilized woman, Ashana."

"How can *they* change people? We do not live back in the beginnings of time when the birds could change back and forth— raven to people, people to raven, and back again." I swallowed their bait.

"No, it's a lot easier. And according to the holy men it never fails." Attu looked to Richard, who offered no help. "They make you crunch down on your knees before a monk. Then one of them takes a little bowl and sprinkles water from it on your head. The monks call it holy water. While he sprinkles, the monk says special words over you. All this makes you Christian. By doing it their way and saying those special words, he . . ."

"Holy *water*? I have never heard of such a thing." I did not understand the explanation.

A mischievous expression crossed Richard's face. He leaned his bench against the wall, lifted his feet in the air, then slammed them down hard onto the floor. Slapping Attu on the back, he said a few quick words to his friend out of the side of his mouth, words not intended for me.

"Holy water on Kadyak only drains out of the monks," the Bengalese said in a low voice.

Attu roared; when he had recovered his composure, he declared sternly, "No baptism for me. Never."

It surprised them that I, too, could say, "No baptism for me. Never."

One evening, after the dishes were cleared away, Richard brought a bowl of hot vodka to the table while the manager and Attu finished talking about a trip to the Ulchena clans. That night Baranov kicked off his boots, leaned back in his chair, and told a story I had never heard before.

"Back home in Russia many people depend on household gods. You have to understand that I believe in the Russian Christian Church. You will be Christians, too, one day. Good teachings. The Truth. But those monks can shake a man's faith.'' He paused, eyeing me and Attu. ''Days like these, I think of my grandmother telling me about old pagan spirits. Long ago in my homeland, each house had its Děduška Domovoy, a Grandfather House-Lord, an old man who protected the family. Great flashing eyes, bushy white beard, long cloak tied with a red sash. The Domovoy, my grandmother said, is usually a long-dead ancestor who was a favorite. He lived in the house. We shared food with him. No one could see him. The people of the house depended on him to protect them from people like . . .'' Aleksandr motioned toward the bunkhouses, turned, and poked through a pile of furs. He pulled out a small white ermine skin, shook it hard, and ran his fingers back and forth to brush up its pile. Putting it in front of the door leading to his room, he laughed. ''That will take care of Ioasaf. He will not . . .''

''How, Baranov?'' Attu said.

And I wondered what purpose Baranov had in telling this tale of one of his spirits. Was he trying to pry the facts about our own spirits out of us? *Wear a mask*, my joncha had begun warning me soon after my coming to Kadyak. I pulled my clan's raven mask over my face, a mask Baranov could not see; and from behind it, wary, I listened.

''That white fur is my invitation to my Domovoy. He will come when he knows we have put it out. You will not see him, but he'll join us at a meal, which is why we put bits of food from every dish on a plate for him. When one of the family dies, the Domovoy shares our grief by howling at night. If the family treats him well, he sees that it has fine crops and healthy cattle. And no trouble.'' My captor grinned, perhaps sensing I had enjoyed the fantasy he had woven. ''We need all the help we can get.''

For all the respect that Aleksandr Baranov paid the God of his Russian church by attending its services, he had surprised me with a tale of a spirit that had nothing to do with the church, its spirits, its beliefs. Only a few days later, when he saw the head monk Ioasaf striding with his aide up the path to our house, he meekly hid the white ermine between some other furs.

''No use irritating the Archimandrite. He thinks I am pagan anyway. He would not appreciate my Domovoy.''

So Aleksandr Baranov has no faith in his Russian spirits. From that moment, knowing I had found a weakness in my captor, I began to take hope. I would never deny Aláyeksan spirits as he had denied his Děduška Domovoy—that was one of the differences between us. Watching Baranov through the eye slits of my mask, I knew he could never understand the force of my spirits.

As winter crawled slowly on, with much darkness and little light, ice-laden winds battered the village of Pavlovsk. Baranov was gone to Kadyak's artels for days at a time. At night, I dreamed of Jabila fighting the waves to come for me. I reached out to him, but he could not find me; my screams drowned in the howl of the storm.

Then, in my dream, I saw a single sea gull rising, falling, buffeted by crosswinds, searching but not finding a log to ride out the gale. Whipped upward by a surging blast, the bird disappeared in the grasp of winds and the waves.

A bird of freedom, the sea gull. It can rest on whitecaps or even breast the winds for a day; neither raging waves nor battering gales will down it. The sea gull survives, a bird whose home we Kahtnuht'ana know is in the sky.

Into my dream entered the image of a mask hung in my parents' japoon—a sea gull carved from cedar driftwood; through it spoke the spirits of Yaghenen: The Tahtna storm is mighty. Shadows ride its winds. Death rides its waves. Despair may come close, Ashana, but remember you have within you the will and the power of the sea gull. Who understands the sea gull's survival? The Tahtna will not understand yours.

In between Baranov's comings and goings, Akoota spent parts of many days at our house, nagged about adjusting, accepting, accommodating. Talk between us seemed to have no purpose until one day she spoke about Natalia Shelekhov's castoffs.

"I will bundle up these smelly old clothes and take them to the bunkhouses for stuffing into cracks in the walls." Akoota stretched the pieces, then rolled them tightly and tied the bundle with a sinew cord.

"Let me walk back with you," I volunteered, embarrassed that she might know of Baranov ripping off the rotten dress and rolling me on the bearskin.

Along the path two or three women talked to Akoota, but none looked into my eyes. With them, as with other women from the work shacks, I still spawned suspicion. We were all hostages, but a gap divided me from the rest of them. As I turned to leave the shed, Watnaw broke away from the others, accompanied me to the door. I felt her hand squeeze my arm and heard her low whisper: "Friend. Sister."

My heart sang at her words; walking home, thinking of Watnaw brought back my earliest memories of the trade parties of her Gulushutna, who came from the islands and coasts far to the south of Yaghenen. To them we traded deer and caribou meat, skins, arrows and bows, quillwork, knives; and from them we received masks, boxes, staffs, anything that caught our eyes. Our people carved and painted, but nothing we created quite matched the art of the Gulushutna; so, by trading with them, my Kahtnuht'ana received many pieces distinctive to the Gulushutna culture. My father treasured his carved speaker's staff with its raven's head; it was all the more meaningful for having been presented to him by a Gulushutna leader at the ceremony ending a trade fair between the Sitka islanders and our clans.

We held the Gulushutna in awe, respect, and not a little fear, for they were worrisome if riled. They were protected by fighters who made themselves fiercesome and otherworldly by wearing headpieces and masks so tall that the men seemed eight-foot figures towering over us ordinary creatures, fighters known for scattering every enemy who faced them. So I had mixed feelings about Watnaw, wanting to draw close to her but at the same time wary about reaching out too soon.

Watnaw and I could understand each other's speech if we spoke slowly, although we sounded different. She was tall, and her thinness seemed due more to a long captivity than what would have been her natural build. Her qenich'eni fell from her shoulders in folds that failed to hide the eagle crest painted on the deerskin in red ocher, black, and brown; the eagle, symbol of her family's high status on Sitka Island, its color once vibrant, had faded.

Defiance, even arrogance, showed in Watnaw's sure stride and the firm way she planted her feet as she talked. When she wore her broad-brimmed Gulushutna hat, she pulled it down over her eyes so that no one could read what she was thinking. Her strong, near-perfect hands grasped objects with the purpose of taking control. Her mouth changed from sardonic scorn to laughter in the face of trouble. It was the mask with which she hid the suffering that churned inside her, suffering that seemed to lie only a little below the surface. I had heard Watnaw joke with Attu and Richard, mercilessly leading them on, appearing almost a fool, then letting go a verbal tirade that left her laughing.

We had seen that same wit and sharp eye in the Gulushutna traders who had come to Yaghenen. It enabled their carvers to shape mosquito masks with pointed beaks, killer whales with lethal might, the raven we knew so well, the strong wolf that framed Jabila's mask, the eagle-decorated houseposts, even the frog with its strong hind feet and haunches. Those carvings caught and combined the spirit of the moment and the essence of the being. Nothing dull or useless trapped the Gulushutna eye and soul: It looked deep into Aláyeksa's spirit world and saw the beings who lived there.

For some reason I still hesitated to begin painting on my caribou hide. But sometimes when I took it out, ran my fingers over the soft, fine skin, I could hear the ancient spirit-whisper, feel its insight passing to me, sharpening my wit to understand and my eye to paint. Slowly, I began to believe that I would create on that hide the essence of being and the immortal spirit of Aláyeksa.

◉ ◉ ◉

8

Nightmare years, those early ones on Kadyak.

"Think no more of your past, Anna. Leave Yaghenen behind. You must become civilized. Russian," Aleksandr Baranov insisted, as he watched me mixing a brown paint for my caribou hide, working it up from pieces of bark. Strangely, he did not question what I was doing—it may have been that he thought I was preparing to redye some of Natalia Shelekhov's old bits of cloth.

Think no more of my past? Angrily I pulled on my invisible mosquito mask and buzzed at the man, "Forget Russia! Think no more of *your* past!"

My words were unexpected; Baranov studied me closely, then said, "Forget Russia? You insult me, Princess Anna. A man can never forget his homeland, his people, his past." My captor sounded irritated, but I could read in his eyes that he still failed to understand the protection my Kahtnuht'ana spirits gave me.

I stabbed at him from behind the sharply pointed beak of my mosquito mask. "Yes, no one can forget home. My people—"

"Silence, you ignorant savage, or you will pay!"

That time I knew I had drawn blood.

"I come from a great country. It has given me the knowledge I need. I have a duty to Russia. All my work must add to her glory." His anger was mixed with pride for his homeland.

He stared beyond me as if seeing into the past. A frown creased his face. Then he brightened. "Come here, Anna." His voice took on a coaxing tone. "I will tell you about Mother Russia."

He had misunderstood me, thinking he could win me by extolling Russia.

"Your country and Gregorii Shelekhov neglect you, Aleksandr Baranov. You have almost starved." I persisted with my jabs. "I know how often your workmen have gone hungry. How they grumble."

Lost in thought, Baranov walked to the window, perhaps imagining that he had returned to Russia and stood on the shore of his homeland. Richard had told me Aleksandr Baranov had a wife and daughters in Russia; I wondered if he was thinking of them. Jabila and my home flowed through me with every heartbeat.

Back at the table, strange expressions flitted across his face. "Mother Russia," he breathed; then, reaching for me, he said sadly, "Come here."

I pulled back, but his strong grasp lifted me to his lap. No switch that day, but he squeezed my thigh as he unfolded a large sheet of paper, traced his fingers across it as he talked.

"In my country, Anna, we call this drawing a map. See how far Russia stretches from this ocean on the west—over here—to this ocean on the east."

I wanted to slide away. But my joncha whispered, *He does not know you. Let him brag about Russia. Listen for a weakness.* And through my mind slipped the thought: The hand that caresses my thigh is the same one that beats me with the switch.

With a satisfied grunt, he settled me tightly against him. "See. This point here. Okhotsk. It is a city on the east shore of Siberia. The harbor where we load our ships and start over the sea to Aláyeksa."

His fingers roamed over the piece of paper. "I lived in Irkutsk. Here. A long way west of Okhotsk. I had my glass business in Irkutsk." His voice slowed. "And Pyotr, my brother, lived there, too. He took over our business when I left for Aláyeksa. I wonder how he is."

Bending closer to the map, he said, "Here is Moscow. And St. Petersburg on the Gulf of Finland just off the Baltic Sea. The Tzarina holds her court in St. Petersburg. Long live Tzarina Catherine!" He shifted me on his lap. "Another time I will tell you about Nikolai Rezanov, Shelekhov's son-in-law. A great man, he is the one who will persuade the Tzarina to grant my company control of all Aláyeksa."

I had an impulse to ask what he meant, for he had told my father that the Tzarina had already granted him authority over all of our country. The fact of his power everywhere in Aláyeksa, his levies of our hunters, left me in no doubt that he had full control. Should I have challenged him? *Better that you do not cross him yet. Wait,* my joncha warned.

"Is Russia no bigger than this piece of paper?" I knew better, but asked anyway.

"No, no." He laughed, thinking my question serious. "First, you must understand that this paper I call a map is just a small drawing of my country. It is like when a man makes a picture of a bird or a baidarka or a person or a mountain. Always much smaller than what it represents. And we Russians measure distance in versts."

Why show me the Russian drawing? I shivered. Had he seen the beginnings of my caribou-hide painting? Keeping my voice steady, I said, "That is different from how we fix distances in Aláyeksa. We measure by how far a man can walk in a day. You say versts. We say yi*l*." I ignored his whiskers scratching my face.

"I know that is the way you Kenai figure. But we Russians have a system; we make pictures like this one. And with these pictures of our country we can tell direction and distance."

Kenai. The man did not know me. Absurd, the way those aliens dealt with maps as the means of knowing where a person is and where he will be going. I came near to interrupting him with talk about the much more efficient method of figuring direction that my people use, our system based on the flow of rivers; but I did not, for it would only mean more argument. What merit would he see in anything so direct as "downriver" . . . "up at a higher elevation" . . . "dach'—this way" . . . "yach'—that way"?

Aleksandr Baranov might talk of picture maps, but his fingers were tracing his rising need for me as they moved between my legs and up my thighs; I felt his hardness.

"I still do not understand about the size of your homeland." I hurried my words to keep his attention on his talk of Russia because I did not want him pawing me. "How can you say it is so big?"

He had sat there tapping the map for a moment. "See this peninsula sticking out from the main part of Siberia? It is like the Kenai Peninsula—Yaghenen, you say—that juts out from the main part of Aláyeksa. Kamchatka—we call ours—about as far east from St. Petersburg as you can go and still be in Russia. Now, if you could pick up the island of Kadyak and put it onto Kamchatka, see—it is only a speck in all Russia. The distance from St. Petersburg, near where I grew up . . . uumm . . . six thousand versts to Kamchatka. Across Kadyak, the distance can't be more than ten versts.''

As he pointed out Russia's mountains, rivers, towns, all the while talking of his homeland, he surprised me in trying to relate everything to Kadyak and Yaghenen.

Baranov's nostalgia for his past and his people mixed with his desire; but that day Jabila's presence stood close. Cringing inside at the hated alien touch, aware that Baranov could be put off if I made him angry, I ran the risk.

"I know that Russia means much to you. You cannot forget your people, your past life.'' I had no trouble letting my thoughts out. "It is no different for me. My home, my loved ones—''

"Stop, Anna!'' he roared at me. "I have told you before, Russia has a great civilization. Aláyeksa is wild and savage. Russians have a heritage—''

"My people, too, have a heritage that will—''

"Silence! Do not cross me! Tzarina Catherine offers your people the means to become civilized. Christian. And my duty to my country demands that I make you people accept Russia for the betterment of all Aláyeksans.'' He brushed me off his lap as if I were a fly.

Rage boiled up at my captor's insults to Aláyeksan civilization, but above the rage swelled my relief that for those few minutes I had saved myself from him, whatever might come later. The mask settled more securely over me; I kept my eyes on him, stayed wary. He stared into the fireplace for a long time before slowly turning to face me. His eyes carried a question; but they appeared different, less glacial.

He turned back to his map.

"Kargopol.'' He pointed to a dot on Russia. "The town where I was born. My father had a small store, sold food and guns and supplies to the village people. He bartered in furs; and I learned about fine pelts from him. I set out a trapline of my own and sent the furs to Moscow, made myself a few kopeks. My father taught me to read and write and how to figure his store accounts. When I had time from work''—his voice lightened—"I climbed our mountains. I found many kinds of rocks—some bright-colored layers in a hillside or in the face of a cliff, some with streaks of different metals.''

I let him dream aloud. As he talked about his home, a sad, bitter note crept into his words.

"My father drudged in his store, from before daylight till after dark. I remember as a child that I seldom saw him at mealtime. But no matter how hard he worked or how well people in Kargopol said they liked him, he never rose above the lowest merchant level.'' His face clouded. ''You see, in Russia people have rank, one class is better or worse than another. All are rated by the levels decreed by one of our powerful rulers, Tzar Peter the Great. The Tzar made it possible to rise in rank by service paid to the state. But being born noble gives you the best kind of rank.

''As for business, like with storekeepers, rank was most important: High rank, and a man got invited to join with others in a select group; low rank, and you meant nothing. It was that way with all merchants. They had a guild. But they only invited men to join who were rich or who had high rank in the city. They never invited me, because I was only a storekeeper's son.''

So, try as he had, my captor could not bury his past; it remained bound to him.

Rank does not exist in Russia alone. Clans of Aláyeksa have men who are wiser than other men, greater hunters or superior leaders. Some people enter this life able to do things better than others, put thoughts into words that draw listeners as other men cannot. Such men rise to leadership, to being qeshqa. My people held my father high because of his wisdom and his story-telling ability.

''I grew to be fifteen and realized that Kargopol no longer held a future for me,'' Baranov droned on. ''I wanted to gain a higher rank than my father had. I dreamed of being more than a storekeeper at the bottom rank of merchants. Traders who came through Kargopol bragged about Moscow—the big stores, huge buildings, travelers from other countries, books of all kinds, parks where a person could play or sit and think, and most of all a chance for a young man to rise to higher rank.''

Much of what Baranov said meant nothing. His eyes turned to me, a sparkle surfacing. ''One day I left home. I walked many, many versts to Moscow. There I stood on the street, not caring about the ankle-deep mud on my boots, gawking at buildings so big I thought the whole village of Kargopol could be stuffed into one of them. Buildings of stone and marble, many of wood. I stared at the crowds of people, thousands of them. And the well-dressed merchants of that great city were out, too. It was a holiday.''

He looked through the window, toward the harbor, perhaps seeing a ship that could take him on a voyage to his homeland.

He faced me again. ''You know, Anna, a celebration was

taking place in Moscow. I had come just in time. People told me the biggest *praznik* in the world was going on. Free food was heaped on stands along the streets. All the wine and vodka a man could drink. Some of the nobles threw rubles to the people from their carriages. Such carriages! Fancy-painted, decorated with gold, drawn by sleek horses, bells on their harnesses. Coachmen sat on the high seats at the front. The carriages splashed mud on us, but we did not care. Women rode in many of the carriages, noblewomen, elegant, with plumes in their hair, ruffles you could not count, decorated with silver and glittering diamonds. I had never seen . . .''

The mosquito mask still securely in place, I stung again. "Dresses as rotten as Natalia Shelekhov's?''

"No, my child.'' He chuckled. "Those dresses would never tear. They were made from the finest material Russia could import from France.''

"And what did the *praznik* honor? A new ship?''

"Heavens, no! Moscow is a long way from the ocean. It was the time our new ruler took the throne: Catherine became Tzarina to rule over all of Russia. I saw it happen. I followed behind the parades of army men and nobles.''

His physical need for me brushed aside, sipping from the mug of vodka Richard had poured for him, Aleksandr Andreevich Baranov stood in front of the fireplace, quiet for a moment. He ignored Attu sitting near the window, listening, saying nothing. Then he went on:

"I will never forget the date—September twenty-third, 1762. Early that morning the massive gates of the Kremlin—you should see it, Anna, the grand fortress of all Russia—swung open. From the streets I had seen the domes of the great cathedrals high above the walls of the Kremlin. Colored domes, shiny, shaped like onions. I remember that day climbing up on buildings along with hundreds of others. I was curious, only fifteen—the same age you were when I found you on the Kenai—and I had to see everything.

"Exactly at ten o'clock the doors of Uspensky Cathedral opened, and Catherine walked down a red-carpeted staircase to the middle of the square. Bands played. Soldiers marched. People cheered. Catherine had on a grand dress of ermine and silver with a train so long it took six men to carry it. The men around her wore red velvet jackets with diamonds, gold, silver sewed onto their clothes. The cannons fired a salute. The wave of sound blasted at me, and I nearly lost my hold.

"Then Catherine put the jeweled crown of Russia on her own head. The noblemen stepped back, bowed to their new ruler. Next, Tzarina Catherine gave herself Holy Communion and decreed herself head of the Holy Russian Orthodox Church."

Aleksandr's eyes fixed on me, but I knew he did not see me. My joncha whispered, *He does not know who you are. It is a weakness you can use one day.*

"The bells of Moscow rang to honor Tzarina Catherine," the voice began again. "Bells sounded from the cathedrals across the city until nightfall, echoed through the countryside. I have never forgotten the sounds: big bells with their deep peels . . . little bells that tinkled . . . The largest bell was called the Tzar's Bell—the biggest in the world, twenty feet high, two hundred tons, so massive its song could be heard across many, many versts. Those bells, the voices of the Holy Russian Church, rang everywhere in the city and up into the heavens."

He paused a long time, both hands gripping the mug, his eyes again staring out the window to the harbor, warming to a past that he would never permit anyone to belittle.

He sighed, then a firmer tone came into his voice. "Anna, as soon as we finish the church on Kadyak, I will have a bell cast. I want the sound of bells to ring in Pavlovsk and across the mountains of Aláyeksa. Bells of Mother Russia, a mark of her civilization.

"You see, Princess Anna, my country has created a rich civilization. Our Tzarina expects every Russian to love and honor and serve Mother Russia.

"That is why, Anna, I have to do important things in Aláyeksa. Build up a rich fur trade. Create a beautiful Russian city. Then the culture of Russia will be able to spread, to change the people of this land. What I do here will make the people at Catherine's court and my country's merchants respect Aleksandr Baranov. And then, my little savage, I will rise in rank, and perhaps receive honors from the Tzarina. Your noble state will help because Russia recognizes the royalty of her capti—" (He had started to say "her captives" but changed his words.) "The people to whom she grants her protection. All for the greatest glory of Russia."

And as I listened to all that bragging, I thought of the wisdom of our Kahtnuht'ana saying: *When the fire-people sit on your back and pound, much hot air comes out of your mouth.*

✿ ✿ ✿

9

Change. A violent force compelled the aliens to change everything that was Aláyeksan. It was not enough that those intruders had stripped our seas and land of furs, forced our submission at gunpoint, held us captive. They clawed and snatched at our clothes, language, habits, beliefs—all our ancient civilized Aláyeksan culture.

The Tahtna seemed to have been born believing they were our superiors. They did not even show respect for our names, names that were full of meaning, precious to us as the only remaining personal link we had with our free lives.

"Attu"—it was no name to force on a man in place of his true one. Before his capture, Attu had proudly borne the name Anakhta-yan, known in his family for generations and given to him at birth. But the Tahtna identified him only by that far island on the Uɫchena chain from where they had stolen him—Attu.

I remember Richard, that English name, to me a nothing word stuck on him by Captain Moore, English himself, a name he no doubt hung on every cabin boy he impressed, marking him for English service. Richard told me his Bengalese birth name, one traditional in his family, he said, his voice a whisper, his right name soft and melodious compared with the hard sounds of "Richard."

My father, Ni'i, a proud man, his name means "sun"; Ni'i— a word quick and easy on the tongue, well-respected among our people. How dismal and hard was the title the Tahtna had put on him, a name I stumbled over with its harsh, un-Kahtnuht'ana *r*. "Raskashikov," Baranov called him.

Why strip people of their true names? Oh, I knew: It was yet another step in breaking us down.

Baranov roamed our land and seas bearing the name his parents gave him at birth. "Aleksandr is an old Russian name, and traditional in our family." He spoke proudly. No one dared strip Aleksandr Andreevich Baranov of his right name.

For me, my captor decreed "Anna, a common Russian name, and easy to say." Over the years, he insisted always on "Anna" as my right name. He ignored my Kahtnuht'ana birth name, scoffed at my wish to keep it—Qaniλch'ey Ashana, for the windflowers that bloom in the meadows of Yaghenen, a name my grandmother remembered from her mother. Baranov tried to tear from me the words and sounds that gave me a special identity, set me apart from every other human being.

How could my captor take away my name? My very spirit lives in it!

I am Windflower. Part of my spirit still roams Yaghenen wild and free, and part of it will wait on Kadyak forever. Until the aliens learn that lach'u, Baranov will never know how to destroy me.

I will never forget the morning Jabila picked the perfect windflower and handed it to me. How he held me close and whispered, "Lovely. Lovely like you, my windflower."

I am Qaniλch'ey Ashana of Yaghenen.

The day I walked back up the slope from the shore to watch the *Eagle* sail from Pavlovsk harbor with Baranov at the helm I felt thankful that I would be rid of my captor for many weeks. And mixing with that relief was the hope that Baranov's ship would be wrecked, that he would drown at sea, would suffer a fate to which he had doomed many Aláyeksans.

As the ship passed from sight, thoughts of the hostage women in the shacks again filled my mind. Never a friendly eye, never a friendly hand, never a greeting. I had tried every way I knew to cross the chasm between us. Akoota was forced to talk to me; Baranov had assigned her to watch me, change me into what he wanted. Once only, while the other women in the sheds glared, Watnaw had whispered, "Friend. Sister." I had bartered for their baskets, talked to their mixed-blood children—the small ones harbored no feelings against me, and they reached out for any friend they could find in this harsh, unhappy village. I brought them small gifts and food that Richard would not miss from the house. But my efforts patched no baidarkas (the Tahtna word had begun to slip unbidden into my thoughts; careful, Ashana, I said to myself whenever that happened, think kayak).

On my walks I gathered seeds, grasses, flowers, more bark

to make paints for the caribou-hide picture; many times, I would stop to look toward the work hovels. I wanted to burst in, talk with the other hostages, but Akoota had warned me that they could do me harm.

"Why?" I had asked her. "They know I am hostage, too."

"Will you never understand how it is here, Anna? You have a favored position. One that is good for you. I've told you before."

"Favored!"

"You do not slave in the sheds. You are not abused by a dozen hunters. The women envy you because life is far better for you than for any of them."

On the warm days, as I walked along the shore, hearing the chatter of the hostage women, I knew loneliness; Akoota's nagging had worn on me. Favored! Baranov had put royalty on me, but I had nothing. I needed to talk to the women. Laugh with them. Sorrow with them.

Isolate me, change my name—each a part of the alien way to break me down, to make me a *perfect* hostage.

One day in deep summer I climbed to the strawberry patch on a cliff behind the village. The plants must have been seeded there years before by migrating birds. I lingered, filling my basket, hoping someone would come. The day before I had noticed two women heading up the path to the cliff; later, I watched as they strolled back with loaded baskets, chattering, laughing, enjoying a moment of escape from the drudgery of scraping skins in the shacks.

Below me, in the square of the settlement, several monks stood talking to a group of women and hunters. They appeared to disagree: The men of the church gestured, sometimes seemed to talk very fast; I could almost hear the impatience in the rise and fall of their voices. Attu shook his head two or three times, no doubt dissatisfied with what he was told to interpret. Mixed-blood children clung to the skirts of their mothers. Then a performance I had never seen before took place: The Tahtna men and the Aláyeksan women stood two by two in line, the men on the right and the women on the left. Led by the monks, they walked toward a small platform decorated with a wooden cross. One of the monks—I recognized him as Father Nektarii—stood in front, the men and women facing him. A couple of the church fathers stood behind the lines of people as if to prevent anyone from running away. Two by two, the couples moved up to Father

Nektarii, knelt before him while his hand passed back and forth across his chest, and he appeared to speak to those on their knees, heads bowed.

Intent on watching the scene below, I jumped at the sound of a voice. "Ashana. It's me, Watnaw." She motioned from behind a rock, and I pushed aside the brush and joined her.

"Lingen-Aka"—she nodded to an Uĺchena woman seated on the ground—"and I ran up here early this afternoon and hid."

"Hid? Why?"

"We had to get away. We did not want to get caught in the marrying down there."

"What do you mean, marrying? The aliens just use us. They do not want Aláyeksan women for wives."

"Well, that is what the monks are making them do. You know, Ashana, they have been angry at Baranov ever since they came to Kadyak—with his letting his men live with the women and not taking them to wife, like the monks say proper people do." Watnaw looked at Lingen-Aka, then turned back to me. "The Russian church says it is evil for a man and woman who share the same bed not to marry. So today they made each man bring his woman. And the monk does the marrying."

"Oleg has been after me to marry with him. But I won't do it." Lingen-Aka stood beside the rock, watching the couples below. "I think this marrying is only for people who have children. And I won't have any with him."

"No, it's not quite that way," Watnaw said. "The monks mean *any* man and woman who sleep together."

Lingen-Aka frowned. "I won't do it. There is no man for me but Anakhta-yan."

For a moment I stared at her, thinking to myself: Ah, she is the reason Attu disappears a few hours some evenings and never tells me where he goes. Lingen-Aka is the one Attu loves?

A half hand shorter than me, nearly as slight of figure as K'i'un and about the same age, pert nose and smooth face, curving lips, wispy strands of straight hair falling across her forehead, Lingen-Aka clung to the edge of the rock, screening herself from eyes that might stare our way. Frail, tiny, already turned woman but too new in Pavlovsk to be hardened, her soft voice made it seem almost as if K'i'un were standing there speaking to us. Images of my brother Seltan's chosen mate came to mind, and the young Uĺchena woman changed into the companion of my flight along a river of Htsaynenq' toward the valley of Sem's clan. Bury the past? Forget those you have loved? Impossible.

My thoughts raced to my captor. I panicked. Marry him? Take him for my second husband? Then I calmed: He had a wife in Russia, and his church would not permit him to take a second one. I could not marry him.

But how could the monks know that some of the men down there did not have wives back in their homeland? The marrying showed no signs of happiness; the performance looked forced, the women holding back, joyless.

I thought of the afternoon when Jabila, young and shy and awkward, had asked my father and mother for me and had brought his gifts. The happiness of our two clans when my parents accepted his bride-price and he took me for wife! I remember to this day my bride time, a time of laughter and joy and color. Jabila and I had our private japoon in the village of my parents. That season will forever remain a treasure, one that I can draw out and look at again and again in the despair of my existence in this alien place. Lingen-Aka should have her hours of pleasure with Anakhta-yan.

Aloud, I said to Watnaw and Lingen-Aka, "Don't either of you marry a Tahtna hunter. It will not change in the slightest the backache or the abuse. And it will not save any lives."

As easily as if the three of us had played together and grown up in the same village, we sat behind the rock, a watchful eye on the path so that no one would surprise us. We talked until almost dusk. The suspicions that had separated them from me were forgotten, gone the age-old rivalries that had kept our peoples apart.

It was late in the day when we said good-byes, our new friendship as fragile as the spider webs that linked one branch to another. I did not want to push myself at them and sever the threads between us. As we hesitated a moment, Lingen-Aka suggested that we talk again two afternoons from then at the same berry patch, a spot easy for the three of us to reach, and away from prying ears; deep in Watnaw's searching eyes I sensed a message I could not read.

The poppy seeds dormant in the winter soil of Yaghenen meadows sprout and become bright flowers in the green landscape. Let this friendship blossom like the poppy, I willed that day. Friendship had seemed impossible in the alien climate of Kadyak until the first whisper had come from Watnaw, "Friend. Sister." At last I saw an end to those long days of solitude on

Kadyak between me and Baranov's servants and the hostages, each of us always on guard and wary of the other.

Sitting on the moss-covered log, I held back from leaving with the other two, needed to warm myself with thoughts of the closeness we had known that day. As happiness filled me, other things I had heard during the past weeks went through my mind. That which one knows limits the range of a person's grasp of what is said; no one can pull meaning from what lies beyond the horizon of understanding. I knew that Richard and Attu had tried hard to broaden my view, shine a light for me on this alien world. Attu, the practical man, dealt with facts; cautious, he had never revealed to me his love for Lingen-Aka. Richard, acting more than one role, tended to be imaginative; from seeing how he handled problems with the kitchen help, I was certain that when he did not know a way out of difficulties he would be able to invent one.

A story Watnaw had told us about a wolf and a wolverine seemed to size up the characters of the two men, both of whom I saw in quite different lights. One day the two animals had decided to race each other down a hill, up another, and along the shore of some distant lake.

''Wolf, you run so fast there is no way I can win,'' said the wolverine, panting, as they came alongside each other. ''But I shall try!''

Then the wolf streaked ahead, but the wolverine rolled himself into a ball. He flashed down the hill, for a ball rolls very fast. He beat the wolf, and they ran away together, laughing and saying, ''May the best runner win.''

As I climbed the path from the settlement on the afternoon I was to meet Lingen-Aka and Watnaw, I could hear the loud voices of Ivan Kuskov and the *peredovshchik* directing the hostages and workmen. Gradually the sound of the harsh commands faded; a rare gladness lifted my spirits as I neared my goal.

Smiles greeted me, warm hands reached out, and only with an effort did I hold back my tears. Watnaw and Lingen-Aka had arrived early and had almost filled their baskets.

''Let us help you.'' Each of my new friends hurried to give me a hand, and soon we had three baskets glowing with ripe strawberries.

Settled under a tall hemlock tree, I waited for the right moment to surprise them. Watnaw plunged immediately into serious talk, keeping her voice low. "Ashana, Lingen-Aka and I have been very careful. And you should know that some of the hostages—"

"Careful? What are you saying?" I asked.

She bit her lip and a flicker of some emotion I could not define gleamed in her eyes. Lingen-Aka made little scratches on her skin by drawing over the back of her hand again and again the thin edge of the long, sharp fingernail she used to split reeds for basket weaving.

"I . . ." Watnaw's deep brown eyes looked into mine, and I knew she was searching for the right words, appearing uncertain as to how much she should share with me. "It's like this, Ashana. Our women and men know that to survive they must do exactly what the Russians demand. But that is not the worst. The worst is when any of our people find ways of doing something extra, and gaining favors."

"I understand that our people must do what they have been ordered to do, but what do you mean by 'doing something extra'?"

"I have watched them in the work huts. When hostages first land on Kadyak, they must learn how to get along with the aliens. They do what they think will protect them: obey orders. And it does not take much time before some of them learn that by doing a little more for the *promyshlenniki* they can expect favors in return. A few bits more food. A better corner to sleep in. Often something the aliens hint they will not get any other way." Watnaw glanced at Lingen-Aka, then back to me. "I have learned to guard against one kind of person most of all, Ashana: a hostage who is nice to your face, but who will cause you trouble and betray you to the Russians if it will gain her little favors. You must understand such people if you want to avoid trouble for yourself."

"As Watnaw says, there are a few of us who will climb over anyone to put themselves in better with the aliens." Lingen-Aka's voice was sad music. "They are the ones who care only for themselves. We know they are dangerous. There have been times I have nearly let myself be trapped."

"I made up my mind long ago that I will not give in. I only pretend to." Watnaw's eyes, deep in their own mask, stared beyond me. "I will strike any way I can at the aliens. There are means. Being late to work. Days I pretend I don't have a good stomach. Don't scrape the otter skin as best I can. Miss a night with the *promyshlenniki*. They will never get complete control of me. Never.''

"Watnaw has been good for us new hostages. She tells us whom we can trust. How to try and match wits with the aliens. She knows ways to hurt, a little at a time, without killing, without making bad trouble for us. She is very careful,'' Lingen-Aka said.

The outer rims of Lingen-Aka's ear were pierced, and she wore labrets made from tiny shells and bright stones. Hers was a face always ready to break into laughter; a slight slant to her eyelids gave her an innocent and rather perplexed look; her wide-apart, shining eyes peered at me from under heavy brows. The worn puffin-skin dress failed to hide her island beauty. I did not sense in Lingen-Aka the strength to endure that I saw in Watnaw; but in spite of what she had been through, the young woman appeared as fresh, yet as fragile, as the spindrift on the crest of a wave.

Lingen-Aka had been watching me; she seemed to be gathering courage to speak to me freely, to realize she could trust me. "You know, Ashana," she said finally, "I am Ulchena. And Akoota, she is Ulchena. But although we come from the same place I have to say that she is one woman we must watch out for. I know she has been through terrible things: The Tahtna broke into her house, killed her family, tore her away from Akutan—that was her island—and made her hostage. Yet she does not seem to have a head of her own. She gives in to whatever the Tahtna demand. I know she does extra things for the aliens. She has allied herself with them to the point that they have set her to watching the rest of us. And I think she is—'' Lingen-Aka stopped and turned to Watnaw as if asking whether she had said too much.

"Akoota, yes. She and I have spent hours together. She has begged me to accommodate, accept, do whatever would put me in better with our captors. A matter of survival, she insists. We grind on each other. I have screamed at her. Told her to be quiet and get out. We do not understand each other.'' I stopped. *Be careful what you say, Ashana, to whom you talk. Stay wary,* my joncha warned me. Much as I wanted those two for friends, open and trusting, women I could talk to without screening every word, a suspicion deep in my mind prodded: Could they be baiting me? I would wait and see.

I did not want to say more about Akoota, and I changed the talk, told them about my goat horns, laughed about failing to carve the animals I saw in them. "Can it be true that only men can bring out the animals living there?" I asked, for even with a sharpened rock I had not been able to scratch a single whisker on the horns.

"It could be." Lingen-Aka laughed.

"Nonsense," scoffed Watnaw. "If a man can do it, you can. Get a sharper rock."

I should have told them that I was beginning to paint the hunting lach'u, but the time did not seem right. I reached into my pouch.

"Here." I drew out my surprises—two cords of sinew strung with dentalium shells and small bird claws mixed with a few pretty seeds. "One for each of you. I made them. Chains of friendship."

They eyed each other slyly, half smiles playing over their faces. Then Watnaw burst out laughing as she reached behind a nearby rock. "We brought surprises for you, too, Ashana. Close your eyes." Watnaw's cheerfulness lightened my spirits, and I giggled as I felt something being placed on my head.

"Now you can look." She stepped back, still laughing. "You would make a very proper Gulushutna lady."

I shook my head and Watnaw's gift fell into my lap; a beautiful hat finely woven from tawny grasses, shaped in the style worn by her Gulushutna clan. It had a wide brim to shed the rain, a high crown, and was decorated with a bold red-and-black eagle design.

Then Lingen-Aka bent down and placed on my knees a small lidded basket made of grasses she had carefully split with her long, sharpened fingernail, then shaped and woven tightly into an intricate white-and-gold pattern. Her gift to me was an exquisite Attu Island treasure. We Athabaskans make large, strong baskets, using birch bark, roots, and whole grasses; but in the Ulchena Islands bark is scarce, and weavers hoard their supply of grasses by splitting each strand into several hair-like ones; their baskets are so delicate they seem born of the island's sea mists.

We thanked one another for the gifts; a warm, strong feeling passed among us, and I buried my suspicions about those two who had reached out to me, past their loneliness and the abuse they suffered. I knew they needed trust as much as I did.

Amid the clatter of the alien house and the din of harsh Tahtna voices, it was often difficult to hear nature speaking to me. But that day, looking toward the sunlit slopes of Kadyak's mountains, the waves below us whispering against the shore, I heard the strawberry leaves at my feet murmuring, speaking to me. And from the far-distant past the voice of Sem whispered, "Be still, my child, and listen."

As Lingen-Aka stepped behind the bushes for a moment to relieve herself, Watnaw moved quickly to my side and tucked a bit of sea-otter fur in my ear. "Ssssh," she whispered, "the sea otter will lead you. . . . A journey . . . Stay close to me tonight." Often when Watnaw spoke, her words were laced with warning and carried messages beyond my understanding. I tried to pull the meaning from what she had said, started to ask, "What do you—?"

Lingen-Aka's voice interrupted us. "We are late. It's time to go back."

We hurried down the path, Watnaw's Gulushutna words dusting another layer over what she had already told me as she whispered, "It is a fact, Ashana. The sea otter knows who wears the fur in her ear."

A shiver passed through me. *Be still and listen.*

10

It was almost dusk as we walked from the berry patch. We passed the Kaydak kashim, a building I had never entered, one that in the old days was used for ceremonies, but later housed men and women held in service for the Tahtna company. Men carrying ferns, grasses, branches, small trees, and feathers walked in and out.

"What is going on?" I asked.

"A festival to honor hunters. A Koniag celebration preparing for winter." Lingen-Aka laughed and ran on ahead of us.

"Come with me now, Ashana," Watnaw's hand gripped my arm.

"Oh, I wish I could. But Baranov has forbidden me to—"

"He is not here. Anyway, he gave us permission to celebrate. It will get the men off to a good start, and the hunt will be a success."

"Can women go?"

"This time, yes. Some of the Koniag women and children will even take part."

I longed to see the dances and hear the songs of Aláyeksa once more, and decided that I would join my friends, despite what Baranov might have thought.

"The Koniags have invited all of us on the island. It took weeks for us to get permission—you know we do not often have time for such celebrations." Watnaw was almost pushing me along, her arm firmly across my back.

Inside the kashim, I settled down beside her on a Kadyak bearskin. At first I felt strange, almost guilty, but I soon began shedding the hostage curse: I belonged there as much as anyone else. Eyes lingered on me a moment; some smiled greetings, others never gave me a second glance. It grew cold outside, but indoors the combined warmth of the fires and the press of excited bodies caused many of the men to shed their parkas. Again I remember that I scolded myself, "Careful, Ashana, do not think 'parka,' think *our* word: bechik'ish nutquni." Some people had stripped naked and were relaxing on the skins tossed on the floor. Overhead, grasses, ferns, and spruce branches decorated the room; the spruce torches spread their fragrance around us.

There was a burst of activity at the door as actors and dancers, their faces masked, filled the center of the kashim. Two young girls took their places, one on each side of the space set aside for dancing. They had spent hours making themselves ready. Before the Tahtna came, they would have worn new clothes for the festivities, but with Aláyeksa stripped of its furs, that night they had to be content with sewing shells, puffin down, bird claws, and beaks to their worn garments. Yet they stood straight and proud, crowned with eagle feathers threaded into strips of deerskin. All the men and women were wearing their decorated hats and masks. Had it not been for Watnaw's gift I would have felt almost naked. The three of us should have taken the time to dress in what little finery we owned, but Watnaw had seemed anxious to get me there as fast as possible, and would not let me stop.

Dancing to one side of the girls, two hunters swung paddles painted with fish, otters, and whales. The paddles in one hand kept time with the loops of supple vines held in the other, loops that were decorated with bird beaks and feathers, squirrel and rabbit feet, bear claws and teeth. The hunters' hand motions were fast and my eyes were drawn to them; then I noticed the helmets—twigs bent in the shape of an Ułchena hunting hat, one slender twig curved down from the top and held between the teeth, symbol of a fish on a line.

A man stood on the end of a bench holding a sinew rope, one end of which was slung over a beam in the ceiling, the other fastened to several crossed spears. From the spears hung a Koniag kayak, pelts, hunting weapons, and seal decoys; the man worked his rope in time with the rhythm of the dancers and the singers, and the objects overhead danced their dance of the hunt.

After a few minutes one of the Koniag leaders sang out, "Young hunters, row to the beach. The animals will come. Brace yourselves for the catch." I added my voice to those of the women around me as nearly a hundred people, singing in different tongues, honored the hunt, while, shrilling through the chorus, wove the whistles that imitated birds and animals.

It was the first time since leaving Yaghenen that I had joined my voice to that of other humans as we sounded the calls of animals and the cries of birds—bear, sea lion, eagle, loon, raven—and, catching at my heart, pulling at me, the call of the wolf, my lost tiqun. From deep inside me came a feeling I had never before known; unbidden tears welled in my eyes and trickled slowly down my cheeks: Aláyeksa was claiming me.

The leader ended his chant. We women grew quiet as the hunters continued the ceremony, rocking and swaying to the beating drums. The ritual honored hunters who would never return, and its strength reached out to those who would range Aláyeksa's forests and seas in the future.

The dance slowed to its finish.

In front of the largest torch stood a stone that represented the burial place of a legendary hunter lost long ago. No one knew where he truly lay, but each clan remembered such a hero. Absolute silence held the gathering as in a spell; even the fire and the torches dimmed. Everyone paused in respect as the servers carried in large clamshells filled with berries and put them on the stone marker. We all grieved for the unknown hunter; but my tears flowed for the young man who had run beside me in the meadows of Yaghenen, his long legs taking one stride to my two, his laughter all that my ears could hear. For a few moments I called back images from my first days with Jabila on the open slopes of Yaghenen. I heard again the throb of Kahtnuht'ana drums; then I realized that the same beat pulsed through the air, in the Kadyak kashim.

The mood changed. Other performers, costumed and masked, danced into the middle of the room; over the heavy drumbeats I heard the shrilling of the seal whistles some men wore in their noses to call the animals to them. Homage to hunters and to the chase itself took the men many times around the fire in the center of the room as dancers from Aláyeksan clans celebrated through the night.

The sights and smells and sounds of The Great Country drove the tears from my eyes and lifted my battered spirits. A few times a certain figure took an extra turn in front of me, brushed close by, a sea-gull mask over his face, his dance pure Athabaskan. I felt . . . Jabila . . . no . . . no . . . I knew many yi*l* separated us. I grabbed Watnaw's arm, and she held me tightly.

Sometime before first light, the dance of the hunt wound to a close, and Watnaw said, "Time for us to leave."

Following her, I glimpsed a lone dancer wearing a Gulu-shutna cape and devil headdress; the man towered above every-one; his dance jerked, twisted, in a swift pattern I did not recognize.

Outside, I started to tell Watnaw I thought Jabila had danced among the performers. I hesitated to raise any question about his presence on Kadyak; instead, I asked, "Why did we have to leave? That next dance was different. I wanted to see it."

"An old Gulushutna devil dance some of my people have added to the celebration." She sounded hurried, anxious to get away.

"Devil dance? Tell me about it."

"In the ancient days my people knew it as the devil dance. Let us just say that for now the devils are the aliens." Her voice was strained, but in the darkness I could not read her face. She went on, "Back then the devil dancers carried sharp, pointed knives, sheathed so only the points showed. As they danced by, they would prick a person. Not deep. Only enough to draw a small spot of blood. Time went on, and the dancers stopped using knives and started pinching. So when that dancer comes in, it is a signal for women to leave. No respectable woman argues about it."

We continued walking as Watnaw described the devil dance, and I realized she had drawn us away from my house and through the woods toward the shore.

"I had better run back. I should not be out here."

Watnaw dropped my arm, stepped back. Bushes turned into moving shadows. Suddenly, arms grabbed me, hands covered my mouth, stifling my screams.

Had Watnaw trapped me? I was betrayed! I had misjudged her! Memories—terrible memories—of having been dragged from Yaghenen flashed through my mind. Had Baranov ordered me to the shacks? Like a snared animal that thrashes and writhes against the sinews, I kicked, pulled back, shoved with my el-bows, my lungs bursting.

"Hurry! Hurry!" The voice was Kahnuht'ana! "Jabila is waiting. We are taking you home."

"No. No. Jabila is on Yaghenen and—"

A strong hand muffled my protest. "Hush. Come."

The half-aloud voices breathed the sounds of home, stilled

my terror, and though how or whence they came I did not know, I followed the men to the beach.

Strong arms encircled me as I stumbled forward. "Qani*I*-ch'ey Ashana," Jabila whispered into my hair, "Qani*I*ch'ey Ashana." I shuddered, knowing Jabila and his men risked their lives for me. I had told him long ago, "Stay far away from the aliens."

For a few moments, we touched, drifting away to the heights of Yaghenen. Swiftly, his hands caressed my breasts, slid gently down my hips, his tongue tasted mine. Our need for each other could not be satisfied in that instant, but his strength entered me. Oh, the joy of standing beside him! But there was no time to savor that joy, no time to linger and talk. Jabila pulled away from me and guided me to his kayak. As soon as I was laced into the middle hatch, he spoke a few quick words to his men and eased himself down into the front position with another paddler behind me. As we pushed off from Kadyak, several other craft came to life on the water.

Not a sound, not a voice from the sea, only the *slk, slk, slk* of the paddles, powerful, rhythmic strokes moving us away from the shore. We seemed ghosts, guided only by the sense of direction in the minds of the men. A fresh following wind breathed over the sea, and shorter strokes sent a different beat through our kayaks as we crossed the open water between the islands. In the faint first light of dawn our shadow boats raced on as one: We had to put as much distance as possible between us and Pavlovsk. As the day became brighter, I could see faces, men from Jabila's village; Seltan did not row with them—the elders and my father would not risk the lives of both my husband and my brother.

The paddles sliced through the waves as the men read the face of the sea, watched the shifting currents that swept the channels, listened for the wind that could either favor us or become our enemy. I willed the kayaks faster to freedom. We neared a large island, and choppy waters hid the other boats from ours as we knifed through the cresting waves. When the others were in sight again, we rounded another large island on a flood current, pushed to the point where the tidal streams parted, and sped on, riding the ebb northward, wary of rocks and sandbars that could endanger our passage.

On a broad stretch of open water, the waves loping and even, I watched Jabila's shoulder and body set the pace with strong, smooth strokes; gradually I dared believe we were not ghost kayaks. I thought back to the day before: Watnaw had known; the tiny fur patch still clung to my ear, and I understood why she had said the sea otter would lead me on a journey.

Questions flooded my mind. How had Jabila and his men planned? How had Watnaw received word? How had they known Baranov was away? That a celebration was being held? How soon would I be missed?

Jabila, you danced at the celebration. My heart had heard the sea gull whisper, but my mind would not believe.

Could raven be bringing back the Light?

We sped past small rock islands, along the coasts of larger ones—the kayaks held formation, ours leading by half a boat length, sometimes a full length, with another craft close on each side, two behind, all within easy calling distance. Leaving a broad expanse of water, we paddled swiftly among islets. The day edged from morning to midafternoon, a day filled with sea and islands, sky and wind, the beauty of Jabila leading the pack that bore me home. We scanned the water behind us anxiously, but there was no one in pursuit . . . only the sea lions calling their greetings.

Later, under cover of night, we beached, pulled our kayaks far above the high-tide line. At a word from Jabila, the rowers scattered, leaving the two of us alone. The wind died down. The incoming tide slapped against the shore, a sound that tugged at my heart as it had never done on Kadyak. Jabila sat hunched over, clasping and unclasping his hands, trying to work out the soreness from days on the paddle. I was afraid to reach out, to touch him, afraid he would vanish into the fog drifting off the face of the sea. I had longed, cried out, dreamed day and night of this reunion, but a barrier now separated us. He seemed a person apart from me, lost in another world. I whispered his name, but he did not hear. Was I scarred forever in Jabila's mind? Spoiled by Baranov's use of me?

Jabila moved suddenly, reached for my hand. "Come. I must walk. My legs cramp." Such strangeness. We were there, together. But too much had happened too fast; too many questions remained unanswered. We could not in a moment bridge the great chasm of time and separation and hurt that had passed between us. We followed the path as it wove through the trees and out to an open stretch of land, where the chill wind made me draw still closer to Jabila, seeking his warmth.

"Ouch!" I tripped on a root, stumbled, pitched forward. Jabila caught me, and, locked in each other's arms, we ended that night of waiting and longing. His kisses, at first gentle yet searching, gradually turned fierce and demanding, driving away all doubt and strangeness that lingered between us. "Nature's japoon" Jabila had called the first cave that had kept secret the love we offered each other. And on that night of our escape, we again discovered a secure niche hidden beneath an overhanging rock, a place of safety and shelter. Tenderly, Jabila slipped my garments from me, his hands gentle on my skin, his touch arousing me, warming me. It was time for our love to burn brightly, time to free the fires that had remained banked for so long. Our love was of this moment, no longer a beloved, flickering memory but a wild flame that engulfed us both, blotting out the island and the seas that would bear us home. Our love restored to us the life we had known together on Yaghenen. I stretched out happily beside my husband. The blaze of our passion dimmed to a quiet glow, and together we slipped into a deep sleep.

With a start, I rolled to one side as a raven call awakened both of us. We tied ourselves into our hatches, and flight that day again began before dawn.

By the time the sun was high we had reached a large island north of the many smaller ones dotting the sea. All morning the paddles had flashed forth and back, forth and back, so fast the eye saw only a blur. *Slk, slk. Slk, slk.* Sweeping overhead, gulls and terns hovered close, as if asking where our journey was taking us.

Then abruptly, out of the corner of my eye, I saw a movement far back and to my right. Whales? Seals? No! Danger. Danger! Humans, not animals. Several kayaks raced after us, black water following. Black water, an ancient sign of peril.

"Danger! Danger!" I screamed at Jabila.

"Tahtna!" He shouted the warning without losing a stroke, and "Tahtna!" passed swiftly from boat to boat. At once I felt our craft speed faster, the strokes stronger and more powerful than when we threaded the strait away from Kadyak; the men had practiced well, and each rower matched Jabila's new rhythm. The sea and sky and islands became our world. I began hearing the sharp intake of breath; the strain was wearing hard on our men.

The deadly pack still followed. Behind me I saw U*l*chena rowers powering the paddles; in the middle hatch of each kayak a Tahtna poked his gun into the back of the front rower lest he slacken his stroke in sympathy for his fellow Aláyeksans.

Slk, slk, slk. The gap between us and our pursuers seemed to widen. Suddenly, out of the depths of the sea, a pod of whales rose across our path. Any other time we would have slowed to watch the great creatures, we would have listened to their voices—the language of the whales singing to one another, telling the companions they were not alone in the vast open sea. That day, we cut to the side to avoid them, and our *slk, slk* faltered. A rower's shout sliced sharply through the air as a whale dived, spreading a wave that upended the kayak on our left which was speeding too fast to change course. We raced on. The rowers could right themselves, for they knew the U*l*chena roll. The men had planned how to maneuver in case of upset, so the kayak at the rear left veered to offer help.

A shot. Another. Four or five more.

An agony of death cries tore at us, then faded away as punctured craft and bloody bodies shuddered, struggling on the surface. Beyond saving, our Kahtnuht'ana brothers would sink into the arms of the nutin'at dnayi, the sea people. It was too late to attempt a rescue; we had no choice but to speed north.

A volley of shots streaked the surface a few boat lengths behind us. The Tahtna had narrowed the gap, drawing close enough for us to hear their threatening orders to the U*l*chena rowers.

Sprint. Row, row. *Slk, slk*. Row, row, row. Sprint. *Slk, slk, slk*. Our paddles churned the water. A few brief words between Jabila and our nearest rowers: He had signaled the kayak on our right to make a quick turn with him around a promontory covered with trees and bushes that came down to the water's edge. We rammed along the narrow cove and onto the shore at a point beyond which the long ridge of the promontory dropped sharply into the water. Huge boulders hid us from the Tahtna as they pursued our two other boats.

The sound of distant shots rent the air. We watched from our hiding place as, out on the open sea, one boat swerved and twisted, the front rower crumpling over as his paddle dropped from his grasp. Another volley, and the second craft jolted. Our qeshqa had decreed the gamble for freedom worth the probable deaths of rowers or hostages. Kahtnuht'ana died for my freedom as the blood of Yaghenen men tinged the water. Only Jabila's strong arm kept me from sinking to the ground in anguish.

We stayed hidden in the brush along the high ridge, while the Tahtna poked at the bodies with guns, sank the kayaks with more shots. The aliens knew I was not among the dead, for they turned back to our island and beached in a cove a long arrow flight from the one into which we had retreated with our boats. The other Tahtna began clambering over the island. One of our rowers drew an arrow to his bow, but Jabila's hand pushed it aside. "No. Don't lead them to us." When our pursuers crawled over a low ridge opposite, Jabila whispered, "Back to the sea."

We moved silently, listening to the muffled stamp of boots on rocks and gruff voices calling to one another. Eyes and ears wary, we crawled and slid down to the shore. The sounds of the men searching for us faded as we dashed over the rocky beach, laced ourselves into our boats, and cut through the breakers, their roar covering the sound of our voices.

We had put many boat lengths between us and the Tahtna before they lined the small bay. Again the race for life or death struck across Aláyeksan waters. We had become a depleted fleet, but as if fresh wind filled their lungs, Jabila and his four last men sprinted, their paddles ripping the water with a strength driven by terror; their arms, their shoulders, their bodies pulling, stroking, working as one. But their strained breathing belied the power; the stress and the long days of rowing—first to Kadyak, then back to Yaghenen—was draining their strength. A short sprint. *Slk, slk, slk.* I felt our pace slacken. The alien fleet gained. Ul̷chena island men, born to the paddles, skilled and weathered on the sea, held the edge in power. Our tiring rowers could not match their ageless endurance.

Shots spattered the water close behind us.

A sharp turn, and Jabila led us into a sheltered stretch of water free of breakers on the north side of a large island. We hastily pulled our boats away from the shore and into cover.

"When they come," Jabila gasped, "our only hope this time—arrows."

We clambered high among the trees, crawled behind one ridge and up onto another. But we were unable to gain time, as we had on the island where the Tahtna had first looked for us; they swung in on the stretch of beach where we had landed. They knew where we were. Harsh voices echoed through the still air. Jabila and his men crouched, waited. *Promyshlenniki* wove in and out among the brush and small trees. Our arrows whistled. Three men twisted suddenly in agony, their guns clattering onto the rocks. Tahtna fell over the cliff in a spiraling devil's dance.

"Danger! Behind you!" Jabila swung round, his arrow flying from his bow in the same instant that a shot felled him. A man from our last boat grabbed him by the arm and dragged him out of sight, his head striking painfully against the ground. I swallowed the shriek that rose to my lips lest the aliens should hear and find me. My rower grabbed me, and together we slid into the shelter of a clump of bushes, then tried to work our way toward the ledge where we thought Jabila lay. Tahtna boots dislodged rocks and sent them crashing down on us. From my hiding place, the drumming of my heart seemed as loud as the surf below; my throat was too dry even to whisper encouragement to my companion.

A shout came from far up on the slope. My rower released an arrow, but not before a Tahtna knife, thrown from the side, hurtled into his chest; he gasped and staggered back, blood spurting from his mouth.

Two Tahtna rushed at me, pushed me to the ground. I kicked, lunged; my scream rose to a high-pitched keening, echoing again and again before rough, filthy hands wrestled me to the ground. I twisted, drew my legs to my chest, kicked out. But I was flung onto my back and my screams died as a heavy boot pushed me down into the dirt and rocks.

A blow struck my head and black water flowed over me.

In those days alone on Kadyak, I had never thought of a life without Jabila, believing that the Kahtnuht'ana spirit people would one day bring us back together. During the nights I roamed and could not find him, nights when I cried out for him, I still knew that, somewhere, he waited for me. Always, he walked with me when I needed him; knowing he lived, I could turn to the shadow-spirit part of me and it sustained me through my isolation and my need.

But that day on the island I lost Jabila. I heard his death cry on the wind, his moan on the surging of the tide.

Alone, standing on a headland facing Yaghenen, I searched the sea. The raven had taken away my Light. K'eghun nu, the red war moon, pulled at me, and from deep within the red waves rose my mourning song for Jabila:

> tide and moon, moon and tide,
> float arm in arm on the sea;
> moon and tide, tide and moon
> float on the breast of the sea;
> blood on the moon, blood on the tide,
> tide and moon float in Jabila's blood.

BOOK TWO

❖ ❖ ❖

⊙ ⊙ ⊙

11

When Baranov stormed onto Kadyak a few days after his men had dragged me back, he roared, "I trusted you, Anna, but you ran away. I ordered you to change, but you did not. Now it is time." His voice snarled in a way I had never heard before, and with each word his whip slashed my back and legs. "We are rid of your savage. My men told me. I have seen you pine for him. Heard you howl at night. But it is over. Behave. You understand?"

Behave . . . I knew the deadly threat, for my mind flooded with Akoota's words, "But worse, Ashana, seven men from my father's village . . . the Russians shot them." Had his killing hand already reached into Yaghenen? Would he kill me?

I forced myself to stand still under the lashes, to bite my lips and not cry out. I did not know where the strength came from until the sea gull sent me its spirit: *Ride out the storm on the sea, Ashana; survive, survive.* The sea gull trembles and disappears in the grasp of the winds, but it always returns. As the Tahtna storm buffeted me, as I searched for my whitecap, it became clear to me that I could make Baranov think he controlled my spirit if I trembled under his whip. I trembled. And as the slashes cut me, the sea-gull mask slipped over my face, its spirit joining mine; I faced my captor with a strength he would never understand.

After the storm, my captor left me alone at night and used a woman in the work shacks. We moved about the house as strangers, the only sounds the muffled voices of the cooks in the kitchen, Richard's few words to his master, Kuskov and Baranov mumbling over reports or cursing the workmen. The welts on my body faded, but the wound searing my heart lay open.

Despair at losing Jabila walked with me in the daylight and

in the dark; and in my sorrow the mourning-woman mask would slip over my face, the eyes mere slits in high cheeks, the mouth clamped in a thin bloodless line. Baranov's house became a burial cave, I the frozen mummy within it.

One day, my captor's ice-blue eyes held a menacing look; I sensed more punishment was coming, but as he started to speak, Ivan Kuskov burst into the room, "Aleksandr, hurry. You have to settle a fight."

"The devil! What the hell is wrong now?"

"The men are fighting. They have guns and knives."

"Aláyeksans or Russians?" Baranov pulled on his chain-mail vest and buttoned his jacket over it. "This vest," he had explained to me, "will stop a bullet." Whenever he wore it, he walked in the company of his trusted men—Attu, Richard, most often Ivan Kuskov.

"Russians are fighting. Hurry, Aleksandr." Kuskov held the door open. "The men are mad about rotten food and short pay. They are out to kill you. You've got to talk sense into them."

Kuskov and Baranov stamped from the house; I was brushed aside like a fly on my captor's nose. All the hatred of Russians in Aláyeksa seethed around Aleksandr Baranov. Ever since he had made me his hostage, I had known of fights among the Tahtna and heard rumblings of plots against Baranov. That day, the plots worked in my favor; my attempt to escape was no longer important in the face of the threats from his own Tahtna workmen. I am only a woman.

Lost in grief over Jabila and all the past, pacing the ancient path that skirted a bluff, I finally sat down to rest against a worn hemlock, one side of which had been deeply scarred by lightning. My hands twisted the ends of my braids as my thoughts flew to the failed homeward flight. My heart throbbed, its beat as loud as the tides pounding the rocks. Jabila was gone . . . gone.

It was almost dark. The crunch of footsteps on the rocks made me wary, and I stood up. Father Emelian was walking toward me, pulling his black robe closer around him as he drew near. Slowly the church father raised his arm, his fingers like claws, and intoned. "Know the words of God to the woman Eve in Genesis, 'What is this that thou hast done?' "

The wind whipped his skirts as he droned on, " '. . . the wages of sin is death.' Know the Kahtnuht'ana man died because of you. His death is your fault."

I stepped back, frightened, for I saw malice in the maniacal glitter in his strange eyes, in the expression on his flat-nosed face.

" 'The wages of sin is death,' " Father Emelian repeated. "You are a sinner. You must suffer God's punishment. You weep for the Kahtnuht'ana man. But you must understand, Anna, his death is your fault."

His death is my fault? Jabila lay dead from Tahtna guns. How could that be my fault? How could the monk accuse me? Yet he kept repeating his terrible words, and slowly I began to grasp the awful message: Jabila had come to Kadyak because of me, come to take me home to Yaghenen, and he had died. Had I caused my husband's death?

The monk cried out, "Anna, you sin. You are an offense to our God. Take his words to heart. ' . . . the wages of sin is death.' "

The shadows lengthened, but still the monk hammered at me, accused me of many things, repeated himself endlessly. But I heard only 'The man died because of you. You are guilty.' Qanilch'ey Ashana of Yaghenen stood accused of murder, the most heinous crime under Athabaskan law. I was shattered. Guilty . . . guilty . . . guilty.

I had found a way to survive Baranov's physical punishment, but these violent charges, hurled at me with no warning, drained my strength and filled me with despair. That day under the old hemlock, Father Emelian settled a terrible grief upon me. In my agony, the monk, no longer human, became the evil side of chulyin. And I heard my father's voice as clearly as if he were speaking from beside the evening fire in Yaghenen: "Long ago, when chulyin lived among a hungry clan, he stole out at night and pecked all the flesh from a whale that had been caught to feed the people. He left only skin and bones for the starving village. Then someone found him out and accused him. In the flash of an eye chulyin turned himself into human form. But before he had changed completely, an old woman reached up and pulled off his beak. So, as a human, he walked the earth holding his hand over his face. He had only a bump of a nose where his beak should be. All people could identify him by his flat-nosed face."

On the rocky trail, the raven-dark eyes of the monk glared at me. And as he turned away toward the village, I knew whose heart hid the evil side of chulyin.

I scrambled down, sliding, tearing my qenich'eni, gashing

my legs and arms on the rocks. Kneeling on the beach, I dug out a mass of soil from the foot of the cliff and blackened my face, a Kahtnuht'ana in grief. Too much . . . Jabila dead . . . my fault . . . guilty . . . murder . . . *blood on the moon, blood on the tide, tide and moon float in Jabila's blood.*

I waited for the high tide to wash over me. The crashing of the waves echoed and reechoed . . . guilty . . . guilty . . . guilty. Then the tide began to swallow me, its icy fingers pushing me down to the land without light at the bottom of the sea. The waters pulled me down, endlessly down. Death at the bottom of the sea, and peace. Songs spread around me, gentle hands bathed my face; they were the voices, the caresses, of the sea people, the nutin'at dnayi.

One day the waves receded, and light streamed down to the land beneath the sea. Voices I knew called me. Not the sea people, for I lay on my furs in this Kadyak house. Lingen-Aka spooned fresh salmon broth into my mouth, and Aleksandr Baranov peered over her shoulder.

"No. No. Can't you see, I'm dead," I sobbed.

Watnaw's strong arm quieted me, and Lingen-Aka soothed me. "No, Ashana, you are here with us." She smoothed my hair, dried my tears. "You have been ill for a long, long time."

Aleksandr's voice reached me, speaking gently. "You have had a terrible ordeal. We were afraid we had lost you." (He had not been so gentle on the day I was brought back from my failed escape.) Surprising, this man . . . did he think, with Jabila dead, I would be any less Kahtnuht'ana? He said nothing about my escape, my going to the sea, and I knew by his silence he was now less certain that he could understand me.

Days later I sat up, still weak, but I knew that the long night under the sea had ended. I learned that Watnaw and Lingen-Aka had rescued me. Father Emelian's madness was more than just my imagination, for the head monk Ioasaf and Aleksandr Baranov agreed that he had lost his mind and that they would send him back to Russia when one of the Tahtna ships came.

Unknown to Aleksandr Baranov, two Kahtnuht'ana hunters slipped away from the shores of Kadyak before dawn one morning, their kayak racing toward Yaghenen. Watnaw told me they had taken home word of the happenings on Kadyak.

And I wondered: Are there Kahtnuht'ana fighters still hiding in the forest, stalking the Tahtna? If so, my father is having his revenge. Dangerous, I know, for it will lead to more killings and hostage-taking, perhaps to my own death. I do not care anymore. I believe my father does not care anymore. If my people were to take to the woods and flee, at the expense of my brother's death, my death, and the other hostages' deaths, this madness would be over. But it is a terrible choice.

"Stay in bed," Baranov had ordered before he left again for Chugach country—the aliens had the idea that to stay in bed meant to recover; and I obeyed when I expected visitors. But there was no recovery from Jabila's death; I paced the floor, longing for the smell of fresh air and the feel of clean earth under my feet; I hummed some of the tunes I had learned at my mother's side, tunes that seemed to wipe away part of my despair.

As days passed, I knew I must force myself to gain strength, take to myself the cunning and wisdom of the ancient hero Qishvet'. I buried my face in my furs and remembered the Yaghenen story:

Long, long ago, in the time of our ancient ones, a strong young man lived in our house. The Eskimo clans raided our villages. They came armed with bows and arrows. They shot many arrows into our village. As for Qishvet', he was lying down inside. He had just returned home from a long snowshoe journey. Our men ran to him. "We need your help." Then Qishvet' put on his snowshoes. They had brown-bear claws tied to the bottom. He took his big war club. Outside, he struck down many arrows. He shot them back at the enemy. They ran away. He chased after them. They shot more arrows. He hurled them back. The lake froze with glare ice. The enemy could not run on the ice. It was too slippery. But Qishvet' could. The bear claws gripped the ice. He ran fast. Soon, he had captured all the enemy arrows. Our people were safe.

Bear claws—I needed bear claws to fasten my spirit.

Some new power seemed to be growing in me: Qishvet' was only a man. I am a woman. I have powers. I must use them. In an instant I knew what I must do. Qishvet' had caught the arrows and hurled them back at the enemy. I must take the alien gun, and it must shoot back at *our* enemy.

Aleksandr Baranov had not beaten me when Watnaw and Lingen-Aka had rescued me; before he left for the Chugach country, he had told me he was going to collect his tribute of furs. But I knew of a different reason: He had claimed a Chugach woman, another leader's daughter, for his use; that woman he left in her village (as he left the woman on Unalaska, whom I had never seen, only heard about), no doubt expecting a deeper loyalty from her people than my being kept hostage on Kadyak was gaining him from mine, for in his letter to Shelekhov that spoke of me, he had also written, ". . . during my long stay at Chugach, the Chugach people gave me a girl for a hostage. On account of that, the Chugach became more attached to me and more confiding." Strange, some of the alien attitudes. From their talk, it sounded as if they believed bedding with an Aláyeksan woman endowed her clan with some special status. If they would listen to Aláyeksan voices, they would know how insulting we consider the act. One man, one wife. One man, a hundred hostage women.

Think no more about the Chugach slave, for that is what she is, I scolded myself. Feel no anger against her, Qanilch'ey Ashana. She lives a hostage agony as heartbreaking as yours. Her despair is no different from that of the nameless woman far off on an Ulchena island or the wretches who slave on Kadyak.

I lay staring at my basket; in it was my caribou hide, untouched for a long time. No voice spoke to me that day: The spirit-whisper had given me instructions, then vanished as the hunting fleet pushed away from the shore. Slipping out of bed, pulling the hide onto my knees, I saw again the story waiting to be painted—the sea hunt. That day I would add a tiny piece of hope. High above and in the center of the hide a brown-bear claw appeared. It took quite awhile. I had started working on the line where the shore of Kadyak meets the sea when a woman interrupted me. She was dressed in finery so beautiful I almost failed to recognize her.

"Watnaw, I . . . I . . . What are you celebrating?"

"I have come to honor your getting better, Qanilch'ey Ashana. We all thought we had lost you, but you have come back to us." Sadness sounded through her words. "We brothers and sisters should never have let it happen."

But I did not want to talk and fussed with folding the caribou hide, then crawled under my sleeping furs. Sometime soon Watnaw must know what was stirring inside me—guns, take guns—but first I needed to work out in my head the message from Qishvet'. So I made a simple remark. "Your hat? I have never seen one like it."

"I wanted to dress up for you, Ashana. Weaving this hat took a long time. I had to hide it from prying eyes, and I have had extra work to do.'' She handed the hat to me.

I ran my fingers back and forth over the ridges of spruce root with reed trim, woven tightly to shed the rain. The hat looked sister to the one she had given me, lost on the beach that night of my escape with Jabila. On the crown, Watnaw had woven in red, green, and black the eagle-crest symbol of her clan; the eagle's body was divided, one half spreading to each side of the hat. Inside each eye, Watnaw had woven another tiny bird, each one a separate eagle symbol.

''I decorated this hat from memory. It is like what I would have woven at home on Sitka.'' A frown crossed her face. ''I had old beads Petrov gave me, but I threw them away. I would not spoil my hat by using his filthy beads.''

Watnaw swung the blanket from her shoulders, ran her hand over it. ''A treasure from home. My father traded one of his red cedar storage chests to a Chilkat elder for it. I remember the ceremony in our village. The two leaders had decided on the gifts. Not a word to their women. My mother fumed. She did not want to give up the chest, but Father said he would make her a better one. She thought a lot of his carvings, knew how long it had taken him to carve it. Everything had to be perfect for him—every eye and limb and claw. 'A bear chest,' he said.''

Watnaw sat quietly a long time, thinking. I heard her whisper, ''Father, did you ever make a new chest for Mother?'' Then she shook herself, ''I came to celebrate. Not to be sad.''

''My family had several of these blankets, but none as pretty as yours, Watnaw.'' One of my greatest pleasures was my friendship with Watnaw, for her talk flowed rich with memories, and we had endured much together.

''This blanket was my favorite. I went off without it when I was taken hostage. Then my father and mother found out I was here and sent the blanket to me.''

''You look like a proper lady.'' My eyes flashed.

Watnaw broke out in a laugh. ''If you say so, Ashana.''

Richard poked his head around the door. ''Why all the noise?''

''You don't need to know everything that goes on in this house,'' Watnaw snapped back at him.

''You may keep it from me now, but I will find out. You look much better, Ashana.'' His eyes passed from the blanket and hat to Watnaw and back. ''You two are up to something, or Watnaw would not come here so dressed up.'' He beamed as an idea struck him. "Nobody else is around. Anakhta-yan and Lingen-Aka want to see you. Let's celebrate your coming back to us, Ashana. I will get something."

Before he returned, I whispered, "Stay, Watnaw, after they are gone. I need to talk to you. We have no time now."

In moments, the Bengalese returned with mugs and a jug of Baranov's best rum. As he began pouring, Lingen-Aka pulled Anakhta-yan into the room.

That day seemed to be the one for displaying hats. Richard's white turban added inches to his height. Anakhta-yan wore his Ułchena hunter's hat. I wondered how many sea-lion whiskers would wave on it if our captor had not enslaved him, if he could have stayed on the Ułchena island, a courageous hunter. Lingen-Aka wore the most elaborate hat of all: A delicately woven cap hugged her head, every inch covered with a lacy pattern of small shells, seeds, bits of ivory and metal. Decorations shone in the tiny holes pierced in her ears. Her puffin-skin parka, decorated with claws and shells, had been repaired and brushed. My friends had dressed in their finery to help ease my loss and cheer my recovery. I fought back tears.

"You know those Russians. They are always doing their *toasting*." Richard handed each of us a mug half filled with rum. "I make this toast to you, Ashana. To your courage."

"Ya. Ya." Anakhta-yan mimicked the Russian toast.

Simple times of pleasure were scarce for us on Kadyak. At first we were hesitant, but we shared a feeling of bravado at dipping into our captor's rum. By the time the mugs were filled a second time, our tongues were loosened, and Anakhta-yan toasted, "Long life to us Aláyeksans."

Then Watnaw added, "To you, Richard, our host today. And to your return to Bengal."

"Thank you. I need a few years to spend on my rice patch." Richard turned away to hide his face, reached toward the corner of the room to brush off a spider web. I sensed he must be close to tears.

"No, no, Richard, leave it." I laughed at him.

"Why? I have to keep the place clean."

"I will tell you."

Watnaw and Lingen-Aka lounged on my furs. Anakhta-yan sat back against the wall. Richard relaxed.

Not ready then to share the story of Qishvet' and what it meant, I began a different one. "We Athabaskans owe much to the old spider woman who spins webs.

"Once in the ancient times, two sisters running through a patch of flowers on Yaghenen spied a butterfly. They reached out to get it. Always, as they were about to catch it, the butterfly darted ahead of their fingertips." I traced the course with my hands, watching Richard's face. "The sisters ran and ran. They survived many dangers. Bears. Big men. Glaciers. Mountains. Stormy seas. But always the butterfly led them on.

"One day, the butterfly was no more. The girls looked for their home. They could not find it. They were afraid. Lost.

"Then they came upon the old spider woman's house. She let them in. There they were safe.

" 'We are lost.'

" 'Stay here.'

"They were happy.

"The spider woman had many sons. They soon returned from the hunt. They saw the beautiful sisters. The young men began to quarrel over them. Soon the happiness of the house was gone.

"The spider woman took the sisters for a walk. 'I can no longer bear my sons fighting over you,' she said. She pushed aside an old stump. Under it was a deep hole. 'Look down,' she said.

"The girls looked over the edge, into the hole. Far down they saw their own father and mother, their sisters and brothers. Then they knew they had run so far they were in another world.

"They wanted to go home. But they had no way to do it. To jump down was too dangerous.

" 'Stay a little. I will spin a web long enough for you to crawl home on,' the spider woman said.

"The girls were excited.

"One day the web was done. The spider woman said, 'When you reach home and the long dark comes again, the sky will fill with snowflakes. The sign of my death.'

"The girls were sad to leave. But they were glad to go home.

"The nights grew into the time of the long dark. It began to snow. No one at home understood why the sisters cried. The spider woman was their friend. She had saved them by spinning her web. Then she died. And, that, Richard, is why we do not destroy spider webs."

Afternoon flowed into evening; my friends exchanged stories, remembered legends; we laughed together.

Then, like a chill wind blowing through the room, Anakhtayan sobered us. "Watnaw, in a little while I leave with a fleet of men to join Baranov. He intends to take land on Sitka Sound.

He told me he sent one of his men, Medvednikov, some time ago to look for a site for his fort. I guess . . . I guess I need to know. What is Sitka like?''

In an instant, Watnaw's anger flared. Hatred marred her beauty. ''Tell Baranov to stay off Sitka Island. He will ruin it just as he has done here. Look at Kadyak: There is nothing left but starving old people and hungry dogs.''

For some moments Watnaw sat on the bed beside me, her head in her hands. Then she drew herself up, her eyes burning, her voice hard. ''I will tell you what my island was like. Attu, you tell your man Baranov—''

''Understand one thing, Watnaw. He is not 'my man Baranov.' I am hostage like anyone here. He forces terrible choices on me, just as he does on all of you.''

''But, Attu, you are more Russian than any of us. You went to Russia and learned to be one of them.''

Lingen-Aka blazed, shook Watnaw by the shoulders, ''Anakhta-yan is as much Aláyeksan as any of us. Don't you forget it. Even if Baranov makes all of us call him *Attu*.''

''Do not accuse me of being Russian. I was only a child. They dragged me away by the hair, yelling and screaming. I do not want this life any more than you do, Watnaw.'' It was one of the few times I had seen Anakhta-yan angry.

Our happy celebration clouded. An angry mood threatened our friendships. In our misery and fears, we five had begun to form a bond that I thought was drawing us closer and closer, and I could not allow it to shatter because our tongues and tempers had been soaked in rum.

''Ai-yi! Ai-yi!'' I claimed their attention, reached out and took Anakhta-yan's hand. ''We are on edge. We are all hostages. We hurt. Quarreling will not mend our kayak.''

The rivalries between our three peoples were age-old, and I feared we might be stirring up those ancient dislikes. That afternoon we had shared our Aláyeksan heritages, shared the tales learned in childhood. Our hostage life on Kadyak—was it part of that long journey that would change us Aláyeksans from being rivals to being partners?

My spider woman had spent herself on her web, and the two girls traveled home on it. Perhaps it was our ties to one another that would enable us to reach out and search for our own journey home. The first step that day was to heal the wounded spirits of my friends so that we could again walk together.

"Come, Lingen-Aka. We will go." Anakhta-yan's voice broke into my thoughts.

"No. Stay." I sat up in bed, tears streaming down my face. I tried for words. My first step was with Anakhta-yan. "Please stay. We all need you."

"Ashana is right, Attu. Stay." Richard shook the jug of rum, refilled our mugs. "I know your anger. Even you, Ashana. Sometimes you think I am Baranov's man. But I, too, have lost my family. We are all hostages. We must keep trust between us, no matter what happens."

My eyes begged Watnaw to tell Anakhta-yan she was sorry for her ill-chosen words. For seconds I saw only hostility and hurt; then she softened, and the warm smile I knew spread across her face. "I am sorry. I'm desperate. Thinking about Sitka. The Tahtna taking it. Killing my people. It drove me crazy. Wild. I am sorry, Anakhta-yan."

The ugly mood passed as she continued. "On a summer day— to answer your question, 'What is Sitak like?'—the sea stretches blue around the island. Tall trees cover the land, some so huge three men joining hands can't reach around the trunk. Clear, cold streams race down mountainsides into the ocean. A beautiful land. Plenty of food. All that we need for the rich life of the Gulushutna.

"Scattered on the shore of Sitka Island stand the houses of my people. Painted carvings on house posts tell you which family lives there. Whale. Eagle. Moon. Sun. Bear. *Totems*, the aliens say. The fun we had! I remember when I was a child running from one house to the other. Feasts. Celebrations. I did not know what the occasions were. I was too young to understand. A good hunt. A birth. A coming of age. A marriage. It did not matter. We ran free. But we were never lost. Those house posts drew us home."

Watnaw relaxed, shed her anger. What an intriguing storyteller she is, I thought, as her low voice sketched pictures for us, and I reached over and put her hat on her head. "You know, we Gulushutna had many families. We did not live just on the islands. The country is ours all along the main coast, from Yakutat Bay to the south, farther than I can tell you. My father was a leader among our villages from as early as I remember. His clan gatherings were the most important. My family was born to that. It is ours."

I knew, I knew. Baranov had an eye and a purpose for young girl hostages from the homes of leaders.

Watnaw paused again, her eyes searching far beyond our room. None of us wanted her to stop. We needed to know about her legendary people. Aláyeksans had feared the Gulushutna. Some of my earliest memories had been of hearing my father and the other qeshqa talk with respect of Watnaw's people, who raided our coasts dressed in masks and armor that no arrow could pierce. Sometimes they stole women, sometimes children. I had no desire to open old wounds or hurt the new one that was just beginning to heal by talking of raids among Aláyeksans, for, as Richard had said, we hostages here on Kadyak must keep the trust between us.

"We Kahtnuht'ana had masks, too, Watnaw," I said. "Plain ones, nothing compared to those made by your people. Tell us about them."

"Just imagine how a Tahtna will jump," Watnaw said, laughing, "when he meets a war party of eight-foot men and—"

"Eight-foot men?" Richard broke in. "You grow them that big in your part of the country?"

Watnaw's laugh relaxed all of us. "Let me tell you how we do it. Come here, Richard. Pretend you are a mighty fighter going out to meet the enemy." Richard puffed out his chest, threw back his skinny shoulders. "First, you hang over your shoulders your war shirt of walrus hide or moose skin. On it you have painted your clan symbol. Over that you hang armor that covers your body front and back. It is made of slats of wood lashed together so tightly with sinews that no arrow can shoot through it. And front and back you paint on the evil spirit, one fierce enough to scare away your enemy."

I could see Richard was taken by what she was describing, because he grasped his neck and asked, "But if I am going to be protected, what about this space?"

"Let me finish, Richard. From the top of your shoulders to above your eyes, covering your neck and face up to your turban, you pull on a collar of carved wood. It has a flap of deerskin to tuck under the top of your slat armor. This makes your head look like your neck, so now you look taller. This piece has slanted openings for your eyes and fierce figures painted on it to disguise the nose and mouth."

"I can already see Richard stumbling under his armor." Anakhta-yan laughed, his anger of a few minutes ago gone.

"You are right, Anakhta-yan. Stand still, Richard. Then, to top it off, every fighter lashes on his tall, carved helmet—it's this, standing two feet or so above your head, that makes the eight-foot man. It's fiercesome the way the whole face leers—the eyes glisten, the mouth, filled with sharp dog teeth, gapes. Human hair or walrus whiskers stream from the top. No way of telling you, Richard, how you would frighten someone if you jumped out of the woods dressed in your armor and headpiece."

Suddenly, Watnaw's hands and fingers became eagle claws threatening Richard's face. Her voice deepened. "Some masks have mouths that are hinged. And when they open, evil spirits glare out." She laughed as Richard shrank back.

"I have heard my father say that much as an enemy might fear a mask with a human face or even a spirit one, nothing is as frightening as bear or raven or sea-lion people rushing at you. Even mosquito masks. There's something about those animals! And that is how we grow our eight-foot-tall men."

"Those brave Russians! They certainly will get a surprise." Richard managed a grin.

"Remember, though, the Tahtna have guns," I cautioned. "Bullets. And bullets pierce wooden armor and skins."

For some moments we stayed quiet. Watnaw, Lingen-Aka, and I hunched on my furs. Richard and Anakhta-yan leaned against the wall.

Then Watnaw spoke again, her voice husky. "I will tell you because you are my friends." Her eyes bore into Anakhta-yan. "I warn you. Do not repeat what I say. Our fighters will dress to scare the life out of the Russians, but the Gulushutna have more guns than anyone knows about. The British and Yankees have traded muskets up and down our coast for years. They had thousands left over from some war they fought against each other. Since that war, both countries have come to Aláyeksa, trading off weapons to my people for furs. Shot, too, they brought us. And powder. Our fighters always say, 'No difference between British and Yankee guns. No difference between their men.' "

"They look alike to me." Anakhta-yan laughed.

"Exactly what the aliens say about us *savages*," I said.

"Drink up!" Richard dribbled out the last of the rum.

As Lingen-Aka and Anakhta-yan took their leave, I motioned Watnaw to stay. We chatted easily till Richard headed for the kitchen.

"Watnaw, lying here in this room, I have thought of many things. Jabila is gone—shot by an alien gun. It is clear that my people need guns, like yours. I am going to steal them. Will you help?"

Watnaw settled down, the big brim of her hat covering her face. I wondered if I had talked too soon, but Jabila had said, "Trust Watnaw."

Suddenly she whipped off the hat, her broad grin telling me I should never have doubted her. "You have my promise. I will help. You know I will."

"The Tahtna do a lot of brawling, lie around drunk. Those are the times we could snatch a gun or two. I will hide them in this house—no one would think to look for an extra gun under Baranov's floor."

Watnaw laughed. "For sure not. What will you do with them?"

"Hand them over to our men whenever they come with meat from Yaghenen."

She paused, elbows on knees, her chin resting on her clenched fist. Then she straightened up and grasped my hands. "We will have to be daring, be the bold eagle. It's the only way we can get guns for your fighters."

We planned details, weighed the risks, thought of what to say if a Tahtna caught us with a gun. After Watnaw had gone I was too excited by the boldness of our scheme to rest any longer. Strength, my Qishvet'. I spread the caribou hide on the floor, painted a small kayak, added bent driftwood hats for the hunters and quick slashes for the sea lions' whiskers. I used up the last of the bark paint to finish the bear claws.

"Let's walk in the woods. I need to talk, Watnaw." Excited by my hope for the gun stealing, I had thought myself recovered; but a tiredness had settled over me, a tiredness that crawled from deep in my bones. My stomach balked at food; my qenich'eni hung loose. The loss of Jabila had made me an ancient one and pushed the days of happiness so far into the past that they seemed never to have happened.

Early morning on that unnamed island in the sea, before we Kahtnuht'ana sped our kayaks further north, my husband had held me close, his low voice caressing me. "Your eyes . . . I always remember your eyes. They dance for me, Ashana. Bright like fireflies."

But now my eyes felt dull, the shine in them dimmed like the fire inside me.

"Ashana, you do not seem to be here." Watnaw brought me back to Kadyak. "Let's keep walking."

"Let them kill me. Jabila is dead."

"I know. The walk will help you, will be good."

"Nothing is good."

Grief had racked me when Baranov first tore me from Yagh-enen, a wild, tearing grief; but in that long-ago time I knew Jabila walked free toward my mother's land, Htsaynenq'. Even though days and nights on Kadyak surrounded me with loneliness, knowing that he lived, I could survive. Then, with the birth of friendships that broke my loneliness—Watnaw, Lingen-Aka—my life turned. But too much had happened too quickly.

"Qanilchey Ashana." Watnaw's strong, calloused hand touched my shoulder. "Come. Let's keep walking," she repeated. Her hair lay in glistening braids laced with shells and thin sinew cords; how she managed to keep so clean living in the hovels, I never knew; her body never bore the stink of the Tahtna.

Down the path, the air streaming over me, my friend beside me, my wounded heart eased slightly; I could speak about my murdered husband. "Jabila told me that our men whisper messages to you when they deliver meat. He said you carry those messages in your head, pass them to others. I did not know until he told me just how much Aláyeksans trust you. Watnaw, he said I should always trust you."

"I am glad he told you. Remember, Ashana, how good it was talking about the spider woman, bear claws, guns. Your illness has left you weak, but do not give up. Jabila would want you strong."

"Are you safe being with me?" Fear for Watnaw prompted my question. "They are watching all of us since the escape. Me most of all."

"Do not worry." The squeeze of her hand on my arm reassured me.

"Do they suspect you of helping me the night Jabila came?"

"No. When I left you, I ran back to my shack. Petrov was waiting. He had been drinking. I told him I came straight from the kashim."

"Are you sure he believed you?"

"Yes. He would have beaten me if he had suspicions. Besides, when Kuskov questioned the workmen, I heard Petrov tell him I had come right home." Sadness clouded her words. "But trust is not enough, Ashana. Not when men like Jabila die. And there will be others."

I had to ask the question that had haunted me since the day I first saw the alien boats racing toward our kayak. "How did the Tahtna know Jabila came?"

"I do not know, Ashana. I try hard not to believe an Aláyeksan told them."

Before I lost Jabila, I had often climbed high on the headland, my heart and thoughts in Yaghenen, willing that my husband's strong arms would wield flashing paddles across the open water to take me home. He could not, but I took comfort and strength in knowing that he lived, even though it was far away. That day, walking with Watnaw, I closed my eyes, not daring to look toward Yaghenen but forcing my attention on the place that bound me.

Baranov's work stations—artels, he called them—with their debris and decay, insulted the beauty of Kadyak Island and its ancient bays. The Russian company had littered Kadyak with workmen's shacks, fish-drying sheds, huts for storing furs. In the old days the islanders were strong, but the Gulushutna, the Kahtnuht'ana, the Ulchena, the Koniags, and others also possessed their own strengths, and the rivalries among Aláyeksan clans were kept in close balance—spears, arrows, and knives against spears, arrows, and knives.

Skirting the buildings of Pavlovsk, hiding behind brush or rocks whenever we saw a Tahtna, Watnaw and I headed up the slopes. An ancient path softened with ferns and pine needles led us to a sturdy Koniag log house. Its grounds were deserted, its drying racks empty. In the seasons before the aliens, they would have been filled with furs, shells, and the trade riches of the Koniags. From ancient times, trade had flourished among the Aláyeksan clans—it was the way we obtained whale meat, skin garments, dentalium shells, and the brightly colored carvings that were so different from our own. My father and our elders would swap tales with visiting traders and listen to stories about the great deeds of other clans; in our turn, we would send men from Yaghenen to barter with far-distant peoples. But that day no Koniag trade goods filled the sheds.

Watnaw and I crawled onto the roof of the Koniag house, looked in, called down through the entrance hole: "Hello! Is anyone here?"

Only the buzzing of flies and gnats greeted us.

We backed down the ladder into the Kashim, pausing for a moment at the bottom until our eyes grew used to the dim light. The house looked as if it must have belonged to an important man: Many feast bowls, carved plates, shells, and beads lay scattered on the floor. The man must indeed have been a great hunter, and his wealth must have come from the sea. Darts hung on the wall of his japoon, next to the backbones of seals, gut sacks, otter skulls, and his carved sea hunter's cap. But the fire pit was not blazing, and the rocks around it were icy cold. The grass cooking basket lay overturned and empty.

"Watnaw! Look!"

In a corner on a stack of furs lay an old man, his skin tightly drawn, every bone showing. Cradled in his rigid arms he held the body of a small boy, whose skin, too, stretched dry over his tiny body.

I hesitated, then bent down and touched the old man's shoulder. "Sleep well, Grandfather." Next to him on the furs lay a half-chewed piece of root. Watnaw picked it up, sniffed at it. "Poison plant."

Aláyeksans have always known this deadly plant, with flowers that have fragile, deep-blue petals shaped like tiny bowls, and green, fingerlike leaves. Our legends describe how great hunters from Kadyak and the Ulchena Islands learned the secret of extracting the poison and used it to coat the tips of their spears when they went on whale hunts. There were many ways to take the poison from the plant, and each hunter kept his secret. It was a secret this grandfather must have known well.

Watnaw and I stood in the kashim, unable to speak. This tired and aged hunter should have been allowed to live out his years in dignity; instead, knowing that the shadows drew close, he cheated the aliens of his labor on their bird hunts, cheated them of his grandson, who in just a few seasons would have reached the age for their levies. Somewhere in Aláyeksa the family who had loved this man and boy slaved for the Tahtna, but we did not know where to look for them; there was no one we could bring back to the kashim to be sure the two received a proper burial. We backed away, not wishing to show disrespect to the old man, wishing we could honor him as he deserved.

Blood on the moon, blood on the tide.

We sat silent on the roof of the Koniag house for several moments, then pulled the gut covering over the entrance and weighted it down with rocks. We turned that building into a burial cave; never again would it know the happy excitement of fearless Koniags as they celebrated their hunt in the ancient ceremonies. The house became the world of the grandfather and his grandson, the roof their sky. They had made their escape. Let no alien disturb their peace.

* * *

"Come, Ashana. Don't make yourself sick with thinking."
Watnaw led me away from the house. I knew her purpose. She
was still trying to bring me out of my grief, keep me moving
until I dropped. Physical exhaustion eases the emotions.

Our footsteps trailed us past a salt-making place, abandoned
because the Tahtna had moved to another site to leach out the
bitter stuff. On one side the sea stretched endlessly away from
land; behind us the mountains of Kadyak, snow-covered on the
high slopes, towered over the once-free island.

I wondered: With all the forces of The Great Country—
mountains that tossed rock and steam high from the center of
the earth, seas that thrashed in maddened waves and threw men
and boats into the arms of the sea people—why could not a
mighty upheaval shake the earth and rid us of the alien menace?
Instead, the intruders kept coming in greater numbers.

The mist spilled into a drizzle. Ahead of us a bear followed
by her half-grown cubs ambled across the path. We paused, held
our breath, as the little ones jostled one another for first place
behind her. The bears were moving upslope, so we wound our
way down through the thickets, glimpsing between the trees and
bushes a small stream that cascaded toward the sea. Hidden in
a grove of saplings near an artel used for farming, we watched
as an old Koniag, now useless for the hunts, roped to what the
Tahtna called a "plow," dragged the thing behind him, digging
it into the ground to ready the soil for planting. A Tahtna, whip
in hand, followed, hanging on to the handle of the plow and
screaming, "Pull harder! Walk straight rows! Stupid Aleut!"
The whip curled over the Koniag's back, bent with the struggle
to rip open the rocky ground.

As we hurried away, Watnaw showed me what she had
clutched in her hand. "Poison plant. Do you want some?" *Do
not touch. Do not eat. All of that plant, from roots to flowers,
is poisonous.* It is a warning that every Aláyeksan child grows
up knowing.

We read each other's eyes, Watnaw and I: We could so easily
have joined that grandfather and his grandson. Jabila lay dead
on an unnamed island. I could end the misery, wipe out the
struggle, taste the same peace the old man and the child already
knew. How tempting it was! I was so tired. Death seemed a
comfort. Death could carry me away forever.

No, Ashana. No, my joncha warned, as the faces of Sem and
Jabila swam before me. *No, Ashana. Not yet. No peace. Not*

yet. Remember Qishvet', enemy arrows, enemy guns. You have much to do.

Gently, I took the pieces from Watnaw, threw them aside, and put my hand on hers. "Friend. Sister. Not yet."

❂ ❂ ❂

12

My father believed that the eyes are the mountain passes into the lach'u, the truth, of what lives within a person. So, as the seasons trailed one into another, I watched Aleksandr Baranov's eyes for changes, some of which were barely visible, some not so hidden. Whether at our table or on our sleeping furs, as time wore on he called me "Princess Anna" and talked often of my noble state, whatever that may have meant to him, just as Attu had said he would.

"Anna, you are Chief Ni'i's daughter. In your village the people knew you as a special young woman." He eyed me with pride laced with cunning; it was the same expression I had seen on his face when he rubbed his hands over an especially fine pelt.

"We Kenai do not talk of *chief* or *princess*. We have *leaders*, men such as my father. Qeshqa, they are."

"Anna, I have told you before. You are not a commoner. You are *Princess Anna.* I want you to be the most important woman in Aláyeksa, just as Tzarina Catherine is the most important woman in Russia."

"How can you say that? I am nothing but your hostage."

"Try to understand. Russian law recognizes your rank. You are royalty among your own people, and our customs allow us to accept your rank in my country."

Contempt spread through me. I did not understand how Baranov could consider me—a woman held hostage to bind the terms of a bargain—as the "head woman" of Aláyeksa, and I did not believe that it would be in the same way Kahtnuht'ana respected Sem as the head woman in our villages. Baranov understood my resistance only from my biting and clawing; he did not truly understand who I was at all.

"Behave yourself. Listen to me. I am taking land on Sitka Island. There, I will build a great city as the capital of Aláyeksa, with a fine house for us. The ships from Russia take years to get here, but they will come, and they will bring furniture and clothes and goods such as you have never seen. Soon my own fleet will bring fine things to us. We will make our house in Aláyeksa a Russian house. Drapes on the windows. Damask on the table. Spoons and forks. Caucasian rugs on the floor. Lamps, bright metal and glass lamps. And you, Princess Anna, I have promised myself, will dress in fine clothes."

Drapes. Damask. Glass. Rugs. Silver. My captor needed such trappings, possessions, to impress the traders coming to Aláyeksa. He needed these things to help him cling to the memories of his homeland, to remind him of a past that *he* did not wish to bury.

"You are like the Tzarina Catherine. She came to Russia from another country, too—her home was in Germany. You come to Pavlovsk from your home on the Kenai. I want you—"

"Yes! You have told me how your empress got to Russia. She was of royal blood, as you say." I wanted to see his reaction to my words, so I dared to add, "Her family bartered her off to your head man, your Tzar Peter. You Russians *used* Catherine. I, too, have been—"

"Listen to me, Princess Anna. How can a woman of high birth better use her royalty than in helping her husband?"

"*Husband!* How can you speak to me of *husband*?" My captor ignored the scorn in my voice. I went on, "The way you Russians believe, a man may have only one wife. You have told me you have a wife back in Kargopol. So, by your own customs, you cannot be my husband."

I sensed that Baranov was baffled, but apart from his brief loss of hold over me, his inner self showed me nothing more. He ignored my challenge and continued to recite his daydreams, his visions of power, sipping his vodka all the while until it appeared that weariness and drink would get the better of him. I need fear him no more that night.

Aleksandr Baranov was plagued throughout those years by his own Tahtnas.

Drunken navigators often wrecked their ships on our shores. Those who did manage to land on Aláyeksa were insolent; they belittled Baranov because of his merchant class. From his earliest seagoing days he had wanted to learn sailing, but the Tahtna captains had kept their skills to themselves. This made Baranov suspicious of all who sailed: "You cannot trust navigators, Ivan. They are all drunks. Take old Pribylov—he was a damn fine skipper when he first explored these waters, but his drinking turned him into a bad risk."

"Yes," Ivan Kuskov growled, "the sailors told me he soaked up whiskey from the day he left Okhotsk. All the men got careless, started drinking vodka. The kegs they didn't drink dry washed overboard. From what I have seen, one ship's captain is as bad as another."

Company workmen—from the convicts dumped at Pavlovsk by the *Three Saints* to the ne'er-do-wells grabbed off the Okhotsk waterfront for shipment on the *Catherine* to the *promyshlenniki* of fortune—stirred up plots and revolts from the moment they landed on Aláyeksa.

The serfs should never have been sent to Aláyeksa: According to Baranov, they belonged to the land in Russia. As out of place as the alien vegetables they tried to grow, they drained more resources than they produced.

The monks, always the monks, shadowed Baranov's dreams. From the day they came off the ship, and Tahtna high and low in rank bowed before them, a circle of alien respect surrounded them wherever they set foot. They criticized everything Aláyeksan—our customs, beliefs, way of living. Every move Baranov and his workmen made was held in disrespect by them. The head monk challenged the manager's authority, for he held a letter from Grigorii Shelekhov telling him to look into complaints and send word home.

"An insult to my right to run affairs here," Baranov stormed. "The monks snoop around, poke into my business matters. They stir unrest with their meddling questions. And they do not try to understand what has to be done. But they had just better listen to me, because *I* am in charge of this colony.

"I sent for a village clergy, common men who understand poverty and hard work. Instead, I got these demanding monks." Baranov could not rid himself of their presence, so he tried to come to some kind of terms with them.

"I must overlook their frailties. They are only men. The Russian Church is a mighty institution, and it must be respected and supported. It is a great civilizing force. I will give fifteen hundred rubles of my own money to help build a church. It will be small, but the monks will be busy with their holy place, and perhaps they will leave me to my work."

Then there were the rival Tahtna fur companies. One afternoon, a *peredovshchik* from Baranov's hunting camp on Yaghenen stormed into the house and began complaining to Baranov. "Lebedov's men on the Kenai—Balushin and Konovalov. I see a hell of a lot of trouble. They have offered our men a bigger share of the fur hunts if they will join Lebedov. And they held guns on us to force us to listen. If we do not join them, they will burn our camps and boot us out," the *peredovshchik* reported.

"Like hell they will!"

Tahtna pointing guns against other Tahtna! I thought. Each band of alien traders, driven by greed, grabs for itself in spite of the words that had often been spoken across our table: "All Russians must work together for the greater glory of Russia."

"You have to hear me out." The foreman's next words struck close to my heart. "Balushin has threatened Chief Ni'i if he does not stop sending men and food to our camps. Fact is, the bastards raided the Kenai villages and took several of Ni'i's young hunters. The chief is very angry. I could not reason with him. He says you promised him protection, but you have failed him. He demands to see you." The *peredovshchik* looked from Baranov to me, then to Kuskov and back to Baranov. "I think the mad old savage will cut off our supplies unless you head north and set the situation straight."

Mad old savage. Anger flared in me, but I knew better than to let loose the scornful words my tongue wanted to speak. I dug the tips of my fingers into the ends of the bench and bit my cheeks to keep from crying out.

"We better take action right away, then." Ivan Kuskov supported the *peredovshchik.*

"That Kenai chief complained about the furs Balushin's hunters steal from him. And his Kenai men being shot—"

"Who died?" I shouted.

The men glared at my interruption.

"Be quiet, Anna, you must not get excited over—"

"My father? Minya?" I dared not ask about Seltan.

"Don't interrupt. It did not involve any of your family."

"Ni'i *is* involved. Your man said so." I doubled my fists and yelled, "Let me go home. I need to see them."

"I warn you, Anna. Be quiet." Baranov shook his cane at me. "Balushin is a liar. He cannot be trusted. I told Raskashikov not to believe him. If there's trouble on the Kenai, your father's to blame."

Blame. The word burrowed into me. Would Aleksandr Baranov never see that Aláyeksa's turmoil came from him and the other alien intruders? I heard my father's words the day the Tahtna brought tragedy to our village: "Murderer! You lie. You do not come in peace for trade."

Listening to Baranov and his man talk, I heard the Tahtna accuse their own men of lying; and if they saw it that way, daq'u, let it be. But from the first, my captor had told Ni'i and our leaders that the Tzarina had granted *him* authority over The Great Country. Russia, he boasted, would protect Yaghenen. But his protection was worthless. Baranov blamed Ni'i for Balushin's raids on my clans.

Questions raced through my head: What did my hostage life on Kadyak do for my people? Had Aleksandr Baranov lied to us when he said he was in charge in Aláyeksa? Could my father ignore promises forced out of him? Could I go back to my village?

My spirits lifted for a few moments, then plunged. If Balushin and Konovalov had control on our peninsula, I would become *their* hostage, and their circle of beasts would probably be more vicious than the one that already surrounded me.

My family, my village, suffered; they were caught in the schemes and quarrels between Tahtna—invaders, all of them, not one of whom had a right to be in Aláyeksa.

After the *peredovshchik* had gone, the pounding in my head eased when I decided that Seltan must be safe from the Lebedov men. Thank Naq'eltani, my brother still walked free! Again, I concentrated on the talk between the two still at the table.

"We do not have enough men to fight Balushin and Konovalov. How do you plan to get rid of them?" Kuskov asked.

"I must avoid bloodshed between Russians. For now, Ivan, I can only wait and bluff." Aleksandr looked out at the harbor. "Lebedov's interference will end. A time will come when he must join me or get out of Aláyeksa." He stroked his chin and sipped his vodka. "Remember, Shelekhov owns this company, and he has strong support at the Imperial Court. If I have not told you before, Ivan, it's his son-in-law. A young nobleman named Nikolai Rezanov. Stingy as Grigorii has been with us, he was smart when Nikolai asked for his daughter's hand. He gave his new son-in-law shares of stock in the company, so Rezanov is one of the owners. Old Shelekhov did it to benefit this trading business.

"I know Nikolai enjoys great respect at the court in St. Petersburg. The Rezanovs are an ancient noble family, reaching further back in history than the House of Romanov. It will take time, but Nikolai Rezanov will convince Tzarina Catherine that it is best for Russia to grant the Shelekhov company exclusive trading and hunting rights in Aláyeksa. That's what he will get for us. Then we will be rid of those Lebedov *svoloch'* for good.''

''High stakes, Aleksandr.''

''Yes, but worth it. I will stop the Lebedov company. I will hold the colony together with my wits and my bare hands. I will have one company in Aláyeksa. I will bluff and wait.''

Our stake had been high, too, Jabila's and mine. Life.

Qishvet' walked the shore with me late one moonlit night some weeks later. A glimmer from a beached umiak caused me to stop, hardly daring to believe that a gun lay there in the open. Quickly, I climbed over the side, pulled the gun under my qenich'eni, and furtively slipped back to the house. An exhausted Baranov snored on his furs, so I dared not pull up the boards where I had begun digging out a cache. Pushing the gun under my side of the furs, I spent a restless night, worrying that in the morning he would find the weapon or sense my impatience to tell Watnaw. But most of all, my spirits soared because I was beginning to strike for Yaghenen with the help of Qishvet's' sharp bear claws!

Oh, it had been easy stealing that first gun. A couple of weeks later, Watnaw snatched a second one. Even though they were stowed in our cache, we worried until we sent them home with a boat returning to Yaghenen. After that, it was a long time before another chance opened to us; guns did not seem to lie handy for the taking anymore. Perhaps the Russians had become suspicious. We waited. We needed to make a more dependable plan.

When there was little food on warehouse shelves and on our tables, when winter's cold made Baranov's bones ache, fear for the success of the settlement pushed his mood into a bottomless muskeg. He withdrew into himself, lived on a few bites of food washed down with vodka. He muttered about the tough, unruly men Shelekhov had dumped on him; and those days I knew that the hostility of his own countrymen stalked him like a lynx. Many nights he tossed on the furs, asked me to rub vodka into his muscles; only then could he rest. I would lie awake, in de-spair over more killings of Aláyeksans. My lost Jabila would walk through my mind, the sound of his voice caressing me, and I would fall asleep, the furs wet with my tears.

My captor sometimes pulled himself out of his black mood and pushed aside his dreams of a splendid Russian house to pen letters urging his company to send a new manager for Aláyeksa; he would talk of a ship that would take him home to Russia. He would chide himself for lacking the skill to find words strong enough to persuade Shelekhov to get a replacement for him, but he still kept on writing in one letter after another how he felt: "My bones ache, replace me. . . . You demand more furs and territory. Please send me ships and supplies . . . I exhaust myself exploring new regions for the Tzarina and for you. . . . Grigorii, I have done all I can for you and for my country. . . . I send riches home to your company while my affairs in Irkutsk go to ruin without me."

As his stay lengthened beyond the first period of agreed service to Shelekhov, one replacement having died in Siberia, another having drowned with a ship lost to heavy seas and poor navigation, Aleksandr Baranov settled into the belief that his God's will kept him at his post.

He would constantly drive his aging body to new activity—huddle at his desk with pen and paper planning greater sea hunts, an exploring trip, the site for his new city. When he was home, he would set his chair to face the bay, stare at boats sliding through the water. Always, forces surged in him, plans birthed and multiplied. His belief in the glory of Mother Russia forced him to work even harder in search of his goal: a higher position on the ladder of rank established by Tzar Peter the Great.

"I will bluff and wait," Aleksandr Baranov had said. And wait he did. Knowing that angry men might strike, he became more wary. Then, when he had the advantage, he struck with cunning and force at his rival fur company, the Lebedov men; after a brief fight, he returned to Kadyak with the leaders of the uprising and shoved them into the stockade.

One morning, while Ivan Kuskov was at the warehouse inspecting the furs, Baranov sat writing reports of his success to Gregorii Shelekhov. Bent over his papers, his great beak of a nose silhouetted against the light, his eyes darting along the lines as he wrote them, Aleksandr Andreevich Baranov seemed to me like chik'dghesh, the kingfisher.

Sitting on the floor close by, trying to carve on my goat horn,

I whispered under my breath, "Chik'dghesh. Chik'dghesh. Powerful. Crafty."

"Speak up, Princess Anna. I cannot hear you."

"Chik'dghesh, kingfisher. That is what you are. In the ancient times—"

"Nonsense, woman. Do not talk foolishness to me."

I wanted to explain to Baranov how the rivalry between the Tahtna and Baranov himself seemed to me to resemble the sharp-crested, fish-stealing bird of our shores. But he would hear none of it, and I sensed it would be foolish to cross him.

✿ ✿ ✿

13

Several of the hostage women down at the shacks jostled one another in their eagerness to greet me; words were jumbled together in a tangle of our various tongues. Their attitude had changed since the day Watnaw and Lingen-Aka had met me and we had watched the marrying. Instead of avoiding me, their voices strident and accusing if they spoke at all, a new feeling reached out from the women; even those still keeping their distance nodded to me. I felt the gap between us closing. Perhaps it was Watnaw's words, perhaps my failed attempt at escape, perhaps because Akoota was not watching me that day. But the women understood that suffering tore at me as it tore at them, that I wore the same mask they wore.

Watnaw seemed nervous as she stood close to me and said in a low voice, "Let's walk along the path to the waterfront." Bent over their fish nets, other women must have thought of my escape with Jabila but dared not speak of it.

A late-afternoon fog had begun to drift from the open sea into the coves of Pavlovsk harbor, making ghosts of the shacks in the village. Few people lingered outside, and we took our time. As we walked, we heard the sound of Baranov's church bell.

"The monks said we had to come to meeting today." Lingen-Aka laughed.

"I am not sure I want to. The baptizing. And the way I feel about their dinning at me." Watnaw frowned.

"No baptizing today. The monks said just come and listen. Let's go and see what they do," Lingen-Aka urged.

"I will go if you do, Ashana." Watnaw took my hand.

I paused: yes . . . no. Emelian's words—"You caused his death"—had never left me. I knew I was not the cause of Jabila's death—the Tahtna were. Standing there I felt strong, ready to

144

meet the monks with a clear head. "Yes, let's go," I said to my friends.

To understand your enemy, you must watch and listen and know him. I would listen to the monks and learn from them more about the aliens.

We lined up in the church, women on the left, men on the right behind the Russian who was in charge of Pavlovsk when Baranov was away. In front, on a raised bench with a cloth over it, lay a big book, and at one side a candle burned in a holder.

"Church candles from Russia. And that's an icon on the wall," Baranov had told me at the time his men had completed the building. "Special religious symbols. Each icon is different. This one pictures the Virgin Mary and the Child, the Son of our God."

When everyone was in place, the monks filed in and began a chant—words in a singing kind of voice, words I had never heard, not even in Richard's pecking. Baranov had told me, "Our church has an ancient beginning, an ancient ritual. We Russians believe in its teachings. Someday you will understand and believe in it, too, Anna."

Suddenly, the chanting ceased; whispers drifted from the monks huddled at one side of the raised bench. The candles flickered. Then two monks paced their way along the aisle between the men and women and stopped at my side.

"You must leave the house of God, Anna."

"Leave? I came to listen."

"You must leave now, because—" Father Emelian repeated, and for a moment I was back at the water's edge.

"No," Watnaw broke in, "we asked her to come."

Lingen-Aka and Watnaw took my arms. A murmur came from the people. I looked into Father Emelian's eyes and, as once before, read madness.

"Come, Anna." Each monk seized an arm and half guided, half pushed me toward the door. "We told you before, you are a woman of sin. And we will not allow you to desecrate the house of God," the one on my left rasped into my ear.

"What have I—?"

"Silence, woman." Both voices assaulted me.

As they pushed me outside and turned back to close the door, the tight, drawn features of Father Emelian's face and the feverish look in his eyes reminded me of the day our elders in Yaghenen banished from the village a man they told my father had gone insane, a fellow whose reason had deserted him and had left his face contorted by forces unknown to us.

"You tell people to come and learn. I came. Why can't I stay?"

"You do not understand, Anna. You are a sinner, and you do not repent."

"You must stay out of Baranov's bed. Stop sleeping with him. That is your sin, too." The second monk's cold voice stabbed at me, and he pulled at his chin. "You must obey the command of God: When a man takes a wife through the Church, another woman cannot be his wife."

"Be an example to the other women. Stay away from Governor Baranov," Emelian intoned.

"From now on just take care of Baranov's house. But that is all."

"That is all I do," I stammered.

"Can't you understand, woman? You are not his wife. Stay out of his bed."

The Tahtna God must know little of men and women in the same house! Nothing of the life of a hostage, who does not have the right to say "I will" or "I won't."

The second monk waved me to silence. "Listen to us, woman. If ever you have a child, it cannot be baptized in the Holy Church. When the time comes for learning, it cannot attend our school."

"Aleksandr Baranov says—" I held my ground. I did not care if any Aláyeksan child ever learned Tahtna; but the monks made me angry, and the anger came out in defense of Aleksandr—a strange twist of hostage life in Pavlovsk.

As the monks turned back to the church, Emelian cried out, "Anna, you sin. An offense to our God. Take His words to heart: 'And if thy right hand offend thee, cut it off, and cast it from thee.'"

Outside the holy place a thick fog rolled around me; torrents of autumn rain drenched me. I saw neither rain nor fog; the monks' treatment enraged me and blotted out caution. Before they pulled the door shut, I yelled, "*Sadana!* Qil'i! *Sadana!* Devil! Evil! Devil! No-good devils! Lazy! Go back to Russia!" What I did not know in Russian, I screamed in Kahtnuht'ana. "Qil'i! *Sadana.*"

I saw Richard watching. "What's happened, Princess Anna? Did the monks sprinkle you with holy water?"

I struck out at him. He evaded me and dashed away. Stumbling, shouting, I chased him into the house, pursued him around the table. In a few moments, realizing how silly the whole affair was, we pounded each other's backs, screaming with laughter.

"Do not be scared. I have no thought to punish you this time, Anna. The monks treated you cruelly, but you were foolish to defy them." Baranov had learned of my dispute with the monks when Richard and Kuskov met him on his return to Kadyak. "I try to be patient with you, but you make trouble when I am gone."

"They called me a woman of sin," I told him, before he could get angry and whip me. Resentment still rankled: The monks had often said that the doors of the church stood open so that all might enter, that everyone had a duty to learn the Christian teachings. But they had put me out.

Baranov looked at me. Light from the blazing logs traced sparks in his eyes. "First, the monks did it to strike at *me*, Anna, not you. You know the trouble they have made. They refuse to understand conditions here in Aláyeksa, argue it is not suitable for their kind of life. Cross me any way they can." He stared into the fire, sipping his vodka. His voice seemed to come from some faraway place. "The real reason, Anna, are my wife and two children in Kargopol. Our church teaches that a man can have only one wife, and that rule holds, even if he no longer wants her."

"I am not your wife, and I told the monks so," I rasped. And to myself I added, *Nor do I want to be.* Someday, somehow, I would escape again from Kadyak and return to my people. I could not join Jabila in life. To stay in Pavlovsk and accept this alien man physically was my lot, but no order of my captor could make me open my heart to him.

I had difficulty understanding the sense behind the Russian one-wife belief, for by our Kahtnuht'ana customs a man could have more than one wife and a woman could have more than one husband, an arrangement our clans held practical and wise: It ensured that families were cared for and work done. And every spouse held an accepted position among our clanspeople, respected for the person she or he was, and for their skills. But not so with the Tahtna: The extra women a Tahtna used received no respect, had no position, no rights, meant nothing in those alien lives except pleasure. And I knew Aleksandr Baranov took extra women. Right here in Pavlovsk, he used another hostage woman. Then, when he came to our own pile of furs, I had difficulty crossing the barriers between us to meet his demands on my body.

"Forget the monks. I have work to do. I have to get ready for the *praznik* next week."

No moon shone over Kadyak the evening of the *praznik*, so under cover of the noise, hoping to find another gun, I hurried down to the shore. Watnaw and I had not yet been able to put together a dependable gun-stealing plan, concern still plaguing us that the Russians might know we had stolen some. But Yaghenen needed guns, and to me that need spoke louder than any danger. So we kept looking, and late one night Watnaw "borrowed" another gun from a sleeping guard; but the night of the *praznik* no guns lay out in the open for me to hide in the cache.

On the way back to the house, the shouting from the *praznik* grew louder. Warnings from Watnaw and Lingen-Aka and my dread of the *promyshlenniki* had kept me from venturing anywhere near the shacks at night. Because Baranov had forbidden me, because I had heard whispers of the horror of the women, because of the boredom of sitting alone in this house, the need to snatch more guns, I became defiant, determined to see Baranov's party, to find out for myself what was happening.

What would Baranov do if he saw me? Were the festivities too crude for his head woman's eyes? I giggled. What would the head monk Ioasaf say to the "woman of sin" if he caught her at the celebration? But he should not be there, either.

Edging over to the building, I found a hole in the gut window and peered into the smoky room. A circle of men tossed a couple of hostage women from one to another, shouting, stamping their feet. A man on a bench drained a mug with one hand, slid the other under a woman's parka. In the jumble of men and the haze of smoke and steam, I did not see Baranov or the women I knew best. Oleg and Petrov stood at one end of the room, laughing, drinking, both pawing the same woman. Then Oleg burst into guffaw, pointing to a hunter bending over a nearly naked hostage girl, taking his pleasure with her. The whole scene disgusted me. I turned away . . .

Stinking hands sealed my mouth, covered my eyes, locked me in a tight grip. A bearded alien face leered into mine; terrible fright seized me when I realized Igor held me alone in the darkness. I was dragged, kicking and pushing, away from the window. Then suddenly I let my body go limp—his surprise gave me a chance, and I scrambled to my feet; but I had gained only a few steps when he dove for my legs, threw his shoulder against my hip, and shoved me to the ground.

"Stop! Let me go . . . ! I'm—"

A blow smacked my face. "Shut up, bitch!"

I wrenched my body to one side, struggled to push away; but my assailant pinned me with his legs, jerked my parka above my waist, and tore at his trousers.

I clawed with one hand, bit his fingers; his grip loosened.

"Leave me alone! I'm Baranov's Anna. He'll kill you!" I screamed at Igor; I knew the man had hated me ever since I slashed his arm with a clamshell.

"Yaah! Haa! Haa! I should care." His drunken laughter shot spittle into my face. "I'm Tzarina Catherine's lover. I'm Count Orlov. Haa . . . Haa . . . Yaaah!"

He pressed against me, dug at my body. Again I found strength to twist under him, scream. His fist sent a ringing through my ears; his hands forced my legs apart. With strength bred of terror, I lunged, smashed one knee into his groin. Maddened, he flattened himself against me. Pinned under him, I felt my strength giving out, screamed again and again, "Baranov! He will kill you! Baranov will kill you!"

The *thwack* of a club crashed onto my attacker's head; he jumped up from me, grabbed someone in the dark.

"Run, Anna! Run!" Attu's voice muffled into a choked gurgle as Igor's hands grabbed for his throat.

I almost knocked Richard down in my frenzy, but he sidestepped me and leaped on Igor like a snarling animal, forcing loose the death grip on Attu's throat. Attu rolled to the side, and Igor turned and pounced on Richard. "You little bastard!"

The pair on the ground was mismatched—the Bengalese half the size of the *promyshlennik*, his body soft compared to that of the muscular hunter. The two rolled, kicked, twisted, until the Tahtna pinned Richard down and drew back his fist to smash his face.

Attu lay on the ground, dead or alive, I did not know. With both hands, I grabbed his club, brought it down with all the power I could muster on the back of Igor's head. Oh, the great strength that poured into me when my friends were in danger! The murdering fist fell limp. Richard kicked the brute away and jumped to his feet.

"Grab Attu's legs, Richard," I yelled. "I've got his shoulders. Let's get inside before the beast wakes up."

With difficulty we carried Attu's limp body into the house,

stretched him out on the bearskin. Richard dashed cold water on the pallid face and rubbed the ugly red swelling that scarred his neck. Bending his head to Attu's chest, he listened for several endless moments. "He is alive," he said, finally.

Relief swept through me. "Raven, you did a good deed tonight," escaped my lips.

Richard gave me a look filled with questions.

We waited.

Crouched on the floor, Richard and I watched our friend through the night. In and out of foggy sleep, I was conscious that every part of my body hurt. When I dozed off, angry tree spirits tore at me, tossed me from branch to branch, thrashed me. In my imaginings, the spirits of the forest joined the circle of beasts and danced gloatingly around me.

First light filled the room before Attu finally roused. He pushed himself up on one elbow; and the bruises on his swollen neck showed an angry red and purple. "Ashana? You all right?"

"Yes. I am not hurt much."

"Lie down. She is fine." Richard eased Attu's head onto the skins.

Too soon for us, Aleksandr Baranov burst into the room. "*Chort's/neem.* What the hell has been going on? Have you three been fighting? Igor staggered into the shack early this morning, mad, yelling he had been attacked by you, Attu. And you, Richard—"

"Igor attacked? He tried to kill us. You should—" I stopped, knowing that I had been to the shacks at night against Baranov's orders.

Richard's words flew fast. "The man tried to rape Anna. Nearly choked Attu to death."

Whatever distrust I had felt for Richard fled. He and Attu had saved me.

In the flare of temper, instant decision had always been characteristic of Aleksandr Baranov. "Bring Igor here. Now!" he ordered two hunters loitering in the yard.

Of me, my captor demanded, "Where, Anna? Where did this happen? Did Igor come in here?"

I looked down at his boots, hesitated, too scared to answer.

"Anna! Tell me what happened."

"It was outside. He was not in the house."

Scuffling and arguments interrupted us as the men marched Igor up the path. Baranov stormed outside yelling, "Lock him in the stockade!" Igor jabbered, pointing to the house, evidently accusing me. Baranov silenced him and followed his men to see that they carried out his orders, leaving the three of us alone.

By afternoon, Attu had rallied slightly. His throat swollen half shut, he could speak only in a painful whisper. I took his hands in mine. "Attu, you saved my life last night. I will never forget."

A faint smiled played around his lips, but his eyes seemed to look beyond me. "Lingen-Aka. Can I see her?"

"I wish you could. But she has been forbidden to come while you are here."

Eyes shut, Attu lay quiet.

All day Baranov stayed away. Work to be done? Recovery from his all-night bout? Perhaps his wrath at the thought of another man touching his woman would gloss over my disobedience.

"Anna, will you never learn?" Akoota started her harangue the next morning the moment she walked through the kitchen door. "I heard about your run-in with the monks. Then last night you left the house and went off alone to the *praznik*."

Her words, her manner, her very appearance, raised my anger. "I do not need your speeches, Akoota. Get out! Go back to your shack!"

"For your own good you will listen to me, Anna." She called me by the Russian name. Her manner of tossing it at me rankled far more than Richard's use of it, raising a barrier between Akoota and me that I never intended to cross.

I held my hands over my ears, but could not block out her high-pitched voice. "I have told you many times, but I will try again. You must watch yourself. Adjust to how things are here in Kadyak. *Obey* Baranov."

"It is easy for you to talk. But I am alone in this house, shut away from everyone. You have your companions among our women. I only wanted to see what goes on during those parties."

"That is none of your affair. It's the lot of the hostage women."

"You are uncivilized for an Aláyeksan, Akoota. You have become an alien."

"Uncivilized? *You* almost got Attu killed last night. Was that civilized? He is still too ill to work, and it's your fault. Richard got into the fight, too. That is what happens when we don't keep our place."

Attu killed? Those words were aimed to crush me.

She went on, "Life here does not offer much, Anna. And how we—"

"I know there is nothing for us here, so what is the sense in your talk?"

"Survival. Our survival. I said so before. I have found a way. Do as you are told. Do not involve yourself in the troubles of others. Obey orders. If Baranov demands something, do as he says. And remember, put out a little more than you have to. Set yourself in better with the Russians. I do. And I gain by it."

Did she inform on Jabila?

I faced Akoota squarely. "You have given up everything to them. Your decency. Your respect. Your heritage. And what do you have in return? Nothing." My voice rang louder, higher. I almost shouted "You hostage spy," but kept quiet.

"Liar. I have made myself somebody here. I'm accepted. Baranov trusts me to look after you other women."

"Look after? You watch so you can inform on us. You are a traitor, Akoota." I understood her visit: Baranov had sent her to find out and report my story, warn me back in line.

I screamed at her. "You are always first for better food, an extra blanket. You are no Aláyeksan! And it shows in your looks. You . . . you Russian cabbage, wide as you are tall. Braids that are sticks." I yanked her hair. "Brown stubs for teeth. If you cannot see what you have done to yourself, I can. And I will never put myself down like you have."

In all our months of talking and arguing, nothing I had said to Akoota ever riled her as much. She stared at me through eyes drawn to slits; and her angry voice spat out her old litany about how we should accommodate ourselves to our captors until I could bear it no longer. I slammed into my room and braced myself against the door. She pounded for a time, demanded I come out. I said nothing. Moments passed, then I heard the outside door close. I was free of Akoota for a while.

"Ashana, sit up. I want to talk to you." Baranov poked me.

The ordeal with Igor and then Akoota had left me sore and exhausted, and I had slept far into the next morning. The heavy hand did not quit; my captor pulled me to my feet.

"Listen to me. I talked to Igor in the stockade today. He is howling like a wolf. Says he found you at the *praznik*. Were you there?"

"No, I was not in the *praznik*." I put as much defiance into my voice as I dared.

"Do not play words with me, Anna. He said he found you by the window. Is that true?"

"Yes. Outside the building."

"Outside. Inside. No difference. I told you never to go near when there is a party. You could have been hurt. Maybe killed. I did not want this to happen to you, but you asked for it."

"I did no such thing," I countered. "Igor attacked me. I did not even see him."

"Anna, any woman down there at the shacks . . . I . . . you . . . ," he stuttered, trying to find the right words. "If you are there, you are part of what is happening. Hunters like Igor don't have a regular woman. And men need women if they are going to produce. So, the company provides girls for them."

Baranov's crudeness toward Aláyeksan women, his *allowing* his men to abuse them, goaded me; I challenged him, "You have told me your company needs those women to pick berries. Dig roots. Clean and stack furs. Tie nets. Sew clothes for the men." I knew their main use, but I baited him.

"They have to earn their keep. That is the way they pay for what we provide."

Like the onion that grew in our woods, there were many layers to Baranov's hostage world; when one layer was peeled off, another was revealed.

"Don't worry, Anna." Baranov broke into my thoughts. "Those women like being screwed. You've heard them giggle and laugh. They're all whores."

The women he talked about: Watnaw and Lingen-Aka, my closest friends. K'atl', stolen from Yaghenen in an alien raid soon after I was taken. Atoon, from the far Ulchena Islands. Sutina, a Copper River hostage, older than the others, quiet but as enduring as the land she came from. Even Akoota, perhaps most of all Akoota. The anger, the resentment, the pain—long held back, covered with a mask—tore loose. The words poured out of me: "Whores? You made them what they are! You stole fourteen-, fifteen-year-olds. Your men force them. You abuse them. Those women are not whores. You talk about civilizing? Dlah!"

"It is none of your concern. I run the company. I order you never to go near a *praznik* at the shacks again. Always stay away at night." His voice beat at me, hard as stone. "Now, listen. You made two problems for me, Anna. I nearly lost Attu, and he is my best interpreter. The company put a lot of money into him; you know we sent him to Siberia. That is where he went to school and learned what he knows. He will pull out of this, but he won't be helping me for some days. I have to go on supporting him meantime, a dead loss, and I have—''

I wanted to challenge my captor again, break into his dronings, but held my tongue. Anakhta-yan's heritage had been destroyed by the aliens as surely as a storm among his people's islands smashed boats against a cliff.

''—a nasty situation with Igor. You made me lose face with the man. I have to reverse my orders and let him out of the stockade. He does not deserve punishment; you disobeyed me. He is raging mad. I am forced to send him to Prince William Sound to cool off.''

Every word angered me. I lashed out, ''Don't you see what you have done, Baranov? The women—''

''Stop bleating about the women!'' He flung his vodka into my face. ''Get out of my house, you bitch. Now! You're too much trouble. Go!'' He rushed at me with his cane raised.

I turned and ran, his curses following me up the path. I did not stop until I was hidden behind the rock that had sheltered Watnaw and Lingen-Aka the day we watched the marrying.

The cold night rain did not soak away my wrath, but a feeling of release settled over me: I had defied Aleksandr Baranov. I had challenged him and escaped without a beating.

During the night, wrenching pain raked my back time and again. I felt alone, Jabila lost to me. The strength that had come to me when I clubbed Igor seemed drained away. Huddled for warmth, dozing, I was roused at first light by a voice calling, ''Anna. Anna. Do you hear me?''

I did not reply, uncertain how I wanted to face the day.

''Anna.'' Closer, ''Answer me, Ashana.''

I would not be able to avoid Richard, so I brushed the dirt from my clothes and tried to straighten my braids.

As he rounded the rock, he stopped, laughed at me, hands on his hips. ''What a mess you are, Ashana. You certainly bested Baranov last night. Put him in a rage. But this morning he has calmed down. Wants you home. Sent me to find you.''

''How did you know I would be here?''

''A talent I won't explain.'' He shook his head, grinned at me in his mischievous way. ''Seems as if I keep dragging you back from some sort of trouble. I can't guess what will be next.''

He twisted his face in an odd way. "You know Aleksandr's temper flares one day, cools the next. It is the pattern with the man. So, come back to the house."

"I will not."

"There is no place else for you to go. Anyone who finds you will take you straight to Baranov." He knelt beside me. "Come with me, Ashana. It is better that I take you back. I'll walk in with you. And listen, if it had not been for you clubbing Igor, I would be dead. Thank you for what you did." He paused, his eyes seeming to plead as he said, "Anakhta-yan needs you."

I hesitated when I thought of facing my captor, but I knew I must help Anakhta-yan, see him through his healing.

When we entered the house, no one called to us; and I saw that Baranov had already gone. In front of the door to my room lay the white fur, the Děduška Domovoy patch. Did my captor seek the protection of his old Grandfather House-Lord? Maybe he thought I was the one who needed the Domovoy's help. A fragment of whimsy from the man of contradictions? He had left a small brown bottle on my furs, a keepsake from his glass factory in Irkutsk. More whimsy? No, I saw the gift for what he intended. I was being treated like anyone else in the village after Baranov had raged at them, then suffered remorse: banished from his presence one day, accepted back the next with a gift. Never admitting fault, his amends made, he assumed all wrong was forgotten.

Baranov had left orders that the interpreter stay in the house until he could handle his work again. Anakhta-yan spent hours lying before the fire locked into himself and far away.

"You have to make him talk," Watnaw said, as worried about him as I was.

"He cannot talk. He can only whisper."

"Then make him whisper. Keep talking to him."

As I brooded again about the many onionlike layers that covered my hostage life, I knew self-pity was taking over; watching Anakhta-yan, I saw those layers beginning to grow around him. Anakhta-yan's inner self had suffered damage invisible to the eye, unlike the ugly gouges Igor had dug into his throat.

I wished for the wisdom of a shaman to reach down and pull out Anakhta-yan's suffering. But I had no such wisdom; I could only sit beside him, spoon-feed him broth or water, and let him know that I honored the bond between us: he the saver, I the saved.

Anakhta-yan's recovery was slow, but gradually his voice began to gain strength, and the day came when he rasped, "Home. I need to go home."

Home for Anakhta-yan was Attu Island, the rocky chunk of earth at the end of the sweeping curve of the Ulchena chain that reached westward into the sea, toward the place where the sun sets—"desolate Aleutians," the aliens called those islands.

"Anakhta-yan, Anakhta-yan." I saw the pleasure in his face when he heard me speaking his true name. I could only bring *home* to the man Baranov had renamed "Attu" by talking, listening, trying to wrest from him the memories of his island, interweaving his thoughts with mine. Just as in my own thoughts when I roamed back to Yaghenen and drew strength from my memories, Anakhta-yan wandered back to the days of his boyhood, when he had clambered over the rocky shore, shaken his little fists at the waves and chased them back into the sea. It had all happened long ago, but during these weeks of his recovery he remembered and mourned his Ulchena Islands. He had not buried his past, and no alien order could make him forget his life before captivity.

Sadness filtered through his memories, but I believe he drew a strength from them that sustained his spirits in the grief that was his constant companion, so I led him on to tell me more of his homeland. Listening carefully, I caught the phrases, stored them in my mind: "Windswept, my islands, pelted with storms . . . waterfalls cascading down to the sea . . . vach kegh—as you would call them, Ashana—big gulls, soaring on the fresh breezes . . . islands, dark gray, the color of burned wood, humped like a pod of whales plunging across the ocean—a chain of islands anchored on an ever-restless sea."

I sensed many times that Anakhta-yan sent his mind far from Kadyak; his vague, drifting manner often left me uncertain if he knew that he lay in front of Baranov's fireplace. As the days passed, and I drew him back time and time again by talking, asking, I gained a respect for his homeland, for his islands and his people.

"We lived at home by sharing meat and berries . . . our houses were huge . . . no one lived alone in a house like the Russians do . . . Mother and Father taught us to share whatever we had. Sharing was a way of life to us, we all grew up with it. . . . Men took a partner for life. And the hunting partners survived by watching out for each other."

"Yes, I know about partners. My husband and my brother became slocin, life partners, on a bright day beside Tikahtnu, a day I will never forget.'' The memory brought both joy and sorrow to me, but whenever Anakhta-yan paused, I kept talking. ''Kahtnuht'ana families grew up sharing, too, just as you did.''

''. . . And the greatest fun of all: when we raced kayaks against the tide, or watched the spindrift sweep across the sea. Have you ever seen the spindrift, Ashana?''

Spindrift. Is that what we children of Aláyeksa were? Spindrift tossing on a sea forever restless, sparkling in the sun one moment, lost to sight the next?

14

"I brought Lingen-Aka this afternoon." Watnaw laughed as she and our friend rushed into the house. "Oleg left to gather furs on the south end of the island, so we have a day for ourselves."

That Watnaw, a chance taker! She dared steal Lingen-Aka away from her work and into my house to see Anakhta-yan in spite of Baranov! I admired her.

"I had to come," Lingen-Aka said, smiling. Anakhta-yan's touch as he took her hands in his and drew her to him carried the same tender feeling that Jabila had for me when he held me close, an embrace I would never again know.

Lingen-Aka's smooth face glowed, her hair shone with candlefish grease. Her presence filled the room like a flower, her smiling eyes saw only the man to whom she clung, and I heard her whisper his name.

"Let's go." I motioned Watnaw to follow me outside.

My Gulushutna friend had little to say as we passed between Pavlovsk's buildings and circled to the back of the village, close to my house, so that we could be the first there if anyone approached.

"How much longer before Anakhta-yan goes back to work?" Watnaw asked.

"Maybe another week or ten days. Baranov wanted to take him yesterday, but he mends slowly."

"Lingen-Aka and Anakhta-yan belong together. But Oleg insists she stay with him. She swims in shifting waters." Lowering her voice, Watnaw leaned toward me as we rested on a dry log. "You know, Ashana, we women make poisoned meat coils— the hunters use them to kill foxes. I want—"

"Meat coils? In the old island way?"

"It's done like this: We take a piece of baleen smaller than the width of my hand. Sharpen one end. Coil it tightly without breaking the bone. Tie it with deer sinew. Next, we take some of the blubber and a piece of the poison plant, wrap it around the coiled bone, poison inside. We leave the balls outside so the meat will freeze. That way the bone will stay coiled after you cut the sinews.''

"I've heard hunters talk of this way of using poisoned coils, but most of our men don't like them. They're dangerous if a *person* happens to swallow one.''

"That's just it!'' Watnaw exclaimed. "Here's a small one. For a man, not an animal.'' She reached into her pouch and took out a ball no bigger than a fourth the width of her palm. "We'll feed them to the Russians this winter. It's small enough to swallow, and in a man's belly, the same as in that of a fox, the meat will thaw. The bone uncoils and stabs his insides. He'll bleed, and the poison finishes him.''

"But, Watnaw, the blubber balls cannot be frozen with bone coils inside them like those used for hunting. You would be in big trouble if you tried that. The Tahtna want their meat cooked. What will that do to the blubber balls?''

Watnaw ignored my question. "Lingen-Aka supports me. And five or six other women. They will help. We'll freeze the meat coils in the winter. So, we'll kill off the aliens. Ashana, we'll get rid of all of them at one time.''

"I understand what you want to do. But think of the risks. You must know you could get yourselves killed. You need—'' Then my joncha whispered, *Caution, Ashana, do not snap the fragile reed of friendship. Remember, Watnaw risked her life for you and Jabila.*

"Don't you want to help us?'' Her voice wove distrust and contempt. "But then you have it so much better—''

"Stop, Watnaw! You know I'm as much a hostage here as you. Of course I'd like to rid Aláyeksa of the aliens, and I'll—''

"Then we will do it! All of us working together, we can do it!'' Her excitement mounted. "We got the idea from the Russians. Remember, they talked of the time the Ulchena hunters died from eating rotten mussels? One hundred men, two hundred, maybe more. Poisoned. Ever since we saw the dead grandfather, I have been thinking we could put poison in our captors' food. That way, they will blame what they eat.''

"Listen to me, Watnaw. Reason out what you are saying. Your plan cannot reach every Tahtna in Aláyeksa. Not in one night.''

"But there are more hostages than hunters, and—"

"I do not think you will get every hostage to help. Besides, Baranov has sent *promyshlenniki* out from Pavlovsk to other artels—they'll be away hunting for weeks. Some for months. Several live on Unalaska. Some have been transferred to Yakutat Bay. As I said, you cannot poison them all in a single night." I chose my words carefully.

Watnaw puzzled, frowns creasing her face. She started to interrupt, but I went on:

"Whatever you do, do not make the Tahtna suspicious. The way I see it, the fox gulps his food, swallows the meatballs without chewing, bone and all. Men don't eat that way. But I have a suggestion."

"How would you do it, Ashana?"

"Leave out the bone. Use only the poison plant and meat. To start with, try only a couple. See how the plan works. If two Tahtna get sick from bad meat and die, who knows where the fault lies? That way we can see how far we can push without getting ourselves into trouble." I said *ourselves* because my hope to rid Aláyeksa of the aliens had never died.

I was concerned about something else: How strong, how reliable, was the trust Watnaw said she had woven with hostage women on Kadyak? But I did see changes taking place among them. Through many seasons of shared suffering they had come to walk the land more nearly friends—a common enemy made them so. I knew some might wear double masks—one for us Aláyeksans, another for the Tahtna. Did a woman who gained favors by passing information to her captors face us with a mask that deceived? And I knew none of them saw as I did Baranov's dedication to his company; I doubted that a few deaths among his workmen would drive him to pack up and sail home.

Watnaw nodded, and I sensed I had covered points she might have passed over or not wanted to face. "Yes. When I first thought of this plan, Lingen-Aka had questions, too."

Using poison raised many doubts in me, but knowing we were having some success in stealing guns, I turned our talk to them. "I meant to tell you, Watnaw—I think there is an easier way to get guns."

My mind flashed back to the time months before when Baranov had ordered me to keep a count of puffin skins. "Anna, I want you to learn business. This will be a start," he had said, speaking in an easier manner than usual.

"Puffin skins?"

"Thousands of puffins nest on the high cliffs. We need good skins to make clothes for the workers. I have ordered the old hunters and the boys to gather enough for seven parkas each. It takes only thirty-five skins for a parka."

"Do I have to go with them?"

"No, Anna, you stay here. Look, I have made a sheet with each hunter's name on it. Just make a mark like this for each bird he brings in." He drew a few short up-and-down lines, like tiny sticks standing beside each other. "See how it's done."

Making the marks would be easy, but I knew how often a man hunting puffins fell from the sheer heights onto the jagged rocks below.

"Qil'i, evil, Watnaw. I feel evil having to count puffin skins for those old hunters who should be home resting by their fires. But Baranov says I have to learn some of his business. So I count the puffins. But sometimes I cannot help adding a few extra marks for a man who had bad luck."

"Good for you. But what have the puffins to do with guns?"

"It is this way. I do my counting at one end of the storehouse. And I see guns piled there. You and I need to find a way to get them out."

"Let's do it, Ashana, let's do it!"

We plotted another night when we might steal guns for Yaghenen. As I heard Watnaw's excitement, I felt the raven flew with me and together we were dropping guns to Aláyeksan fighters across The Great Country.

In the doorway Lingen-Aka slid from Anakhta-yan's arms and ran to me. Her whole being glowed with happiness. The mystic spirit that lives deep within a person and is allowed to appear beyond the mask only when joy comes from the heart shone in her eyes.

"Anakhta-yan will be as good as ever in a few days. Thank you for taking care of him." Lingen-Aka smiled, her warmth reaching out to me. "He is kind and gentle. I love him."

"He saved my life, Lingen-Aka. He has told me how much you mean to each other."

Suddenly all her desperation poured out. "I hate Oleg. Remember the day we hid behind the rocks? He wanted me at the marrying, and beat me that night for running away. He drinks all the time, stinks of vodka. He drags me around the shack, making me dance until I can't move. Whips me if I don't sing with him. Terrible songs. He wrestles me in his bunk till—"

I held Lingen-Aka close to me for several moments. One of her hands looked different somehow: The long fingernail she had shaped and sharpened at the edges, the fingernail with which she split her reeds for basket weaving, had been broken off. Every Uℓchena basket-maker guards her long nail from cracking and breaking, because it takes a long time for the nail to grow out, and skill to shape it. Lingen-Aka's fingernail, the pride of her hand, was gone. Her fingertip was reddened and swollen.

"I broke it in one of my fights with Oleg. I cut him and it put him in a rage. He beat me until I passed out. When I came to, I was tied to a peg beside his stack of furs. And he was gone."

Watnaw echoed Lingen-Aka's bitterness. "The alien curse batters every woman. It will be a long time before Lingen-Aka can split reeds for her baskets, and I grieve with her. A beast, that Oleg. And Petrov, another. He ties me down. Crawls back and forth on my body. He has a whip and beats me if I try to push him away. He takes me whenever he has the urge, and invites any other *promyshlennik* who wants a woman to use me when he is done. I have about come to the end of what I can stand. Another time, I'm not sure if . . ." Her voice trailed to nothing. She turned her head away but not before I saw her tears.

My own life, if I could call it one, with Baranov never sank to the level of the abuse in the hovels. My rape was rape by one man. But how thin that line between our abuse. I had only to remember that the rape of Aláyeksan women was actually approved by the trading companies and the Imperial government in St. Petersburg—from those who boasted of ranks, royalty, and marble palaces and prided themselves on their "great civilization."

Over and above the Tahtna boasts, Baranov's words rang through my head: "And men need women if they are going to produce work. Those women like being screwed. You've heard them giggle and laugh. They're all whores."

I knew that "great civilization" was a monster wearing two faces. As I put my arms around my friends, I could not hold back tears of despair, for I wept hearing Watnaw's terrible words: *Batters every woman . . . batters every woman . . . batters every woman.*

Faced with a late hunting season, Aleksandr Baranov sent out the Uℓchena, Koniags, and Kahtnuht'ana fleets for furs, and forced the old men to go on puffin hunts. With the most important of his company's affairs set in motion, he sailed on the *Olga*.

His time away would be long because, as he had said before leaving, "I am going to pick a site for my new capital. One worthy of Mother Russia."

Baranov's quest took him to the outlying artels. At each post, including Yakutat—where the serfs had made little or no progress in farming—Baranov found only anger and sloth. Not one artel met the needs for his new capital. He then sailed the *Olga* southward along the coast into the Gulushutna country of Watnaw's clans on Sitka Sound.

Before leaving Pavlovsk, Baranov told me, "Hovels, that is all we have. Russia's capital in America must be a place of majesty and grandeur, with a harbor that fronts the sea-lanes of the North Pacific. Pavlovsk lies too far off.

"I must control the trade of Aláyeksa, every Aláyeksan fur. Only through me will foreigners be able to buy what they want. I must collect Russia's rightful *yassak* from every pelt. Her Imperial Majesty's treasury will overflow with tribute from my furs. The Shelekhov Company directors will grow rich. Then they will understand why I have fought so hard all these years. And I will build a home to rival any nobleman's house in Russia."

Always his dreams came back to "a capital, a rich trading center, that will grow up around a square of bricks—all Russian cities have a central square—protected by thick walls. And church bells will ring out over Aláyeksa."

Late in 1797, following Baranov's Russian calendar, he found the spot he wanted in Watnaw's Gulushutna country—a high promontory on Sitka Sound under the shadows of Mount Edgecumbe, the peak so named some years before by England's Captain Cook but renamed by the Russians the past year or two to "Gora Svataya Lazarya"—both sets of aliens unheedful of the true Aláyeksan name for the mountain guardian of Sitka Sound's waters. The land and sea it watched over teemed with animals, and the aliens planned on reaping a fortune in furs along the coast of the mainland as far south as any Ulchena had ever paddled his kayak. It was here that Aleksandr Andreevich Baranov hoped to fulfill his ambition, and build Russia's *kremlin* in Aláyeksa.

The day the *Olga* returned to Pavlovsk harbor, the Tahtna toasted the success of their find, and Baranov's mood rode high. What he said to Kuskov surprised me: "You have seen St. Petersburg, Ivan. A grand city. But the foggy bottoms of the Neva River marshlands are nothing compared to the mountains, the forests, the harbor I discovered on Sitka Sound. Majestic country. Now I must try to get the Kolosh chief to give up that high promontory where his fort sits. The spot I discovered. I will take it.''

Majestic! Baranov himself found Aláyeksa more majestic than his homeland!

> yuyqush, yuyqush
> across the sky
> low to high
> shadow-spirits ride

> shadow-spirits ride
> high to low
> across the sky
> yuyqush, yuyqush

I stood on a Kadyak headland facing north. Yuyqush, the northern lights, wore shimmering bands and shafts, streamers of color that floated high above me, taking me far away from the hurts of Pavlovsk.

Quietly—I had not sensed his presence—Aleksandr slipped his arm around me, whispered words of love as he drew me close. For that instant, he forgot he was captor, I almost forgot I was hostage. Warm parkas covering all but our faces, we watched the dance of lights spill around us a whiteness not of this world.

''I cannot say how many times I saw these heavenly celebrations in Siberia, Anna.'' His arm tightened around me. ''You, too, must have seen them in the Kenai sky.''

I kept silent. My captor thought to open a way to my heart through a glory common to our northern lands. Oh, I did remember the bright, still nights of Yaghenen, when our families watched and wondered at the brilliance of yuyqush, but I would not share the spirits of that glorious sky with my Tahtna captor.

As I stared into the night, I tried to draw a meaning for my existence from the shifting patterns of light. It seemed that I heard a faint whisper coming to me from a long distance away, borne on the delicate hiss of those drifting curtains.

Ashana, our people live because you serve the alien. Remember why you are here.

As we walked slowly down to the village, Baranov's arm still around me, we paused to look back at the wonder of the sky.

Ashana, our people live because you serve the alien. A strange calm came over me, and I knew that on this night, for once, I would serve my captor without a struggle.

⊛ ⊛ ⊛

15

On Yaghenen, we divided time by the running of the salmon, by the warm and cold seasons, and the rising and setting of the sun. The birds measure time by flying south at the start of the cold weather, returning north with the warm breezes. The animals change the color and texture of their coats as the seasons change. Time may be measured in different ways. The Tahtna write a set of numbers on a paper and call it the "Gregorian calendar"; it measures their time in what they call years, months, weeks, and days.

In the past I had counted time by Baranov's absences from the island: when the days were long, the nights short, the weather warm, he would be gone for many weeks. Sometimes he would be trapped by a storm and forced to stay away through the times of sleet and gales; at others, he was gone for only as long as it took him to sail around the island.

Then, in alien Pavlovsk, I began measuring time by the growth of the niłdulchinen within me. Through the tangled strands of my hostage web, another strand looped its way: That night, when Baranov and I had watched the northern lights together, had been the first time I had not fought my captor, either in my mind or with my body. I knew soon after that my blood had mingled with his, but I did not tell him, nor did I share my secret with Lingen-Aka or Watnaw: that I knew within me grew the seed of Aleksandr Andreevich Baranov, my half-breed child, my niłdulchinen—no, *our* child.

Jabila was dead. Was it not time to stop contending with Baranov, to know the relief of giving in? But, oh, the shame of bearing the Russian's child . . . the rage that I had let myself be trapped, and the hopelessness of being forever linked to him.

One morning, just as dawn was breaking, I found myself

unable to sleep and stole out of the house. The drifting mist and fog blotted out the sundogs, and I could find no comfort in my mother's words—"always, the sundogs lead our people." On the headland of Kadyak, looking homeward, I searched the seas for strength, but not even the sea lions called to one another. The morning's peace was broken only by the cry of a child from the shacks. Ever since I had come to Kadyak I had been troubled by the niḷdulchinen—children of two worlds, bred by Tahtna fathers, born to Aláyeksan mothers, children neglected because their mothers slaved until all hours and their fathers hunted the seas for weeks and months at a time.

How different were the lives of the small ones in our Kahtnuht'na families, where parents, grandparents, aunts, uncles, and friends watched over them. I worried about the future of the children of Kadyak—lost creatures, wild at an early age, frightened; some with exquisite faces, others dulled by neglect or marked by the ravages of a European gift to Aláyeksa: syphilis. I placed my hand gently on my belly, wishing that I could keep secret the niḷdulchinen within me, carry it home to Yaghenen; I wanted to push time back to before the night of yuyqush. I would never rid myself of the baby I carried, as some women did, but how could I face myself every day, trying to be mother to our niḷdulchinen? Why had I let myself feel any warmth toward Baranov?

As I turned back toward the house, the cry of another child, one whose mother's duties had driven her to the work sheds, drifted to me on the winter wind.

"Where have you been, Anna? You were not in bed when I reached for you." Baranov straightened up from the papers on his desk and shook his steel pen at me, the ink trailing a thin black line down the palm of his hand.

"I could not sleep, so I went for a walk." I looked him straight in the face. "The way the babies cry so much down in the shacks troubles me. You must—"

"Those women." He cut across what I tried to tell him. "They do not know how to care for babies. They pay no attention to them."

"How can they? They are always at work," I flashed back at him. "Or the men are at them. You do not give the mothers time for their children."

"Enough of that." He started to wave me away, then asked, "Tell me, what is the puffin count?"

I thought quickly. "Four men have finished. Others will be done within the next few days."

"How many have you marked down?"

I showed him the markings for each man. He ran his fingers along the columns, apparently adding in his head. "Good enough. You are learning business. Just keep at it." He handed back the papers. "Now, leave me. I am busy on plans for Sitka."

"Put aside your plans for a moment and listen, Aleksandr. I am going to have a baby." It was one of the few times I had used his first name, but he did not notice it.

He jerked back, braced his hands on his desk, spat out, "No, Anna! You can't! I won't allow it!"

At that, I lost control. I could not help myself. Despite Baranov's affection the night we watched yuyqush together, he had not changed toward me. Hostage I was, hostage I remained. I had kept quiet for many weeks about the new life, about his seed growing within me, not daring to disturb him and not wanting to share my secret.

" 'I won't allow it!' you say," I sobbed. "But just what can you do about it, Aleksandr Andreevich Baranov?"

Seizing my shoulders, he shook me until I turned dizzy. "Be still! The cooks will hear you!"

Was he concerned about me? About his child? No. Aleksandr Baranov's distress rose from the fear that siring a child by a hostage woman would damage his image with the other aliens in Aláyeksa, with his company superiors in Russia, even with his wife in Kargopol. In the days that followed, he cursed Grigorii Shelekhov for not sending a replacement to take over the company management in Aláyeksa before such an event could entrap him. But he did not lash out at me again, and a calmness settled over us. I avoided outbursts. We lived in silence.

The longer the silence, the greater my fear that my captor might kill me rather than admit to a Baranov niⱡdulchinen. And always through that fear coursed the growing revulsion that Qaniⱡch'ey Ashana of Yaghenen bore the child of her people's killer.

Early one morning, my joncha came to me for the first time in months; and listening to it, I knew the lach'u of our ancient tradition of loving our children: *The child is yours, Ashana. Accept it. Protect it. Love it.* My revulsion slipped away.

I reminded myself that the Tahtna had few rules of conduct in Aláyeksa, but one they held inviolate: one man, one wife—a bond created by the Holy Russian Orthodox Church that could not be broken. Nothing prevented a man from taking another woman for his use, but she was shunned and her children were unrecognized.

On Yaghenen, a man could take two or three wives; it was the ancient and accepted way of life among Athabaskan clans. Always, the children born of each union received the love and protection of the clan and were shared with the family. No stigma was attached to them.

As the months of my pregnancy went on, the monks pretended not to see me, pulled tight their sacred skirts so that I would not accidentally brush against them as we passed. They ignored me, but as my bulging stomach bore obvious witness to Baranov's indulgences with me, their anger against him mounted.

Baranov stormed home one day after the church service and broke the silence between us. "The monks still do not understand how things are here. Father Juvenal attacked me in church, called me 'sinner.' Ridiculed me in front of my men." My captor glared at me as if I were to blame, but he did not touch me.

A report was brought in late one day that caused Baranov's already bad mood to deepen and turn more sullen. The food bowls cleared away, his pipe in his mouth, he tipped his bench against the wall. "I have to replace two men." He puffed several times, then went on, "Oleg and Petrov must have eaten rotten meat."

He watched the smoke rise from his pipe awhile in silence. "I hope this does not set off an epidemic like that time on the hunt, when the Aleuts found mussels on the beach, thousands of them. They had not eaten for a long time. Gorged themselves. I don't know how many men died that day: a hundred, two hundred. They were only Aleuts. But I cannot afford to lose Russians the same way."

Watnaw and I had not talked about the poisoned blubber or the gun stealing for some weeks. Instead she and Lingen-Aka and I had dreamed about my baby. I never learned if they had anything to do with what happened. But Baranov's words frightened me, and I fought to control myself.

Mask your face, cautioned my joncha.

Hoping that my voice did not betray my worry, I asked, "Oleg and Petrov? How did it happen?"

"I am not sure. They got sick yesterday. Complained their throats burned. Vomited a lot. This morning they were dead."

In my head there was a pounding as if k'eltemi thundered across the heavens. Murder. Murder. Murder. In Athabaskan law, murder has always been the worst offense one human being can commit against another. Murder is hideous, but my friends had been driven to it if that is what happened. It troubled me deeply that Aláyeksan women could be reduced to the level of killers.

"You do not look well, Anna. What is bothering you?" Baranov's eyes, the tone of his voice, his mastery at reading people's faces, struck new fear in me. I willed my mask to cover my fright.

"My stomach has been upset. Too much salt in the soup. It made me sick till I got rid of it." I fought for words to take his mind off Oleg and Petrov; I must not let him suspect my concern that our poison was the cause of their deaths. I almost said *meat* instead of *salt*, but caught myself in time. We Kahtnuht'ana did not know of the white, grainy substance until the Tahtna brought it, insisting that it be used to improve the food.

"Eating that soup is like gulping dirty seawater. It nauseates me. I have no stomach for the uncivilized stuff."

"You act like a child, Anna," he chided me, as he had many times. "You must learn to appreciate fine foods. Salt is necessary to raise food out of the ordinary. Every civilized table uses it."

"Yes, I know your concern for improving my taste. But some things I do not believe I can handle. Salt. Cabbage. Smelly old dresses. Civilization!"

"Well, my dear savage, between me and Richard, we will keep trying." Forgetting Oleg and Petrov a moment, he guffawed at my outburst.

"Salt is bitter; I will not use it."

I regarded salt as a symbol of resistance and rejected it all the time I was a hostage. Baranov, no doubt, saw it as a step in civilizing me, perhaps as a symbol of conquest. That day, it served to turn my captor's mind away from Oleg and Petrov. While he worried about salt, I saw the faces of our murdered hunters, the image of Shila, the young Kahtnuht'ana felled by Tahtna bullets; I heard the echoes of Soleviev's musket, as he killed with one bullet eight helpless Ułchena men tied back to back; the cries of hundreds of hunters driven by Baranov's *promyshlenniki* over treacherous waters and lost forever; the moans

of abused hostage women and the wails of their niÅdulchinen.
And through it all, I heard Baranov talking of salt and cabbage.

Haunting my mind was the question, What will be the fate of
the new life within me? In our Kahtnuht'ana clans the child
belongs to the mother. It is a concept as deeply ingrained in us
as the one that allows property to pass through the mother. What
would happen when Baranov went home to Russia and confronted the company men or his wife and daughters in Kargopol
with a half-breed child by a savage mother? It could destroy
forever his hopes of gaining higher status in Russia. Then, too,
Baranov had always enforced Shelekhov's old rule that children
fathered by Russians in Aláyeksa must stay with the mothers
when the fathers returned home.

Some women saw this as abandonment; if Baranov left me,
and I could go home to Yaghenen, it would be a release. My
family would blot out all remembrance of alien blood, raise my
child as Kahtnuht'ana. If my child were a son, Seltan would
train him in the ways of manhood: We believe this to be the
responsibility of the mother's eldest brother. My people fear a
father cannot be severe enough to train his son in the hard and
difficult skills of survival and hunting in the way an uncle could.
I longed for my child to run wild and free over Yaghenen, while
I took my rightful place at home.

"I will not go to the burying for Petrov and Oleg."

"Princess Anna, you will come with me." Baranov's order
sounded almost polite.

"No. I will not. The monks insulted me. I told you how they
chased me out of their church building, threw me to the ground.
I will not go."

Baranov shook his head. "That was not right. I told you so.
They called me 'sinner,' too. But today we forget all that. Today
we pay respect to the dead. That is why we have funerals. I want
you to come."

"Respect? I do not—" To spill out my disgust about these
men, to let Baranov know I did not care about their deaths, could
raise questions. Questions lead to suspicion. Suspicion leads to
digging. If the aliens dug, they might find that the deaths of
those two were not accidental.

So, on a little piece of ground the Tahtna had set aside for
burying their dead, I stood at the head of the women, Baranov
at the head of the men. As the monks read from their ritual
books and chanted, workmen lowered two bodies wrapped in

old skins into holes, packed rocks and dirt over them, and pounded small crosses into the ground at the head of the mounds—one for Oleg, one for Petrov. I had wondered whether the monks would rave at me that day. They did not. Their decency must have been because of the performance of respect for the dead, the "funeral," as Baranov called it. But the demonic eyes of Father Emelian fixed on me as I turned away. I ignored him, and caught the knowing glances of Lingen-Aka and Watnaw.

"Aleksandr, our child will come with the breakup of the ice in the streams. That will be soon. You must have a birthing house built for me."

"Birthing house? I told you I will not hear of that way of doing things.'

"I need one. A private place where my child can be born."

"None of that! This is not the Kenai." His eyes narrowing, he pushed at his forehead as if to wipe away the thought. "You will have the child in bed in this house. The way a Russian woman would."

"That is not the healthy way to have a baby, lying flat in a bed. A woman's body has to—"

"Quiet. I do not want to hear about it."

"But you have to hear. It is your child, too, and I need—"

Angry, grumbling to himself, he stamped out of the house.

I felt the need for the fresh air of late winter. It was raining, and I was about to pull on my waterproof gutskin when Akoota came in. "Stay, Anna. We need to talk."

"I have nothing to say to you."

"You listen. Aleksandr Baranov worries about the child."

"He worries? He has not shown any concern."

"Perhaps you do not give him a chance. Remember he will claim his child. If you insist on a birthing house and anything happens to the baby, he will hold it against you. It will be bad for any woman who helps."

What did she mean, *claim his child*? I did not want to ask her, so aloud I said, "Watnaw and Lingen-Aka will help me. They are not afraid."

"Those two. They had better be afraid. They are up to no good. And their work . . ."

Her words faded. I wondered what she knew of the deaths of Oleg and Petrov. If she suspected Lingen-Aka and Watnaw, how long would it be before she carried the tale to Baranov? The more I saw of her, the stronger was my suspicion that she had been the informer the time Jabila came to take me home.

"You had better obey Baranov." Her eyes hardened.

For the good of my child, I pushed all else to the back of my mind. "No, Akoota. We Kahtnuht'ana provide a special place in which a woman may birth her child. No men are allowed there. It is a clean, dry birch-bark house. Inside it, we dig a shallow hole, lined with ferns and leaves. It is over this that the baby is born."

"We cannot do such a thing here. There will be no birch-bark house for you."

"Have one built, then."

"Nonsense."

"It is not nonsense. My mother told me how it has always been done. That is the way—"

"Baranov orders the way we do things in Pavlovsk."

"What does he know? He is not a woman. My mother said that to birth a child a woman must squat, but keep her back upright. Her weight pushes the baby downward. That way birthing happens with the least struggle. You know as well as I do it is unnatural lying stretched out. The baby gets no help. I cannot risk having mine that way."

"Anna. Anna." She tapped her foot to emphasize her words. "You do not listen to me."

"Why should I?"

"Baranov ordered me to tell you how it is with Russians. Their babies are born in bed. You do not have a choice."

"Akoota, you know by Kahtnuht'ana ways the babies belong to the mothers. This one belongs to me. It is my body. I have a right to have my child born our natural way."

"Right? Right? What right, Anna?"

I had nothing more to say. For the rest of the afternoon I heard Baranov's words speaking through Akoota. When she left, I had little doubt that my child would be born according to alien custom. No Russian would build a birthing house for me, and no Aláyeksan dared.

That night I seemed to struggle deep in a forest looking for Jabila, but could not find him. Only the beasts. The circle closed in on me. Tails lashed. Eyes burned. I screamed the silent screams of my stormswept night.

Baranov was shaking me. "Anna, Anna, wake up."

I was shivering, breathless; my heart pounded.

"What were you dreaming about? You rolled around. Made

strange noises." Baranov's arms pinned me down. Escape from that man was no more possible than escape from the beasts that encircled me in my nightmares. And I struggled to remember the shaman's words the night of yuyqush.

"Go back to sleep, Anna. I have work to do early in the morning." His heavy arm over me, he soon snored. But dread mixed with longing for Jabila and the wish that the life in me were *his* child kept me awake. I ached for the release that Lingen-Aka and Watnaw knew on learning of the deaths of their tormentors.

One day, Aleksandr Baranov surprised me as he packed for a trip to his artels—"An inspection," he said. (Attu had told me the real purpose was to levy men and lay plans for the fight to take land at Sitka.)

"The finest fox pelts brought in from the last hunt." Baranov handed me a pack of furs. "Have them sewn together for the baby's blanket."

As our hands touched, my endless anger wavered. My child's father drew me to him; I knew a breath of happiness.

His eyes lingered on me. "Anna, I want our child to be as beautiful as you." Voice faltering, his usual mood of command dropped away. "We have had bad times. But this child . . . I mean to say, you count for much . . . I love you, Anna."

For those moments, we were two human beings whose thoughts wove intimately around the life we had created. I rested my head on his shoulder, and his arms tightened around me. Hearing him speak of love, a fleeting sense of release came to me.

When I had first arrived at Kadyak, Baranov slept on a stinking pile of furs; a couple of years later he ordered what he termed "a proper Russian bed" to be built. His ship's carpenters carved four posts, pegged them together with a framework of slats on the sides and ends; over this framework they interlaced strips of walrus hide and tied them securely. Akoota sewed a pad made from castoff pieces of old gut parka and stuffed it with moss, dried ferns, and pine needles; Baranov smoothed it down over the walrus strips. On top of everything he threw the cleanest of our sleeping furs; I heard him mutter, "Blast Shelekhov! When will he send a supply ship? These old bones need the feel of sheets."

It was on that strange bed that I birthed my son; Baranov's

only concession was his permission to allow Lingen-Aka and Watnaw to attend me. Akoota hovered in the room, intent that I perform the birthing as our captor had ordered, while Lingen-Aka grasped my shoulders, comforting and reassuring me, for I was frightened. As little girls, my curious friends and I had peeked through the cracks in the walls of birch-bark houses, listening to the panting, the groans, the cries of the women giving birth. But from what my own mother had told me I knew that it was those who did not cry out during the birthing who received the most respect. That day in Baranov's house I heard Sem's voice echoing through Watnaw's words.

"Steady. Easy, Ashana."

"Bear down. Hard." Lingen-Aka stroked my forehead. "Harder, Ashana, harder."

"The head is coming."

"Take a deep breath."

The baby coursed its way through me. I heard Lingen-Aka's excited cries. And then: "The baby's here, Ashana. It's all over. It's a boy."

With glazed eyes I watched Watnaw tie the cord in two places, and could not help wincing when she raised her knife and severed the cord that bound the baby to me.

Oh, Sem, why couldn't you have been here to welcome this grandchild? A long-legged, black-eyed Athabaskan from a daughter who would have made you proud in the birthing: no foolish shrieks, no cries.

The name for our child? I dreamed of a Kahtnuht'na name, one with a special, private meaning for me at the time of my child's birth: after a beautiful place, an important event, a natural force or being. Sometimes when I had stood in the early dawn looking north to Yaghenen, I heard my mother's voice: "You are never alone, Ashana. The spirits of our ancestors protect you. Long ago our Athabaskan people walked east from far, far in the west. Then back to Yaghenen. Lifetimes of travel. Always the denedi belik'a watched and led people home. Our ancient tales tell us so."

Denedi Belik'a! Sundog!

"I name you Denedi Belik'a," I whispered in my son's ear. "Some day you will lead us home."

As he slept beside me, my thoughts for him flew: Strength I will give you, my son. Kahtnuht'ana lach'u I will teach you: the beauty and courage told through our legends, the mystic rhythms of our songs, the beliefs practiced in our rituals. All this will I give you through the years of your growing up, Denedi Belik'a, sundog of the dawn!

Brusquely, Baranov brushed aside my Kahtnuht'ana name. "We Russians give names with meaning," he said. "My son will be named for his saint's day, Antipatr, and after me, Aleksandreevich, son of Aleksandr. No one will call him any name other than Antipatr Aleksandreevich Baranov."

My child, born of an Aláyeksan mother, bore a Tahtna name. Akoota had warned me, ". . . he will claim his child."

With Denedi Belik'a's birth, I was no longer alone. Whatever name Baranov put on him, he remained mine, tiny, helpless, dependent; yes, dependent on me, Qaniłch'ey Ashana of Yeghenen. All the months of my agony, of worrying that I would not want this child and could not love him because he was also my captor's, faded to nothing the first time I looked at him and heard his cry.

As my joncha had instructed, I promised Naq'eltani I would protect and teach my son. Someday . . . qezahda, in the future . . . we would go home to freedom on Yaghenen.

As if to remind me that my son had alien blood, during the passing weeks his skin turned a shade lighter than mine, and his small body took on the square shape of his father's. But his eyes and hair remained black; nursing him, I imagined him pure Athabaskan, saw the two of us living in a home on Yaghenen, filled with laughter, stories, and the smell of roast mountain goat. I held him tightly. My tears falling on his tiny face startled him, and he cried.

"Shh, shh, my little one, my Denedi Belik'a. Go to sleep. It is not your fault," I whispered to him.

New life brings hope and happiness, whatever tragedy surrounds it; and the baby reached out to everyone who came to see us. Ivan Kuskov jiggled my son on his knee, sang strange songs he called "nursery rhymes." The cooks came from the kitchen countless times during the day to "check on the little one." Anakhta-yan and Richard appointed themselves "uncles." Not to be outdone, Lingen-Aka and Watnaw claimed themselves "aunts." I whispered his name to them, and the uncles and aunts hummed "Denedi Balik'a" under their breaths. Even Akoota brought a finely woven Ułchena basket in which to store his tiny clothes; and in the wonder of the child, our differences lost their sharp edges.

From the moment Aleksandr Baranov first held his new son, he claimed Antipatr Russian; his affection for the child was unbounded. Seeing the love he had for our baby, that strange new feeling for Aleksandr Baranov, that quiet peace I had known the night he held me close and spoke the word *love*, rose through me again.

"A fine son you have given me, Princess Anna," he told me more than once. "We must work together to bring him up the proper way."

He walked with the child in his arms, sang him to sleep with words he said his mother had sung to him:

> "A—a, lully, a—a, lully
> Why, O wind, dost thou roar
> Why dost thou not allow little
> Antipatr to sleep?
> Sleep my dear little son.
> My little gray-blue dove.
> A—a, lully, a—a, lully!"

As he rocked the little one, I heard him murmur, "You will grow up, Antipatr Aleksandreevich Baranov, and in a few years I will send you to the Naval Academy in St. Petersburg. You will learn from Russia's best teachers."

"The Naval Academy in St. Petersburg." My heart froze at the words. I took no joy in his song. Would not Baranov honor the Shelekhov rule that children of Aláyeksan mothers and Tahtna fathers must be left in Aláyeksa? Would he dare face scorn in his homeland by taking Denedi Belik'a with him when he left? Or would Denedi Belik'a and I perish first?

⚙ ⚙ ⚙

16

In the center of the earth our dead gather: We know this for truth, because when our dead move, dance, or work, the earth under our feet trembles; when they are angered, the ground around us shakes, the mountains spout ash and throw rocks, the tides spill over our shores. I had felt no shaking of the earth since Jabila died. As the seasons passed, I wondered at the quiet at the earth's center, for my husband was known as a man of action.

The shadow-spirit, the body, the breath: From ancient times, we Kahtnuht'ana have known that every person is made up of these three parts. That day of our failed escape, Jabila's shadow-spirit did not walk with us, did not warn me of my husband's coming death. Perhaps Jabila appeared too suddenly that night of the celebration at the kashim; perhaps we were together too brief a time for the spirit to make its presence known.

Thinking of my husband, I turned my face up to the cloudless blue sky. It was a rare day for Kadyak, which at this time of year was usually fog-ridden. And I knew Denedi Belik'a was in good hands, for Watnaw had come that afternoon and said, "I have made this jacket for your son, and it needs fitting. A good aunt needs to spend time with her nephew. The day is beautiful, and you should be outdoors. Don't worry, I will stay with him."

On such a day at home, Seltan and I might skim across the waters of Tikahtnu in his kayak. I can still see us running on the beach, hear his quick laugh as I lost my balance before settling in the little boat. My dreams waft me—or is it my shadow-spirit drifting beside me?—to a mountainous region on the trail by the river leading westward toward my mother's Athabaskan clans. I dream Jabila has gone with the other hunters to track caribou north and west of our village. I dream of tending my house, of talking with my husband and brother when they ask for my ideas on plans that affect us all. In imagining the work and pleasure of a free life among the mountains, I sense the calming of my shadow-spirit. And in my fantasy, the small friends of my childhood mingle with those unborn children, Jabila's and mine, who will never know the sunshine of the earth. And always I see the face of Jabila, sometimes close enough to touch, but too often far beyond my reach.

Sanity or insanity?

A long time ago. Jabila is lost forever.

The shadow world of the forest and the mountain spirits presses close—forest noises change into the growls of the šdónályášna, promising danger to evil men. Someday the šdónályášna's huge, hairy arm will reach into my captor's sleeping room while he snores, and the monster will drop poison into his mouth. The šdónályášna will stuff the alien into a bag, sling him over his shoulder, and walk away. My troubles will be over. Mighty is the lach'u of the terror of this monster. Kahtnuht'ana hunters do not like to talk about him, but in my imaginings I drop squirrel tails from my parka along the path, a sign for the šdónályášna to come to me; if he does, I will swallow my terror and instruct him to destroy the Russians.

Alone, I wandered some distance along the shore, then began climbing the slope, slowing my steps to watch the swimming and leaping of the salmon as the glistening fish jammed the stream from one bank to the other. I recalled the many seasons in the past when I had seen this marvelous sight, for always ts'iluq'a—the spring salmon run—brought the fish from the sea to spawning grounds far inland, and our raven people once again knew raven's gift of food to them.

Suddenly there was a flutter of black above me as a small raven flew out of a nearby tree. I followed it.

A mist slipped over the sea and hid the distant northern horizon where Yaghenen lay. The shadows had lengthened since I had climbed the slope from Pavlovsk. The raven flew close; and following it, wrapping myself in memories of past life, I spent the afternoon on the headland with my heart in Yaghenen. I had long strived to convince myself I must pull away from the day the aliens had killed Jabila, yet the memories of our short life together could never be put to rest. Anguish for his loss would live with me forever. I shook my head, trying to rid myself of the echo of his cry as he fell on the unnamed island, but it was no use. The raven glided up into the highest trees and was hidden by the branches.

Many nights I had awakened screaming, felt filthy hands stifling my cries. Sometimes I had hoped for a message telling me where Jabila rested; other times I thought it better not to know, for I might try again to join him.

I wept. I knew of no Kahtnuht'ana ceremony to honor my dead Jabila. Who had made the new clothes for his death journey? Who had washed and dressed his body? Who had built the pyre for his burning? Who had pierced his stomach to release his spirit? Who had gathered his ashes and bones and buried them? Where was his grave, with the pole to mark it?

Fluttering close again, the raven led me along a stream spilling toward the sea. Lower down the slope, dense patches of fog hung close to the ground, pressing in on me, making my world silent except for the tumbling waters or a falling rock my foot had loosened.

I stopped at a place from which I could see the bay, wondering if Kuskov or Richard had any word about Baranov's return to Pavlovsk, for dread of my captor never ceased to stalk my mind. The raven perched on a shrub for a moment, turned and looked at me, then flew up into the branches of a young birch. From a knot on the birch where the raven sat, Jabila's face peered out at me! Shaking, I moved slowly toward the tree, but I had gone only a few steps before the image faded back into the bark. I heard a rustle in the leaves. The raven took wing, flew low over the trail and out of sight.

Far down the slope, across the ravine, a figure was kneeling, tightening the thongs of his leggings.

"Chulyin, why do you trick me so?" I sank down, buried my face in my hands; my throat tightened, my breath came in quick gasps. The image plagued me—the image of Jabila's face on the tree trunk. I could not let grief go on tearing at me like this.

Sanity or insanity?

Mindslip?

Wiping my face, straightening my braids, I stood up. Slowly, I turned and looked across the ravine. Fright seized me. The figure stood slender and erect. The ghost of Jabila! How? Why? I knew Jabila lay dead on that unnamed island that I would never see again.

The figure below stepped forward, then stopped, as if looking for a person he expected to be there. Straight, immobile, a caribou band around his brow, an Athabaskan fringed shirt clasped at the waist by a belt of caribou hide: Could it be a totem cut from cedar?

But I saw it step forward!

I stifled my cry. My heart willed my feet to hurry down the trail, but my mind held me rooted to the spot; I had suffered too long the truth about Jabila. Edging downward, wanting to believe, yet not believing, afraid to cry out, "Jabila, Jabila," I stared into the fog for a long time, unable to force myself back toward Pavlovsk.

A short distance ahead, there again was the figure of Jabila. It was no image: He walked toward me! Stopping a few steps away, he held out his hands. "Qaniłch'ey Ashana."

I fell against him, sobbing his name. My heart pounded, but not as loudly as his. I clung to him for fear he would vanish.

My husband's arms crushed me to him. "Qaniłch'ey Ashana."

We pulled back, only our hands touching, and for some moments simply stared at each other. I found it impossible to make an opening in the layers of imaginings I had woven around myself, impossible to believe my husband had returned from death. As if he were blind, his fingers brushed back my hair and trailed across my forehead, rested on my cheekbones, then played back and forth across my lips. He tilted my chin gently, his kiss the soft caress of a snowflake on a leaf.

"Have you really come back, Jabila?" I whispered his name, lingered over the word, afraid if I spoke too loudly the sound might shatter the image and he would disappear forever.

"Yes, Qaniłch'ey Ashana, my windflower."

We touched lightly, our bodies strange to our hands.

Long ago, Qishvet', my people's great hero, had met the enemy. They shot him full of holes, but they could not kill him. Was Jabila another Qishvet'?

My joncha whispered, *Jabila is alive. Do not doubt. Love him.*

The question had to be asked. "How is it possible you live?"

"We hid in a cave. I knew nothing until long after my men rowed me home. Our shaman said the bullets nearly snuffed out my life. Our whole clan worked to keep me alive."

K'eghun nu. The bloodred tide that had haunted me since that day faded, and I whispered, "Qishvet'. You must be the hero Qishvet'."

"No. Not a hero. Just me. My men said I raved about you. I

was sure you were dead. Ashana, I had to see you.'' His heart beat with mine.

"But are you safe? Coming to me? You took a terrible risk.''

"We are never safe, Ashana. I rowed in the crew sent here with Yaghenen's levy of meat and fish.'' He gripped my hands tightly, his voice lowering. "This time every man in the crew belongs to my band. I trust each one.''

"Watnaw and I have talked. We worry. Didn't there have to be an informer the night you took me away?''

"Yes. There must have been a traitor on Kadyak. Your father, all of us, think so.''

Higher on the slope, Jabila stopped, his voice lifting. "Ashana, my windflower, it seems that a cave is always our japoon.''

We crawled inside our haven, a shaft of light sifting in from an opening overhead. Jabila pulled me against him. On the island that night of our flight, I had lain in my husband's arms, scared that Baranov's use of me had dulled my feelings and left me a worn woman in the eyes of my lover. But that day there was no such worry between us; Aleksandr Baranov did not exist: I belonged only to Jabila. Wrapped in the love we had known in Yaghenen, we wiped away the lost seasons. The afternoon sun warmed our naked bodies, and our melting together in love spanned the abyss from death to life. At my lover's touch, my whole body rippled and surged, my feelings beating at my very heart as the echoes of a song beat over and over against the walls of a hidden cavern.

"Jabila. Always.'' I searched his face, ran my fingers along his shoulder, down his sides, over the taut muscles of his legs.

"I have so longed for you, Ashana.'' His voice softened to almost a whisper. "Many nights I think of our time on Yaghenen. I lie awake, unable to sleep for wanting you.''

"We had no time to talk that night on the island. I must know about K'i'un and Seltan and you. Didn't you find a place in the land of Sem's people?''

"We stayed through one winter. They took us in, but they were upset. They feared the Tahtna would track us to their villages. Use guns on them. In the spring we could not stand being so far away from our own people, yours and mine. We went back to Yaghenen, and I felt closer to you.''

A shadow passed over Jabila's face as he whispered, "Seltan's wife . . .'' He seemed unable to say more.

"K'i'un?''

"You must know, Ashana . . ."

"No! Is she dead?"

"Not dead. Several seasons after we came back to Yaghenen, a Tahtna hunting party surprised her snaring squirrels. Dragged her into the bushes. Raped her. Many times. She tried to run. Fought them. They broke her arm. Dug the labret out of her face with a knife. She bears a long scar, from forehead to chin."

"Not my beautiful K'i'un!" I screamed. My cry was for K'i'un, scarred and broken, K'i'un, whose freedom I always dreamed about. "How is she?" I managed to stifle another cry.

"Drawn into herself. Lives like a shadow. Her wounds have healed, but she is scarred deep within even more than on the outside. She and Seltan had two small ones, but she lost the baby she carried in her that day. The Tahtna killed it. It was stillborn. She can bear no more."

As my husband held me, I heard K'i'un sob, her cry the ancient words: *Sh'una yula, una yula, come to me, come.*

I needed to grieve, but Jabila's time with me on Kadyak was short; and after he was gone, I would have many days for mourning. I could not go home to K'i'un, and from my shock came the words, "I have suffered every day for all of you. Lost hope. I have even thought of taking the poison plant."

"No, Ashana."

"My joncha warned me, *No*. And I saw your face and Sem's and heard your voices."

"I have sat on the headlands many times. Imagining I could see you on Kadyak." His lips fluttered across mine. "I have even paddled my kayak out of the cove, headed to you, then forced myself back."

"My mother and father, how are they?"

"Your mother stays alone most of the time. She has changed, she lives within herself." He paused. "And your father has a hard trail to walk. Our qeshqa have been badly divided for many seasons. Some of them demand we cut off food and meat from the Tahtna and refuse men for the hunts. Others argue that the bargain must be kept. I see the drain on Ni'i. He has aged much, Ashana."

"You and Seltan? How do you avoid Baranov's levy?"

"Your brother and I and a few other young men stay away. We do not live with our families. But at night we bring meat and fish to our people like the wolf did for the starving villages. We do our part, so that they may eat and can send the levies of food to Baranov. That way, you hostages will be safe."

"But, Jabila, you . . ."

"Your father believes the aliens still think I am dead. And they do not know that Seltan and the rest of my men exist. We keep it that way."

"Is there hope for us?"

"Yes, Ashana. We look ahead to a time on Yaghenen when we will rid ourselves of the Tahtna. Your father's bargain with Baranov was forced. It rests on no bond of loyalty. Our qeshqa still fear the alien guns, as we fear for the lives of you hostages. For the lives of our people." He stopped, searching for words. "I am sure that you sometimes hear of Tahtna hunters who simply disappear. No trace. No bodies. A small group. One here, another somewhere else. Gone."

"Ey'utna? The bad one?"

"Yes." Jabila laughed. "We resist, and we will never stop resisting. We must never give up hope."

"Resist. Yes, I have heard Baranov raving about trouble on Yaghenen. He lays the blame on Ni'i."

My lover breathed deeply. "It is better that I do not tell you anything more about what we plan. That way, if the Tahtna ask questions, you know nothing they can force out of you."

What courage my Qishvet' had! Jabila had risked his life in our attempt to escape, and Kahtnuht'ana had died. Alien bullets had slashed through his body like arrows through Qishvet', tearing ragged gashes on his arm, on the left side of his chest, across his hip. I traced the terrible scars gently.

My thoughts shifted. I stirred in Jabila's arms. "Jabila, you said to trust Watnaw. It is time you know: She and I have three more guns for you. They are—"

"Ashana. It is too dangerous. Do not risk your lives stealing from—"

"The Tahtna think we women dare not touch their guns. I found one in an umiak. Watnaw *borrowed* one. We pick them up whenever we know it is safe."

"It is never safe." His arm tightened around me. "Are you the ones sending guns home with our rowers?"

My eyes gave him the answer.

"Ashana, I must—" I put my fingertips over his mouth, and Jabila knew it was useless to argue with me.

The long day had sped toward evening, and the shaft of light dimmed.

"It is dusk, Qanilch'ey Ashana, and my men expect me."

"I think by now Watnaw has the guns in your boat. I will run to the house and make sure."

He shook his head at me; his smile reminded me of my young lover as he swam beside me in a lake on Yaghenen. "Only you and I know of this place. None to see. Just the sky and the trees . . ."

"And the wind, and it will never tell."

Stand on the headlands, Ashana. Shout it to the winds. I want all this land to know: *Jabila came back to me. Jabila's my husband. Shani Jabila, summer rainbow! Jabila! Jabila!* I long to sing my love to all Aláyeksa, but my voice must remain silent. My mask must always keep me hidden from the enemy; I must guard my actions while I search eyes and faces to read what schemes the aliens are brewing, to ferret out any suspicions they might harbor about me. Despair, yes. I will know days of despair. But now I also know: *Jabila lives. Jabila lives!*

BOOK THREE

✧ ✧ ✧

❂ ❂ ❂

17

The trees, the waves, the wind, even the grass at my feet, sang with the message: "Jabila lives!" In the distance the sea lions called to one another: "Jabila lives! Jabila lives!" And my heart answered.

Paint the sea hunt, the ancient Athabaskan spirit had once whispered. Shaking out my caribou hide, spreading it flat, I dipped my fingers into my stone paint dishes: They held my dark berry color, the brown made from bark, the green so faint I was not certain it would show on the hide. I had spent hours making those colors, but still had much to learn. Boats far out to sea jumped to life on the painting. The women on the shore, the trees and the mountains, were all beginning to appear, to tell our story: The nanutset of the hunt, the lach'u of the moment, the tragedy of the lost hunters depicted for all to see. My own spirit rekindled as I worked. I painted more than just the hunt: K'i'un, Jabila, Seltan, those three who walk with me in spirit, are there, too. But first Jabila took his place in the upper right corner, high above the rest, with his arrows and bow, his headband, his Athabaskan clothes, just as I had seen him a few days past, standing by the birch tree; and I draw Seltan beside him. My hand refused to picture K'i'un injured, for I still saw her as a young Kahtnuht'ana beauty, trusting and unscarred. *Tell the lach'u of the story,* the spirit insisted. For a long time I watched the sun as it passed through its high arc in the sky; then, dipping my fingers into the brown color, I began painting K'i'un as Jabila had described her to me, ruthlessly scarred.

Absorbed in putting my memories down on the caribou hide, I did not know how long Watnaw had been waiting beside me until she whispered, "Ashana."

I wiped my fingers, leaving the skin flat to dry, and again told

Watnaw of that morning on the trail the last time I had seen my loved ones; told her of K'i'un's tragedy. Watnaw and I talked until it was almost dusk. Finally I said, "Watnaw, I have finished a new cache." She followed me into the house, helped me shove the bed to one side. "Down there. I pulled these boards loose and dug out a place."

"Ehu, terrific! A safer spot than under the old fur pile. No one would think Aleksandr Baranov had guns hidden under his bed. Very crafty, Ashana, very crafty."

"I lined the hole so the guns will not rust. The ferns are from behind the house. I used sea grass, too."

Watnaw bent down, patted the lining firmly into place, measured the length of the hole. "It's perfect for those long guns!"

Warily, we quickly replaced the boards, pushed the bed back; then the two of us sat and laughed at the thought of Baranov sleeping over guns stolen from him, our hands covering our mouths to keep from waking Antipatr.

"Ashana, I almost forgot. I have something to tell you. But let's get out of the house."

First making certain Antipatr was sound asleep, Watnaw and I ran to the beach. A cutting wind skimmed the shore, drawing aside the fog's blanket, and the waves splashed our feet. The last rays of daylight turned Watnaw's face a chalky white and played across the misty shapes of hovels, boats, and trees.

I knew what was always first on Watnaw's mind, and I said, "I heard about Skaoutlelt selling land on Sitka Island to Baranov. Isn't he the clan leader? Why would he do such a thing?"

"Ashana, the old man saw a pile of Baranov's shiny stuff. He wanted it. He sits on his promontory and does not understand that he has allowed the aliens to invade Sitka Island. He is greedy. Skaoutlelt has led the clan so long he feels he has the right to do what he wants. I know none of our other clans would sell land to the Tahtna."

Some time past, Kuskov and Baranov had bragged and laughed with their men, and I repeated their talk as closely as I could remember it. "Medvednikov found a safe harbor on Sitka Island, but it is low ground. I did not fire a shot to get it," Baranov had said.

"Low? That is not a good spot for our fort." Kuskov had not seemed pleased.

"*Chort' s/neem!* I discovered the best site—the high promontory looking out to sea. But the Kolosh had their own fort up there. They would not let me have it. So I traded my stuff to

Skaoutlelt and got myself a foothold in that country anyway. A fit harbor for now.''

"Stupid savages," one of the other men had said. "You certainly fooled them with that worthless old brass.''

Baranov's men admired his besting the Gulushutna on Sitka Island. But as they toasted his success, I had sensed in my captor's mutterings a doubt unheard by Ivan Kuskov and the others. His tone had been questioning; and as if he did not want his men to hear, he said quietly, "I may have gotten my foothold on Sitka too easily. Skaoutlelt agreed to my terms without much argument. And it worries me.''

Chik'dghesh, Kingfisher, uncertain of his conquest?

By late spring of the year 1800, my captor could boast of Fort Saint Mikhailovsk. In it were new shops, warehouses, quarters for the *promyshlenniki*, a wharf where the trading could take place, and space for his office. The passion for a new capital that had burned in him for years transformed his sketches and the images of his mind into the structures that made the village truly Russian—part of Aleksandr Baranov's homeland created on the shores of Sitka Sound.

"Fort Saint Mikhailovsk, my new capital. I will make it a trading center unequaled anywhere else in this part of the world. I will have a port on the sea-lanes. My city will show the power of Mother Russia.''

Chik'dghesh. Chik'dghesh. Kingfisher roaming The Great Country. Stealing whatever he wanted.

Watnaw's eyes glistened. "But something good is going on, too. I hear that Kotlean—Skaoutlelt's nephew—talks against his uncle.

"When we were children playing on Sitka, Kotlean was always the leader. Always serious. Always fierce. Even as a small boy, he spent most of his time shooting arrows and throwing his spear. I have a feeling he is one of the young leaders who will put down greedy old Skaoutlelt. And it may happen very soon.''

"What do you mean?''

"A big fight is coming, Ashana. I think my people will take back their land on Sitka. They will kill the Tahtna. Burn their fort.''

"Watnaw, you should know what else I heard last night." I chose my words carefully. "Baranov told Kuskov he worries about Fort Mikhailovsk. He worries that his *promyshlenniki* will leave the fort to hunt and fish. That they will not stay on guard, and the fort will be left wide open. They're not soldiers. They're hunters. He told Kuskov he fears your people.''

Watnaw grabbed both my arms, whispered as if fearing the Tahtna might hear. ''Ashana, you mean there is a chance Fort Mikhailovsk might be left unguarded?''

Facing her, I nodded. A message passed.

''I must send word to Kotlean, but I will forget who told me.''

I returned to my plot. ''Watnaw, the guns. Our fighters on Yaghenen will need them. Let's take some. Now. Tonight!''

''We will, but later. The long days tire the guards. I have noticed that they start drinking by late afternoon, so they will be drunk soon. Then we can meet at the storehouse.''

Later that night Pavlovsk lay quiet, its guards sated with food and drink. Making certain Antipatr still slept, I slipped over to the storehouse, where Watnaw and I untied the door and stepped inside. A pile of puffin skins waiting to be counted lay at one end of the room, alongside stacks of otter furs. I ignored them. Against the wall leaned several guns. Each of us took a couple, along with bags of shot and powder. We were turning to leave when the crunch of boots sounded on the rocks outside. We flattened ourselves on the dirt floor.

The door was flung open. A *promyshlennik* cursed; he must have thought a workman had carelessly left the door ajar. The shadowed interior held its secret as we hid behind the furs.

We heard mumbled words, Tahtna oaths, and a snort of disgust. I nudged Watnaw, but we dared not move. Did he sense our presence?

Time slowed, the darkness hung heavy. We waited. The dull thud of boots thumped across the floor, followed by the sound of skins being dragged toward the outside. The door slammed, and in the quiet we heard the knots that held it closed being tied.

We lay still for some time, holding our breaths until the man's steps died away.

''The man is a thief,'' I whispered.

''He must have dragged away several furs.''

We tried the door, but it held.

''We're trapped, Watnaw.'' I did not speak my other thought— we will be caught here in the morning.

''The window,'' she whispered.

''It is too high. Too small.'' I groped for the lower edge of the gut-covered hole and pulled at the skin, measuring the opening. Watnaw crawled around trying to find a loose board; but they had all been pegged tightly, and we had nothing to pry them with.

"We'd better not get caught in here." Watnaw voiced the fear I kept inside me. "I do not want to face another whipping."

"Watnaw, our only hope is the window."

"But you said it was too small."

"I will squeeze through some way."

We stacked a pile of furs under the window, wide enough for both of us to stand on. Pulling at the gut covering did not loosen it. I dug my fingers into the smaller inside frame, broke several fingernails. We were about to give up and try something else when the frame slipped toward me a little, then the covering loosened on one side.

"Careful, Watnaw. Don't tear it," I whispered.

"Yes. Slow. Slow. It's coming."

Tugging, feeling with our fingers, we gradually worked the window covering loose. "Here." Watnaw cupped her hands into a support for my foot, and I raised myself onto her shoulder. The rush of fresh air in my face braced me. I pushed my head and shoulders into the opening, forced my body, but it would not pass through. I tried to pull back.

"I'm stuck."

Watnaw tugged at me, and we crashed backward onto the floor.

"Give me another boost."

I reached one arm through the opening, twisted my body so that one shoulder slid through the hole; then pulled the other out at an angle. I wiggled my hips upward and into the opening; then I stuck. Bracing my hands against the outside wall, I pushed hard, stretched. Suddenly I tumbled out, landing on ferns and shrubs that broke my fall. But the breath was knocked out of me, and I could not move for a short while.

From above, I heard Watnaw's half-whispered "Ashana? Where are you? Get me out of here."

The knots holding the door shut resisted me, and I broke my last fingernail before I saw how the cords had been looped around each other. In the darkness, my fingers followed the leather straps around and around until I had worked the knots loose and pulled them apart.

Watnaw had already jammed the window frame back into place and dragged the furs to the spot from which we had taken them. We grabbed the guns we had come to get, slid them under our qenich'eni, then stepped outside and retied the door knots.

Once back in my own house, I pulled up the boards covering our cache. Watnaw handed me the guns and powder, then we carefully hid them under grass and ferns and laid the boards back in place. Our loot safely cached until it could be sent home, Watnaw and I relaxed by the fireplace for a few minutes, in high spirits. Our guns rested in the safest of all places—under Baranov's bed.

"I am not a good thief, Watnaw. I was scared all the time."

"You wiggled out of that window as if you knew exactly how."

"Yes, but I am still shivering."

"No talk about tonight, Ashana. Not to anyone."

"You know we have an excuse: The thieving *promyshlennik.*"

"Yes, and if anyone prods us, we will just say we were walking home and saw a workman go into the storehouse and carry out something. But we could not see what he had."

"Baranov may pry at me. But I will tell him the horror of Igor scared us, and we ran home."

We felt happy that the Gulushutna were planning to take back their land whenever they could, and oh! the excitement over our gun stealing! It was a stride toward home. When Aleksandr Baranov returned to Kadyak, we pulled on sea-gull masks to cover our glee, ready to ride out his wrath if he should find some guns missing, for sea gulls are among The Great Country's best survivors.

For days I held strictly to my rule of never talking to anyone except Watnaw about the guns, the meat coils, anything linked to *escape*; but I knew moving guns to Yaghenen must involve some of the men from here or those who rowed in with supplies.

I pondered *who*; then, the Kahtnuht'ana Tema and the Ulchena Agagasik came to mind. I knew they were the pair I needed. There was a big point in their favor: Whenever the two men rowed a hunt together, they brought back a larger catch of seal or otter skins than when they teamed with anyone else; the Tahtna never failed to notice, so they allowed the two to row in the same kayak, hunt after hunt.

One night, Tema sat alone on the shore sharpening his harpoon. And I heard the raven speak. "Ashana, it is safe now to break your rule of no talk. Tell Tema you need him, and why." So, I told him of my gun plan, and he was eager to help.

The season progressed from spring into middle summer; Baranov, who had gone from Yelovi Island to outlying artels, would not return until the cold season. Watnaw and I continued planning with Tema and Agagasik, and we grabbed as many more guns and as much shot as we dared. We watched. We read the signs of the sea, the sky, the winds, waiting until they would be right—the sea calm, the moon's dark side toward us, the sea lions still, the winds from the south low and quiet.

Even when nature favored us, we still had to be wary of the guards. Then the perfect afternoon came: Long before dark, the guards lay flat and snoring; with the sea favoring us, I said, "Tema and Agagasik, now is a good time to row to Yaghenen."

Guns and powder safely stowed inside their kayak, the two hunters slipped down to a small cove partially hidden from the village, bending low against the boat as they headed out. Tema would stay on Yaghenen; Agagasik would flee farther west to Akutan Island, his home in the U*l*chena chain.

Two men escaping. Guns for my people!

Screened by shrubs, Watnaw and I watched as the hunters skimmed smoothly into the main channel. Few craft were on the water, and I felt that my plan was succeeding. Several more kayak lengths, and the hunters shot around the headland and out of sight.

"We have done it, Watnaw!"

"Your plan is a good one."

"Tomorrow night, we will go to the storehouse, take a few more guns. Hide them, and wait until the right time for another escape."

Our hearts sang; our spirits skimmed the waves, flying with the sea gulls above that lone boat. For days as we went about our work, our thoughts were on the men in the kayak racing north to Yaghenen with our guns.

And then the word came.

Several Tahtna baidarkas returning to Pavlovsk had recognized Tema and Agagasik and ordered them to join the hunting fleet. Instead, the great hunters had turned aside, rowing hard. The warning crack of a gun, then another, was followed by several shots, no longer in warning, that ripped across the surface of the sea. Our men did not stop, but they were tightly strapped into their boat, and there was no escape. Tema and Agagasik slumped down; their kayak, torn through, took the bloody bodies of the men and their guns to the depths of the sea.

Was it my fault they had died? Could I have planned it differently? Had I misread the signs? I had cost two trusted men their lives: Tema, a brave Kahtnuht'ana whom I had just come to know, and Agagasik, an Uℓchena who seemed more shaman than hunter.

One night Denedi Belik'a cried out suddenly; restless, rubbing his eyes, he quieted only when I tucked him under my furs; the touch of my hands, the sound of my voice, helped him slip away to wherever slumber takes a child. Disturbed, restless myself, not wanting to waken him by moving about, I stepped outside.

The village lay in darkness; the only sound was the splash of water against rock, sometimes a sharp crack like the echo of a gun, sometimes a soft whisper. Unmindful that I had climbed the slope away from the village, I leaned against a rock and felt the night world wrap around me. Voices swept through the trees. I listened as Athabaskans have always listened since the days of our most ancient ones, and the language of the forest filled my ears.

As the night voices rose and fell and grew in me, the trees disappeared, the island of Kadyak faded away; a force took hold that I had sensed only dimly in the past, a force that left behind the body and breath of Aleksandr Baranov's hostage woman and bore her shadow-spirit upward to the high slope. A snowfield stretched across the mountainside farther than human sight could see. I tried to run toward the mountaintop; but the snow lay hip-deep, and I broke through at every step. Somewhere on the whiteness, I was stopped; I struggled again to run, but I could not move. Dotting the white expanse stood monsters, two and three rising up in the place where before only one had been. The snow deepened. Bitter cold burned me. Sounding from among the voices of the night, the qegh nutnughel'an, the spirit of the recent dead, spoke with Agagasik's voice. My grasp of his Uℓchena tongue was faulty, but on the snowfield that night I seemed to understand every word. His voice poured out with urgency; then suddenly his words were lost as the snowfield jerked and heaved. Chaos shook the mountain. The monsters whirled in a maddened dance. I tried to scream, but my dry throat could not even whisper.

The force I did not understand moved me down the slope and into my house. I fell into a heavy sleep on the furs beside my child, and in my dreams the qegh nutnughel'an, again in Agagasik's voice, spoke to me from the shadows.

Before I awakened the next morning, my son had crawled from the furs. My first thoughts tried to recall the voices, the words spoken high on the slope. What had been Agagasik's message? As my child's demands intruded into the day, I could not remember what the voices of the night had said to me, try as I would. I knew only that the qegh nutnughel'an had talked to me, as they had spoken to my people since the beginning of time. From such talk our shamans drew on the wisdom of the Athabaskans, and they remembered.

That night I had heard such wisdom, but the next morning I could not remember. I was no shaman.

✦ ✦ ✦
18

Korabl! Korabl! Ship!'' Excitement over a vessel—the first in more than two years in our harbor—raced through Pavlovsk, and all work stopped.

Baranov swung Antipatr to his shoulder, and the three of us rushed from the house. A man who seldom showed emotion, Baranov choked, unable to speak when he recognized his own *Phoenix* dropping anchor at Pavlovsk. Many seasons before, his ship had sailed from Aláyeksa to Siberia half-painted; the day of its return, fresh paint glistened on her new deckwork and cabins; tightly woven white canvas replaced the sails that had been patched together from skins, old trousers, and rotten cloth for its first voyage home to Okhotsk.

''They said I could not build her.'' Baranov handed Antipatr to me. ''But look at the *Phoenix* now. She has sailed those stormy seas to Siberia and back.''

Jumping into a umiak, he ordered Ulchenas to row him to the vessel to greet Captain Ivan Podgasch.

Headed home to Russia, the *Phoenix* had carried many thousands of rubles' worth of Aláyeksa's finest furs, along with alien men who had finished their contracts with the company. That day she sailed in bringing molasses, sugar, tea, flour, foodstuffs to satisfy Tahtna hunger; Russian jackets, pants, cloth, boots to clothe their bodies; rum and vodka to quench their thirst.

Captain Podgasch saluted Baranov, a smile playing across his whiskered face. ''We bring news for you.'' With his German sense of order, the skipper did not waste time in idle talk. ''Here, a bundle of letters for you, Aleksandr. They will tell you better than I can what is going on.''

Excitement crowded Baranov's words. ''Remember, I told you a long time ago we would have one company in Aláyeksa.

All the Russian hunters would have to join me or get out. It is happening. It is happening, Princess Anna. Just listen.

"Dear Sir:
   "Alekandr Andreevich:
   "In reading this letter you will wonder perhaps when you notice it is signed by so many, among whom you will find many of your sincere friends. You will be glad when you know the reasons.
   "Ivan Larionovich, Mr. Golikov and Mrs. Natalia Aleksoevna Shelekhov notified you May twelfth that a new Company of Milnikov and Company was formed at Irkutsk for trade on the high seas and on land. The above-mentioned Mr. Golikov and Mrs. Shelekhov merged their American Companies on such conditions as to form one Company.''

He shook the paper, roared, "See! I told you! One company! Old Gregorii could not pull the companies together, but his wife has.'' He went on:

   "Thank God for everything. We want to add that we are very glad to have you for a manager in the Northwest. We beg you to stay and to let us see our plans executed, which are outlined in the above-mentioned note, given to Emelian Grigorievich. If boredom or a conclusion that our plans are impractical will make you quit your position and if you will return to Okhotsk next year, please turn your duties over to Emelian Grigorievich. We are grieved to make this resolution and we make it only to avoid the difficulties that might arise otherwise due to the long distance. In case you will remain we beg you to go ahead with our plans as to: Agriculture, settlements, upkeep of the ecclesiastics, missions, and settlers. We are expecting to receive in our main office of the American Company of Golikov, Shelekhov, Milnikov and partners your detailed report about all this. This report is expected . . . with the Right Reverend Bishop Ioasaf.''

Baranov snorted. "The ecclesiastics! I heard Ioasaf's complaints before he wrote them down: "You hold back food from us, but you eat well. . . . The company sent cows, and you let the dogs eat the calves. . . . The winds howl through our shacks; you enjoy a warm house.''
   "Much worse, Anna, he accused me of distorting the aims

of the government. That would be treason. So, with the partners begging me to stay on, they couldn't have put much stock in Ioasaf's report.

''We are ending this letter by wishing you good health and success in all your undertakings and remain respectfully yours. Dear Sir, Your obedient servants and partners.

''Look at the names, Princess Anna. Important people, every one. Ivan Golikov—the old man's been in the company from the start. The Dudorovski family. Even Zubov, one of them the Tzarina's last lover. And, of course, Natalia Shelekhov.''

Yes, Natalia of the rotten, sea-green dress. But that night I said nothing to dispel Baranov's moments of satisfaction. One pleasure he had not expected: The message to Archimandrite Ioasaf called him back to Irkutsk for further training.

''Smart asses,'' Captain Podgasch had sneered about the three cadets he had delivered to Baranov. Midshipman Gavril Terentyevich Talin, arrogant (though why he should have been is beyond figuring: Podgasch said the young whelp had failed most of his studies at the Naval Academy and had been sent to Aláyeksa so that experience could make up for lack of brains), strode through the village, the other two following, parading their bright uniforms and brass buttons, their naval caps raked over one eye.

Midmorning on the shore one day, shrieks sounding like the night revelries in the shacks ruptured the stillness and yanked me from my clam digging. I grabbed a club and slipped toward the screams. Beyond a cluster of shrubs two young hostages from the shacks, K'atl', a commoner from my own Yaghenen, and Sutina, a woman of the Copper River clans, had been fixing old knots and replacing worn lines when three sailors had shoved the women to the ground. None of them saw me moving in. Kicking, twisting, K'atl' tried to squirm away from her attacker. Nearer the water, a sailor had Sutina pinned down, her qenich'eni shoved up to her waist, his penis swollen and red. I thought Sutina had lost the fight, but just as the alien mounted her, she kneed him; he roared, and the seed of young Russia spilled onto the sands of Aláyeksa.

Just then Talin saw me and rushed at me before I could hit him with my club. ''I have one for myself,'' the midshipman crowed, twisting my wrist, forcing me to drop my stick. I pulled back, ducked under his arm. He tried to push me to the ground, bragging, "Aha! I love a wildcat!"

"*Sobaka!* Dog!" I yelled, butting him in the stomach as hard as I could, so that his legs gave way and he fell into a pile of fish nets. Without thinking, I tossed a couple of the nets over him; as he kicked and tried to paw his way out of the tangle, I threw on a couple more. In a few moments he was as badly entangled as any sea creature caught on our beaches. The fracas between Talin and me had startled the alien attacking K'atl'; surprised at the mess Talin was in, the devil jumped up. K'atl' scrambled toward me. We grabbed Sutina's hands and dashed for the safety of my house. Looking back, I saw three Tahtna naval officers, faces scratched and uniforms muddy, one cap twisted backward and two on the ground. What explanation would they give Captain Podgasch for their disarray? In Kaht-nuht'ana, "ta*l*in" means whale, but no respectable whale in Aláyeksan waters would claim kin to such a rascal as Midshipman Talin.

The months piled together; I wondered many times if our fracas with the Tahtna naval officers had turned Talin's mind to enmity toward everything in Pavlovsk, to revenge—for trouble brewed on Kadyak Island, and the midshipman always seemed to be sloshing in it. Insolent, he challenged Baranov's authority: "Naval officers should govern this colony. Not some worn-out civilian." He flaunted rank: "Tzar Peter the Great's *ukaz* granted our officers rank above lowly merchants like Baranov."

A drain on Baranov's power walked these shores in the person of Talin. He found sympathetic listeners in Father Nektarii and a few other monks; they plotted, fomented unrest and devilment that struck at Baranov more sharply than the hostility of the monks during their early days on Kadyak. Ioasaf's old complaints were dragged up, decorated with new words by Talin even though the meaning remained the same: bad food, hard work, freezing huts, women. And always, at the root of the matter, poor management.

As if nature agreed with the complaints, The Great Country unleashed a severe winter. An angry sea people cut us off from the food of the deep. Kadyak Island writhed and twisted in misery. Hunger gnawed our stomachs, dragged us through the swamp water and deep into the bog; starvation was no respecter of men or rank, naval officers, *promyshlenniki*, monks, managers—all suffered alike. Cold pushed us close to death, as each faction struggled to crawl out of the muskeg by climbing onto the shoulders of the others.

Deep in his mental bog, Aleksandr Baranov strove for footing, for a way to feed the people. When supplies from the *Phoenix* were down to the last crumbs and the warehouses empty, desperation settled over him. As the morass seemed about to pull him under, Nektarii and Talin stalked onto our porch with men they had persuaded to defy Baranov. I took Antipatr and retreated inside, away from Talin's hungry-lynx eyes. Through the open door I heard Talin and the monks talk as if they had taken control of Aláyeksa: No more levies for the fur hunts. No more unpaid work for the company. No more days without food.

"Food? Let Nektarii feed you? Talin, you take command? What food can you give the men?" Baranov roared at the collection of Aláyeksans and Russians confronting him.

At night, the threats hanging over him, his spirits down, Baranov would worry aloud to me. "No hunters, no furs. It could end, Anna, all my power in Aláyeksa. My power could drip away like water from a gut bag punched full of holes."

The monks and Talin might accuse Baranov of holding back food for his own family, but as the months passed, our household reached the edge of starvation, along with everyone else on the island. The head Russian dared not leave Pavlovsk for fear that the unrest would flame into open rebellion and the plotters would act on their threat to seize control.

As the naval and church men drew more hunters and workmen into their talks, the thoughts stabbed into my mind: Should I slide from under Baranov? Join against him? Rid Aláyeksa of his alien power? Settling on a bench by the fireplace, the logs blazing high, I saw a demon face in the flames, Emelian seeming to push me down. I pulled back against the wall, rid myself of the wild thought that had come to me only moments before. The criticisms of the monks, the arrogance and deceit of the navy officers, made my choice clear: My fate with them could be much worse than what I had with Baranov, great ill to my child certain. I counted for little in this alien settlement; but I refused to be an accommodator, even though I was forced to put up with a life that was not of my own choosing.

The Great Country drew back its furies and demons. The skies cleared, the fog lifted. In the distance, we saw a ship easing into our bay; and an alien vessel dropped anchor. On board the Yankee *Enterprise*, over food and drink, Baranov bargained stacks of otter, seal, and fox furs for the ship's cargo of food, guns, and other provisions to meet his needs. So, backed by supplies, my captor once again proved that he alone could fill empty bellies. But in the piling of the cargo in the storehouses, he failed to notice that a few guns took flight for Yaghenen.

It was Talin's and the monks' gut bags, not Baranov's, that, punched full of holes, had dripped dry.

A banging on the door drew me from the table where I was talking with our cook, Richard hovering near as usual.

"Help us. Our children at Kiluden Bay starve." A Koniag woman fell into the kitchen, her bony hands outstretched toward me. The skin of her face and neck had scaled and dried almost like that of the grandfather in the kashim.

She need not tell me why the people of Kiluden Bay hungered. I knew. Aleksandr Baranov and his men just a few weeks before had again raided the villages, skimmed off the remaining able-bodied Koniags who had hidden from the other levies, and left the old and unfit behind to starve.

Many times I had listened in anger as the Tahtna and their trader-visitors scoffed at the Koniags and the Ulchenas for not storing food against the months of hunger. The Ulchenas and Kadyak Islanders had always walked a harsh route to survival. Then, the Tahtna with their pretended claims of *civilizing* us Aláyeksans had deepened the ruts of hunger by draining the villages of men at the seasons when they should have been hunting for their families. The thin threads of survival had been stretched to breaking; I knew when the Koniag woman said the children of Kiluden Bay starved, all the people of her village faced death. Always they gave their last food to the small ones.

"Give us food," the woman gasped.

A feeling of purpose stirred in me. The message of the qegh nutnughel'an still eluded me, but the Kiluden woman's presence brought to the surface the feeling of purpose I had known the day following my night on the snowfield.

Masking my anger at the brutal cause of her plight, I turned on Richard; with all the authority of Ashana, *princess* of this house, I surprised him with a command. "Go to the storehouse. Order the workers to sack up food for this woman's village. Share what we have, if only a little. Get it to Kiluden for her."

Richard scowled, "You know I cannot do that, Anna. Without orders from Baranov, no servant can take food from the storehouses."

"Do it now. The children starve," I ordered him.

"No, Anna. I will not." The use of "Anna," the tone of his voice, told me we did not talk as friends.

"Yes, Richard. You will go to the storehouse for food."

The Bengalese folded his arms across his chest, braced his feet, set his jaw. "You have no right to order me to do anything."

I was shocked. The trust Richard and I had woven between us through the seasons since he and Anakhta-yan had rescued me from Igor seemed to be tearing apart. I set a bowl of leftover salmon on the table, helped my visitor to the bench. "Here, eat this."

Her head barely above the food, she pawed the fish into her mouth with both hands. I raged at the cause of her suffering, scolded Richard and through him Baranov, his face merging into and out of that of his servant as I glared across the table. "You do not care that people starve . . . little ones . . . you get enough . . ."

Richard spat back. "I do care. But I told you Baranov has ordered no one to open our food supplies to outsiders. It is not for me to say."

"You Bengal devil! Kadyak Island people are *not* outsiders. This island is her home. Their men have been taken away. There is no one—"

"Sure they are gone. People go hungry. That is life in Aláyeksa." Richard continued to defy me. "We never have opened our food stores to them before."

"This time, Richard, a woman in my kitchen begs for food." I stabbed my finger at his chest, backed him against the wall. "I demand that her family be fed."

"You do not realize, Anna, if you feed this one, we will have endless streams of people coming here. Feed one, you feed them all. Yell if you want, I will not get food for them."

Richard had known hunger as a child; he had told me about his father trading him off for a bag of rice. After the fear and the meanness we had faced on Kadyak, he shocked me, for he knew that we Aláyeksans were stolen at gunpoint. Perhaps his attitude did differ from ours; perhaps he looked on this island and our people through eyes that saw us as Baranov did, though I failed to understand how he could. Richard might be Baranov's servant, yet he had become a friend to us; he had laughed and hurt with us; he had risked his life to save Attu from Igor. I had thought that Akoota's cowering obedience was peculiar to her;

but that day it showed in Richard, too. Even with starvation in this house, he denied the Koniag to accommodate his master. I saw only the servant Richard, the slave of Aleksandr Baranov.

Does captivity strip human beings of compassion for those less fortunate than themselves? Harden us to deny tragedies when they face us? I knew that hostages could seldom fend off the forces beating on them until they lost the will to survive, ceased the struggle to help each other, descended to the level of compliant and unresisting animal, stripped as they were of every shred of dignity.

"I will see about it myself. I should not have expected you to take any risk."

Having gulped down the salmon and seeming somewhat revived, the woman gathered the few remaining crumbs into a fold of her ragged shirt. My hand on her arm, we hurried through the door and along the path.

At the storehouse, I met surprise but no hesitation. The women working there helped me fill a large basket with dried fish, berries, and meat; and just because I asked, several hostages carried it to a umiak. A feeble wave of her hand and my visitor settled into the boat beside the basket, clutching it to her.

Before she reached my kitchen, the starving Koniag had already walked the length of Kadyak's rocky shore, climbed steep trails, pushed her way through brambles—a hard, long walk for a man in good health. Desperation had given her enough strength to walk to my door. I shuddered; had I listened to Richard, the woman—who could never have forced herself back up the slopes and over the rocks—would have died in my own kitchen.

Defiance?

I could do nothing else. I had made up my mind. Baranov boasted of me as Princess Anna, his head woman. I took my authority and used it for what I knew was right.

"I will not allow it!" Baranov had blustered when I had told him about my first niḷdulchinen. With our second child on the way, we argued less. I was more tired than I had been with the first one, did not have the energy to discuss a birthing house and stopped asking Baranov about it after he had ignored me three times. We had both lived on the edge of starvation that winter, and we dared not waste strength in bickering.

Long ago, on Yaghenen, Seltan had picked a perfect, egg-shaped stone out of his tangled fishing net and handed it to me. "A shesh, good medicine, for you, Ashana."

I still had the lucky stone, wrapped in soft skin in the bottom of my pouch of Yaghenen treasures. One day I took it out and licked it, rubbed it with a piece of soft deerskin. Its white face laced with gold streaks gleamed in my hand. My shesh had eaten the ptarmigan feathers I had fed it during the past year. Oh, I knew the soft down wore out, crumbled to dust, but I chose to believe what I was always told: To keep a shesh happy and lucky, feed it. So I did, wrapping it with soft white down plucked from a freshly caught ptarmigan. Well fed, my shesh would favor the new niłdulchinen with health and strength. Nothing on this island lived beyond the grasp of starvation, and the baby I carried needed as much good fortune as I could give it.

"Uncivilized superstition," Baranov chided me. But in his own way, he tried to ease the coming of the baby. He brought me a roll of nankeen cloth from the *Enterprise*. "I will teach you how to sew the garments, Princess Anna. Antipatr had only furs, but this child must start life wearing civilized clothes."

In the spring of 1802, I bore him a daughter in his Tahtna bed here on Kadyak Island. As he had chosen the name for our son, he chose the one for our girl. "Irina Aleksandrovna. A good Russian name. You might guess, Princess Anna, Aleksandrovna means daughter of Aleksandr."

From the first day the infant lay in my arms, I saw the face and eyes of my mother, the look and sounds of a tiny Yaghenen baby. So, for my far-distant mother, my baby's Kahtnuht'ana name would be Sem, star.

Following the birth of Sem, the village survived for a time on the cargo from the *Enterprise*; when those supplies drained to nothing, Pavlovsk faced starvation again. The hunts produced little. The garden patches sprouted and soured, and even the cabbage failed. The pigs and cattle the Tahtna tried to fatten for table fare shrank to skin and bones, easy prey for starving dogs and hungry bears.

Some seasons earlier, Baranov could have blamed misfortune on Talin and the monks, but during all his years of stripping Aláyeksa, he should have blamed himself. He did not listen to the forces around him (and if he had listened, he would not have believed). When the gentle sway of trees shifted to angry cracking and howling, the šdónályášna shook their fists in rage at him and his aliens because they had insulted the land and the seas of The Great Country.

Many forces of Alýeksa joined with the šdónályášna. I knew

the tsayan dnayi, rock people, battered the aliens and that the ey'utna, evil bogymen, took their measure of justice by tipping rocks onto the *promyshlenniki*. But the greatest anger of all was released when the ezhi'i dnayi, north wind people, and the nutin'at dnayi, sea people, joined forces; invading waves and demon winds swallowed hunters, drove animals to shelter, beat us all down to a desperate level. Baranov feared for survival on Kadyak—survival for his headquarters, his men, his family, himself.

It was a mystery to the aliens why a rock would suddenly fall on a Tahtna, why one hunter died, another disappeared. Those deaths Aleksandr Baranov tried to explain by Tahtna beliefs: "Scurvy. Not enough food. They weaken, stumble, bump their heads. Die of exposure."

But Aláyeksans knew.

Late one evening, Attu and Baranov and I sat talking as the ezhi'i dnayi pounded our cabin, pushing through every crack to force their way inside. The nutin'at dnayi drove the surf in mountainous waves against the headlands. No ships could reach us; the storehouses stood nearly bare. Baranov's heavy woolen clothes were worn to shreds; he was forced to wear the caribou-hide trousers and jacket of Aláyeksa. We allowed the fire to burn low, held back logs to conserve wood. In the dull glow, in our Aláyeksan garments we three looked much alike. A stranger could not have told Tahtna from Aláyeksan.

Attu reminded us of the times of hunger at home on his Ulchena island: "The old died first. They starved so there would be enough to keep the young ones fed in the bad days." Neither Baranov nor I said a word, our thoughts on our two children asleep in the next room, worried about their fate. "Remember," Attu continued, "we uncles and aunts will save your children. We may starve, but we will give our food to keep Denedi Belik'a and Sem alive."

That night Aleksandr Andreevich Baranov did not chide either Attu or me for not using the Tahtna names for his son and daughter. He knew that in the time of hunger, in the presence of death, the lives of our two little ones would depend on the strength of Aláyeksan uncles and aunts.

A whistling sounded in Baranov's fireplace. "A whistling sound in the fire pit, a good omen," my father always said. On Kadyak, we had need of a good omen; and it came from Anahkta-yan.

After Anahkta-yan had gone, Aleksandr grasped my hand.

"Do not worry, Ashana. For you and the children, the last crust of bread. As for me, I'll boil the old tea leaves again."

His eyes, his voice, his touch, spoke tenderness, and my tired feelings lifted a little at his caring.

Daq'u. Let it be.

"Attu, I cannot hold off any longer," Baranov said to his interpreter a week later. A new respect was in his voice, for he could not so soon forget Attu's promise for the children the night we three had talked. "It is only a couple of months till the end of the year. We cannot live without supplies. Head two baidarkas to Unalaska. You take one, and I will put Max Solnikov in the other. I have written a message to Larionov. You know he's the company man there. I have not heard from him in months; maybe all of them have starved. We'd better find out if one of our ships has left supplies for us."

Attu returned hungry, bringing only messages and a letter. "Larionov believes we have lost the *Phoenix.* His men found boxes and kegs and papers. A lot of wreckage has floated in that he says could only have come from our ship."

"Do not tell me, Attu. Not my *Phoenix.* The men. Supplies. All at the bottom of the sea." Baranov groaned.

Then, when Attu told him that Archimandrite Ioasaf had gone down with the ship, Baranov slumped onto his seat by the table, his head bowed. "We lived in disagreement, Ioasaf and me. But I would not have him end that way. He was a man of the church." Baranov's eyes fixed on me. "The Archimandrite never came to terms with Aláyeksa." For a moment, I thought Aleksandr Baranov might have come to grips with the Russian error in my country, but he continued simple-mindedly, "He never understood what I try to do here."

He read and reread the long letter from Larionov, parts of it aloud.

". . . As it happened I sent out one ship, waited vainly for the other to come and am sitting here now without having any ships at all. We have only three bags of provisions left for all of us. . . .

"Among other things you are writing to send you tea, sugar, and also vodka. I would be sincerely happy to ship these to you, but believe it or not, I forget how the tea tastes.

I am without tea since the New Year and am drinking used, old tea leaves boiled over again. . . .''

A Tahtna without his tea hungers like a dog without his bone.

"Sometimes, I think it is just that I am too old to get along with the likes of Talin. But Larionov sees the navy men the same as I do. Pesky. Meddling bastards. Arrogant. Listen to this, Richard:

". . . God punished you and me with these government employees. I have also troubles with the one that is here. They always put first what they call their honor and make us responsible for everything because we are traders. Often he threatens me and my partners with the Emperor, and there is nothing I can do about that. My lot is to endure, because this is my state and position in society . . .''

For a couple of moments, Baranov ran his fingers over the sheets, clicked his tongue against his teeth. He read again:

". . . You write that your government employees and 'holy' monks stick their noses in business matters that do not belong to their duties and are the cause of troubles among the Islanders and Russians. That does not surprise me. The management and promotion of trade for the benefit and glory of the Fatherland is entrusted here by the government and by men in charge of Company's affairs to managers and not to these people. Now you must insist upon that more than ever.''

"From what I saw on Unalaska, Talin would fit in with Larionov's troublemakers," Attu threw in.

"Ship Talin over there today." Richard laughed.

"No. Larionov sounds too decent. I will not push that navy *svoloch'* off onto him," Baranov said. "The authorities back home should never have sent those young whelps to us. We will have to work out our own problems. Remember the old saying— *God is too high and the Tzar is too far.*''

"Another piece of news, Aleksandr," Attu said, finishing his report. "The company has sent a new man to work for you— Ivan Banner. He would not ride our umiaks in the storms, so he is sitting on Unalaska waiting for a bigger boat and better seas.''

With a break in the heavy seas and battering winds, two umiaks with caribou meat from Yaghenen paddled into our harbor. The next day the smell of a beached whale drew men to the spot downshore; the owner of the first spear hurled into it out at sea was entitled to the whale. The man was notified, and quickly blubber and strips of meat lay ready to be divided among all in the village. Once again, starvation lost its sharp edge.

After the seas had settled, three large umiaks from Unalaska brought Ivan Banner and a few men to Pavlovsk. With his possessions came two weather-soaked kegs of vodka; and as men gathered to hear what news the boats brought, raucous toasts echoed through the Kadyak night.

"It is my duty to inform everyone that all Aláyeksa belongs to a new and great enterprise, the Russian-American Company. We hold this charter signed by Tzar Paul back in 1799. Before I left Siberia, the great new Tzar Aleksandr confirmed it, and he directed Nikolai Rezanov to send it to you." Ivan Banner handed the charter to Baranov with the words, "Long life to Tzar Aleksandr!"

As the men raised mugs to their Tzar, I watched Baranov's face and remembered his words: "I will have one company, Anna. Until then, I will hold Aláyeksa together with my hands. Bluff and wait."

Chik'dghesh. Chik'dghesh.

Banner jumped onto a bench and motioned for quiet. "I toast another great Russian. The man who has brought this rich land into the empire of Russia. Aleksandr Andreevich Baranov. Our great Tzar has named Baranov the colonial governor over all the territory from Yakutat to Kamchatka."

Roars filled the room: "Governor Baranov! Governor Baranov!"

The newcomer had difficulty making himself heard as he stamped his boot on the bench. "Silence! Silence! I have more."

Some moments passed before the men finished their toasts and quieted.

"Step up here on the bench with me, Governor Baranov."

Eager hands hoisted the new colonial governor up beside Ivan Banner.

"And, now, the special honor. Tzar Aleksandr has decreed for you, Governor Aleksandr Andreevich Baranov, the Cross of St. Vladimir. Your reward, Rezanov reported to me, from Mother Russia for your loyal service through hardship and want."

As Ivan Banner slipped the ribbon over Baranov's head, the

gold medal set with a jewel sparkled against the worn brown jacket. Mugs of vodka swung high in salute to Baranov's honors. Unable to speak, tears rolled down Aleksandr's face when his *promyshlenniki* began singing the song he had written to commemorate gaining his foothold on Sitka Sound at Fort Saint Mikailovsk, and I caught the words: "wild tribes tamed . . ." These drunken, raucous aliens! Who are the *wild tribes* needing to be *tamed*?

Baranov's song finally ended, and the noise of stamping feet shook the cabin walls. My head pounded; above the din rose my babies' screams of fright as Watnaw held Sem and I clutched Denedi Belik'a to me. Whatever the word "governor" meant, whatever honor the gold piece shining on Baranov's chest held, his children were unimpressed. We tried to lull them to sleep, but each time one of them quieted a new toast to Aleksandr Baranov boomed out, to be answered by a chorus of voices.

When the last man had staggered out of our house, a red-eyed, flushed governor of Aláyeksa grabbed his Antipatr from me, danced around, tossed his son high in the air. As happened so often when he talked to Antipatr, I knew his words were directed at me. His eyes glittered; his voice mixed disbelief and pride, sometimes his words came out slurred and garbled, sometimes they rang loud and clear. ". . . All companies in Aláyeksa are one. . . . All under your papa. . . . The great Tzar made your papa the colonial governor of Aláyeksa. . . . The Tzar sent me this!" He took Antipatr's tiny fist and clamped it around the new medal. "Feel it, my son! The Cross of St. Vladimir! . . ."

Chik'dghesh. Chik'dghesh. Chik'dghesh.

After the children had finally quieted and dropped back to sleep, Aleksandr turned from gazing into the embers in the fireplace and slipped the ribbon holding the Cross of St. Vladimir over his head. As he caressed the gold medal, his eyes burned with a smoky glow I had never seen before; I sensed he was trapped by the honor the Tzar had draped over his shoulders. Fascinated by the object he held in his hand, my captor stroked metal and ribbon and laid them on the table, murmuring, "A beginning . . . nobleman's rights . . . rank . . . mine." Then he grabbed my shoulders with clammy hands. "Princess Anna . . . you, the governor's woman. Mother of the governor's children." He stumbled over the words, his voice a jumble of drunken, fevered emotions.

Clumsily, Baranov took me twice, muttering before sinking

into unconsciousness, "Princess Anna, you will see why you . . . important to me. . . . Antipatr and Irina . . . live noble . . . when I take my children home . . . to Russia."

Voices sounded out of my past. Echoes of Attu's voice the first day I had stood in this house, a scared and shivering captive. "Aleksandr Baranov has need of your rank. You will see." Later, a few days before Denedi Belik'a was born, Akoota had raged at me. "Remember, he will claim his child." And once long ago, Aleksandr had looked deeply into my eyes. ". . . Love. . . ."

When could I run with my little ones to Yaghenen? Would Baranov's power ever be broken now that he had received new authority and honors?

I soon had reason to forget pity for myself. One day, I noticed a commotion at the shacks. Watnaw broke away from the group. "Ashana, I need to talk to you."

I put my arm around her as we turned away from the buildings, walked out of the village and down the beach in the twilight.

"Akoota will not . . ." Watnaw's voice faded as her eyes avoided mine.

"What about Akoota? She came to the house yesterday."

"She is dead, Ashana."

Slivers of ice jabbed through me.

"One of the *promyshlenniki*?"

Watnaw held back a moment; tears streamed down her face. "We have all been hard on Akoota. I despised her for giving in to the Tahtna the way she did. For teaching young ones to give in. And I let her know . . . we all did. Even yesterday I sneered at her."

"I was hard on her, too, Watnaw. I resented her, snarled at her every time she came. Accused her of betraying Jabila. Oh, Watnaw, how did it happen?"

"Attu found her awhile ago. Behind the shacks." She stopped, wiped the tears from her face. "For several days we had been making blubber balls with poison for the fox hunts. We did not intend them for people."

"She did not . . . ?" I could not finish my thought.

"I do not know how many she ate, but Attu found a half-eaten one in her hand. She had vomited all over herself. She must have suffered terrible agony. Just before she died, she whispered to Attu, 'I can't stand any more . . . I don't want to live.' "

Akoota had crossed the line beyond hope.

The thought flashed through my mind: I am free of Akoota's dinning, free of her pecking. But I swallowed my mean feeling. Who knows the battering that drove her to do what she was forced to do on Kadyak? She made no friends, knew we despised her. She spoke only to beat into us alien words she must not have believed herself. Always alone, she could walk no further.

Shaking, Watnaw and I sat on the beach; our tears poured out for a life wasted, one we did not understand, a woman we despised. In the fading light, the tide drew away, flowed back again, lapped our feet. The drizzle fell unnoticed. Regret and sorrow filled me. Why did I not have the wisdom to talk through Akoota's torment? Reach into her depths and understand her? For a long time, we stayed silent.

"Ekdu. Watnaw, I wish we were back to our ancient beginnings," I finally broke in. "I would change myself into a raven and fly home. I would show my village the good side of chulyin, and banish all the evil, the monks, and the aliens."

"I would be a sea gull. I am always hungry, and they know how to fish. They survive best." As we turned back toward the houses, Watnaw took my hand. "You belong to the raven clan, but you are hummingbird. You could fly back to your flowers on Yaghenen."

"Yes, and no one can ever hold a hummingbird in his hand."

"Akoota. What was she?"

"I don't know. Perhaps a sparrow." Icy shivers again crawled up the skin of my back, and I shook myself.

"What is it, Ashana?" Watnaw put her arm around me.

"Listen. I hear the qunuje*l*en, the dead who cry from the grave."

Later that day, all Aleksandr Baranov could say to me about his lost, dependable informer, was "Poison plant. Dangerous. I will teach the islanders a better way to trap fox."

Before dark, I watched the men carry Akoota's body to the hole dug for it in the Russian way. Dressed in her patched parka, her death-face as grim as her life-face had been, she seemed no farther away than when she had stood shouting beside me in Baranov's house. As we hostages stood beside the grave, my head rang with the keening of the mother and family mourning the boy's murder the day on Yaghenen when Baranov had claimed me. Akoota left no family to grieve for her. The thought of her suicide, my own meanness to her, a longing to escape this prison island, left me crying too much to sing; and as we do at a mourning, I began to talk a song of death for Akoota. I kept my voice low, and all of us—Lingen-Aka, Watnaw, K'atl', then Sutina, Atoon, many voices—joined together, wrapping Akoota with our sorrow, regrets, guilt.

Our song faded, and Watnaw began a story. "Long ago, the raven creator set about making human beings. He wanted them to live until the end of time. He carved and carved and carved from rocks, but he could not shape human beings. He rested, then tried again. His tool broke. Then, he gathered leaves together and created people from them. He showed a leaf to the human beings and said, 'See this leaf. You are like it. When it falls from the branch, there is nothing left. And that is why all the clans of the world know death. If people had come from rock, there would be no death. You are unfortunate. You are not made from rock. Leaves you are, so you must die.' "

We placed Akoota in the grave. Dirt and stones closed her forever from our sight.

A crumpled leaf had fallen.

❂ ❂ ❂
19

Usually Watnaw carried herself with solid, watchful dignity, but one day she came to the house breathless, and asked, "Is Richard out there?" Watnaw pointed to the kitchen.

"No. He has gone to the storehouse." I looked at her a moment. "What is it, Watnaw?"

"Remember the eight-foot Gulushutna fighters Richard shivered about?"

"Yes. And I remember Baranov said he feared them."

"They have taken back the land Skaoutlelt sold."

"What!" I stood up so quickly I almost dropped Sem.

"Kotlean planned, just like I said he would. My people listened. They waited. Baranov's men got careless. Medvednikov sent most of the aliens out to hunt furs. It was a warm June day, and the rest just lazed around." Watnaw's eyes narrowed, and her voice hardened as she settled herself on the bench beside me. "One by one, so not to stir suspicion, my Gulushutna sisters left the fort. The few Tahtna men and their Ulchena women inside the stockade lay in the sun, played and giggled with little ones too small to walk.

"Then, my brothers struck. Skaoutlelt knew he had done wrong in trading Sitka land to Baranov, and the old fellow joined Kotlean's attack. The Tahtna were no match. My Gulushutna had plenty of English and Yankee guns. Our fighters burned that alien place to the ground."

"Burned Fort Saint Mikhailovsk?"

"Yes, Ashana. Our fighters topped sticks with pitch and lighted them. Threw them over the walls. The attack did not last long. Our men got inside the fort. Shot all the Tahtna. Took some Ulchena women captive."

Ulchena women long held captives by the Tahtna, then captured by the Gulushutna. Would it never end?

Watnaw stared eastward toward Sitka Island; her thoughts, I knew, reached out to her blood-soaked homeland.

"Your people have done it, Watnaw. Sitka is free. We need a potlatch." I grabbed Watnaw, and we swung around the room in an Aláyeksan mockery of the Tahtna *prisiadka*, half squatting, kicking out first one leg, then the other, jumping, shouting as we circled. Then, Watnaw hanging onto Denedi Belik'a's hands, me holding Sem, we danced another round, fast, faster.

A big step in Aláyeksa's journey home! Our talk was mingled with laughter, and every hostage on Kadyak walked straighter, proud of the freedom of some of our people.

In the storehouse, counting puffin skins, I marked the sheets for the men who had brought the birds in, then slipped home with my qenich'eni covering a gun and hid it under the floor.

Early the next morning, alone and looking toward the north, I sent my message on the wind: Men of Yaghenen, strike!

His Fort Saint Mikhailovsk burned, his dreams smoking ruins, the colonial governor huddled with Ivan Kuskov one evening in the main room of the house, questioning a couple of badly shaken survivors: Maximilien Solnikov and Vassili Tarakanov. Solnikov had escaped and hidden, but Tarakanov had been seized and put to work cleaning fish, then was forced to watch the torture of Russian captives. Tarakanov himself had been rescued only because an English ship's captain in the waters had outwitted the Gulushutna fighters. That night the laughter of our children went unheard. Baranov's honors seemed crumbled to dust, and my captor struggled to keep himself from again sinking deep into the bog.

He downed a big mug of vodka and asked, "Vassili, what happened on Sitka Island?"

As if not wanting to remember, Tarakanov sat grim-faced, shaking his head. Solnikov answered for him, looking Baranov straight in the eyes. "Some of us more experienced hunters tried to warn your man Medvednikov, but he said enough time had gone by that he believed the Kolosh were peaceful. For weeks before the attack, he talked only of the fur hunting, how many pelts he would have in the storehouse before heavy weather set in." Solnikov hesitated a moment. "I remember telling him the woods were so quiet it made me nervous. The day it happened

I was upriver tending traps. My woman Atoon and several others had been sent out to clean skins.''

It seemed only a short time ago that I had watched Atoon stand with Solnikov on one of the marrying days. Hearing the men, I could not hold back my fears; and I called on someone I had not thought of the past season: Naq'eltani, have you allowed Atoon to be killed?

I broke into the men's talk. "Atoon—Where—Did she come back with you?''

"Yes. We were two of the lucky ones. We got away alive.'' Solnikov's words faded to whispers. "We hid in a cave, survived on a few berries. She is here with me.''

"Sit down, Anna. I must hear about my men.'' The flash of Baranov's eyes drove me to one side.

Tarakanov took over, told of the attack as he saw it. "My boats were about to close in on a small herd of sea lions when Erlevski and Kochessov came racing down the slope, yelling 'The Kolosh! The fort's burning!' To the south we saw smoke streaking the sky. We headed back to help, but a line of Kolosh canoes cut us off. We beached. Kochessov and I ran for the woods. You would not believe, but huge masked men ran us down.'' He stood up abruptly, turning to the window, seeing again the Tahtna defeat. "They tied us together and threw us into one of their war boats. The next morning they herded us into a pen with other captives. They had Erlevski in there, too.''

For some moments Tarakanov was unable to finish his tale. He seemed to still see the war armor and masks, the eight-foot fighters Watnaw had described. I was thankful Attu had not been sent with the war fleet to Sitka, but had been with Baranov on one of the Ulchena Islands.

"I thought they were going to attack me, but they dragged Erlevski into the middle of the clearing. Then the torture began, Aleksandr.'' Tarakanov gulped half a mug of vodka to deaden the pain of his memory. "A masked Kolosh with a shiny new Yankee hunting knife peeled the skin off Erlevski's knees, all the way down to his feet. The sun burned into the raw flesh.'' Another slug of vodka, two more. "Thank God, he passed out. The pain was terrible. He hung on the post unconscious till he bled to death. And then another masked heathen cut Erlevski's head off and stuck it on a pole.''

"Not only that, Aleksandr.'' Solnikov picked up when Tarakanov could not go on. "We watched them scrape off men's fingernails—Kochessov's and two others. Scrape a while, then stop. Haw-haw at the screams. Scrape until the blood seeped through. Over on one side, they held down three or four of our hunters, stabbed them with sharp sticks, drawing blood. All those savages laughed like fiends. When a man became unconscious, they flung cold water at him to revive him . . . tied several to posts . . . held a contest shooting arrows into the center of their eyes.'' Solnikov clamped his hands tightly on the sides of the bench, threw his head back a moment. ''I cannot tell you the screams, the agony, the horrible deaths.'' He paused. ''I am only alive to tell you because the Englishman Barber made a deal with the savages, bartered for my life.''

Baranov, head down, said nothing.

''Long ago, Aleksandr, I saw the Aleut youngsters brought to St. Petersburg. I admired their Aláyeksan artifacts, their native dress—fascinating. And I wanted to come to Aláyeksa. Then here in Pavlovsk, I talked to Watnaw and other Kolosh, learned more about their masks and painted carvings. So different, the Kolosh artistry, from anything I knew. In those days, it interested me far more than the furs. I planned to collect as much as I could and sell it in Russia.'' Solnikov stopped again. ''But I have seen too much of their torture. I have lost all interest in collecting any Kolosh stuff. Wouldn't go near them to trade. Too dangerous.''

Ah, the burning, the killing, the torture. But what drove the Gulushutna to such measures? If the Tahtna had stayed in Russia, none of the bloody deeds would have happened.

''So, the Tzar made me colonial governor! So, the Tzar gave me authority over all Aláyeksa! So, the Tzar blessed me with the Cross of St. Vladimir!'' Baranov pounded the table. ''But he failed me. He did not send enough guns and men and ships to defend Sitka.''

The light from the candlefish lamp seemed to multiply the wrinkles in the governor's aging face. The furrows in his forehead deepened. His eyes were hooded. His nose sagged over his upper lip. In the weeks that followed, he brooded over his loss, walked the paths of Pavlovsk leaning on his cane, his bald head dripping with rain, unmindful that from behind their masks hostage Aláyeksans dared dream of freedom.

''I know the Kolosh got their guns from the English and the Yankees. Damn their hides. They never lost a fortune in furs like I did.''

Many times, Baranov spilled out to me parts of his past, a

past that had cut him so deeply he could never forget it. As a young man Baranov vowed he would become a wealthy fur trader; with his brother Pyotr, he roamed the Chukchi region of northeastern Siberia for three seasons. Severe winter storms lashed them and their hired Chukchi hunters, but the brothers garnered a fortune in pelts. They had traded guns to native men who killed many more animals than they could have done with arrows and spears. Then, as the heavily laden Baranov caravan headed from the Siberian wilderness south and west toward Irkutsk, the Chukchis turned on the Baranovs and took all the furs. The guns traded to the natives cost Baranov his fortune in furs and almost his life. "The Chukchis taught me: Never trade guns to savages. I have always held to that."

Long after Baranov's snores throbbed in my ears, a storm raged inside me. We Kahtnuht'ana had surrendered to Tahtna guns. The Gulushutna did not. Why? The reason lay beside me. Aleksandr Baranov bargained with my people for furs and meat and hunters, but refused to give them guns.

I wished that my people on Yaghenen could be Aláyeksan Chukchis like the Gulushutna. A familiar thought took hold of me once again: Oh, for the power to become a raven, to fly home, bring guns, show my village the good side of chulyin. Our Yaghenen hunters would become Aláyeksan Chukchis, and the raven would lead my people to freedom.

○ ○ ○
20

From the time they could walk, my Denedi Belik'a and Sem—half Kahtnuht'ana, half Tahtna—played and tussled outdoors with the other small niłdulchinen when the warm weather came. I watched them as they romped; as with children everywhere, the difference in speech, in appearance, in clothing did not seem to inhibit them. The young devised a common language, understood one another much more readily than we adults, whose different tongues were blurred with an overlay of Tahtna, English, German, and smatterings of Richard's Bengal speech.

Since the birth of my children, their impish grins, their hands reaching toward us had drawn out the gentle side of a father who could squander the lives of hundreds of men without another thought. I never forgot the afternoon a few months after Irina's birth, when her frightened screams echoed through the house. Aleksandr and I rushed to the room where she slept to find four-year-old Antipatr leaning over his sister, pummeling her with his little fists.

"Stop it!" I grabbed him. "Why are you hitting her?"

"You told me she would play with me." He tried to break from my grasp. "But all she does is sleep or cry."

Aleksandr had picked up his daughter, rocked her in his arms to quiet her. "Son, you will have to wait till she grows bigger. Once you were little like her. You could not play then, either."

Antipatr had slipped from my hands, stood facing us, eyes blazing. With Irina cradled in one arm, Aleksandr took her brother with the other hand, led him to a bench, "Antipatr, you must be gentle with Irina. She is very tiny yet, and cannot stand you being rough with her." His fingers played with Irina's curly black hair. "Only brutes hurt those who cannot defend themselves. Antipatr, I will not have my son being a brute."

He pulled his hand away from Irina's hair with a grimace. "What is this grease you have put on my child's head, Anna?"

Ever since her birth, I had tried to smooth out my little Irina's curly hair, the same color but finer than my own. I wanted to be able to braid the strands once they grew long enough, so I rubbed her hair with bear grease, but always the curls defied me. "I am only trying to straighten her hair. I need to braid it."

Aleksandr laughed at me, rubbed his bald head; the fringe over his forehead made it resemble a mountain capped with a shiny glacier. "You did not know me when I was young, Princess Anna, but I had wavy hair, too. And my brother Pyotr's grew curly just like Irina's. It is in the Baranov blood."

Antipatr defied us, arms folded, feet apart, jaw set. A little Aleksandr Baranov.

His father could not hold back a gusty laugh. "There is a lot of Baranov in these two." He nodded in satisfaction, pride in his voice. "Plenty of Baranov."

I reached for more bear grease, for only with a great deal of brushing and smoothing would our little girl's hair yield to braiding.

"Ashana, you can't make a savage out of our child . . . greasing her hair to make it straight! The Baranov hair curls, and you won't change it."

"I cannot braid twisting hair. I need it straight, or the braids will not hang right."

Suddenly, Aleksandr and I burst out laughing. Little Sem rolled away from us, her eyes questioning; no doubt she was wondering what spirit had handed us to her for parents. And Aleksandr's arm around me felt warm.

But those gentle times in our home were few.

Smoldering like the fiery timbers of his lost outpost, blazing up at the slightest breath of wind, the indignity over the defeat at Mikhailovsk bedeviled my captor day and night, breeding drinking bouts that grew longer, harder. His language became offensive, his treatment of my body harsh. Without warning, while the children slept and the servants were gone from the house, he would burst into our room, strip and force me; sometimes I cried out, but in his besotted state he little knew or cared who I was. I believed that in some way he sought revenge on me for the Gulushutna uprising. Sore and bruised for days afterward, my only relief came when duties called him from Kadyak. At times like that, I pleaded to my joncha, "Help me escape from this place." I allowed myself to drift back to the days when

Jabila and Seltan had fished in the mountain streams. On Yagh-enen, I ran free.

During the time Aleksandr Baranov was gone from Kadyak to fill umiaks with stacks of furs and to levy men for fighting his way back onto Sitka Island, the children, removed from his oppressive Tahtna influence, drew closer to me. It was a time when Kahtnuht'ana legends and beliefs came alive through me, brushing Denedi Belik'a and Sem with nanutset, our early history, to breathe into them the spirit of my Athabaskan ancestors. Free to do as we pleased, I bundled up my two children and we climbed the slopes above the village. Here, seated on the headlands, I felt free to weave for them the same strands of lach'u and nanutset, truth and history, that my mother had woven for me.

One day, as we stood beside fish-drying racks full of salmon, I told my children the origin of our salmon ceremony, a lach'u my children must know, as salmon has always been one of Aláyeksa's most important foods.

In the long-ago ancient times, a very rich leader had a daughter. He told her not to walk near his fish trap. She had a mind of her own. When her father refused to tell her what was in the trap, she did not obey. At the fish trap, she saw a king salmon. She talked with him. Time passed. The talk kept on. Little by little, the girl changed into a fish. She swam away with the salmon. The rich leader searched and searched for his daughter. He never found her.

The seasons made their cycles. Ts'iluq'a, spring salmon run, filled the streams again. The rich father took many fish from his trap. Most of them he tossed on the grass. He cleaned them, packed up all the cleaned fish. He stood up to go. He saw that he had forgotten one little fish. He went to pick up the one left behind. To his surprise, there was no little king salmon on the spot. Instead, a small boy sat in the grass where the man had seen the fish. He watched. He saw in this child a likeness to his lost daughter. He walked around the boy three times. He knew this was his grandson. The rich man talked to the child. The boy told him everything that needed to be done if the people wanted to keep enough salmon for them to stave off hunger. He told how to fix sticks into racks for drying salmon. He warned that to keep the salmon from falling off the drying poles they must pour fresh water over them.

So the little boy told the very rich man about the salmon

*ceremony. He said it should be held every year to pay respect
to the salmon. He warned that if such things were not done, he
would never return with the salmon.*

"Did the grandfather ever see him again, Mama?" Denedi
Belik'a asked.

"Yes, he always came back. My village celebrated every
year."

Sem snuggled close to me, "Tell it again, Mama."

So, standing there, one arm around Sem, one hand on the
fish rack, my eyes sometimes on my boy sitting in the grass, I
told the story again, slowly, making certain my two would know
how to care for the salmon and never go hungry.

Throughout the seasons of my captivity on Kadyak, some days
spent painting on the caribou hide, some days walking by the
streams and shores of this island, I felt the strength of my family
reaching out to me from Yaghenen. My body stayed strong from
climbing the rocky trails, the hands of the wind sometimes pulling me on, sometimes pushing me back.

More than once, I remember, Watnaw told me, "Ashana,
you look as young as you did your first season here. How is
that?"

And many times Baranov would eye me closely across the
table. "You do not age, Princess Anna. Your hair shines. You
stand straight. Your eyes flash—more when you fight me than
any other time," he would say, laughing. Then, serious again,
"I mean it. Your eyes flash like they did that first day I saw you
in your village. Your skin stays clear and fresh. Other women
look dumpy. Pocked. Wrinkled. How do you do it?"

I did not answer his question, but fixed my eyes on his bald
head. Age was closing in on him.

And Watnaw worried me when she put herself down. "My
hair seems dull. My braids have been brittle for a long time.
You always keep your hair so beautiful, Ashana."

To my friends, I said, "I have indeed aged. It may not show
on the outside, but I feel it on the inside."

Lingen-Aka sensed more clearly than Watnaw what it was
that kept me from falling apart. "You stay young-looking, Ashana, because you have Jabila. It is a matter of love and hope.
Without them, anyone withers, loses the life spirit."

"Yes, Lingen-Aka, I have Jabila's love, and it pulls me
through the bad times. You have Anakhta-yan's love; that gives
you hope—like a lamp shedding light in the night."

Sewing puffin skins was not to my liking, so I asked for help when the children needed clothes. Atoon had learned on her Uℓchena island how to cut and stitch together the fine downy undersides of the birds; she made each of my children puffin-skin garments, and I can still hear Baranov storming at me the day he saw them.

"I will not allow my children to look like a pair of damned idiot birds. Hell! They will *not* wear puffin skins!"

Atoon took one look at our captor's angry face and fled.

My mosquito mask, unused for some time, settled over my face. "What would you have them wear, Aleksandr Baranov? You said Aláyeksans could never wear fine furs or deerskin. You said they had to wear puffin skins. You ordered it."

"Not *my* children, Anna. You have the white cloth I gave you before Irina was born. Use that."

"It was sewn up long ago. To wrap Irina the civilized way, as you said."

He muttered to himself, went to the back room, returned with a deerskin and an armful of fur. "Here. Make some decent clothes for them."

I stung back, "A decent fur for an Aláyeksan? Stealing from your company? Never! Puffin skins are what you ordered many times. Only puffins for Aláyeksans." I knew what would sting the most. "Better clothes for our son? Never! Mothers of other niℓdulchinen will hate Antipatr and Irina."

"Silence, woman!" He yelled at me. "Do not call my children *niℓdulchinen!*"

"Niℓdulchinen. That is what they are. Mixed blood."

"Sew up the deerskin and the fur. Today!" Baranov threw the pieces on the floor.

"I have told you, the other children will pick on Antipatr and Irina if they have better clothes."

"Everyone must learn that these are the governor's children, that they are of a higher rank." Baranov stared hard at me. "Don't you understand, Anna? You are of royal blood, a princess. Act like one."

I dared not push my captor further.

So it was that I worked those first pieces of deerskin clothing my children were to wear, lost in the remembered dream of how my mother used to sew with me, aching with unshed tears for a mother so far away, so unknowing of her grandchildren. But it was sheer joy to slice the soft pelts with the ulu, to pierce the tiny holes with my awl, to thread the sinew cords and seam the pieces together. I took pleasure, too, in cutting the hide into narrow strips for the fringes that adorn some of the Athabaskan garments—beautiful as well as useful. They help the water to run off in the times of heavy rain, and the fluttering strands around the neck keep the mosquitoes from pestering.

When Baranov was at the house, the children sat on his lap or tagged along after him wherever he went, wearing their fine, fur-trimmed deerskins. But when he was out of sight, off the island, I changed them back into the puffin-skin garments, and the mothers of the other ni*dulchinen understood.

As Denedi Belik'a grew, his body stretched upward. Even though it seemed he would be taller than Baranov in a few years, tall as I was tall, his body carried more than a trace of alien stockiness. "Baranov blood," his father bragged.

Sem looked pure Kahtnuht'ana—her flashing black eyes, the color of her skin, the way she moved her small, quick feet. But when her father bounced her on his lap, he would croon, "Curly hair. Bright eyes. You will be a fine Russian lady, my little one."

The ni*dulchinen of Pavlovsk needed a friendly hand, a voice softer than the strident tones of parents with few moments to father and mother them, parents whose time at home was taken up by babies in arms and toddlers, the only ones who escaped the toil of the camp.

Some days, after the ni*dulchinen finished the work set for them, I would gather several and find a grassy spot. From the ragged circle of children, eyes would follow me, seeming to plead in silence; I sensed wariness and fear, for they knew nothing of a human's kindly attention. This alien settlement, a place of hard labor from light till dark, was no home for little ones. I tried to breathe into each one the first beginnings of the spirit of our people.

Other days, I took them high on the headlands, told them to lean their ears against the rocks. All nature spoke; the farther we wandered from the alien village the louder its voices. Some of the waifs heard, some did not. I knew from past walks and from my storytelling that the closer they could be to nature, the better chance they would have of hearing her many voices. Because most of the ni*dulchinen were not Kahtnuht'ana, I drew legends and truths from all across Aláyeksa. Their questions, the quick smiles, the way they opened themselves up to me when we walked a distance from the village, let me know they passed on to me their trust, a precious strand threading through their sere existence on this island.

One day Lingen-Aka brought some dried grasses along with her, and while the boys played, she showed the girls how to weave one of the small U*I*chena baskets, splitting the reeds with her newly healed fingernail. At home with their clans before the Tahtna came, each girl would have grown up weaving in the tradition of her mother; here they watched a young woman from faraway Attu Island weave her basket in the way her mother had taught her, the work so fine one could barely trace the intertwining of the different reeds.

On Yaghenen, we believe that all nature has a life and speaks to us if we take time to hear.

"Listen to the grass. Put your ear down to it." I knelt on the grass, showed the children how. "What do you hear?"

A small girl looked up at me, pleasure in her eyes. "The grass sang to me. Running water."

Another whispered, "Spring wind."

A third, a thin little boy, hair so matted it looked like a cap of rags, face spotted with dried snot and mud, put his ear to the tip of a blade of grass, listened.

All of us watched him.

"I hear it." He pushed against the stem, held up his finger. "Sssh!" A broad grin crept across his face as he sat back. "It said, 'Run. Be happy. You will eat tonight.' "

Like the early spring blossoms of Yaghenen, my two children grew and flowered; their laughter rang through every room of the house. Denedi Belik'a was growing up, had learned to be patient with Sem, taught her to walk. Her giggles when she pulled from him and fell to the floor were music to me. They reminded me of the long-ago days when Seltan and I had played on the floor of a distant house. I would take my small ones onto my lap and tell of those days. Sem, learning her first words, never tired of hearing about our shaman dolls.

"If either Seltan or I lay sick"—my children's eyes sparkled the minute they knew I was talking about the k'enin'a dolls; neither of them seemed to breathe during the telling—"the shaman would darken our room, then dance to our bed jingling his rattles and holding against his chest a doll for each of us. On his long sleeves and on his cape, he wore shells and bones and claws and bright stones. They made a lot of noise as he danced fast, fast, faster, so fast you could not see him! All at once, he stopped. Pushed the dolls hard against our chests. And they disappeared!''

"How, Mama? Where?'' my son asked, round eyes shining.

"I do not know, Denedi Belik'a. The shaman said they went inside us.''

"Oooooh.'' Sem's whisper was filled with wonder.

"The next night, the shaman came back. He danced first one way, then the other, singing and jingling, dancing faster than the first night, so fast he looked like one big blur of feathers and furs. Then, *woosh!* He reached down, pushed his hands hard on our chest, yanked them away quickly. And when he stood up, he had a doll in each hand. Seltan and I felt better right away, because the dolls took away our sickness.''

Denedi Belik'a grasped my hand, turned his face up to mine. "Where did the shaman keep his dolls?'' Always the practical one, my little boy's curiosity dug for facts.

"In his pouch or high up on a peg out of reach of prying fingers.'' I patted his small hand.

"What did they look like, Mama?'' Sem asked.

It had been a long time since I had seen the shaman's k'enin'a, but their images tumbled through my mind. Dolls with carved faces, the faces of my Kahtnuht'ana people. There were k'enin'a with straight hair, others with braids, but none bald like Baranov. Some had jade labrets in their lips like the one K'i'un had worn. They had dresses of deer or squirrel skins, jingling chains of dentalium shells and copper, and on a few the gleaming gold metal the Tahtna loved. Many of the girl dolls had tiny chains hanging from their earlobes. Boy dolls wore embroidered belts and bands, carried quivers filled with arrows. Some boy dolls would be seated in the birch-bark canoes of the Athabaskans, others in the skin kayaks like the Ulchena ones, for we Kahtnuht'ana had lived by the sea so long we had absorbed and mixed the crafts and skills of Anakhta-yan's people with those we inherited from our own ancient ones. Always, the dolls wore small moccasins or footed leggings of white deerskins embroidered in the Athabaskan style.

Hugging my two close, I was filled with dreams of the warmth and happiness in my parents' home.

"Each doll had a joncha all its own. My brother and I knew the dolls jumped down from their shelf and danced at night.''

"How did you know?'' Denedi Belik'a asked.

I paused a moment, thought back to those nights when Seltan and I would lie awake. "It is hard to put into words, but we knew they were there in the dark. I think they heard a music we could not hear. Sometimes, if we woke up in the middle of the night and were very quiet, we could hear them singing.''

''You could?'' Sem's eyes glowed.

''Seltan and I tried very hard to stay awake till they danced close to us, and we could watch them. We were sure we saw them. Then, early in the morning, before first light, the dolls danced back to the shaman's japoon, hopped into his pouch, and stayed quiet when grown people woke up and walked around the house.''

''Can we see them, Mama?'' Denedi Belika's eyes searched mine.

''Someday, son. Someday, I hope to take you home—''

My children slid off my lap; holding hands, they danced around the room as wildly as ever did any shaman's k'enin'a, then sat giggling at each other on the Kadyak bear rug by our fireplace.

I had not been aware that Richard paid any attention when I told my Kahtnuht'ana stories to my children, but, that day, when Sem and Denedi Belik'a laughed and rolled on the floor, I realized he stood in the door watching. His arms shielded something from me.

''May I, Ashana?''

A few weeks after we had quarreled about giving the Koniag woman food, Richard had apologized; we began rebuilding trust between us. The day of my storytelling, he held out two small objects: dolls carved from driftwood, hair and eyes painted on, fine-stitched clothes made in a style that mingled Bengal and Aláyeksa.

Denedi Belik'a rushed to Richard. ''Are you a shaman?''

Richard laughed. ''No, Antipatr, I am no shaman. I made these dolls for you and your sister to remember me by.''

''What do you mean, Richard? Are you going away?''

''Yes, Qanilch'ey Ashana. The governor has promised that he will buy my passage on the next ship sailing to India. He will let me go free. I need to go home to Bengal''—a rueful smile escaped him—''and see if my rice patch is growing.''

Pensive, Richard watched the children a few moments, giving me time to recover from the shock of his words, for he had not mentioned his need to return home for many months. Sitting on the floor in front of us, Denedi Belik'a tried to explain the dolls to his sister, who cuddled one and cooed to it in a language only a doll could understand.

"Are you parents still living, Richard?" It was a stupid question. How could he know?

"I am not sure. I have not been to Bengal for so long I can hardly remember anyone." He did not take his eyes off the children and sat down beside them. "I hope I will have a few years to spend at home."

To hide my tears, I walked to the window and gazed toward the harbor. Richard and I had flown at each other in anger, defied each other; yet, that day, he brought gifts I would never forget, and tears came at the news of his leaving. Directly in front of me on the path I saw the monks plodding one behind the other through the mud, holding their skirts above their ankles as if not to soil them with the slush of Aláyeksa. Richard (called "heathen" by the men of the church), with his toys that delighted my children, had done more for Denedi Belik'a and Sem than those black-frocked, flint-faced monks who professed the *civilized* Tahtna religion. I shivered, mindful of the three who played on my living-room floor, thinking back to the time when Denedi Belik'a was but a baby and they branded him "child of sin." All of them had railed against Baranov, accused him of endless sinning, yet their hands always grabbed his offerings. Father Emelian was missing from the procession that day, for at long last a ship had finally taken him to Siberia—"for his health" his brother monks said; but I will never forget the real reason for his banishment.

Neither could I forget that the enmity of the monks had been directed against me since the day they set foot on Kadyak. They had come to Aláyeksa to save its people, for they saw us as "heathen." They accused me of standing in their way, demanding that I be an example to other "heathen." The greatest insult to me lay in their condemning my bride-price marriage. Insulting, too, was their blaming my presence in this house as being somehow my own fault. They insisted I was a symbol of the savagery of all Aláyeksa.

The pleas of Sem and Denedi Belik'a, "Story, Richard, story," brought me back to the present. Richard hugged the children close, set them in front of him, each one holding a doll.

"I have time. I will tell you a story about monkeys back in Bengal. I saw monkeys every day when I was your age, and—"

Denedi Belik'a interrupted, "Monkeys? What's monkeys?"

"Sssh. Do not interrupt, and I will tell you." He smiled at

me as I slipped into my room, leaving the door open so that I could hear his voice as I worked on my basket weaving.

"Monkeys are small brown animals with long tails. They hang by their tails from branches of trees. They have bright eyes and people sort of faces. They chatter a lot. They are covered with short fur, not soft and thick like your animals in Aláyeksa."

Through my door I saw Sem cuddling her doll, her eyes never leaving Richard's face. Denedi Belik'a was stretched out on the bear rug, his chin propped on his hand.

"In my home in Bengal grow huge trees. Wide trees with many branches like long, long arms or legs. Banyan trees we call them. You do not have any in Aláyeksa. The little brown monkeys live in the branches. They jump from branch to branch and from tree to tree all day long. And like I said, they hang by their tails. They chatter so loud it sounds like many people talking, everyone at the same time.

"One day a peddler came by the banyan tree. A peddler is a man who carries a pack and sells the things he has in it. The peddler was so tired he fell asleep in the shade of the big banyan tree. His pack was full of red caps, and he wore one so people could see what he had to sell. He snored so loudly the monkeys stopped chattering and listened to him. Many people had slept under their tree, but never a man with a red cap who made small thunder.

"One monkey said to another, 'Who is the strange man down there in the shade of our tree?'

" 'I do not know,' said the leader of the monkeys.

"One braver than the others jumped down, pulled the pack open. All the red caps fell out. He snatched one, put it on his head, and raced back up the tree. The other monkeys chattered at the one with the cap. Then they swung down from the branches by their tails. They all jumped to the ground. Each one grabbed a red cap and stuck it on his head. Then they ran up into the tree again. The branches of the banyan shook with all of them jumping up and down and back and forth. The monkeys chattered so loud they woke the peddler.

"He rubbed his eyes and looked up. At first, he could not understand what he saw—monkeys with red caps! Then, he reached for his pack to start his peddling. The pack was empty.

"He shook his fist at the monkeys. 'Bring back my red caps, you thieves.'

"They hung on the limbs, chattered back at the man standing

down below on the ground. It seemed to the peddler that the monkeys were laughing at him. 'Give them back! Give them back!' he screamed.

"The monkeys just kept on chattering. They hopped about and swung by their tails from the branches. The peddler kept screaming at them. Finally, he got so mad he jerked off his own cap and threw it down on the ground. When the monkeys saw him, they stopped chattering. Then they jerked off the red caps on their heads and threw them down.

"The peddler was so surprised he could not believe what he saw. Every one of his red caps flying down from high among the branches of the banyan tree. And as you can guess, Denedi Belik'a and Sem, the peddler did not stay around. He grabbed his caps and stuck them back into his pack. Then he ran on his way. The monkeys soon forgot about the peddler with his red caps.''

Several mornings later, on the table by each child's bowl rested a small red skullcap. Richard had cut them from the old Bengal cloth I had seen covering his pile of furs all the time he had been with us. The sewing must have taken several nights. Denedi Belik'a and Sem rushed into the kitchen to find Richard, the caps pulled tight on their heads. There was no keeping them on the floor. They perched on top of the table, climbed onto benches to swing from clothes pegs on the wall, all the while chattering in Kahtnuht'ana-Bengal monkey talk.

◉ ◉ ◉

21

"I will return to Sitka."

"Attack Sitka, Aleksandr? Another big fight? We are not ready." Kuskov had argued for months against Baranov's plan.

"It would be insane to attack the Kolosh before the company sends us more men and cannon from Russia." Banner's arguments were the same as Kuskov's. "You cannot do it without a ship with guns big enough to knock their fort to the ground."

"Nonsense. I have levied Aláyeksans, and I will levy more till I get all the men I need," Baranov had countered, his words backed by his authority. He was *governor of Aláyeksa*.

For months the planning, the arguing, the talk had gone back and forth across our table, the hour always late before Baranov settled beside me for the night. The need to build a kremlin for Russia in Aláyeksa consumed most of his energy for many seasons. Then one morning he told us what he had decided. "Enough talk. We will make do with what we have." His command cut off open opposition, whatever Kuskov and Banner might continue to say between themselves.

During these days, it was only his two small ones who could pull Aleksandr Baranov away from his work, from envisioning his new kremlin. He would snatch a few moments to tell a story, give a kiss, bend over his children before they fell asleep, then go back to his planning.

One night he lifted Antipatr from his sleeping furs. His roars brought me running to the door. "Anna! These damn things on Antipatr's fingers! What have you—" Roughly, he pulled off five tiny finger masks that K'atl' had carved for our son, her own idea of how she thought the súslíga, the spirit-of-the-barking-dog, must look.

"My mother made me masks like these. My first masks. We

232

used them for dancing,'' K'atl' had said. ''I made these for Denedi Belik'a so he could learn what they mean. When he is bigger, I will carve him a raven.''

Together, K'atl' and I had taught Denedi Belik'a how to slip the little masks onto the fingers of his right hand, how to control them. He had run around the room, laughing and barking ''Wa?-wa?-wa?,'' for he understood the lach'u of the spirit-of-the-barking-dog. ''You can't see them, Mama. They're running ahead of me. Down the trail. I hear them. Wa?-wa?-wa?'' A moment of fun, an easy story for my son to grasp, and he loved the masks—as did every child who owned them, for they were light and easy to move. In his imagination, Denedi Belik'a believed he was that spirit running ahead of men on the trail, leaving no track, barking all the way, just as the fathers of Yaghenen came home and told their children about the súslíga they had heard but not seen.

''Savage superstition. Damn foolishness.'' His father held Antipatr close to his chest, my son's sleepy-eyed head over his shoulder. ''What the hell are these things?''

Old Half-Man Mask slipped over my face, and his caution and wisdom spoke to me: *Qanilch'ey Ashana, do not challenge your captor. Remember, use your divided mind.* With each word, I could almost hear Old Half-Man tapping his foot on the high mountain of Yaghenen, where he still lives. *Tell your captor only what you want him to know.*

''Playthings,'' I replied.

''They look like some of your savage stuff to me. No one will teach my children heathen superstitions. I forbid it.''

I stood there, and, dividing my mind, I knew how to meet his ''I forbid it.'' Over the seasons I had come to understand the power and wisdom behind my Old Half-Man mask: Useless to argue with Baranov—let him think he is having his way, but make certain the children are taught Kahtnuht'ana wisdom.

''I told you long before the children were born that you must put away your uncivilized notions. There must be no more of this!'' He shook a súslíga mask in my face. ''Stop! Now! I order you. Disobey me, and I will take the children away.'' There were glaciers in his voice.

Baranov flung the little masks into the fire. Antipatr stuffed his fingers into his mouth, tears streamed down his face as he ran from the room.

''See how your foolishness upsets my son.'' My captor twisted the blame for our child's tears onto me. The life of the nǐʎdul-chinen of Kadyak was twisted indeed.

Aleksandr Baranov completed his plans to grab a new site in Gulushutna country. My heart was saddened by the hundreds of men he levied for the fight on Sitka Sound. There would be more killings and yet another rape of Aláyeksa's land and people and sea. I knew all the old scenes would be repeated yet again in Gulushutna country: hunters seized for a fight they did not want, families torn apart, wives and daughters snared and used by aliens.

Watnaw grieved, doubting that her people would survive, even doubting that they had enough guns to beat back the aliens. Anakhta-yan foresaw a future filled with cruelty for the Gulu-shutna clans, cruelty inflicted by the same father who had told his small son, "Only brutes hurt those who cannot defend them-selves. I will not have my son being a brute."

The village of Pavlovsk never fulfilled the governor's dream of a grand Russian capital. Apart from its size, it was no better than any of his other hunting artels that dotted the coves and bays and were vital to his fur gathering. Its sagging shacks and buildings were a sordid and somewhat embarrassing array, not worthy of Baranov, the Tzar's Imperial builder.

"The time has come to move on Sitka. We will make do with what we have. I will drive the savages off that high promontory and build a fort we can defend, or I will die in the attempt. I know I can depend on you two when I have to pull things to-gether," Baranov complimented Banner and Kuskov.

A _promyshlennik_ thumped onto the porch and in through the door. "A Yankee ship is coming."

"A ship?" Three voices sounded as one.

Baranov and Kuskov rushed out, Banner followed, and kay-aks paddled them to the _O'Cain_, which was dropping anchor in Pavlovsk harbor. Far into the night, Baranov and his clerk stud-ied the _O'Cain_'s supply lists. The ship carried everything he needed for his fight against the Gulushutna—food, cannon, cloth, knives, guns.

"I do not know how you can pay his price. Thousands of Yankee dollars? We do not have enough furs," Kuskov pro-tested.

"Sitka will give us the best otter ranges; we _have_ to move in. Joe O'Cain is here. I will find a way to get our provisions."

Baranov sat back, never happier than when he was putting a deal together. "You've had a good many long days, Ivan. Go to bed, get a few hour's sleep. We have a lot ahead of us tomorrow."

Puffing on his pipe, a new vigor in his step because a supply-laden ship rode in his harbor, Baranov paced the room, the only sounds the crackle of logs in the fireplace, the moan of the wind, the steady thump of his boots. He paid no attention to me as I stood at the window and watched the moon floating red in a sullen sky.

What hour he came to our bed, I do not know; the next morning he left for the *O'Cain* before I awakened. He did not come back for several days. I knew from Baranov's talk to me about his trading business that his bargaining with the Yankee trader would end only when the governor gained his way.

Finally, he strode into the house. A happy, vodka-soaked Aleksandr Baranov swung the children around. "I got the ship-load of supplies. Cannon, too. Nothing can stop me now, Princess Anna. I will blow those Kolosh off my land."

"Where did you find enough furs to trade O'Cain?" I avoided talk of the killing to come.

"Didn't need them. Old Joe hung tough. And Jonathan Winship, his first mate, argued right along with him. Smart for a twenty-year-old Yankee. Joe is partners with the Winships, traders from around Boston. They have been in the China trade so long Jonathan cut his teeth on it."

"But how did you get O'Cain's supplies without furs?"

"Simple, Anna. I knew the first day what those traders wanted: furs to sell in Canton. So I pushed the talk around to our being partners in otter hunting. Rented them a crew of my Aleut hunters. Made the Yankees promise to pay each Aleut a stipend for his furs—no slave dealings for me. We will share the take. Fifty-fifty. If they come back with a profitable load, I might do it again. Let them take the risks for a change."

As he sat here on Kadyak working over figures and plans, the flickering light from the fireplace wove patterns on the walls. Settled cross-legged on a small bearskin, my hands busy with sewing, watching Baranov, I struggled to restrain myself from flying at him for his gross act: *renting* the children of his land.

Children! I almost panicked at the thought that young niĬ-dulchinen would make up part of the crew the Yankee would take far south to kill otter. My son was of mixed blood. Would the day come when his father would rent him to an alien for profit? And Sem? What of her? Another mixed blood to serve in the shacks?

His deal agreed on, Baranov sent umiaks to bring in the ablebodied hunters; O'Cain and Winship sailed from Pavlovsk with their rented human beings, heading south for a season's catch of sea otter.

Months later, one day in March, the alien O'Cain anchored in our bay, his ship stuffed with furs.

"Profitable for all of us." Baranov chuckled as he penned notes for the report he would send to his company office in Russia, telling of the supplies he had *earned* from Joe O'Cain.

Dividing the stacks of heavy pelts, with no talk of rewarding the Aláyeksan hunters, posing terms for a future venture, Governor Baranov and the traders fell into days of drinking and toasting.

A short time before the *O'Cain* would put to sea, Attu and Richard stood on our porch. "Will you be leaving with Captain O'Cain?" Attu asked.

Richard glanced away. "No, I will not."

"Baranov promised you some time ago, and I thought you might go home first chance."

"I want to be sure I get back to my family. I saw things I did not like sailing with Moore—O'Cain was his first mate then. Boston men bringing slaves from Africa." Anger and a questioning fear seemed to trouble Richard. "I will not go on a Yankee ship. I do not want to be traded off as a slave again."

With the cargo of the Yankee trader now his, and cannon from the *O'Cain* bolted to the decks of the *Catherine* and the *Alexander*, the colonial governor ripped his final levies from across The Great Country, pulling into camp the many hundreds of men he would lead to Sitka Sound and the attack on the Gulushutna clans.

Another event seemed to signal that fate again favored Aleksandr Baranov. A few days before embarking on the *Catherine*, he came to me with a stiff parchment bearing the gold seal of Tzar Aleksandr of Russia. "This paper, Princess Anna, raises me to the rank of collegiate councilor. A very high rank in my country's civil service. I am now the equal of an abbot in the Russian church. A colonel in the military service. Now, Antipatr and Irina have the rank they deserve." His excitement boiled over as he shared his pride with me. "Yes, I have rank equal to that of captain-lieutenant in the Tzar's navy. I have waited so long for recognition. Never imagined how great I would feel.''

In an instant, his face saddened. "If only my father could have known.''

More honors, more power. Baranov does not need me. I remember saying to myself, Why doesn't he let me go home?

In the bundle of papers with the Tzar's parchment came a letter addressed to "His Excellency, Collegiate Councilor, Governor Aleksandr Baranov. . . .'' He read that Captain Urey Lisianskii in command of the *Neva* would soon put in at Pavlovsk to pick up furs for the China trade.

"Damnation!'' he snarled as the meaning of the next lines hit. "How could my company do it? Sending Nikolai Rezanov. He will be here before I can build my capital. The man knows nothing but marble palaces. Beautiful rugs. The finest of foods. And what can I offer? The poorest quarters. Little food. No silver on the table.'' He stared at the letter. "Sending Nikolai Rezanov to inspect this colony!''

I had heard Banner and Baranov talk of that alien, a man of higher standing than either of them.

"Princess Anna, Nikolai Rezanov owns an interest in my company. He is a director, a man who helps manage its affairs. I have told you he had a great deal to do with getting us the only trading rights in Aláyeksa.

"He is a smart man, and he enjoys great respect at the Imperial Court. The letter says he is a high chamberlain now, the highest rank for anyone outside the Tzar's own family. The nobles held a feast celebrating his new rank and his appointment as leader of the first Russian voyage around the world. When he comes, you will understand what I mean when I say we Russians will civilize your people. Rezanov is bringing fine paintings and rare books. Scientific works and drawings of ships. Everything for a school that will teach the children of Aláyeksa.'' Baranov's fingers traced the lines on the page in front of him. He said to me, "Nikolai Rezanov has done more than anyone else in St. Petersburg to make the Russian-American Company a great trading company.''

Rezanov? Another chik'dghesh?

Before Baranov boarded the *Catherine* and headed his fleet of over three hundred kayaks and umiaks toward Sitka Sound, he gave instructions to Ivan Banner. The most important: "When Captain Urey Lisianskii comes with the *Neva*, send him to me

at once at Sitka. I need his cannon. And Nikolai Rezanov—
when he comes, treat him well.''

Antipatr must have felt an echo of Kadyak's grief, for as his
father gave his daughter and son a last hug before leaving to
board the *Catherine*, he dropped something into his father's
hand.

Aleksandr looked at the object, turned it over. An egg-shaped
lucky stone wrapped in ptarmigan down, tied up in a gray mouse
skin I had helped him find.

''A good medicine, Papa. To bring you back to us safe.''

Aleksandr gripped the stone, glaring at me, anger flashing in
his blue eyes. He started to speak, clamped his mouth shut, then
spat out, unable to contain himself, ''I ordered you: Do not
teach my child stupid superstitions. I forbid it. Stop!''

I had heard those words before. My captor had roared them
at me when he had torn the tiny súslíga masks from our son's
fingers.

''Papa,'' Antipatr insisted. ''A shesh for you. I made it.''

His knuckles tensed around the gift, Aleksandr stuffed it into
his pocket, grabbed his son, picked up Irina under one arm, and
left the house. I could hear anger in his every step. But men
were waiting for his order to put to sea, and he had no time to
counter the lach'u I was teaching my children.

I followed them to the harbor, where the three of us watched
Governor Aleksandr Baranov's sails until they disappeared in
the distance.

''Keep Papa safe.'' Antipatr sent his wish across the water to
his little shesh.

Messages passed swiftly across Aláyeksa. In ways never understood by the Tahtna, words flew between clans many yił
apart as if on eagle wings. We on Kadyak always learned what
went on all across The Great Country. But words did not ride
the eagle wings from Sitka Sound; they were borne by a few
Ułchena who had slipped away from Baranov's camp.

One of the men came to the house, and both Watnaw and I
asked, ''How did Kotlean do it?'' As the tragedy was unfolded,
I better understood what my father had gone through on Yaghenen.

''Kotlean and Baranov bargained for the high promontory by
the sea, and Kotlean accused the governor of many things:

''You talk of protecting Aláyeksans? You hold free peoples

captive. You speak of civilized life? You rape our women and steal our young. You want to trade with us? You steal our furs.''

Kotlean charged that the alien taking of land on Sitka was stealing, but Chik'dghesh Baranov argued that he had *bought* the land.

Kotlean scorned the alien leader. ''You know you gave us nothing. Just junk and worthless old brass.''

Backed by his huge fleet—hundreds of boats and levied Aláyeksans—Baranov figured he could end the bargaining and begin an attack whenever it suited his purpose.

So, in between talks with Kotlean, the governor set scores of his men to gathering a rich harvest of sea otter.

''Theft,'' the Sitkan charged, his words becoming sharper.

''There is plenty of space for all of us.'' Baranov shifted his stand.

''We want no Russians on Sitka.'' Kotlean's stubbornness matched Baranov's.

''I must tell you, Kotlean, the Tzar of Imperial Russia has granted me authority over all Aláyeksa. The Tzar will protect your people, and he requires—''

Protection? My Kahtnuht'ana had certainly learned how great the ''protection'' of the Tahtna was.

''Your Tzar may praise you, but he knows nothing about us. As for you, Aleksandr Baranov, you are a common thief.''

The messenger laughed as he described to Watnaw and me the governor's struggle to control himself, his angry face turning from red to purple as Kotlean pressed the charges.

''My men have watched you. You burn our homes. But first you steal our headdresses, our masks, our clothing—''

''I have given you good value for everything.''

''Good value? You even looted the ancient copper shields that our men traded for in the far-distant past—treasures beyond price from the clans of the Copper River far north of here.''

I knew the alien robberies enraged Kotlean and his people, most of all the theft of those ancient shields. Some of them hung in the Pavlovsk storehouse, and Watnaw and I had admired them many times. She told me the Sitkans had given twenty or thirty sea-otter skins for each one. ''Our artists cut these lines into the copper. They are symbols of my people. Baranov should not have taken the shields.''

The parley closed late in September. I doubted my captor would ever forget Kotlean's sarcastic remarks: ''What of the sacred dolls used in the shaman's dance? Of no use to you, but still you could not help stealing them.''

Talk had become a broken spear.

The red moon hung in the sky over Sitka Island, a sign of war to my people, the k'eghun nu, known from ancient times.

The bargaining a failure, Baranov's waiting fighters—Tahtna with hundreds of levied Aláyeksans—began firing on the Sitkan fort. The powerful cannon of Lisianskii's *Neva* backed the men fighting with small guns. The Ulchena told Watnaw and me that Kotlean put on his warrior outfit, topped by his fiercesome black-bear mask, and led the eight-foot fighters. Her people fought bravely to hold their high promontory, drove many of the attackers into the woods, even shot Baranov in the arm. ''And you should know, Ashana, Kahtnuht'ana men fought with them. That's why some of us Ulchena rowed away: We did not want to shoot other Aláyeksans just to help the Russians.''

But the Sitkans could not evade the *Neva*'s cannon or the invading forces. The walls of their fort were knocked down and the aliens set everything on fire.

''Watnaw, your people had to flee into the woods,'' the Ulchena told us, describing the end of the fight. It was the children who suffered the most from that fight on Sitka Island. When the battle ended, many of them lay dead inside the fort. And to this day, men differ as to what truly happened. Tahtna claim the Sitkans killed their own children and dogs so that the men and women could flee silently, safe and unburdened. Gulushutna claim that the Tahtna guns murdered their children before they could escape with them. Whatever the facts, I could not help but wish our Aláyeksan peoples were as immovable as the high mountains that frowned on the aliens wherever they set foot in The Great Country. But none of us were.

Watnaw's agony over Sitka poured out in a flood of tears, and the loss she suffered released my own grief. Faces blackened, we mourned together as sisters over our lost people.

Captain Lisianskii returned to Kadyak for the winter and set about making repairs on the *Neva*. He needed an interpreter, so Baranov *loaned* him Attu. And Anakhta-yan took as much interest as Lisianskii in hearing the story told by a Tahtna *promyshlennik* from an outlying artel, interpreting between the hunter and the captain as he asked questions about an event the hunter had seen a few years back: the creation of an island. He had been with Ulchenas on a fishing trip when they saw a great smoke rising up out of the sea. For nearly a year they had watched the smoke, until suddenly a blaze had burst above the water. A few weeks later an island lay on the surface of the sea, where none had been before. Violent eruptions continued for a long time, finally slackening till there were only occasional wisps of smoke to be seen. The captain was an observant man, who spent much of his time drawing pictures and making notes about what he had seen and heard. "I read years ago about the process he describes—it is a volcano. But I have never talked to anyone who actually saw such a thing happen," Lisianskii wrote in his journal.

I captured the story on the inside border of my caribou-hide painting, drawing in part of what my own grandfather had told me of new lands he had watched rise to the surface of the sea with much smoking and a hail of rocks. Anakhta-yan helped me with some of the details.

In June, Captain Lisianskii and his men boarded the *Neva* and sailed out of Pavlovsk harbor on the long voyage that would take him home to Russia. Banner sent with him boxes containing reports and messages to be handed to Baranov on Sitka Sound. Those Tahtna left behind and hostage men and women watched as the ship passed the fort, receiving a salute of cannon as the custom of the aliens required whenever their ships arrived or departed.

The *Neva* carried away from Aláyeksa the work of our clans: our finest clothing of white deerskin, cut and embroidered in the Athabaskan style . . . Ulchena gutskin capes . . . salmon-skin boots . . . Chilkat blankets . . . sacred dolls and rattles . . . the masks that were the many faces of Aláyeksa: the eagle, bear, whale . . . goat-horn spoons and ivory carvings—and a raven-headed speaker's staff.

Gifts, the Tahtna claimed, from the Aláyeksans.

Stolen, we knew.

Anakhta-yan and I sat on a bluff above the harbor watching the ship being loaded. "All those things will be nothing more than curiosities in Russia. The aliens won't wear them, won't use them," he said.

"Have some." I handed him pieces of smoked salmon. I wondered if he would say anything about the years he had lived captive in Russia. I waited, then decided to coax him a bit. "Tell me, what will they do with all of our things?"

"Paw them over. Stare at them. Laugh about what strange creatures we are. Every piece will go into a case or on a shelf. Likely soon forgotten about. And they will never understand us." He shook his head, "Ashana, did I ever tell you about the time I gave away one of Aláyeksa's finest pieces?"

"I don't think so." I handed him more salmon.

"Well, you know Baranov sends Aláyeksan boys to Irkutsk in Siberia. They have to learn Russian so they can be interpreters for the company. Shelekhov started it. I was taken there to learn it, too, then they took us to St. Petersburg to show Tzarina Catherine *her new children.*"

Sadness crossed his face briefly. "The thing that hurt the most was the Ulchena hunter's hat the men made me give the Tzarina. The finest I had ever seen. Stolen, I knew. The owner must have been a daring hunter—daring until a Russian murdered him for his hat.

"The Russians made me put it on. I felt like a traitor, walking in front of the court wearing a man's treasure, something to which I had no right. I was stolen from my home on Attu when I was only eleven, so I was still not old enough to be a good hunter.

" 'Welcome to St. Petersburg, my children.' The Tzarina's voice was strong, used to commanding people.

" 'Thank you, Your Imperial Majesty.' I had been told to address her with those special words. Then I bowed low, looking straight at her feet, which peeked from under the sable robe she wore over her dress to keep her warm. The dress, I remember, was blue velvet trimmed with sparkling jewels.

" 'Your Russian pleases me. I, too, come from another country, from Germany. I know how hard you have worked to speak so well,' she said, 'I treasure your gift, and it will please me to hear about it.'

"I hated telling the alien ruler about the hat, but the Shelekhov men were listening and they had threatened to hurt me if I did not tell the story as they had instructed.

" 'This piece of carved driftwood is a hunting hat, worn by the greatest hunter of our clan. He has caught at least thirty-seven sea lions. I know this because the hat has thirty-seven sea-lion whiskers attached to the back, one for each catch. The man spent a lot of time polishing the driftwood, bending it to fit his head. He wears it to shield him from the sun out on the sea. These inset pieces of ivory—'

" 'Where do you find ivory?' the Tzarina asked.

" 'Our hunters take ivory from walrus tusks, Your Imperial Majesty.'

" 'And I see that the driftwood is fastened in the back. How was it bent so?'

" 'Your Imperial Majesty, the driftwood has been steamed and then bent into shape and tied with sinew from the legs of deer.'

" 'Oh, deer live on your islands?'

" 'No, Your Imperial Majesty. We trade with Kahtnuht'ana of Yaghenen for the sinew we use in our sewing.'

" 'Ah, yes, trade.' She nodded, smiled, handed the hat to one of the men close by, and dismissed me. 'Now I will hear from the man who speaks for Gregorii Shelekhov. I understand Mr. Shelekhov has sent me a petition about trade. I must give my attention to him, for trade is important to Russia.'

"One of the court attendants called out in a loud voice, 'Mikhail Matvyevich Buldakov.' The words seemed to come from high in his mouth. I remembered to step back as I had been told."

Anakhta-yan shook his head at me. "Ashana, we Ulchena children stood in the Russian court that day, and none of us could believe the words we heard roll out of Buldakov's mouth—big talk about all the Aláyeksans Shelekhov had captured to be new children for the Tzarina. He said schools had been built, but you know there aren't any. Then, he told about our fine furs and the *great civilization* the Shelekhov company had brought to Aláyeksa. As you have said, Ashana, when the fire creatures sit on your back and pound, a lot of hot air comes out of your mouth.

"Ashana, you cannot believe the huge palaces in St. Petersburg—marble that looked like ivory. Winter there is blistering cold, with freezing winds off the Neva River. Artists painted the inside walls of the Tzarina's palace the colors of flowers—pink, yellow, blue, and leafy spring green—to make the Tzarina think of warm seasons. The palace had one thousand rooms, each of them bigger than our greatest Ulchena leader's whole house. It seemed to me that buildings were built inside other buildings so no cold winter air could freeze the people who lived there."

Anakhta-yan's friendly smile spread wider. "I must tell you about Tzarina Catherine. You can never imagine who she reminded me of. My little grandmother! My grandmother had black eyes; Catherine's were blue, more blue than Baranov's. The Tzarina sat high on a platform in a golden chair with a tall carved back. All around her stood her people, men and women in clothes trimmed in fur and gold and shining stones. She wore a tall crown and the candles in the room made it sparkle. Then, the court's high chamberlain, who wore a dark-red velvet suit covered with what I was told were diamonds, ordered us to kneel to the Tzarina. She called the man Count Orlov.''

I burst out laughing, reached up, and shook Anakta-yan by the shoulder. I knew about Orlov. ''Remember the night you and Richard saved me from Igor? He bellowed at me, 'I'm Tzarina Catherine's lover. I'm Count Orlov. Haa . . . Haa . . . Yaaah!' ''

⊛ ⊛ ⊛
22

It was the time of low tide. A leader's daughter had married a man. Soon, he wanted other wives. He put his wife out on a big rock. There he left her. The tide came up. It reached her feet. She sang a song, low and sorrowful. She pulled her legs up under her. The tide came higher. Soon, it reached her knees. She sang another song. The tide rose higher and higher. The water came up to her waist. She sang another song. The water reached her chest. The tide still rose. The water got to her mouth. Then, she sang the last and saddest song. She sank into the water and became a sea otter.

As often in the past, I heard my father's voice telling the story; but this one I could never understand.

Jabila—always I held him high in my heart. Then, why the doubts that plagued me that summer, why the questions that I saved to ask him when he came? Loneliness is as deadly as the poison plant, it can sicken the heart; Baranov's long absence at Sitka would have been the perfect time for Jabila to visit me, and when he did not come I let many doubts cloud my thinking.

Why had the elders of Yaghenen decided to stay and bargain with the aliens that long-ago day? Why hadn't they fled into the mountains in the far north? Why hadn't they fought to the death? Although I knew it was the power of the guns that had driven them to their choice, deep despair made me ask those questions over and over. My life was wasted. Anguish lived with me.

It was in that miserable state that Jabila found me.

"We came late last night, my men and I. We brought a large boatload of meat. I waited. Too many people around all day." He seemed to notice nothing of my misery as he swung Sem high in his arms. "I see no trace of Tahtna blood in this child, except maybe her curly hair.'' Jabila laughed at Sem's face smiling down to him.

"She could be ours, dear one. She looks pure Kahtnuht'ana.'' I spoke in our own language, quickly so that Denedi Belik'a would not catch what we said and pass it on to his father.

"Does Governor Baranov think so?''

"No. He sees her only with Russian eyes.''

I longed to hold Jabila close; but with Baranov's son there in the room with us I dared not. It was still daylight and anyone could peer through our window. Ivan Banner's sharp eyes missed nothing. I covered the window with my caribou hide, but we still sat far back in the room, out of sight.

"I must leave early tomorrow, Ashana. We waited in the mountains till Captain Lisianskii sailed. I hoped Banner would go with him, but he did not, so I came anyway.''

"Jabila, I heard you were on Kadyak, and I worried. You took a great risk. What if a *promyshlennik* had recognized you?''

"The times between seeing you are too long, Ashana. I had to come.''

That night I wanted only to sit quietly by Jabila's side, but I was restless. Through all the seasons of his coming to Kadyak, I had never felt the strength to confront my husband with the questions that cut my heart: Where did our leaders get their power and authority over our clans? The men, like my father, made the decisions that controlled our lives. They organized and sent our parties of men to hunt or to fight. The women gathered berries and trapped squirrels. Men chose the sites for our villages and camps. They trained the boys who would one day become leaders. The girls learned to sew. Our men gave the orders: All that our people did for a single day or for an entire season lived and died with our men. Men alone sat in village councils, keeping all authority to themselves.

Why did we women let them?

Neither my mother nor any of Ni'i's other wives had dared question his order that day, the order that sent me down Tikahtnu to Kadyak as hostage to Aleksandr Baranov. Before the aliens came to our village, my parents had agreed that Jabila take me as his chosen one; his family had wealth enough so that he need not work for a year to pay a bride-price for me; his gifts to my parents were sufficient to make his claim. I could never accept my father's failure to honor the pledge between Jabila and him, a violation of Kahtnuht'ana traditions as ancient as our clans are ancient. Nothing could change the fact that Jabila had been my husband since the day he gave his bride-price and we had joined our lives. Why didn't Jabila fight harder for me?

We women were mere objects—property—owned and traded or bartered by men as they trade or barter a stack of pelts. From Baranov's talk, the faraway alien peoples tied their clans together by marriages ordered for their children, often before the small ones could stumble about on their own feet, bartering them in trade as Tzarina Catherine had been bartered to be bride for the Russian Tzar Peter, who hated her and whom she could never love. The greed for power dictates the action.

I keep asking myself: Do leaders of all clans across the world barter young women without regard for the fact that each one of us is a human being, has a mind capable of choices?

I know that a woman's lot depends on the whim of the men before whom chance may throw her. Women live trapped in coils they can never shake off. That lach'u spread heartache through me. We Kahtnuht'ana women may pride ourselves that rights to property pass through our mothers, but those rights deal only with *things*, the objects one generation inherits from another.

As I mulled over all this, I finally understood the last part of the sea-otter story: *And then one day the sea otter saw her husband's boat skimming over the water. She swam after it a long way. The man did not know it was his wife. Finally, when the time was right, the sea otter dived. She swam very fast, right underneath his boat. She reached up. She took a bite out of the skin of the boat. She took another bite, then another and another. All day she nipped little bites until the water began to fill the boat. It started to sink. Soon, her husband drowned. That made them even.*

Careful, Ashana, my joncha whispered. *You have no wish to sink Jabila.* No, I would not, I whispered back.

We needed to keep a good feeling between us, so at first all I said was, "Jabila, I know our people on Yaghenen, the clans of my mother, do fight back. You have told me of Tahtna hunting parties that disappeared. I hear of others, like the one the Tahtna lost on Yaghenen after the monks accosted me." I paused, sensing that my husband could see into my mind.

Jabila simply smiled down at Sem, who was tugging at the fringes of his sleeves, her tiny face tilted up to his. Denedi Belik'a watched them as he pulled his toy across the floor; and I knew that soon Jabila and I would not be able to meet at night, not with my son close by. I worried that soon he would say to

Baranov, "A strange man comes. He is from far away. A place my mother tells us stories about. Who is he?"

Hurt that Jabila ignored me, still fighting my doubts and questions, I blurted out, "Don't you listen to me?"

He bent down, gave Sem a pat on her bottom as she ran toward her brother. Turning to me, his voice calm, he finally said, "Ashana, I know how you hurt."

"Hurt. *Hurt*." I stopped. "Will there never be an end to this hurt? Why do Aláyeksans give way so easily?"

Horrifying, those words. Our minds filled with memories of that day Jabila had given me up to Minya, of the failed escape when his blood had spilled on the unknown island.

"Yes. We did give up too easily." Outside our window, we heard the hurling surf of Pavlovsk harbor. "If we could go back to the time you were taken, I would fight. I would die before I would let the alien make you his woman."

My anger still smoldered, and as my husband reached out to take me in his arms, I drew away, then faced him again and asked one of the questions that plagued me. "Go back? It is easy to say now. Why didn't you move us far into the mountains before the guns came?"

"Your father—"

"I do not want to hear about my father. You had paid your bride-price. We had started our life together. You . . . you . . . you should have killed me rather than let me go." My voice broke, and I turned away to hide my tears and bite back other hard words. I knew my husband risked his life every time he landed his kayak at Pavlovsk to share our brief moments of love, but the poisoned years of loneliness, boredom, and terror that had been festering in me spilled out. Sem and Denedi Belik'a had seen me cry, had heard me rage before, but they had never heard the torrent of words that slashed the air that night, words they could not understand, names of people they never knew. Frightened, my children ran to the kitchen.

For whatever reason, Jabila let me storm; he must have known my great need to say what had been festering in me so long. In the distance, I suddenly heard the cry of tiqun, but I knew wolves did not roam Kadyak Island. Jabila belonged to the wolf family; his brothers, who had rowed with him, watched and waited in the ravines beyond the village; soon he must leave me.

"Listen, Ashana. I do not have answers for us. But there is more I must tell you. Changes hang over Yaghenen. Ni'i has lost his leadership. Minya has taken his place, but Ni'i still speaks as an elder.''

Jabila reached into his pack, pulled out two pairs of white deerskin moccasins, with long fringes and the finest embroidery I had ever seen. ''Gifts from my second wife, Nidoc. She made them for you and your son. Her tokens of her respect.''

''Second wife, Jabila? A new wife?''

''Yes, Qanilch'ey Ashana. Nidoc. She is from Htsaynenq', where we fled so long ago. Sem's country.''

Both of us had always known there would be another wife, even two or three. An Athabaskan with Jabila's wealth and stature had need for more than one wife to look after his home and do his work. With me away, he needed another wife more than most men; oh, I should have been in his house. I was quiet a long time; I was the first one he had loved, I was the one who should share Jabila's life as first woman. And I could not help thinking, had Jabila's new wife so taken hold of his life that I was only a memory?

He sensed my struggle, knew my agony.

''Ashana, Ashana.'' His words came gently. ''You are my first wife. Always you will be first. Nidoc knows that. Everyone does. Nidoc wants to be a friend to you.''

''I need to go home with you, Jabila. I am lost in this Tahtna house. Some days I cannot see my way to—''

I was glad my children were out of the room, that they could not hear my next questions, for they showed the anger and hurt storming in me. ''Jabila, does your other wife mean so much that I am only a memory? Am I a woman you need only when you come with the meat to Kadyak?''

Jabila held me tightly, stroked my hair, his arms strong sinews binding me to him. ''You know that I treasure you as my first love.'' His eyes searched mine. ''Everyone on Yaghenen honors the memory of you as my first wife.''

''Memory! That is all I am. I am dead on Yaghenen.'' Bitter tears flooded my eyes. I became the abandoned wife on that lonely sea otter's rock, the icy water creeping up on me.

''No. Not a memory. Always, for me, you live.'' He crushed me against his chest, murmured, ''Ashana . . . my wife . . . my first love.''

For a long time I held myself rigid, while he brushed my hair back from my face, dried my tears.

''Ashana,'' he whispered, ''Qanilch'ey Ashana of Yaghenen, remember the meadows, the flowers, the lakes. They are

still there. Unchanging. I go there. I see you. I talk to you."
Then he began coaxing me back to him. At first I did not even
listen; but finally, my head began to clear; slowly, my storm
receded. Oh, I was so ashamed. No Athabaskan woman of worth
wastes time feeling sorry for herself the way I had done, never
when the risks are so great. My husband had almost given his
life in one escape attempt for me. As his arms went around me,
I relaxed for the first time.

"And you, Jabila . . . my husband." I could not deny him.

But I must have brought up some long-held doubts in his
mind, for Jabila surprised me by asking, "What of this man
Baranov? What do you feel for him after all the seasons here?"

Did he have doubts about me, that he could ask such a question? What did a hostage feel? Fear . . . hatred . . . contempt . . . But then, I *had* borne my captor two children.

I kept my voice as even as possible as I answered. "I am not
a wife here. You know that. Baranov has a wife in Russia, in a
village he calls Kargopol. And in Alóyeksa, he uses other
women."

His arms tightened around me, but as I pulled away, I heard
him whisper, "You did not say how you feel about him."

My angry doubts almost rose to the surface again. "I have
no feeling for that killer. I am hostage. Captive. Baranov holds
me against my will. Every day I force myself to live with that."

"Are you sure you do not feel for him, Ashana?" He persisted, "You have lived with him. Here. Many seasons. Had
children by him. Hasn't all that made him a husband?"

I swallowed the harsh words that came to my tongue; I knew
the pain that tore him, too. "No, Jabila. If this were Yaghenen,
and I had taken a second husband according to our customs, we
would both accept him. But here, I have no choice. I dare not
tell Baranov 'I will' or 'I won't.' "

Dusk fell on Pavlovsk. We could scarcely see the mist-
shrouded figures working along the waterfront; it was time to
light the stone lamps. That night I lit only one and set it on the
floor in the far corner so it would not silhouette our shadows.

Deep in thought, Jabila watched me. "Ashana, I will never
understand what kind of people think they have the right to take
us over." His voice lightened. "But I see one good thing coming out of it all."

"What good?"

"The Gulushutna, the Koniags, all of us Alóyeksans, have in
past years raided one another. No more. Kahtnuht'ana, Ulchena,

Gulushutna—we will stand together until we drive the aliens out.'' Whispering so that Denedi Belik'a would not hear, he repeated what Watnaw had told me. ''Remember, I promised you that we would resist. My men and I fought with the Gulushutna on Sitka. We will fight again.''

As he spoke, I watched Jabila's long fingers roam over the contours of the samovar Lisianskii had left as a gift for Governor Baranov. He lifted the cover, tried the spigot. This strange pot did not belong in Aláyeksa. It was alien, like this house and all its trappings. On my wrists I wore Aláyeksan shell bracelets, gifts from my mother and father, given to me to mark the summer of my passage into womanhood. The last time Jabila had held me in his arms, he fastened in one of my ears a k'enkena, a dentalium-shell necklace that hung close under my chin and was attached to the other ear. I treasured it not only because it came from my husband but because the shells came from the living sea, could trace their lineage back a million and more years, so vast an expanse of time that it makes the time of the aliens on Aláyeksa seem less than a day.

The strangeness of the furnishings receded in the dimness, and I saw again the firelight of my Yaghenen home. Qenq'a, we call our log houses, the shelters in which we live the greater part of the time. Like most Aláyeksan houses, my father's had been dug into the ground to half the height of a man to ensure that we would be warm throughout the months of cold, when the rain and sleet and snow lashed our peninsula. The men in our village had sweated over splitting logs for our house, pounding hard on their spruce wedges. Others had smoothed the timbers for the inside walls, so that we children would not get splinters in our bottoms, for we always ran naked in our houses, just as Denedi Belik'a and Sem did whenever their father was absent.

Our qenq'a was huge, six trees long; several other families shared our home. Each of my father's wives had a separate japoon, built on to the main house with an opening to the inside. During the cold season, when nights were longer than days, blazing logs lighted and warmed our home. It was a time of teaching the nanutset and lach'u of our Athabaskan people, the dena'ina sukdu, the legends of our people, that have come down to us from past generations. A qeshqa, my father had great knowledge, and an imagination that roamed further and wider than that of most of the men who sat beside our fire and told their sukdu.

"Ashana." Jabila shook my arm, and my dreams faded. "You seem so far away."

Outside a summer breeze tapped on our window. I opened the door a little, to let fresh air push aside the stale smells. Denedi Belik'a and Sem squeezed past me. "Look, Mama, see the grandfather in the moon." My son pointed, and Sem chimed in, "Hello, Grandfather. We love you."

For several moments we watched the bright circle high in the sky; as we closed the door, both children insisted, "Tell us the story, Mama."

"Not tonight."

"Please, Mama. Richard always tells it when the moon comes out."

I looked at Jabila. He nodded. I tucked the furs around my small ones, and the two of us sat beside them while I told Richard's story from Bengal.

"A very long time ago, a grandfather lived with his granddaughter. He was very rich. She was very beautiful. The most beautiful girl in the kingdom. Suitors came from all over, but none pleased her. The most successful man, she said, talked only of his money; but he gave none at all to the poor. The thin one talked only of food; he was hungry all the time and could never eat enough. Another man talked only of his books; he bored the girl.

" 'I will not marry any of them,' she said. 'I want to marry the prince who lives in the moon.'

" 'Prince in the moon?' Grandfather asked. 'How do you know there is a prince in the moon? I cannot see him.'

" 'You cannot see him because your eyes are dim with old age, but I know he is there.'

"One beautiful, moonlit night, just like tonight on Kadyak, the moon shone, shedding its golden rays, lighting the spindrift on the sea. The princess called to her grandfather, 'Look, Grandfather, the golden rays make a path down to our shore. And a little man is running on them toward us.' 'Do not be foolish, child,' her grandfather chided. 'There is no man running on the moon's rays.' 'Oh, yes, there is, Grandfather. Come, let's go to meet him.' She took the old man by the hand and ran toward the shore of the lake, to where the moonbeams ended. 'See Grandfather, here he is.'

"Standing on the tip of the moonbeams was a little man all in golden yellow; his face, his hands, his hair shone golden in the moonlight.

" 'Foolish girl, come back inside. He is not real.'

"The little man spoke. 'Princess, the prince in the moon sent me for you. I am his messenger. He wants to marry you just as you want to marry him. Will you come now?'

"The grandfather grew very angry. 'Foolishness!' he roared. 'You are not real. You are not from the moon. Come back to the house, Granddaughter!' That made the little golden man very angry. He took hold of the grandfather's cloak and dragged him upward on the moonbeams. The princess held on to her grandfather's hand and skipped along. Soon, she married the prince of the moon. They lived happily ever after.

"The grandfather sits on the moon, guarding it. Happy, too, that his granddaughter made a wise choice. And the grandfather and the little golden man became good friends, but sometimes they quarrel; and the little man gets very, very angry. His face grows very dark, and it is at those times that we have the dark of the moon. Then, while they have their good times, we enjoy the bright of the moon."

Richard had told the Bengal tale to Denedi Belik'a and Sem over and over until it had become a favorite.

Sem yawned, laughed, turned her face up to me. "Someday I am going to marry a prince on the moon."

Like the grandfather, Denedi Belik'a had doubts, but his words sounded heavy with the sleep he could not fight off. As we closed the door to his room, a flash of jealousy crossed Jabila's face. "It seems that Richard has become more a part of your children's lives than I have."

I started to say sharp words about men—Baranov, Richard, Ni'i, Banner, even Jabila—to burst out that the only certain thing in the lives of women is the uncertainty of men. Then I looked at the lines of suffering that had begun to drain from my husband's face the glorious freshness of his youth.

The sea-otter wife got even with her husband; but I would not inflict more hurt on Jabila. That sukdu ended: *The sea otter swam to some other country. She was never seen again.* Ashana, let your cruel doubts, your harsh words swim away.

Jabila and I were first loves on Yaghenen, and the distance and time that had separated us could never again be allowed to shatter our passion.

His touch felt as gentle as the sea breeze; he whispered, "Qanilch'ey Ashana, my windflower."

Oh, the golden wonder of that night alone! Our bodies touched, hands caressed, lips and tongues explored. Passion rose and thrust us across the abyss of space into an explosion of brightness.

Then he was gone.

❂ ❂ ❂
23

One clear, bright day I took my caribou-hide painting with me to an open space high on a ridge, where a flat shelf of rock thrust outward. Far below, waves chased one another across the sea, broke high against the rocky masses of the shore. I studied my painted figures, and eventually found a way in which I could make the sea beyond the bay look more as it really was—living, moving, eternally restless. My blues and greens, made from berries and grasses, would give it depth.

Standing on a jagged outcropping of rock a short distance away, unaware that I was near, her eyes turned toward Sitka Island, Lingen-Aka spoke to the wind, willing her words to fly to Anakhta-yan, who was still there with Baranov. Wanting to capture the essence of that moment without disturbing her, I painted quickly; as I brushed her shape in with my finger, her spirit brought more life to my painting. I retouched many of the figures and saw that now the picture was beginning to tell its story.

As I draped the caribou hide over a flat rock, I had a few moments of freedom the stale air of Pavlovsk never allowed me. Kadyak lay below, and, to the north, beyond snowcapped peaks bright in the sun, waited Yaghenen, where myriad flowers graced the meadows. And borne on the wind came the whispers of my beloved Jabila: "Qani*l*ch'ey Ashana . . . Qani*l*ch'ey Ashana. Sh'una yula, una yula, come to me, come."

Lingen-Aka still seemed lost in thought, so I watched the bay. A large ship searched the channel, drawing as close to shore as the alien vessels dared come.

"Oh, Ashana, I am happy that you are here." Lingen-Aka turned toward me, pointing. "That must be Lisianskii."

"No. It has to be the second Tahtna ship. I have never seen that one in Pavlovsk harbor before."

"Second ship? What do you mean?"

"Before Baranov headed back to Sitka Sound, he received a message telling him Nikolai Rezanov would soon sail in. He is an officer in the Russian-American Company. I forgot he was coming. The ship down there was to be the *Nadeshda*, bringing Rezanov."

Lingen-Aka and I hurried down to the waterfront and watched Ivan Banner greet the newcomers. As the men exchanged salutes and courtesies, I felt Nikolai Rezanov's eyes sweep over everything—the people, the hovels that made up the capital of Russia in Aláyeksa. Would he be an ally to Aleksandr Baranov, or did he plan to send the governor home to Russia?

Ivan Banner had ordered Richard to be the waiter for Rezanov's visit—serving food and drink, clearing the table, keeping up the fire—in Banner's own quarters, where the newcomer would be lodged. Richard hated being demoted from the governor's house, and in the evenings unloaded his anger to me.

"His Excellency, this brass-and-spit Nikolai Rezanov"— Richard's voice dripped sarcasm—"says the poverty of this place upsets him. He expected to see a civilized town—houses, food the same as he has in Russia. He asked Banner straight out if the blame for such crudeness rests on Governor Baranov."

Those aliens blame Aleksandr Baranov? When no company ships came from his homeland with supplies and men for two, three, even five years at a time? Though my captor was wrong in being in Aláyeksa, he had struggled hard for Mother Russia. The storehouses, the shipyard on Yelovi Island, the church, the artels, were all built because he poured his life into the company, even at cost to his health. Many times, I had seen him become discouraged by the lack of support from the men in Russia, who grew rich on his shiploads of fine furs. But always he would slog ahead, mutter into his vodka, "Russia will come to respect and honor the name Baranov."

I stopped myself: What was I doing, defending the governor? Me, the hostage woman, side with my captor? Had I been captive so long that I saw with his eyes? Strange, those twists in my thinking, as distressing as when I would call my children by their Tahtna names instead of their Kahtnuht'ana ones.

"Others are catching hell from Rezanov, too," Richard said, as he hurried into the house one evening to tell me more of what he had heard. "Today he started on the report the Shelekhovs made about building a school. Taking thousands of Aláyeksans into the Russian church. He called in the head monk. 'Where is the school? What do you teach?' The holy man said, 'School? We have no school.' Rezanov dug at him. 'Why don't you carry out your responsibility and teach the children? You let them grow up savages.'

" 'The company has received many complaints from you criticizing Governor Baranov. But it is clear to me, now that I am here, you have sat in Pavlovsk when you should have built churches out among the people. Most of all, you should have opened a decent school.' The monk mumbled excuses. He told Rezanov that Father Juvenal had been sent among the natives and that they had murdered the holy man."

Richard's mood shifted. "Much of the time I am angry at Banner for the way he treats me. But I tell you, Anna, he does take the side of the governor. This evening he told the high chamberlain that Pavlovsk would have fallen apart years ago if it had not been for Baranov.

"You know, His Excellency asked Banner if he would take over the management of the company, seeing Baranov has asked to go back home so many times." Richard laughed. "Ivan said, 'God, no. You would be foolish to replace the man. Aleksandr Baranov is Russia in this land.' "

Richard's next words shocked me. "His Excellency Nikolai Rezanov requires that in a few days, you, Princess Anna, must appear before him."

"Me?"

"Yes. You are the governor's woman. The royal one among us. Rezanov insists that you talk with him."

"No. No. No. I do not want to be displayed." My mind whirled, for I had no desire to appear before that high-ranking officer of the Russian Imperial Court. Richard and I spent the afternoon arguing; he kept repeating he had orders to bring me to the high chamberlain.

Lying awake late at night, I tried to climb into the mind of that nobleman. How would he see me? As an ignorant savage? Uncivilized barbarian? Meek woman?

I had another concern: If I went, how should I dress? There was another of Natalia's old gowns in her chest, stronger than the one that had been torn on the bench. But I knew I would look out of place in the eyes of the high chamberlain if I tried to make myself into some kind of alien court lady I knew nothing about. I could have my friends lend me their jewelry to spark up a worn dress, but I would not ask to borrow it because we had all agreed to keep our copper and rich stones hidden from the eyes of everyone who intruded into Aláyeksa. We had learned that the aliens grasped at whatever we wore that looked of value to them, and my joncha warned me not to make the nobleman an exception.

I spent a couple of restless nights trying to think how to avoid the meeting, but Richard's message that I must face the Tahtna could not be denied.

I would not wear Aláyeksa's finest treasures, yet I saw no reason to appear ordinary when I presented myself to Rezanov. I was *not* ordinary. I was Qanilch'ey Ashana of Yaghenen, daughter of a high-ranking qeshqa of the Kahtnuht'ana.

I made up my mind. If the Tahtna insisted I was a "princess," I would play the part. I would carry the honor of the Kahtnuht'ana clans into the presence of Tahtna nobility. I would not face Rezanov as a humble person. My ancient heritage and that of Nikolai Rezanov would meet on an equal footing.

I would wear my deerskin trousers and the beautiful white deerskin qenich'eni embroidered with moose hair and porcupine quills, given me by my mother and father and cherished through all the seasons of my captivity. The trousers were so worn that the feet had to be cut off, but I would wear Nidoc's lovely moccasins. And, too, I would wear Jabila's dentalium necklace, and my embroidered head- and wristbands. Watnaw would braid my hair and make it glisten with candlefish oil, weave into it the downy feathers from an eagle's breast.

Excitement spread swiftly through the village as soon as the people learned that I had been called to speak to the nobleman. Dread walked side by side with the excitement. Why? What does the Tahtna want? Does he intend to use you? We always dreaded that the aliens would think we women relished being shared among them. Does he want to inspect you, to see what kind of a *savage* Baranov lives with? Does he want to get information out of you?

Sem and I joined the women scraping skins a short distance from the shore. I had finally faced the fact that my meeting with Nikolai Rezanov could not be avoided, but that did not lessen my discomfort about it.

The first words of encouragement came from Lingen-Aka.

"Remember, Ashana, you are head woman among us. Show that man our Aláyeksan pride."

"That is right. We have all heard the Tahtna men brag about their royal people. Their ceremonies. Now, we will show them we Aláyeksans know ceremony." Watnaw added her support.

"Just what I was going to say," Lingen-Aka agreed, giving her fox skin an extra fierce slash. "Ashana, remember you told me what Baranov said: Always, when the Tzarina Catherine left her palace, carriages and horsemen and noblemen and servants and her people lined the streets."

Sutina recalled the day the nobleman had landed on Kadyak. "Rezanov was greeted with ceremony. The guns fired. Banner and the Tahtna saluted him. The monks even bowed to him. It showed respect, they said."

"We Aláyeksans will show you proper respect, Qanilch'ey Ashana." Lingen-Aka laughed. "We will line your path when you go see that alien. Our people will show ceremony."

"How can you make the stranger understand you? He does not know Kahtnuht'ana, and your Russian probably will not fit with his." Sutina voiced a concern I, too, had.

"I do not intend to speak Russian to him. I will speak only Kahtnuht'ana. Richard will interpret."

"Yes, Richard." Lingen-Aka's puzzled look vanished. "That is why he has been so busy fixing your raven crest on a pole. You will have him carry the staff for you."

"My father used his eagle-crested speaker's staff for ceremonies. You do the same. We want you to speak for all us Aláyeksans," Watnaw added.

The size of my task! How could I open Rezanov's mind and make him understand us? How could I open his mind to the wrongs he and his company did here? The last point I was certain he would never want to face, and the first might be impossible, for he would see us as a confusion of many diverse clans with differing tongues and customs and dress. The Great Country displayed a vast array of lands and climates, and an equally varied range of human beings. Would it be possible in one short meeting to bring Rezanov to an understanding of this boundless region?

When I awoke on the morning of my visit to Rezanov, my joncha had been speaking to me, and I picked up the words. *This day,*

Ashana of Yaghenen, you will tell the lach'u and nanutset of Aláyeksa to Nikolai of St. Petersburg.

Shortly before I left to walk to Ivan Banner's house Sutina and Watnaw slipped in.

"You look beautiful, Ashana. But do not wear those white moccasins on the muddy ground," Sutina said.

"They are part of my dress. I must wear them."

Watnaw had finished my hair, had braided in the tiny eagle feathers. She smoothed my qenich'eni to make certain no wrinkles marred its beauty, put on her cloak, and left.

"We will do it my way." Sutina laughed, a mischievous grin flickering across her face as she disappeared into my sleeping room and returned with my worn old moccasins.

"No, Sutina, those are too shabby," I protested.

"Sit down. Slip on the old ones. I will carry the white moccasins and you can change on the step of Banner's house. I will be right behind to help you. It will only take a moment."

By the time I stepped from my house, the sun had stripped away the night's mists. Kadyak welcomed me with one of its rare, cloudless days. Beyond Banner's house, the spirits of the mountains, their green forests and blue-white glaciers, watched over us.

Proud to be speaking for all the clans, I followed with firm steps behind Richard, who carried my raven-headed speaker's staff. His worn clothes clean and patched, his body held as straight as my staff, he took easily to his role.

So quietly I could hear the lapping of the waves over their footsteps, my friends came from behind trees, houses, shacks. The event I had dreaded became a ceremony of respect. Tzarina Catherine, riding along the streets of Russia, could never have felt more love from her people than I felt that day. Not bowing as aliens do, my people stood tall, and their eyes looked deeply into mine as I passed.

From behind masks that would impress, sometimes frighten the alien newcomers, Aláyeksans watched. A few masks carried a humorous message meant to make fun of the visitors. Others were designed to insult those who, in their ignorance, would not understand. Any knowing person could identify each clan by the way it rendered the bear, the whale, the eagle, the raven—whatever the spirit, hand, and eye had chosen.

"Our people will show ceremony," Lingen-Aka had said. Oh, how splendid it would have been had my friends been wearing the real treasures of their clans, but on Kadyak that day most of their masks had been hurriedly carved from bits of driftwood or fashioned from pieces of skin, decorated with old strips of hide, feathers, even grasses and reeds; they had neither the time nor materials to make new ones. But I saw each for what it was meant to be: colorful, full of meaning, alive with the spirits of Aláyeksa.

One of the first people to greet me was Watnaw. Her neck-piece was a small eagle crest she had carved from driftwood and fastened to a deerskin band decorated with eagle down. The grieving-woman mask—haunting with its sad eyes, its downward-sloped red and black and brown lines calling to mind the hurt of a wounded eagle—covered her face, for that day her heart sorrowed with her people at Sitka. "Do not be afraid. Be strong," she whispered.

Ulchenas wore driftwood masks, most of them formed like human faces, strong, disciplined, with heavy eyebrow ridges and broad cheekbones, but many were otherworldly, skeletal, their eyes deep-socketed and mournful: The Ulchena Islanders had suffered most at the hands of the Tahtna. One mask wearer whispered, "Courage, Ashana, courage."

The man known as the best dancer stood with several other Kadyak Islanders; he wore fringed furs decorated with foxtails, a headdress of fur and feathers; his face was painted red and black, and chains of bear teeth and shells hung around his neck. Dignity and loss spoke silently from a group of old hunters wearing the triangular headpieces of the Kuskokwin people; one was wearing a seal mask, and from its smiling mouth with its sharp wooden teeth slipped the words, "Your brothers stand beside you, Ashana."

My eyes rested on Lingen-Aka for a moment; she seemed ready to take my hand and walk with me. Her long braids were half hidden by her Ulchena cap, made of a woven cascade of shells. Her face, under its disguise of paint, seemed worried.

From among my Athabaskan brothers and sisters, the mask of tiqun spoke to me: "Steady, Ashana. Yaghenen's spirits walk with you."

I wanted to shout aloud with joy, throw myself at tiqun, but I dared not, for even to look at him could signal to the Tahtna watching us that the man they believed dead had returned and stood that day in defiance of them all. Nor did I dare confront the men who stood beside Jabila; they, too, wore the masks of tiqun. "My band. I trust every one of them," Jabila had said that day in the cave high above Pavlovsk.

Near the end of the path stood a hostage boy. He had remembered the mosquito mask from his father's home; it had been hastily carved, and he wore it unfinished, but the young artist had captured the essence of the mosquito spirit: The mask, with its fierce long beak poised ready to strike, seemed alive. And I hoped it would one day strike against Tahtna.

Standing on the steps to Banner's house, I turned for a last look at my people. I gathered into my memory the colors, the designs, the shapes, for I knew many of them would take their places on my caribou-hide painting.

For an instant, I was back on the snowfield the night the spirit spoke to me with Agagasik's voice. Not until that moment had I been able to recall it. Aa', yes. I remembered, and took courage. The message carried four commands: *Stay angry at your captors, Qaniłch'ey Ashana. Remember your friends. Build with them a family of trust. Tell Aláyeksa's story to the four winds.*

Sutina helped me slip my feet into the pure white moccasins. Richard rapped loudly on the narrow spruce door. The shocked look on Ivan Banner's face as he stared at my assembled people cannot be described.

With a ringing challenge in his voice that set the tone for the meeting, Richard of Bengal announced: "Qaniłch'ey Ashana, Princess of Yaghenen. To see His Excellency, Nikolai Petrovich Rezanov of Russia!"

Aa', Richard. You played your part well. Other actors might have better trappings, but no one could best your performance.

My staff-bearer stepped aside, and Councilor Banner motioned me into the presence of his guest, who was seated at a plain plank table. Out of place in that Aláyeksan setting, the High Chamberlain Nikolai Rezanov wore a dark-blue coat decorated with braids and medals, his clothing dull in comparison to the brilliant, living colors of the feathers and furs that lined my pathway. Sitting erect, Nikolai Rezanov passed his eyes over me; the flicker in them told me I had surprised him. Strangely enough, even though I had dreaded facing the Tahtna nobleman, supported as I was by the spirits of my friends I knew I could match wits with him. His power came from the court of Imperial Russia; my power came from the people of Aláyeksa.

"Princess Ashana? I understand your name is Anna." The high chamberlain motioned me to a chair. "Perhaps we can talk more easily if you sit on my left." He made no mention of my people outside.

"Anna is the name the Russians call me. But my Kahtnuht'ana name is Qanil̃ch'ey Ashana, and my people call me Ashana."

"A pretty name, but I presume that I should use Anna as the governor does."

"I prefer my own name." I looked directly at him as I took the chair he offered. I had the feeling that ordinarily a native woman would have been expected to stand in his presence; but he must have realized that our meeting had commenced on a level different from what he had assumed it would.

He hesitated, rearranged papers on his table. Do alien men always shuffle papers when they lose the edge? Could I have put the nobleman off balance?

I waited for him to speak. He did not, so I made the first move. "I welcome you to Aláyeksa, Your Excellency, and wish health to you and a speedy return to your homeland." In my mind, I willed him back in his country with his entire retinue, for I had no reason to proffer friendship to the newcomer.

"Governor Baranov has written the company several times that he wants to retire to Russia." He carefully avoided using my name. "Unfortunately, three different times, accidents or sickness have taken the lives of replacements appointed for him."

"Yes, I know. Aleksandr Baranov grows old and worn in the service of your company."

His manner eased. "I came prepared to hear complaints from your people. But at our artels and trading posts, Aleut men have told me conditions are good. On Unalaska, they only requested that, if a new company man comes in, he treat them as well as they have been treated in the past.

"From distant villages, the word has been the same. 'Governor Baranov is a good leader. A fair man. Works hard.' " He looked straight at me; his next words drowned all doubts about his purpose: He sought information. "How do you see it here on Kadyak? Does the governor work hard?"

There was a brief silence after Richard finished his translation, while I settled my thoughts before answering. "The company dominates his life. Always, Aleksandr Baranov drives himself to the limit for it. Never a day that he does not talk of the need to make the company successful. To honor Mother Russia."

We spent time on Russian affairs in Aláyeksa and my captor's dedication to his duties as manager and as colonial governor. I stuck to facts, and Ivan Banner supported what I said.

Then the high chamberlain probed more deeply. "As I said, Aleut men told me conditions are good. They must be satisfied."

"Satisfied, Your Excellency? *Satisfied?*" The word was insulting. "What else could they say?"

I hurried on before he could interrupt. "Every man you talked to was a captive. A hostage. A man levied for sea hunts or other duties for your company. Their words were spoken out of fear for your guns. The lives of their families depend on how well they work for Aleksandr Baranov. The talk you heard pleases the ears of the company. The men dared not speak otherwise. They would be shot if they told the truth, and other hostages would be taken."

"But I am told the men are far better off with us here than they have ever been. I have learned that before we Russians came many families in Aláyeksa died of starvation. There were times known as the months of hunger. Now, because of us, that has changed. They have work and food."

"Some months of hunger, yes, that has always been. But nothing like what our people suffer since the *promyshlenniki* came. I will tell you, Your Excellency, of losses your company has caused Aláyeksan men. You must know that Governor Baranov levies eight hundred, eleven hundred, fifteen hundred men at a time for his sea hunts. In one season, hundreds of these men die at sea.

"Their families starve; their children die. From a party of a hundred men, twenty drown in a day. Many times on the hunts the company runs out of food. Our men have to hunt food on their own. Often they find nothing. Your *promyshlenniki* have killed off vast herds of our animals. Our men have eaten rotten mussels. Poisoned themselves. I remember one party because friends of mine hunted with it; one hundred and forty died over a single night. Many times your *baidarshchiks* have ordered hunters too far out in open water on heavy seas. In times like that, the whole hunting party goes down. Thirty-two baidarkas with sixty-four men were lost not long ago.''

Purposefully, I kept my eyes away from Ivan Banner, looked straight at the stranger, whom I intended to inform of the facts. ''If you would spend a day with the women whose men have gone down and listen to their keening, you might understand what you Russians are doing to Aláyeksans. You must have seen Ivan Kuskov's listings of Aláyeksans lost on the sea hunts.''

Rezanov's face tightened as he stroked his chin. ''I know that life in the wilds is harsh at best. People suffer. They need our help, and I—''

''High Chamberlain Rezanov, walk with me on Kadyak Island,'' I cut in. ''See the villages empty of men. Look at the crippled hunters crawling back from puffin hunts ordered by your company—too hungry and weak even to care for themselves. Learn that mothers have no food to feed their children. Hear them cry. Hold the babies when they die because their fathers hunt for Baranov and there is no food in their shacks.

''Look at the waste. See the stacks of rotting furs. You slaughter far more than your ships can carry. Starvation and death live in our villages because of your company.''

He held up his hand to quiet me. ''Be patient, Anna.'' No doubt to discipline me, he used the Russian name. ''Our great civilization will soon replace the wild life of your people. The Russian-American Company leads the way. You will live to see Aláyeksa civilized.'' (Was he ignoring what I had just told him?) ''All of you are passing through a harsh period, but better conditions lie ahead. That is why we Russians have come.''

Better conditions: Guns. Levies. Rape. Families torn apart. Animals slaughtered. Skins rotting. Images of what the Tahtna had brought to our land and seas flowed through my mind. How could I put those images into words, restate my meaning in a stronger voice so that he would hear and understand?

My anger rose, but I controlled myself. ''Your Excellency, your civilization differs a great deal from mine. Who can say which is the better?'' I spoke slowly, paused, then went on. ''I know why you Russians, the other aliens, come to Aláyeksa. You want our furs. Aláyeksan men mean riches to you.

They have the hunting skills and courage on the seas your men do not have. Furs. That is why you come. Your concern to give us civilization? That is the shame of you aliens. Your talk does not fit what you do."

I listened carefully as Richard translated my words: even with my limited knowledge of Russian I detected that he tended to soften some of my message. With a quick aside, I directed him to repeat exactly as I spoke. His face a mask, he nodded.

"I assure you, Anna, my government takes care of her people. Since we discovered you, you belong to us. We will look after you." Rezanov shook his finger at me. "You must understand that civilizing people takes time. You savages must be patient." He straightened in his chair. "The civilization it has taken Russia centuries to build will be yours within a few years, if you follow our teachings. I am sorry for the deaths, but suffering goes before better days. It is not easy building a nation. The church will lead the way. The monks have begun the work among you."

"In case you have not noticed during your short stay here, Your Excellency, I must tell you that the monks from your homeland have spent most of their time and strength in conflict with Governor Baranov. They found conditions far more harsh in Aláyeksa than in their monasteries. They complained about the food. Their quarters. Everything. They interfered with Baranov's work in every way they could. But they grabbed at his rubles for building their church."

Memory of the terror inflicted on me by Father Emelian sprang into my mind ready to spill out. But I held back, for at that point I wanted to bear down on the truth about the monks without giving the high chamberlain any grounds for charging that my words rose from personal insult.

"I know of the difficulties between the colonial governor and the monks. Yes, and of their failure to establish a school. But I have issued an order: Conflict between the church and the Russian-American Company will end. A school will soon be started for all children in Aláyeksa."

Oh, he sensed hostility in me, for he tried to appeal to my motherly instinct. "I understand you have two small ones. They can attend our school."

"Your Excellency, my children may never go to your school."

"Why not, Anna? The governor's—"

"The monks insist that couples living together get married. It makes the children legal. Not like Antipatr and Irina—children of sin, they call them."

Banner began to speak, but I waved him aside. "You know Governor Baranov has never married me. He beds me, so the monks tell me that I am a woman of sin."

"He cannot marry you. The church will not permit it. He has a wife living in Kargopol." It was as if His Honor swallowed each word and found it as bitter as sourdock.

"Yes, I know. Aleksandr has told me."

Banner finally broke in, "Useless talk, Anna. Do not bother His Excellency with—"

"No, Ivan. Let her speak her mind." Rezanov brushed aside his host. "That is why I asked her to come here."

"The monks hold that my boy and girl are children of sin. As I told you, they say I, too, am a woman of sin. They say Antipatr and Irina cannot be baptized in your church, that they cannot go to your school."

Red creeping up his throat, over his face, into his hair, Rezanov tried to hide the stiffening of his body as his voice lost its warmth. "We will see about that." His eyes became almost hooded, and through the slits I knew he was trying to understand me. Banner's horrified expression told me I had made an enemy of him for speaking Aláyeksa's lach'u.

Banner cleared his throat, his unspoken anger filling the room. He picked up his gun and stepped to the window. "I will have my men order those people away." Behind his guest's back, he motioned me to tame my talk.

"No, Ivan. Let them stay. Remember, Russian law recognizes Anna's royalty. Those Aláyeksans do, too."

Nikolai Rezanov seemed relieved to get off the subject of my children and the monks; ignoring what I told him, he repeated himself. "Civilizing people takes time. You savages must be patient."

I sensed we had come to the end of our talk, and I rose to my feet. *Stay angry, Ashana,* the voice of the spirit of the recent dead sounded through my head. *Stay angry. Tell the four winds.*

Like the cold breath of the snowfield that spirit-filled night, my voice came out crisp and strong. "Mother Russia has forced herself onto our land, saying she brings us civilization and better conditions for our bodies. Her monks drone that they bring salvation for our spirits. The fact is, Your Excellency, that Mother Russia *kills* our bodies. Her monks *destroy* our spirits. Be that as it may, Nikolai Rezanov, I tell you that long after you Russians have gone from these shores, our people will be here. We will endure, and we will prevail.''

BOOK FOUR

◇ ◇ ◇

⊚ ⊚ ⊚
24

Long ago, when I was a child on Yaghenen, my grandmother became very ill, and could not answer when we tried to talk with her. Worrying, hurting deeply, Seltan and I remembered a summer morning before sunrise when Grandmother had taken us to a mountain stream some distance from our village, her favorite secret place. There, she had us strip and dive into the cold water three times. On the edge of the deep woods, she taught us two songs: one to sing at dawn, one after sunrise. That wisdom has been known by Kahtnuht'ana from ancient times: To those of us who listened and could hear, songs came into our heads from the wind, the sea, the rocks, from the animals and the birds—gifts to us from their spirits. Each song belonged and was treasured forever by the person who first heard it.

No song could pass to another by being inherited, but it could be earned. So, to pay her, as Grandmother had ordered, Seltan caught her the fish, and I picked the basket of berries. We walked on each side of her, hand in hand, back to the village. As we went along the trail toward home, she told us, "There are special songs for luck in hunting, to take sickness away and burn it. We know songs for everything, and the most special is the song to give long life."

The songs worked.

The day that Grandmother lay ill, Seltan, crawling away from the narrow japoon where she suffered, had whispered, "We must get up early in the morning. She needs us to sing for her."

Before sunrise the next day, we ran to the stream. As Grandmother had taught, we stripped off our clothes and sat chin-deep in the water, facing the ridge over which the sun would rise. We sang the first song before dawn, then, as the sun climbed over the ridge, the second. That day we ate nothing until the sun went down, for that is what Grandmother had told us to do.

For three more mornings, we sat in the icy water and sang to the rising sun. On the fourth day, Grandmother opened her eyes and smiled for a moment. Within a few days, she joined us at the evening fire.

That is the way the songs worked. That is how I know.

My two small ones had been robbed of my grandmother, so I taught them the songs she had taught me. As happened with many people from Kahtnuht'ana villages who were trying to listen and learn their special song, Antipatr could never hear one.

"Mama, it does not make sense," he had said more than once. "The rocks, the water, the sun, the animals—they make their own noise, but they do not sing. I cannot hear them."

Much later, when he learned the word "superstition" from the monks, Antipatr told me that our belief in songs that healed sickness was "just superstition." At the school, the men of the church had shown him songs drawn on lines on pieces of paper. "*That* is the way music comes. It is written out." Nothing I said changed his thinking, but I wondered, from where back in the beginning of the Tahtna people, did they get their songs?

When Governor Baranov returned to Pavlovsk from Sitka Sound, he seemed full of dread that no alien could count himself safe outside the fort he had built in the land of Watnaw's people. The disappearance of some of his Tahtna workmen in the forests had etched fear into my captor's mind. He seemed unable to explain the losses. But Aláyeksans knew: Sdónályášna? Ey'utna?

"I wore my chain-mail vest under my shirt every day. More than one bullet bounced off," Aleksandr bragged, and Antipatr looked with awe at his father's arm, scarred by a Gulushutna bullet. He said nothing to me about his fight at Sitka and evaded my questions; I could only judge how close death had stalked him by that healed wound.

"I put Ivan Kuskov in charge of the workmen. I ordered them to build a strong fort with warehouses, a wharf, quarters for all my men, and a big house for us. I will take all those books and maps and fine things Nikolai Rezanov brought me here at Kadyak. As soon as our boats can be caulked and the baidarkas sewn up, I will move my headquarters to Novo-Arkhangelsk. With time, Sitka Island can be made livable and safe for Russians.

"Phew. You smell bad." Irina had held her nose when her father had first come home and reached to take her onto his lap.

Sweat-soaked, with vodka-laden breath, sodden woolen jacket and pants, and wrinkled leather boots, the governor of Russia in Aláyeksa looked no better than his roughest *promyshlenniki*. He made repeated trips to the sweathouse before his daughter would let him hold her.

"I have been away too long, little one," he said as she cuddled against him, the strangeness that grows with absence melting. "I am building a big new house for you and Antipatr on a beautiful island. I will have a tutor to teach you and your brother." He held her tightly; she rested her head against his arm. "And for you, Irina, a governess. You will play the piano. You will grow up to be a fine young Russian lady."

Over Irina's curls he called to Antipatr, who was studying a navigation chart on the desk. "I will see that you have a sponsor for the Naval Academy at St. Petersburg."

"Can I go tomorrow?" Antipatr asked.

"Do not be so eager, Son." Baranov laughed, ruffled our boy's hair. "You have studies to finish before you will be ready."

A mist seemed to rise from the earth and separate the three of them from me as Baranov talked to our children. "You know your papa holds the rank of collegiate councilor. And these medals"—the lamplight played over the Cross of St. Vladimir and the Order of St. Anne as he took them down from their pegs—"have been given him for services to his country. Your papa has earned them.

"These honors make you children of rank," he continued, as he slipped the ribboned medals over his head. "I want you to listen carefully, for you two are entitled to the best Russia has to offer. I know it has been hard for my little ones with me away so much. But the work has to be done. Now, with my new capital at Novo-Arkhangelsk, I will send my helpers out to inspect the artels and the villages, and I will have more time for you."

A look of satisfaction I had seldom seen warmed Aleksandr's face. "Many men from ships around the world will come to buy furs from your papa. They will eat at our house. When we move to Novo-Arkhangelsk, I plan to live the way a Russian of rank should."

He talked on of his new capital, his plans, his children's future. Did this mean that as they grew older, my boy and girl would be separated from me?

Being no part of Baranov's plans that day, alarmed by his talk of the Naval Academy at St. Petersburg, the governess, the fine young Russian lady, I slipped into the sleeping room, picked up a goat horn and carving stone, tried to bring out one of the creatures I saw living in it. But the stone kept slipping, and the lines scratched on the surface did not bring a single animal to life. My mind spun with the question: Was there any place for me in my children's future?

When he had first returned from Sitka Sound, Baranov had talked at great length about his winter with High Chamberlain Nikolai Rezanov.

"You should have seen the two of us at Novo-Arkhangelsk, Princess Anna. The nobleman with his fine clothes and grand ship. Me with no decent clothes, living in a leaky hut and slopping around in muddy water. The Aleuts to be fed. The *promyshlenniki* grumbling all the time. That bastard Kotlean threatening to strike. Luckily for me, Nikolai had to write reports to the government on his round-the-world expedition and to the company about Aláyeksa, so he spent a good part of the time on his ship. With God's help, we survived through the bad season, Rezanov along with everyone else."

Those reports the Tahtna write: There is never any end to them.

"I worried what he would say about me. Then, one day, he handed me some of his notes to read. Anna, Nikolai gave me credit for pulling the settlements through all those difficult times." A smile touched Baranov's face. "And on Grigorii Shelekhov's head—may his soul rest in peace—Rezanov put squarely the lies Grigorii had sent to the Tzar to promote what he wanted: the school he said he built in Aláyeksa, the converts to the Russian church, the number of people he had added to the Russian empire. Give the high chamberlain credit for understanding the truth about his father-in-law. Those claims of Gregorii's were all groundless lies."

The aliens seemed far from agreement among themselves. That Nikolai Rezanov, the son-in-law of Shelekhov? What split in the family would his report cause?

"He did not spare the monks, either. He made a long list of their shortcomings: failure to carry the message of the church into the hinterlands; failure to learn the Aláyeksan tongues; failure to educate the people. He blistered them in language as hot as a steaming samovar." Baranov chuckled.

"Remember Talin, Anna?" Baranov's question reminded me of Podgasch's arrogant young naval officer. "The government sent the navy men to help build Russian America, but they spent all their time griping over harsh conditions. Worked to stir up revolts against me. Rezanov reported all this.''

I feared what the alien nobleman might have said about my meeting with him; but, doubtful as I had been, Rezanov's words to Baranov praised me. ''Anna is an honest woman. A beautiful princess. I saw the support the people of Aláyeksa gave her. An astonishing sight. But her people must remain hostage in order that we can speed our civilizing them.''

The nobleman had praised me, but he had buried the truth about the destruction of Aláyeksans under the name of civilization.

Alone with Irina and Antipatr for months on end, teaching them the Kahtnuht'ana nanutset, the lach'u, the sukdu, I willed them to accept their Athabaskan heritage. When Baranov returned from his long absences, he would drown nearly all I had taught them with the excitement he raised by his talk of far lands, his promises for the future.

When my mind struggled to sharpen my teachings, I sought help from Watnaw and Lingen-Aka, for they had become sisters to me. We shared our moments of happiness, our many griefs, trusted our feelings to one another. One afternoon, wanting to talk with them, I found them soaking skins in the urine vats and waited. Later, while they washed themselves at the beach, I told them Governor Baranov talked of moving me and the children to Sitka Sound.

''When?'' Watnaw asked.

''Not till summer. He put Kuskov in charge of the work. The fort and the company buildings come first. It will take a season or two before his house is ready.''

''We cannot let you go, Ashana. We have too much . . .'' Lingen-Aka choked; she reached for my hand and gripped hard.

My news upset Watnaw, too, for she said, ''We depend on each other, you and I. The hostages, too. We are a family. All of us. We need you in Pavlovsk. The guns. . . . We still have work to do,'' she said, finishing Lingen-Aka's thought.

''I will not be leaving for a long time yet. Many things can happen. Baranov may decide his children will not be safe at Sitka.'' I tried to ease their worry.

''Yes. Something could happen to change his mind.'' Lingen-Aka strove to push aside what she had heard.

''We will find a way to keep you with us, Ashana. Lingen-

Aka and I may hide you under the floor in Baranov's sleeping room.''

Silent for a few moments, I watched Watnaw. Usually a steady presence, that day she could not hide her distress; something more than what I had said was troubling her. I had to lean forward to hear her next words. ''The Tahtna may build their fort where my people have walked and hunted for ages, but they will never drive the Gulushutna spirits from Sitka Island. Every totem of my Gulushutna people on Sitka Sound breathes with the spirits of the children left behind. Every totem has been washed by the tears of my sisters. The Tahtna say my people killed the littlest ones so that our men and women could escape. Our people know the Tahtna guns murdered them.''

Lingen-Aka slipped her arm around Watnaw. ''We understand how you grieve. The sorrow of your people is our sorrow.''

''Terrible. Children killed. No blame lies on your sisters.'' The man responsible sat inside my house with my children on his knee! How could I comfort Watnaw?

''Ashana, if you are taken to Sitka, I want you to know my Gulushutna people. Find support in them. If they fight again and beat the aliens, perhaps you can be free.''

Out in the harbor, tushei crawled toward us across the face of the sea. There was no healing, no way out of Watnaw's sorrow.

As we walked slowly along the path, Lingen-Aka asked, ''Why didn't Baranov send Anakhta-yan back here with Solnikov and Atoon and the others?'' She turned, stared into the mist. ''Why was he left at Sitka?''

That night, I forced myself to tell Lingen-Aka of the many times Baranov had bragged of Attu's value to him as an interpreter, explained that he would be gone a long time because the governor had sent him far south to explore the region he said had a great stream called the Columbia River and then to the California coast—places where the Russians expected to find sea otter and land on which to build more of their settlements.

Anakhta-yan could not choose to stay with his beautiful and gentle Lingen-Aka, and it took strength to tell her that Baranov had often said, ''That woman is valuable. She has the most skill tying and retying the fish nets. She is quick. We depend on her. Good to have a woman around who is not always complaining, one who can laugh. I will never let her tie herself down to a savage.''

It would have been more to the point, Aleksandr, I had thought when first hearing him pronounce her doom, if you had said what was truly in your mind: Lingen-Aka's beauty draws the men. And she serves the men the way they need to be served.

"Lingen-Aka," I said, "Baranov will waste your life before he will allow you much time with Anakhta-yan."

She grasped my hand, sobbed against my shoulder.

No healing. No answer for Lingen-Aka's sorrow.

Some seasons earlier, having learned of the death of his wife in Kargopol—a message that had drawn from him words of relief rather than sounds of mourning—Baranov had penned a request to the head man of his company seeking legitimate status for our children. Much later, he held in his hand a copy of Tzar Aleksandr's *ukaz*, a decree making legitimate and giving rank to the boy Antipatr Aleksandrovich Baranov and to the girl Irina Aleksandrovna Baranov, the children of Colonial Governor Aleksandr Andreevich Baranov.

Irony wove through the message, for the *ukaz* had also changed a passing phrase of Baranov's into official recognition: I had been created "The Princess of Kenai" in the records of my captor's homeland. Antipatr and Irina, because they bore the blood of Yaghenen leaders, had been granted noble status among the Tahtna.

When I had first come to this house on Kadyak, I had cried out, "Princess! What does it mean? Whore? Prostitute?" Attu had warned me, "You are not a common hostage. Aleksandr Baranov has need for your rank. You will see." The *ukaz* had given me my place. Tzar Aleksandr had marked Qanilch'ey Ashana *a valuable property*, belonging to Baranov.

As late spring flowed into summer, the governor ordered the transfer of his headquarters from Pavlovsk on Kadyak to his new capital, Novo-Arkhangelsk on Sitka Sound.

For weeks, I had wanted to make a request; and now, knowing that he would soon leave Kadyak, I did: "Novo-Arkhangelsk is so far away. I must see my father and mother before you take me there."

"I will not hear of it," he boomed at me. "Every band of hunters I send to the Kenai meets trouble. Hunting parties get wiped out. Besides, I know Kenai men fought with the Kolosh." His flint-hard eyes pierced mine. "Your people keep up their supplies to me, but I do not trust any of them. You will not leave

Kadyak until you go to Novo-Arkhangelsk.'' I pleaded for several days, but he paid no attention to my efforts. The governor had not softened with the years; and his openness with his children did not translate into ease toward me. Even though my status as princess had become official, this hostage drew no favors.

A couple of weeks passed; I voiced another hope. ''I will need help in the new house. You have told me it is much bigger than this one.'' His jaw set, he tried to ignore me; but I continued as calmly as I could. ''Watnaw and Lingen-Aka have helped me most here. They know the ways in this house. They are good with the sewing. The children like them. We will need them in the new house. I think they should—''

''No Kolosh from this island will go with us. And you know Lingen-Aka has duties here. They will both stay on Kadyak.''

His stony words killed my hope of visiting home, Watnaw's longing to return to Sitka, and Lingen-Aka's yearning to find Attu. My captor knew the lach'u behind my words.

Before he left, Baranov loaded his ships with most of the goods and supplies of Pavlovsk, leaving the company men here with only enough guns to guard us and for the hunt. This was a loss for me; for a time, no guns flew back to Yaghenen. The governor sailed for Sitka Sound without us, heading one of the largest Ulchena fleets ever gathered, friends of mine among those levied. I painted a few more baidarkas on my caribou hide, then added a Tahtna ship with the governor standing at the helm; but later the same day, I told myself that he did not belong in Aláyeksa, and painted him out. By the time he sailed, my captor had poured himself so completely into plans for his new capital that he already viewed Pavlovsk as nothing but a minor artel.

The site of power had been moved.

Time on Kadyak drifted. I counted puffin skins until the sight of them seemed to suffocate me. Several men had fallen from the cliffs where the puffins nested, a few had died; the injured survived, their broken limbs healing in tormented positions. As I listed the skins turned in by each hunter, I thought how striking the birds had been when they were alive: raven-black backs, snow-white stomachs, stubby red beaks, and large feet that looked useless but could cling easily to the harsh windswept cliffs. Then I pushed aside thoughts of the day when Baranov would send for us, for my heart always led me to Yaghenen.

Could the men in the next boat bringing supplies take me back? Could I hide in the boat? Yes, I would talk with the men. They could take me home.

I waited. No boat came.

Then, from Novo-Arkhangelsk, Ivan Banner received the governor's message and his order: "The Kolosh have made peace with us. Commander Kuskov has built well. We have a strong fort. Our house is finished. Send my family to me."

I remember my thoughts as I faced Banner. Should I hide? Do whatever necessary to keep me away from Baranov and Sitka? Then a different idea struck me: I would be among the Gulushutna. Might I find another Watnaw among them? Would the Gulushutna fight again? Could I escape to them, as she had suggested? Those thoughts made the move a little easier, even though the choice of staying or going was not mine.

Men loaded the ship with all our personal possessions, along with boxes containing the books and paintings and trappings Nikolai Rezanov had brought to Kadyak to establish a school and to settle *civilizing* influences over Aláyeksa.

No ceremony marked our departure. Along the waterfront, a few men watched as workmen stowed the last bundles into my umiak. Denedi Belik'a and Sem had questions but no regrets, eager to join their father in his new home. Lingen-Aka and Watnaw and I had said our good-byes in the house, sheltered from staring eyes; none of us wanted to stand on the open beach and face my leaving.

Before I went, I gave Lingen-Aka my goat horn, a few images barely scratched on the surface because my hands had no skill and could not cut into the bone to bring out the animals and people I saw living there. I gave Watnaw my painted caribou hide to hold until I came back and could finish it. If I never returned, I knew she would make certain it would someday find a home with my people; it was my story of Aláyeksa, and she would pass it on to Seltan. The children and I were forced to go, but I would not trust my painting to that ship; I feared the Tahtna sailing boats, knowing well that too many sank.

As the Tahtna ship carried me eastward, past the familiar shore-line of Pavlovsk and farther away from Jabila and my people on Yaghenen, I had forebodings about the sea—so vast, with no land in sight; I had no concept, as one day merged into another, how far the sailing ship was taking us from land; the North Pacific threatened to swallow us. All my life I had heard men tell of braving that vastness, where for days nothing could be seen but water that lashed with a strength greater than men knew how to describe. Our sea hunters did survive, in their kayaks and umiaks, riding the waves with mastery and courage that flowed in the blood of Aláyeksans, who lived with the sea. No such understanding favored the alien sailors.

Frightened, my children clutched me, both of them heaving with a sickness none of us had ever known before. The thick blackness in the small space below the deck where the sailors had put us, the pitching and turning floor, filled me with the sickness, too; I could do nothing for my small ones, and I wondered if we would survive. My spirits sank, and I believed that the end would come out there on the ocean, far from my Yaghenen loved ones.

On Kadyak, I had fought against my hostage fate; but now, helpless, my life and the lives of my children dependent on men whose skills appeared questionable, I drifted. Not only a physical illness possessed me; my mind seemed without moorings as to time and space. The endless sway and pitch made my children retch till they had no more to heave into the bucket that spilled its contents onto the floor. Miserable and vomiting, I was too weak to lift my head. Rarely, a sailor would bring water and another bucket. Time slowed. Imprisoned in that stench-filled, endlessly rocking box, I did not care if we ever reached Novo-Arkhangelsk. Better we let our spirits join those of the sea people, sink to the bottom into the arms of the nutin'at dnayi.

One afternoon Antipatr rolled over me and off the bunk. Through my haze, I saw him squatting in the corner by the porthole, heard his weak cries, "Mama, Mama."

The door to our cabin opened and a sailor entered; I sat up. He put cold water to my lips and Sem's, swabbed the cabin as best he could, but the smell of vomit remained. When he reached down and picked up my son, I was too weak to protest or to ask where he intended to take my child.

How long we had been on the ship I did not know, but one day I sensed a change. The ship steadied; for a time it moved slowly, then stopped. The door opened; framed against the light stood Aleksandr Baranov, Antipatr at his side in a blue uniform, my son clean and smiling.

"They told me you have been sick, Anna. And how is my Irina? Poor little one."

"We have had a terrible voyage." I sat up as Baranov took Irina in his arms. "It is over?"

"Yes. You are at Novo-Arkhangelsk. The sailors told me you have been very ill. They said it seemed impossible to help you." He paused, took my arm to steady me. "I am glad you are safe."

For once in my life I welcomed the sight of Aleksandr Baranov. Our hands touched as he reached for one of my packs; his eyes, warm and protective, lingered on mine before he picked up the bundle and started across the deck. And in me stirred a softness I had rarely felt for him on Kadyak.

"Antipatr. Those clothes. Where did you get them?"

"Mama . . ."

The captain of the ship interrupted, "Governor Baranov, that boy of yours will make a fine sailor. We did not have a uniform small enough for him, so my men cut pieces from their worn-out ones and made one for him."

My son looked as if he were growing into a young man. I wanted to hug him, but he straightened his small shoulders, and I held off.

"There he is." The captain spoke with pride. "The newest sailor for the Russian Imperial Navy."

Did I see my son strut a bit across the deck? More Antipatr than Denedi Belik'a?

From the small boat taking me from the ship to shore, I gazed at the sharp peaks towering beyond the new village. I saw the majestic beauty that had struck Baranov as far more splendid than the muddy land surrounding St. Petersburg. The high promontory I had heard so much about rose from the water's edge. On Sitka Island, Baranov had built his new settlement: The fortress with three towers, a huge structure, rose up straight in front of me. To one side and below it, I saw workmen's quarters, storehouses, and other buildings, all made from hewn logs. The Russian flag whipped in the breeze. A bell started ringing. How many times had Baranov said, "I will have bells?"

The flag, the bell, did not speak to me as my captor no doubt wanted them to, for my attention was drawn to the beach. It was strewn with carved cedar totem poles and house posts, some charred by fire, others rudely chopped into pieces, most of them shattered and splintered remnants of the dignity they once bore. No longer did the posts rise skyward, guarding each family's house as they had when Watnaw and Kotlean had raced along the shore and through the forest.

"Heathenish idols. I ordered them destroyed as soon as we took the promontory," the conqueror of Sitka Sound bragged to the captain as I stopped for a few moments, staring at the totem pole lying nearest me: A brown bear carved exactly like the one Watnaw had described on her father's box sat on the base of the pole; above it, a land otter tilted its nose upward. A red-winged flicker, then a dogfish perched higher. My eyes lingered over the carved images. Near the top, the smiling sea lion belied the fate of the owner, who had not had time to finish his family's history. A smooth empty space at the top awaited the carving that would complete the totem's record. For a sickening flash, I saw in that uncarved space a kingfisher, its long beak pointed upward, its eyes staring over Sitka Sound. Chik'dhgesh, chik'dhgesh! Mindslip? Insanity?

Ashana, hide your distress, my joncha prodded me. I looked around for a familiar face—Attu, but he hunted far away. Richard. No greeting from Richard? I had many messages from Kadyak for him.

"Where is Richard?" I asked, shortly after stepping into the new house. I could not shake the sight of those houseposts and totem poles rotting on the beach; I was glad Watnaw had not come with us; for she had been so proud to describe them for me.

"Richard?" Baranov hesitated a little. "Oh, yes. He's gone."

"Richard gone? When?"

"Some time ago. I sent him home on an English ship sailing to India."

"I should have said good-bye." I turned away. There was no use letting Baranov see my sadness over the servant whom I had mistrusted at first as nothing more than my captor's slave, a young man who through the seasons drew closer to us Aláyeksan hostages than to the Tahtna workmen. He had become a trusted member of our Aláyeksan family.

Long ago, he and our friends had toasted me. That day from Sitka I sent my own toast across the ocean to him: Richard, may your parents be alive, and may you be happy with your rice patch in Bengal.

The children resisted going to bed the first few nights in the big house. Men called it "the governor's mansion": a huge building of peeled logs, with a dining room, living room, library, sleeping rooms, and an office overlooking the harbor. The sights and sounds of Novo-Arkhangelsk opened a whole new country for Sem and Denedi Belik'a to explore. The shift from Kadyak was easy for them, and as the days passed I saw how they were drawing closer to their father because he took time to fit them into his busy hours.

On sunny afternoons, Antipatr and Irina raced the length of the porch and down the steps to check each of the sixty guns that guarded Novo-Arkhangelsk. It mattered little that few of the men who serviced the guns could understand our children's mingled Tahtna and Aláyeksan; children speak a universal language understood by warm hearts all over the world. Only occasionally did they get a cuff on the ear from some brusque fellow who hated his post or resented being separated from his own children.

"You have a strange mixture of people here. I have never heard so many different tongues."

"Princess Anna, nearly one thousand people live in Novo-Arkhangelsk."

I remember Governor Baranov looking out at the harbor from the large window of our residence, and I can still hear his voice. "I will never again be caught by the Kolosh or anyone else. I have control everywhere in Aláyeksa. I have forbidden any foreign ships to trade guns to the natives. Every trader must deal through me for Aláyeksa's furs."

The laughter of Antipatr and Irina broke into our talk as they raced through the dining hall with its large fireplace, then danced around on the raised platform where those of Baranov's men who knew music could play for the receptions he would host when important visitors came to his capital.

"We like when the room talks to us, Mama." Irina listened and laughed as her voice buffeted one wall then another. Ivan Kuskov had built the governor's house according to Tahtna ways, a huge cavernlike place, in which voices echoed and reechoed. "It will be quieter when the damask drapes and the tapestries and rugs come, Anna. They will mute the sounds. Our next ship from Okhotsk should bring them," Aleksandr explained, whenever I complained about how exposed we were with nothing but gaping windows in the walls.

More than once I had difficulty getting my son to shed his uniform when it needed washing.

"You cannot take this off. The captain gave it to me. I have to be ready if I'm going to sea with him."

"Antipatr, the captain will not want you with him in such a dirty uniform. Look at the mud on your legs."

He pushed my hand back. "I can brush it off. You can't . . . ."

"A good sailor keeps his outfit clean and obeys orders."

"Yes, Antipatr. Do as your mother says." Aleksandr supported me. "Someday you will be an officer in the navy. You must learn the proper way to dress."

Aleksandr Baranov's pride in both Antipatr and Irina had grown as they had grown, most noticeably since the day on Kadyak when he had received word that Tzar Aleksandr's *ukaz* granted them legitimate and noble status.

"I have always called you *princess*," my captor said one day. He took special pride in me: in Novo-Arkhangelsk the change in my status served his official need for a first woman for Russian Aláyeksa. Although he wrote to his company ". . . I taught her to sew and to be a good housekeeper. She can be trusted in business matters," hostage I had lived at Pavlovsk, and hostage I remained at Novo-Arkhangelsk. In my greater isolation, my divided mind sent me escaping to Yaghenen, and with those brief happy memories of home was mingled a longing for Jabila, a longing that almost overwhelmed me.

On Sitka Sound more than on Kadyak, the faces, talk, and dress of Mother Russia forced themselves into my days and nights. The part of my mind that lived here listened and watched, cautious and wary as always. The tasks Baranov prided himself on having taught me kept me working inside for hours; I missed the outdoors, the open slopes a few steps beyond Pavlovsk village, friends walking beside me. Would Novo-Arkhangelsk's Tahtna layers make me more alien as the seasons merged one into another?

To keep from slipping into the Tahtna frame, I kept telling myself: Weave your strands strongly around me, my Athabaskan beginnings. Guard me from slipping into an alien being. Hold me fast to the lach'u of my people.

The young man who followed Aleksandr Baranov into our living room directed the servants to carry boxes of books and paintings upstairs to the library room. They came and went, bending under the heavy loads. An hour before the evening meal, Aleksandr called the children and me to him.

"I want you to meet a young sailor Captain O'Cain brought to us. A Yankee, Abram Jones from Massachusetts. He will tutor Antipatr and Irina."

The stranger greeted us, his voice low and pleasant. He was slight, his face tanned from outdoor duty—he looked like all the other Yankees and English who sailed in to Aláyeksa, and I had the feeling I had seen him before.

"Princess Anna"—he lingered over my title—"Abram will live with us. Tell the servants to make him comfortable in the sleeping room next to Antipatr's. He knows some Russian, but I want him to speak only English to Antipatr. I do not much like it, but English is the language of trade. My son must speak it."

Aleksandr took Antipatr's hand, turned to his tutor. "I think you will find my children bright, but there's little learning for them in this country."

"The men around the company tell me how quick your children are." Although Abram's voice sounded pleasant, it seemed uncertain. "From what my ears tell me, your boy and girl already know more than Russian. I see a sparkle in their eyes. They will learn fast."

And I remembered the chickadee of Kadyak, that other young man Baranov had assigned to teach me his language. Ah, Richard, I do miss you.

Novo-Arkhangelsk pulsated with Aleksandr Baranov's will to create a center of Russian culture. The governor had begun building his dream from that rough settlement. My captor's kremlin rose up from the high promontory commanding the harbor; its tower held a light much stronger than the one that guided the ships at Kadyak. The storehouse was piled with furs, and the sound of hammer against metal rang out from the workshops. There were quarters for the Tahtna men, an inn for guests, and shacks for the Aláyeksans. And the Russian church more than anything else had settled the alien presence on Sitka Sound.

One place, a strange, small building, drew me: I could not resist the tempting odor that hung around it. "It is the bread we bake," the workmen there told me. I watched the men pour little seeds—"wheat," they called it—into a large bowl, pound them into small bits with a heavy hammer, stir water and salt into them. Hours later, after much mixing and kneading, they shaped loaves and shoved them into a covered section of the fire pit to bake. I have to admit I loved the smell of fresh-baked bread.

That once baggy-trousered, poorly clad manager, bedeviled by monks and navy officers at Pavlovsk, presided over Novo-Arkhangelsk in his dark blue suit during the evenings he entertained his guests with Russian music. The alien trading vessels brought supplies that filled the storehouses, added many new things to the governor's house. "More ships land here than ever did at Kadyak. Men come from all over the world—English, Yankees, some Poles and Finns and Swedes, a few French and Spanish," Baranov said.

They came for furs, dined richly on meat and bread and vodka, joked with Aleksandr Baranov, and raised mugs to toast him: Winships and Campbells of New England, Astors of New York, English captains from Liverpool and Bristol.

The harbor served another need for the traders: Baranov had built a shipyard, and ships could be repaired while the men bargained and ate and drank. It was managed by a Mr. Lincoln, another alien import who came when O'Cain's ship had sailed in with Abram Jones.

Most traders no longer dared deal directly with Aláyeksan clans. The power of my captor had become absolute in ways and across regions that had not been possible from Kadyak. The honors represented by the Cross of St. Vladimir and the Order of St. Anne endowed him with a distinction that impressed the visitors. The alien traders spread word far beyond Aláyeksa of the power, the achievements, the hospitality of the Tzar of the North. Instead of trying to evade him as they had so often done when he ruled from Kadyak, they sought him out to bargain for the wealth of our seas and land. They needed the skilled Uɪchena hunters, the men over whom Baranov had sole dominion, the men he *owned*.

Those sea captains from far places! Free to sail wherever they would, bragging and independent, they came to Novo-Arkhangelsk fevered with lust for furs, always furs. Their scheming matched Baranov's, and together they plotted more robbery.

"I will rent you my Aleuts. In return, you will pay the Russian-American Company fifty percent of all the pelts you take, clear of all costs to me."

To avoid looking as if he were dealing in slaves, the governor and the traders agreed to pay each hunter a token amount. I viewed this as an insult. The aliens pushed our men to the limit, disregarded the danger, the loss of life, ignored that it was only because of Aláyeksan skills that they were able to reap such a rich harvest of furs. The venture ended with yet a further insult to our men: The *baidarshchik* in charge wiped out any payment owed the Aláyeksans: "You know that to keep a hunter costs the company a lot of rubles.'' I never learned if they were paid anything.

So it was that the world of the Tahtna grew, reached further and further, ignoring and insulting The Great Country, ignoring me, ignoring the terrible blood toll that growth was taking in animals and Aláyeksans alike.

25

I often heard a sound by the big gate, a crying like that of a hurt animal. One morning I slipped past the guard and saw several women standing in the shadows. Large labrets drew out their lower lips almost to the size of spoons. I had always pictured Watnaw's people as strong and free; but those women, faces worn and soot-blackened, garments streaked, looked closer to death than to life. They stared at me in surprise, backed away; and I realized my Tahtna dress frightened them.

"Stay, sisters." I spoke in the Gulushutna that Watnaw had taught me.

They covered their heads, turned, and ran. I sickened at the thought of how they must have seen me—an Aláyeksan woman in Tahtna trappings.

"Those women are the ones who killed their children before they fled the fort. Have nothing to do with them," Baranov scoffed when I asked him about the visitors. "Do not forget. Captain Lisianskii had to gun their fort to run the savages out. They could not hold it against us. They killed the dogs and children to make their escape. Cowards, they are. Brutes."

"I am told it was your guns that killed the children." The lach'u fit, and my captor must hear it.

He scowled, "Keep your place, Anna. It is none of your affair."

"None of your affair" rang in my head all that day, and before nightfall I was determined to make those women my concern; my own agony made me recognize their suffering. How could I get them to stay and talk to me? How could I ease their anguish?

As I put my two to bed that night, I pulled them close, held them a long time, knowing that each day I lost a little more of their hearts to their alien father. Must every Aláyeksan mother lose her children to the will of the aliens?

The sight of those grieving women stayed with me, and I needed the strength of Watnaw, K'atl', Sutina, and Lingen-Aka added to mine. Oh, my sisters on Kadyak, I would cry out, it is hard for me to bear not being with you, not laughing and crying with you, knowing I cannot reach out and touch you.

"Lingen-Aka?" Anakhta-yan had asked me when he and Solnikov brought the Aláyeksan hunting fleet back from far south. "I hoped she would come with you."

"I asked Baranov to let her come. He would not. He does not want the two of you together."

"I know. I know. It tears me, Ashana, thinking of her alone," Anakhta-yan said despairingly. "I should have tried harder. Taken her and headed to my islands. We could have hidden from them. But how many would the Tahtna have killed as the price for our freedom?"

It was no accident that Aleksandr Andreevich Baranov had ordered Watnaw and Lingen-Aka to stay in Pavlovsk village. On Sitka Island, I was unknown and alone. My captor required me to hold myself above the workers and the household servants, who did almost everything needful in the governor's residence. I could no longer walk into a workroom to talk with friends as I had on Kadyak, no longer could a woman slip into my house and confide a personal sorrow or laugh with me. There were no more small potlatches with my friends.

My failure to reach Watnaw's sisters troubled me, and several times I caught myself chanting the ancient phrases that came back to me after Jabila told me K'i'un had been abused, "Sh'una yula, una yula, come to me, come." As the days passed, I sang those words, tried to send them to the women outside the gate; my need to talk to them became so great I knew I would defy the warning that no one would be safe outside the stockade. Perhaps there was danger or death for Tahtna; but I did not believe there was any revenge toward me in the hearts of those mothers grieving for their children. These Gulushutna women needed me for a friend, and I needed them. Our clans differed, but we were all people of Aláyeksa. *Remember your friends, build with them a family in trust*—the qegh nutnughel'an had told me through Agagasik's spirit that night on the snowfield.

I thought I was singing "sh'una yula, una yula" under my breath, but one day Irina heard me. "What did you say, Mama?"

For some reason I held back, did not answer her. She insisted. "Why do you sing those words? They are not Kahtnuht'ana, are they?"

My arm around Sem, we settled down on a bench in the book room. "Sh'una yula, una yula? Yes, Sem, they are Kahtnuht-'ana. They are ancient words from the time of the beginnings of our people. I use them to reach out to others in trouble and draw them to me so I can help them."

"Sh'una yula, una yula. I like that, Mama."

"I always think, Irina, of the words calling—"

"Calling who, Anna?" Aleksandr's voice was like a stone crashing against a cliff. "Foolishness! Never talk such foolishness in my house. I have told you many times. I will not hear of it."

"Why, Papa?" Irina had no fear of her father.

"Because it is nonsense, that is why. You have more important things to learn." He glared at me. "Princess Anna, we must teach my daughter to live like a lady. This is a Russian house. You must manage it like one." His voice changed, became cunning. "Take a hand in sewing Russian clothes for yourself. For the children. You do fine work. Teach a couple of the women what you want done so you will have help.

"You do mean something to me, Princess Anna. I want us to have a better life here, and—" He paused, lost in thought. It seemed he was on the verge of saying more, but then he turned abruptly to the papers on his desk and was silent.

Proudly wearing his clean uniform, Antipatr strutted along the waterfront with Abram Jones, who talked of ships, sails, the men from alien ports. Irina often tagged along, too, absorbing everything told her brother. Words from the lingo of the waterfront began to turn up in the playtime chatter of both my children. At times, I heard the tutor translating a sailor's navigation book into words Antipatr could grasp and repeat. Always, Irina hung around them; much as I resisted seeing any difference between the two, she did seem to learn the new words faster than her brother.

On clear days, Abram sometimes took my son on board ship for a short voyage, leaving Irina behind. She would run into the house shrieking, "They left me, Mama! I want to go!" then slam the door, angry at not being included.

Faced with his child's outbursts, Aleksandr would lift our sobbing daughter onto his lap, run a clumsy hand through her hair. "There, there. Do not cry, Irina. Sailing is man's work. Not for girls." (Echoes flashed through my mind of another girl, long ago on Yaghenen, who pleaded with her brother until he took her with him to sail on Tikahtnu in his kayak.)

"Be patient. You are Papa's girl." Aleksandr dried her tears. "You will learn how to be a lady in a beautiful house. You will know how to serve tea. To sing. Even to play the piano. Let your brother do the men's work. I want you to become a fine lady and dress like one."

"I don't *want* to be a lady. What *is* a lady?"

I caught Aleksandr's glance across the top of Irina's head, and read in his eyes what stirred in his mind: His child knew no ladies; *princess* I might be by *ukaz*, but in his eyes I had not yet learned to be a *lady*.

Sitka Island's forests teemed with the best of Aláyeksa's animals. Late one afternoon, a Tahtna hunter brought in a wolf whose hind leg had been caught in a metal trap. The animal had chewed the limb half through in his frenzy to escape before the alien bullet crashed into his heart. Sem and I stared down at the tiqun, its majestic face twisted in death. Tiqun, who should run free, who called from the hilltops when the bright moon filled the sky. Tiqun. I reached down, touched the bloody leg; I felt the scars on Jabila's body beneath my fingers. To keep from crying out, from letting the hunter see my agony, I turned and walked away.

My husband's voice flooded into my mind as clearly as if he stood at my side. "Do not harm the wolf. He is my brother." As I looked back at the magnificent creature stretched on the ground, the feeling came to me that there on Sitka Sound, even in my loneliness, Jabila walked with me. "It was the time of the new moon in early spring. Food was short. No animals or plants had come from their winter hiding. Two women from different clans went out from their villages to look for something to eat. They walked and walked, one of them carrying her baby. Finally they made camp for the night. In the morning, they left the baby in camp, and went out to set squirrel snares. At night, when they came back to camp, they could not see the baby. In the tent lay a big wolf." Jabila's voice surrounded me as he told the long-ago legend.

" 'Come, I will show you where the baby is,' said the wolf.

"He led the way from the shelter to a little bed of spruce boughs that he had kicked together.

" 'Here. Your baby sleeps.'

"The woman picked up the child. It started to cry.

" 'I put your baby on a bed where he would sleep. He was crying when I came into camp.'

"Then, the next morning the wolf said, 'I will stay with your baby. You go hunt the squirrels. I am hungry, too.'

"The mother of the baby came back with her squirrels. She prepared them. She shared them with the wolf. Then she went out to set more snares. The woman from the other clan came back with her squirrels. She did not share them with the wolf. In a few days, the second woman disappeared.

"The mother of the baby caught many squirrels. Each day she shared them with the wolf. Soon, she had enough to feed her whole village. She said, 'I must go back now. My people are starving.'

"The wolf said, 'I will go with you.'

"She said, 'You may come with me, but do not come into my village. The hungry people might kill you.'

"He said, 'I will stay on a high hill where I can see your village. You will never starve again. I will bring food to you in times of need. As you did for me.'

"Ever after, when the people of the village were hungry, they would hear the howling of the wolf from high on the hill. The mother and her growing son would go out. They would bring back enough food for the whole village. And so it is that tiqun is our brother. He cares for us."

As the *promyshlennik* dragged tiqun toward the shack to take his pelt, the breeze stirred the heavy fur, and its richness shimmered in the sunlight as if its myriad hairs were crowned with tears.

Governor Baranov continued to complain of the Gulushutna women lingering and wailing at the gate to the stockade and ordered his guards to send them away. They kept coming back, showed no fear. I wondered how long it would be before an alien shot one of them. I planned to slip out and warn them, prodded by my need to tell them of another sister held hostage on Kadyak, my friend Watnaw, hoping one of them might remember her.

But why be devious? The next time Baranov complained, I confronted him, "I know why they cry."

"They have no cause to stand there wailing."

"You killed their children."

"That is not so. The savages killed them themselves, so they could escape." His anger mounted, his face reddened.

"No, Governor Baranov. The hunters say your guns killed the children, and then you burned the fort."

"Silence, woman. I have told you before, it is none of your affair."

"I know how to stop the crying," I persisted. "The Gulu-shutna have ceremonies for their dead. Those children had none."

My captor's face remained unchanged, but I saw from his eyes he had heard me. "All right," he said, "how can you stop them?"

I took a long look at him, then with as much dignity as I could muster, I made my point. "They will never stop until we return the remains of the children. Not until they have the bones of their dead."

"The small ones have been buried," he flashed at me. "Decently. We had to do it."

"Dig up the bones, Aleksandr. I will carry them to the mothers. Only then will they stop keening at the gate."

"Nonsense. Heathen. Against my church. I will not do it."

"Just give them the bones of their children. They can hold the ceremony, and they will stop keening. I know they—"

"Never will I understand the savages."

Three or four days passed. The wailing continued; but Baranov said nothing more to me until one morning across our table, he conceded, "It is being taken care of today. I have men digging for you."

"I will have Attu come with me. He speaks Gulushutna better than I do."

Alongside the common grave from which the men had dug them lay the remains of the children of Sitka—charred and burned hand bones, fleshless legs and arms, skulls so small I knew them to be those of babies, a few strands of scorched and twisted black hair. Attu and I took those scraps, dirty and muddied, cleaned them as best we could, and packed them into deerskin pouches. Then, dressed in our oldest Aláyeksan clothing, we blackened our faces and raked our hair down. We, too, were in mourning.

When the keening started again the next morning, we walked through the gate in full view of the guards and the governor. Three women had come. Rain had fallen, and they were wearing their outer garments. Each head was covered with a spruce-root

hat like Watnaw's that partially hid their faces, and over their
shoulders hung cedar-bark capes.

At first the women were wary, but they did not turn and run
from Anakhta-yan and me. With their eyes fixed on our bundles,
they moved toward where we stood, then questioned us about
the pouches, each word spoken out of the deep pain from which
it had risen.

We spoke slowly. And when the grieving mothers understood
what we carried, they stretched out their arms for our poor bundles, fingers clutching with hope while knowing that for them
we carried no hope. They clasped the bones of their children to
their breasts.

"It hurts, friends. Anakhta-yan and I had no part in your
children's murders. We know how you suffer."

"An awful deed. May the Tahtna perish." Attu spoke the
hope of all of us.

One of the younger women, her face lined with grief, raised
her head, stared at Anakhta-yan and said, "The buildings the
aliens have put on our land will not stand. Someday, they will
be no more."

The oldest of the three women peered at us; tears filled her
haunted, deep-set eyes until they became swimming black agates. Her white knuckles grasping the little bag filled with her
child's bones, she spoke. It was Watnaw's voice I heard. "My
people will wait. The eagle will strike. The fort will burn."

I wanted to talk with the mothers, but they left us standing
there and moved slowly along the path that would take them
high up the slope. The women of Sitka did not look back. From
their bowed heads and stooped shoulders, I knew they protected
the bones of their little ones from the cold and icy wind blowing
off the sea.

A thousand tiny feet seemed to patter in the storeroom upstairs.
Strange sounds for indoors, as if flocks of birds of the island
had flown through a window and were dancing above my head.
I listened. Sounds I was far more familiar with—footsteps, giggles—made me climb the stairs quietly in order not to disturb
the two, who I was certain made mischief. Just as I opened the
door, Sem threw a handful of Aleksandr's choicest trade beads
high into the air over Denedi Belik'a. The glee on their faces,
the fun they were having, almost kept me from interrupting, but
I dared not let their father come to the storeroom for trade beads

he valued above others—beads he had spent much time choosing—only to find a sack of them scattered on the floor.

I had watched Aleksandr hold two or three in the palm of his hand, saw his eyes fill with their sparkle, heard him tell Sem of their great worth. A couple of greenish-blue beads would pay for three to four deer or caribou skins. Two beads would buy three to nine beaver pelts, or one large bearded-seal pelt. A seal bladder of beluga fat could be traded for a dozen fine beaver pelts, which in turn could be bargained away for two or three beads from a cunning Tahtna. The aliens also bought food with beads—a large fish, the best salmon, could be had for a single bead.

I shook my head, smiled, as my children threw more beads and shrieked with laughter at the odd feeling as the beads rolled all over their bare bodies. Flock of birds indeed!

"Axdi!" I struggled to keep a straight face. "Axdi!"

They stopped their jumping in midair. "Mama, we will put them back."

We scooped up Aleksandr's beads handful by handful. Most of them were blue, several a dusky green, a few red or white, all about the size of my little fingernail. Irina giggled when she scraped off a few imbedded between her toes.

"Ouch!" Antipatr winced, pulling a sliver of wood from beneath his fingernail. Would the Tahtna never learn to finish wood so that it did not leave splinters? A few beads had slipped into cracks in the floorboards, and we had to leave them. Hopefully, Baranov's fading eyesight would fail to notice those that we could not retrieve.

I had always resisted trade beads in any of my sewing, though I knew some women had begun using them. I much preferred Aláyeksan shells and quills. But perhaps, here among the sacks of beads Aleksandr had hidden in his room, I could find a way to spend part of my idle time, even to teach Irina how we Athabaskans embroidered. Already, I could hear what my captor would say: "No. I will not have you waste valuable goods on such primitive work. I will soon have colored thread from Russia. Embroider like you should, the Russian way. You and Irina need more dresses. Spend your time on them."

I had little choice in the matter, could not say "I will" or "I won't," so I backed into a way to satisfy my need to keep busy. One day, Baranov out of the house on his business and the children gone to Abram Jones for their learning, I climbed the stairs to the storeroom and took out a piece of deerskin I had kept hidden. I had not decided what to use it for. Another painting? I thought of my painted caribou hide, safe with Watnaw on Kadyak. When would I finish it? But I was on Sitka Island. Should I make a gift for a friend? A headband for Anakhta-yan? Wristbands for Nidoc, who had sent me her beautiful moccasins? A fine piece to send home to my husband?

I longed to show Irina how to embroider, but it was a risk not yet to be taken. She was an open child, filled with excitement at learning new things; I would not burden her with the need to conceal from her father that we had used his precious beads, for I doubted she could hold back. "Papa, look. See my beadwork!" would drive him to roar at me in front of her. My own child, when can I be full mother to you? Take you to Yaghenen? You, whose eyes question me. The songs, the stories, our heritage, must you lose all that? Must you lose faith in me?

That day, as usual when I was alone, Novo-Arkhangelsk faded and memories of Yaghenen flooded my head. As my mother had done with her shells, I began stringing Aleksandr's beads, one at a time, on a sinew thread. When I had a solid line of green, I placed it on the tanned hide, making it look the way the stem of a flower would look—the stalk of a quani*l*ch'ey ashana, a white windflower. Then, taking my awl, I punched a tiny hole in the bottom of the hide, threaded the sinew through the opening, and tied it securely in the back. I did the same for the top of the "stalk," leaving enough play for it to curve gently and look as natural as I could make it. To secure the line of beads, I punched a hole between every bead or two, pushed the sinew thread through it and again tied it in the back. Slow, monotonous work.

Finally, my fingers tiring, I put down the piece. But then I remembered my mother saying that when a woman first learned this kind of embroidery she often got bored, felt like stopping. And that was the time when she had to pick up her thread and continue, because it is in this way she learns to stitch and tie very fast. I sighed, and went back to my work.

Stitch and tie, stitch and tie; undo the mistakes that creep in, even if it is only a tiny petal that misses being stitched correctly. Do it until the work is perfect. This is the only way a woman's sewing will improve, will give her pride in what she is doing and lead her on to do more. The beautiful designs she will come to create will make the people of her clan share her pride in them.

It took me months to make the windflower piece; often, when

I was alone, I took my embroidery from its hiding place behind a loose board under the rafters. I needed white beads for the petals in the center, but there was only one small bag of them, so I dared use only a very few. I wondered if these white beads were more valuable than the rest. In order not to use many of them, I embroidered other flowers on the same stalk—red, blue, yellow. I even added one I had imagined—a withered blossom in a dull tan shade, for which I found some dried seeds to take the place of Aleksandr's beads. It was quite an unusual stalk of blossoms, even for Yaghenen! Most of the trade beads were blue, so I made my background blue, like the radiant sky of home, and placed a strip of green at the bottom for the grass. The next time, I would do the sky and the ground first, then fill in the flowers. Or I might stitch a piece showing our trees and mountains—all straight lines, perhaps up-and-down peaks and valleys in a design exactly like our Athabaskan quill embroidery.

One day, more than a week after I had sewn in the last bead, I ran my hand over my work—the beads, big and clumsy, did not lie as smoothly as the porcupine quills of my mother's embroidery. I must do my work more carefully the next time, make finer stitches and tighter ties, if I would have a creation that would have been pleasing to my mother's eye.

"Aleksandr, please, when the men bag the porcupines for meat, tell them to bring me the quills."

"Nonsense. You do not pay attention, Anna. I will not have you waste time. Wait for the Russian thread and goods. You need them if you want to sew fine things."

But in those days, I could only dream of my mother's fingers, skilled and quick, making the porcupine-quill embroideries; working with the deerskin had opened my mind to a pleasure long lost to me. My mother sat with me. And I saw one of the older women flatten the quills between her teeth, dampening them with saliva so they would bend easily. She prepared them that way for my mother because her own eyes had dimmed too much for embroidery stitching herself; but the old woman wanted no idle time, and over the years her teeth had worn nearly to the gums with working the quills. In exchange for her flattened quills, my mother prepared her friend's food—tender meat, mashed berries, the soft part of the sarana root. My mother folded the flattened quills—back and forth, forth and back—to form a band of mountain peaks. Sometimes she sewed her pattern on a loose mat, other times she made bands of the fine sinew, wove the quills over and under the threads. Always, she hid the threads—the mark of an expert. She knew how to tie down her work with stitches so small they could hardly be seen. She had learned this from her mother, just as all my father's wives learned from their mothers. When I started my piece, one of the people I had in mind to send it to was Nidoc, but by the time it was almost finished I decided not to: The work did not lie smoothly enough, and the stitches must be finer or Nidoc would get the wrong impression of Jabila's first wife.

I did not belong in Novo-Arkhangelsk, and I had no Aláyeksan friends, for Attu had again been sent south with the hunting fleet, Solnikov in command. Baranov and Kuskov talked constantly of their great creation on Sitka Sound. Traders sailed into the harbor in big ships, and with the Tahtna toasted the new kremlin of America. Every few weeks more of the giant evergreens in the Gulushutna country fell, and alien axes hacked them into boards for another building. The alien work did not kindle any pride in me; the new capital, the new fortress, the guards at the gates—men whose watching eyes and booted feet reminded me of the guards around my house on Kadyak—held me firmly hostage, and there was no way to escape to the Gulushutna.

Consumed though he was with Novo-Arkhangelsk and his trading ventures, Baranov did take time during the evenings to enjoy the furnishings of his house, the books and paintings. He would spend hours in the book room with Antipatr, talking about maps and navigation charts, planning ahead for the St. Petersburg Naval Academy. Although Aleksandr did not share as much time with Irina as he did with her brother, his will to mold her into a Russian lady burned with greater intensity than it had back in our old house.

I, too, spent more time with my children, followed their interest in books in order to keep them close to me. But they were turning away from things Kahtnuht'ana, and more and more I recognized that I was losing them. They were becoming aliens. The mist that had begun to separate us in Kadyak became denser, and my children's turning aside cut me sharply.

Aleksandr and I lived a strange life; the chasm between us widened, although he must have thought our relations improved, for he kept telling me, "In Novo-Arkhangelsk, Princess Anna, you are truly the first lady of Aláyeksa. We have a great house. We have servants to do all of the work, and you can manage them. Soon, more fine goods and clothes will come from Russia.'' Sometimes his voice softened, and he put his arm around me, ''Princess Anna, you are beautiful. We have the best years ahead of us.''

When he used me, my passion dull and unstirred, my feelings icy, he paid no attention to how I felt, but poured out his manhood as if into a vessel, his revelry with my body an affair that began and ended in him. I hoped it would never cause another child to grow in me. I thought of other Aláyeksan women filled by the *promyshlenniki*; their sanity stretched to the limits of endurance, they took every means possible to keep their niłdulchinen from growing up to be taken for the alien slavery; it is whispered, some were even killed in the womb. And was not that way out just as painful as mothers starving seven- or eight-year-old children to keep them from the levies of Governor Aleksandr Andreevich Baranov? Dreadful forces were at work, terrible to think about.

Spindrift, Anakhta-yan called them, those Gulushutna children. And what of my two, their hearts and minds riding the crests, only to sink and be devoured by the waves a few moments later?

The ship that docked at Novo-Arkhangelsk's wharf brought the cargo Baranov had long expected; damask, drapes to keep out the night, coverings for the table, clothes to replace his worn ones, materials and colored thread from which to make clothes for the children and me, books, food supplies, an ample stock of tea. And kegs of vodka. Always, when a ship sailed into the harbor, excitement filled the settlement.

But a few weeks later, the excitement brought by the ship and its goods was overshadowed for the governor by rumors of the same moody discontent and plans for revolt he had faced on Kadyak when his *promyshlenniki* had attempted to rise against him.

At noon one day, the air still chilly even when the spring sun favored us for a few hours, Ivan Kuglinov, Aleksandr's nephew and secretary who had replaced Kuskov, hurried into the office with a workman he called Mukin, a name I had never heard on Kadyak. Baranov, busy with reports, scarcely acknowledged the intrusion. About to enter the office, I stopped before anyone saw me and listened.

Ivan started to speak, but the workman interrupted, ''Your life. You're in danger, sir.'' Furtive, glancing from Baranov to

Kuglinov and back, the man hesitated, twisting the fur cap in his hands.

"Go on," the governor ordered, leaning against the back of his chair.

"Like I said. Your life. You not be safe." Again he hesitated, wary over what he was revealing. "The night guards, they plan to kill you. They—"

Baranov came to his feet. "Kill!" he boomed out. "Kill me? How do they propose to do such a thing?"

"They got me into it. Maybe twenty others," he said, looking back at Kuglinov.

"Just tell him the rest. Don't worry. We will keep it to ourselves," Baranov's nephew reassured.

"In August, when all the ships have gone, they'll come in the night. Kill you. Your son. Take your woman and girl."

Silence filled the office for some moments, the only sound Aleksandr's banging the desk top with something heavy. "I do not understand why I have not heard of this if so many are plotting."

"I doubted the story, too. So I wanted you to hear it first-hand," Kuglinov said.

"Write up a sheet of notes for me, Ivan. Have Mukin sign it or make his mark with you as the witness. I will lock it in my desk."

A couple of weeks later another workman brought word of the same plot. Then Karpinski, a hand from the wharf, came to our door early one evening before Baranov returned from his inspection of the harbor and warehouses. He and Kuglinov waited impatiently, a few words passing between them; I had observed that Baranov's nephew carried on his duties in a quieter manner than had Kuskov, having much less to say in the presence of other people than the former clerk. The two followed the governor into his office and closed the door.

Restless in bed that night, Baranov talked to me. "It is true. Two of my own men, a bastard each one. They have organized several workmen, with the idea of killing me. Seizing guns and supplies and a ship, then sailing south." Aleksandr was obviously worried, for I could hear it in his voice. "They complain of the hard work. The wet and cold. The bad conditions. Mukin says they intend to take as many women as they can lay hands on."

"Are you sure they have gone that far?"

"Enough has been said over the past weeks to convince me.

Ivan believes he can find out the names of the others. He is doing fine work for me. He is loyal, so I trust him. Princess Anna, this terrible plot includes you, too.'' My captor's voice softened, and he took my hand in his. ''The men say that you and the children will be killed at the same time. Or worse—they threaten to take you and Irina with them.''

Perhaps a Tahtna revolt would give me a chance to escape. ''I . . . Aleksandr . . . how could . . . I have always feared the Tahtna men's quarrels,'' I said, trying to mask my real thoughts.

''I ask myself the same thing. How could anyone think of killing Antipatr? Irina? Killing you, Princess Anna?'' His words sounded harsh.

''Always, my fear has been for Irina.'' I could barely whisper for the terrible images that rushed into my mind.

''None of this will touch you or the children. We know enough to keep ahead of the plot.'' Aleksandr tried to reassure me, held me close. ''I will order those bastards locked up before they can attack any of us. It was different when they tried to kill me on Kadyak. I have trusted men guarding the house.''

Governor Baranov felt much more secure when Captain Jonathan Winship dropped anchor in Sitka harbor, knowing the Yankee trader brought supplies and food and guns. Saying nothing to Winship and the other guests of trouble on Sitka Sound, Baranov planned with Ivan that they would seize the plotters during a feast at our mansion, a time when he knew the traitors would relax, drinking and singing; if they got drunk enough, perhaps they could be taken without bloodshed.

One evening early in August, Winship and his officers were invited to our house for a night of revelry. The beacon above the second story sent its light far out over the Sound. Mugs of hot punch that Richard had taught a servant to blend in a way the governor enjoyed preceded the dinner. Our kitchen hands served vegetables grown on the company farm, steaming baked salmon, and fresh bread from the bakery. On the raised platform, at one end of the dining room, musicians played balalaikas and sang. The traders and Baranov feasted happily, unaware of the governor's worry about the plot brewing among the *promyshlenniki*. Then the balalaikas sounded the opening notes of *''Pyesnya Baranova,''* Baranov's song, and the guests rose and sang the old words written by their host, words I had first heard on Kadyak. As the men at our table settled down to more drinking, a messenger slipped in and spoke quietly to Baranov, who excused himself and went outside.

Later, in the quiet of our sleeping room, I rubbed vodka into the governor's shoulders to loosen his muscles. "Ivan and I know those men," he said after a while. "They put on their celebration, just like we thought they would. We waited outside. Then, at an agreed signal, we grabbed the devils, and that killed their revolt in a hurry. Princess Anna, I thank our saints and my trusted nephew. A bit of a tussle, the quick twisting of their arms, but no bloodshed."

Aleksandr sat up, drew me close. "Princess Anna, why? The men know I do not ask any favors. They had no reason to . . ." He seemed uncertain what more to tell me and turned sideways so that I could rub his neck and the base of his skull.

"A dozen of them had met in the guards' quarters to drink. We put them up against the wall. Took every gun they had. I have locked them up till I can ship the lot off to Siberia. The government will punish them. Severely. You know I hold the *ukaz* of the Tzar that appointed me governor in Aláyeksa. Revolt against me is treason against the Russian government. It will likely cost those fools their lives."

Whenever Baranov talked of the levels of authority among Tahtna, the harsh means used in his country to control the people, punishments cruel by Kahtnuht'ana standards, I thought how simply my clans managed their affairs and went about the day-to-day business of living. The tradition of sharing made only a few direct rules necessary. And those rules rested in common sense. We had no reason to create many different rules to manage people, rules rooted in mistrust rather than trust. We knew the benefits that lay in turning our energies to gathering and sharing The Great Country's resources in order that our men and women and children might better live as one with our land and sea.

"My own men." He beat his fist against his hand. He shook his head. "Not savages. My own men. Russian. Murder my son and daughter."

For the next couple of weeks, Aleksandr spent more time with Antipatr and Irina than he did at his desk, talked to them but kept the troubles with his men to himself. He sketched ships and sails, avoided taking Antipatr to the wharf. He had more stories for Irina, and at night she resisted being put to bed until her father had told her one. To me, he talked more of his concern for our safety than he ever had at Pavlovsk.

Late one evening, the children asleep, Aleksandr told me that he must send us back to Kadyak: He had caught other Tahtna men plotting against us. "I have arranged for Abram Jones to go with you. He will continue the lessons for Antipatr and Irina. I have written instructions to Ivan Banner, who will assign special guards for you, and will be in charge of everything you and the children do."

He seemed unusually moved. Another plot to kill? His own men revolting again?

"I remember when those men came," I said, concerned for Irina and Antipatr. "You said then they were the worst of Siberia. Many of them criminals."

"Yes, Anna, a tough breed."

"They were bad men in Siberia. Why would they be any different here?"

"I gave them a chance no one else did. I thought they would change, but trouble is all I get."

I remember my concern when he talked of sending us back to Kadyak. More than anyone, I knew how much of himself the man poured into his mission for Russia, the long hours, the risks. Trouble with the traders, fights with the Gulushutna, unrest among us Aláyeksans—these problems he fumed and fought against; but they did not touch his heart as did the revolts by his own countrymen. He seemed like a giant bird unable to fly, his wings fouled by grease.

I had found myself defensive of my captor two or three times before, had even seemed to take his part when I told Rezanov that the governor gave his life to his work. Was concern becoming compassion? Not exactly. Always, weaving through my thoughts, were the questions I kept asking myself: Why always so much unrest? Why the constant hatred of one Tahtna for another, even among the monks? Was not Baranov's heavy hand responsible?

Aleksandr Baranov held me close that last night on Sitka. Again I sensed feelings beginning to rise unbidden in me, a softening toward him strange for me; and I found myself wondering if perhaps our many seasons living within touch of each other, the fact of the children we had given life to, the stresses between us that we did seem able to surmount, had interwoven to draw us together in ways over which I might have no control. Two fine children, yes, but I could never forget that Baranov's stubborn will bent our people to his uses. Then my joncha spoke to me; and, oh, I became uneasy about what was happening to me that night, about the alien ways that were taking hold of me, about denial of the Athabaskan human being that I was.

Body: Many times mine had been forced to wear alien clothes; when would it come to *like* those Tahtna coverings?

Mind: Many times on the point of yielding under the power assaulting it, my mind seemed able to pull back; when would it finally break and submit?

Shadow-spirit: This, the third part of my Athabaskan being, drew back my wandering self and allowed it to return to me. When the softness toward my captor would begin gnawing at my resistance, my shadow-spirit touched me and its strength drew me away from the wanderings. Ehu! Never, never, doubt my shadow-spirit. But oh, the danger, when I gave even a moment to the Tahtna, a never-ending cause for despair!

"My Princess Anna," Baranov whispered, as he told me of the plans for the voyage, assured me that a good ship would take us from Novo-Arkhangelsk to Pavlovsk, talked mostly of Antipatr and Irina. "The work here will keep me many months. My children are growing fast. They must be properly trained. They will spend the better part of every day with Abram and learn what he has to teach them. I insist that Antipatr know English. I wish him to take his place among important men."

I badly wanted to say what I thought about their learning, but that last night I held back, not daring to risk one of Baranov's explosions and the chance that as punishment he might keep me from sailing with my children.

"Princess Anna, I am growing old." He turned to me, "I'm growing old, but I have never gotten over my need for you."

He brushed his mouth across my face, kissed my ear.

"The duties to Russia and to my company demand so much. I know I have neglected you many times."

His hands roamed under my nightdress. "Anna, you are more beautiful than when I first found you. You are the only woman I know who grows more beautiful." His arms held me tightly. "I know I am aging, but you seem younger. I will miss you the cold winter months. Anna. Anna."

A trace of feeling for him began rising in me again, but my shadow-spirit touched my heart with cold, and the feeling faded at once. Perhaps knowing that the next day I would leave caused the mosquito mask to slip over my face.

As Baranov slid from me, my tongue turned stinger. "All your other women, Aleksandr. The Chugach. The one on Unalaska. The women you use in the shacks. Did you call all of them *Anna*?"

Surprised at my sudden, stinging words, my captor shoved

his knee hard against me, pushed himself up on one elbow. I pulled away, for in his anger he had raised his fist. "Anna . . . there's no reason . . . it's none of your affair." His words jumbled together. His fist dropped. He lay back on the bed.

In the last light of the long day, the sun reached through the window to play on the lines of his face. His anger turned to pleading. "Anna, Anna, can't we come to terms on this, our last night here? Forget everyone else?"

"Bitch," Igor had called me that day when I was first dragged before Aleksandr Andreevich Baranov. I hated him then. So, if holding firmly to my resolve to stay angry at my captor until my death made me one, then "bitch" I still was the day I left Sitka Island.

26

As our ship dropped anchor in Pavlovsk harbor, I knew the message of my return had gone before me; as always, word had sped swiftly between Aláyeksan clans separated by many yíl— even now Tahtna do not know how it is done. Silence had bade me farewell when we left Kadyak for Sitka Sound. On my return to Pavlovsk, as I came on deck, Aláyeksan shouts and cheers rang across the water, growing louder when the children appeared beside me.

"Who are all those savages?" Abram Jones's voice shook. "What is going on? Will they attack us?"

I ignored him a few minutes. Let the man suffer.

Denedi Belik'a answered him, "Those are our friends."

"Mama, look at them! They are all dressed up." Sem waved from the edge of the deck, leaning so far forward I grabbed her skirt to keep her from falling.

As the umiak taking me to the shore nudged the side of the Tahtna vessel, I saw smiles on the faces of the rowers, men I recognized from my many seasons here. Eager hands helped me from the boat and passed me from one person to the other, the varied tongues of Kadyak greeting me. Watnaw almost squeezed the breath out of me, and Sutina and K'atl' threw their arms around both of us. Looking for Lingen-Aka to give her Anakhtayan's message, I remember thinking, strange that I could not see her with my other friends, and I reminded myself to find her before the day was gone. Behind us, a large umiak slid to rest, carrying the children, more belongings, and the still-frightened Abram Jones. He stayed on the craft, under the pretense of helping unload, until he saw Ivan Banner speaking to me.

Back in Pavlovsk, the house not so huge, not so alien, as the governor's mansion in Novo-Arkhangelsk, I had returned to the

familiar. I felt more secure, for again I could stand on the headland and look northward beyond the islands to Yaghenen, and
Jabila walked closer to me.

My women friends came in a body to the house, bringing
wooden bowls and baskets of food and gifts. At first they seemed
a little stiff, although our separation had not been long enough
for us to become complete strangers; but we soon warmed to
one another.

"We honor you with a little potlatch, and celebrate your safe
return to us." Watnaw took charge of the festivities as men and
women thronged my house. It was a day of reunion for us Aláyeksans—Koniags, Ulchena, Kahtnuht'ana, Chugach, Eskimo,
Gulushutna, and a few Ageluht'an. Even a contribution from
the Tahtna: Mr. Banner himself offered a toast to the health of
the absent Governor Aleksandr Andreevich Baranov. A half
smile played on my face as I saw Abram Jones sticking close to
Banner.

Each clan added a different flavor, a variation of color, a
distinctive tone according to its practice of the potlatch. Among
the gifts for me were several articles we had previously hidden
from the eyes of all aliens: one of Sutina's hammered copper
bracelets, Watnaw's blanket from her Gulushutna village with
its strong Chilkat pattern, a new deerskin qenich'eni from my
Kahtnuht'ana relatives, an exquisite, tightly woven basket—an
image of slim Ulchena fingers with long sharp nails splitting the
reeds into threads finer than the Tahtna or the English or any
other Aláyeksan could make flashed through my mind.

My heart jolted. Still no Lingen-Aka?

As if they sensed my question, my friends closed in tighter
and swept me into the circle of dancers, and amid the clamor of
the celebration it was impossible to stop anyone. I missed hearing Lingen-Aka's soft voice, her laughter. I chided myself: Why
didn't I find her right away, the moment I stepped ashore?

During the feasting, I asked Watnaw, "Lingen-Aka?"

She silenced me with her glance and a downward motion of
her hand. "Not now. I will tell you when the others have left."

Later, as we had done so many times when we needed to talk
alone, Watnaw and I settled before the fireplace in my house.
She spoke quickly, in broken phrases, and I did not interrupt.
We had so many things to speak about, but Lingen-Aka came
first.

She told me that late one night two *promyshlenniki* had burst
into Lingen-Aka's bunk, and dragged her from the other women,

who cowered with dread that the men would force them to the shack, where the singing and drinking had turned into an orgy. Tossing Lingen-Aka from one to the other, pouring vodka over her head, they danced her wildly from man to man, tore off her clothes. As she reeled naked back and forth between them, crying and screaming, a *promyshlennik* pulled her down onto the table and drove his penis into her in full view of staring excited eyes, each man envisioning himself in the man's place. Roaring at his conquest, squeezing her mouth shut to cut off her screams, the first one raped her, then rolled aside; other hands reached out, and a second half-clad Tahtna flung himself on top of her. Another, then another, used Lingen-Aka, chewed her breasts to bloodied skin and flesh, spat out streams of blood mixed with saliva and vodka. Half crazed, semiconscious, she lost even the strength to cry out for mercy.

On the beach the next morning, the Ulchena hunters found the body of Lingen-Aka. They summoned women of their clans, who wrapped her in a gut sack. Silently, our people watched from shore as the kayakmen disappeared westward into the haze across the face of the sea to place Lingen-Aka into the arms of the nutin'at dnayi.

Before the aliens came, the Ulchena would have wrapped her body tightly in layer upon layer of skins and laid it safely in a cave far out of reach of marauders. With the coming of the Tahtna, the Ulchena were forbidden to put their dead in caves; but in the depths of the sea, spirits still lived whom the Ulchena could trust. Lingen-Aka rests with the sea people.

A few days after the little potlatch, Watnaw met me on a point overlooking the harbor. No questions were needed. She gave me more details of the tragedy; her voice did not break, but stayed low and ominous like the measured beat of a drum. There was no need to fret over our status—hostage, slave, concubine. We knew exactly what we were. Nothing had changed during the years to lessen our despair.

Lingen-Aka had refused the marrying, spurned the men's advances. *Promyshlenniki* jokes about her and Attu had become common, for the men had decided they would make an example of her in case any other woman held herself to be too good for them. Hostage women lived knowing that an orgy could at any time unite yet another of them with Lingen-Aka.

So much for the protection promised by Aleksandr Baranov. So much for the Tzarina Catherine's words: "I notify you that in visiting the islands inhabited by Aleuts, you must treat them kindly. Do not molest them in any way.''

Aláyeksans knew: *God is too high and the Tzar is too far.*

My caribou painting hung on one wall of the house. When Watnaw heard I was coming home, she had unrolled the hide, sewed hanging loops on it. She and Lingen-Aka had pegged it up. The unfinished nanutset of hostage Aláyeksa stretched before me. I traced my fingers over the ribbed qenich'eni of my lost parents as they stood on the shore of Yaghenen the day my life as hostage began. I put my face up to Jabila, standing beside Seltan in the pass to faraway Htsaynenq'. I counted the kayaks that left Kadyak's shores for the sea hunt, mourned with their women. Only then did I dare look at Lingen-Aka, whom I had painted as she looked that day watching Rezanov's ship make its way into the harbor; I covered her image with my hand and stood a long time weeping for the sister who was no more.

Sitka. Vivid scenes flashed through my mind, people and places demanding to be remembered in Aláyeksa's nanutset: the scarred totems and house posts on the beach . . . the bones of the children . . . the trade beads . . . aliens renting the hunters. The caribou hide was becoming crowded, but I would paint in whatever remained to complete the story.

Late one evening, shrieks pierced the air, jerking my mind back from its wanderings, and I knew another woman suffered at the hands of the aliens. Rage burned away caution. Pulling on old clothing and a pair of salmon-skin boots, I ran to Ivan Banner's house and pounded on his door. Sleepy-eyed, a shadow of Baranov in his white nightshirt, Banner peered out at me.

''Anna, what do you want this time of night?''

''Down there!'' I yelled at him. ''Your men are killing a woman.''

''*Nyet.* Just a little *praznik.*''

''I hear her. Listen.''

A woman's high-pitched cry came to us, cut off by shouts and drunken laughter.

''Hear that!''

''Anna, those men have had their fun for years. They need it. There is no problem.''

''Come. We must save her. Now!''

''You always make trouble. Go home and be quiet. I warn you, Anna, don't put yourself in bad with me again.''

"You will not make them stop?" I yelled at him, his closed-in mockery building rage in me until I wanted to claw his face.

"No reason to. The men have a right to a *praznik*."

"But Lingen-Aka . . ."

"An accident." His arrogant voice pushed me back as he slammed the door in my face.

I stamped away from Banner's house. From the shadows of the trees, the forms of Watnaw and other women, a few Ulchena hunters with them, emerged, all of them scarcely able to keep from rushing in to rescue the victims of this orgy, but holding back because they had waited to hear what Banner had told me.

"He won't help." I motioned Watnaw and several others to follow me. Taking time to grab sticks and run for masks, we crept toward the women's screams, stopped long enough to agree that we would swoop in silently, as the hawk attacks its prey.

The door was ajar, no guard in sight. I pushed it opened, slipped in, my friends behind me. Holding a lantern high, his back to us, the guard stood guffawing, enjoying the tussling shadows on the furs at each side of the room. Through the smoke, the stench of dirty furs mingled with sweat and homemade vodka. No one heard us. Watnaw grabbed the light as I clubbed the guard on the back of the head; we gagged and tied him before he regained his senses. Our hunters jumped on two half-dressed Tahtna—one trying to crawl under the furs, the other swearing oaths I had never before heard—clubbed and bound each one while Watnaw and I rushed the women out of the shack.

Ekdu! It pains to this day! The women we held were Sutina and K'atl'. Watnaw wrapped her cape around the shaken Sutina, who seemed to huddle into herself as if wanting to disappear. Her voice was filled with shame, "I never wanted you to see me like this."

And K'atl'—named by her mother in Yaghenen for the soft, fresh powder snow—at first drew away from me, would not let me put a comforting arm around her. I knew how she felt—sullied, violated, as dirty as the filthy snow lying around the Tahtna hunting shacks, snow dishonored by animal guts, rotten food, and human waste.

Sutina, older, inured by past ordeals, seemed to snap back more quickly than K'atl', whom I watched carefully. I took charge of K'atl'; she had been stolen from Yaghenen before her parents could teach her much of the lach'u of the Kahtnuht'ana, and she had little inward strength she could draw on to sustain her through a crisis. Only with gentle compassion could I lead

her back, make her know that her body might be abused, her
breath almost stifled, but her shadow-spirit would remain as
innocent as that fresh powder snow her mother had seen the day
she was born.

K'atl' needed me for a long time, whether we talked or just
sat working quietly—tying fishnets, scraping skins, patching an
old garment or sewing a new one. And sometimes I took her
with me to the storehouse, taught her to count puffin skins and
mark them down to the name of each hunter.

Ivan Banner insisted on blaming and punishing his men's assailants, disregarding what had happened to K'atl' and Sutina,
for they were merely *two hostage savages earning their keep*; their
first duty was to satisfy the men; they were wrong to resist.

For several days, Banner called men to his desk, lined up
women in front of shacks, questioned everyone. But who would
name the Tahtna men's assailants? None of the Aláyeksans would
speak, and the Tahtna did not know, for our masks had hidden
us.

Justice for all Russia's children: "Do not molest them in any
way." Times without number I thought of the Tzarina's words
that Richard had told me.

Justice. Banner decreed that one hostage be shot. His men
quickly carried out the order.

And gentle Lingen-Aka lies in the arms of the sea people.

An uneasy truce settled over Pavlovsk. Aláyeksans knew the
Tahtna who had abused and murdered; they waited, picked the
time, struck. A boat tipped over. Alien hunters disappeared, no
bodies found. Another, known by the Aláyeksans to have bru-
talized Lingen-Aka, died from poisoned meat; two more per-
ished from the same cause. Banner never knew what happened
to his *promyshlenniki*.

But our people knew.

Sem. My daughter grew tall and straight, a beautiful Kahtnuht-
'ana. Even though she was the child of Governor Baranov, so
many men hated him that I was fearful for her. How many
seasons would pass before she, too, would be grabbed and
abused?

I had found no way to escape to the Gulushutna in Sitka;
despite the conflict there, the governor's house was closely
guarded. Realizing that nothing had improved for us hostages
in Pavlovsk, the fear for Sem rising, I became almost desperate
in my need to escape.

* * *

I had Abram Jones to deal with, and I divided the children's time so that he was satisfied and I had more hours free to be with them. The young man had not seemed well on Sitka Island; his sickly spells were more frequent here; and he complained much about the wet climate and harsh conditions. To him, Kadyak was a land of crude and uncivilized ways far exceeding the acceptable. His troubles, often soothed with rum, took much of his time and eased the relationship between us, for they made him less demanding as the children's teacher.

"Denida Belik'a and Sem. Gather your friends. Perhaps they would like to see the old beaver pond," I suggested one day.

That morning, a small group of niłdulchinen walked with the three of us to the pond not far from Pavlovsk. Several of the children who had listened to my stories before had disappeared—some sent to uncles and aunts, a few grown old enough for company work levies, others being hidden right on Kadyak. A number were new to me. Shy, somewhat wary of me but trusting Denedi Belik'a and Sem, they had little to say. As we followed the trail, my voice low, I asked them easy questions about the trees, the sky, the sea. They began to open to me, and by the time we reached the pond seemed ready to listen to the lach'u and nanutset of our peoples.

A few smiles touched thin faces when Sem asked, "Mama, will you tell us the lazy beaver sukdu?"

"Do any of you besides Sem know the story?"

"Yes, Mama." Only my son answered.

"I will tell you the lazy beaver sukdu." I arranged the children in a circle on a grassy slope overlooking the pond.

"Two uncles took their nephew hunting in the old style. They were mean old men, and they always said their nephew was lazy. They chopped a hole in the top of a beaver house and put him inside to watch for the beavers. The beavers did not come. The uncles got tired, so they decided to go back and get the nephew. They found him asleep instead of watching for beaver. One of the uncles said, 'Such a lazy nephew is not worth having.' They covered the top of the beaver house and left him there to die.

"Soon, two beavers came out of the water. They walked into their house. They looked at him: 'A lost man. Cold and hungry.' The beavers went up to the nephew. One of them started talking to him. 'They left you here because you are lazy and sleep all the time. But we will help you. Then you will have more ambition than they do.'

"The beavers started a fire. They killed one of their beaver slaves. They cooked him. Then they fed him to the nephew. 'You will be a mighty hunter now,' they said.

"The nephew promised he would never hunt beaver again. Then he stood up. He went home.

"He really scared his uncles. They could not understand how he escaped from the beaver house. Time went on. People noticed the nephew was no longer lazy. They saw he was a good worker and a mighty hunter. No one knew the cause, or why it was that he never hunted beaver again."

The ni*dulchinen, sensing the freedom of the outdoors where they could not see an alien, were eager to hear more. Each clan of Aláyeksa has its own story of the beginnings of its people, and I needed to stretch my teachings to bring in the nanutset of our different clans. It would take time, but those little ones must learn before they grew older and were lost in the service of Baranov's company. Some of them, like Denedi Belik'a, were clearly of mixed blood. But in Sem, my Kahtnuht'ana features stood out clearly—she had black eyes, was slim and lean, finer boned than most ni*dulchinen; only her curly hair marked her as being half Tahtna. Denedi Belik'a walked with the same heavy footfall his father had; Sem stepped so lightly that her feet left only the faintest shadow of a print on the grass.

A change in the early morning air told me that summer would soon fade into autumn. The warm breezes had taken on their first crispness, and already birds had begun to wing their way southward. One day, when there were no classes with Abram Jones, I planned a trip with my children to pick berries for our winter supply. We found a couple of large baskets for me, smaller ones for Denedi Belik'a and Sem. I filled one with food, as we planned to be gone overnight.

As we started away from the porch, Watnaw appeared; she whispered, "Jabila and his men have brought meat. Follow the path to the berry patch beyond the pond. The Tahtna never tramp through there. That is where he is waiting."

My heart pounded. A rush of feeling spread a softness through me I had not known since Jabila had come to me before Novo-Arkhangelsk. I wanted to shout my love high into the sky, but I needed to mask my emotion from the children. I tried to walk along naturally, calmly, my eyes filling with helpless, happy tears. My children, eager for the ripe berries, raced ahead uncaring.

Denedi Belik'a and Sem knew Jabila only as "uncle." The time would soon come when they must be told the true relation between us, but I dared not yet explain it.

"Ashana." Watnaw took my arm. "If Banner asks about you, I will tell him you needed to pick berries. That you had too few for winter. Do not worry."

As if we met every day, Jabila joined us on the path; we strolled along together like a family. By the time we reached the berry patch, I could act calmly, and the children did not notice the hunger in our eyes. Jabila laughed with us, helped fill our baskets, gathered ferns and boughs for the children's beds. When first I had seen him waiting, I had to struggle to keep from rushing to him, passion burning deep within me for the tall, handsome man whose image had come to me many times through all my seasons on Kadyak and Sitka Sound.

In the shelter of a cliff, we built a fire to soften the night's chill. The whisper of the tree spirits spoke of their pleasure at having us come to the forest; I felt them close to me. It was a good time to talk about trees, not people. "Denedi Belik'a . . . Sem . . . listen. The tree spirits you hear singing and talking make trees very special to us Athabaskans. After dark, other spirits come alive in the forest. You can hear trees walking around—it is a time when they come out to find where wrong has been done and to make it right. In the morning, the trees are back in their places. Their night spirits sleep. In the daytime, different voices speak."

"Trees move around?" Denedi Belik'a's voice turned skeptical, echoed that of Aleksandr Baranov.

"Don't be stupid," Sem scolded. "You've seen a big tree blown down, roots sticking up in the air. The bad spirits did it."

In the fading daylight, we watched the shadows of the trees moving in the breeze, listened to the voices of the forest, trusting that Jabila had chosen a spot where the bad spirits would not fight with the trees during the night. The warmth of the fire spread around us, but the warmth that suffused me rose out of my desire for Jabila.

As Sem lay on her pine boughs, I could see her wide-open eyes gleaming in the firelight. She whispered, "Mama, you know those spirits Jabila talked about? Are any of them šdóná-lyášna?"

I did not want to scare her. We Dena'ina Athabaskans know that several beings invisible to us live inside the trees; some are thieves and steal food; sometimes they make people disappear. Many Yaghenen tales describe the immense footprints left along the trail leading to Tikahtnu; no self-respecting Dena'ina would pass that spot without leaving an offering on the hollowed-out rock jutting up next to the trail; those who failed to make the gift could never count on a safe journey. But that night I did not want to fill Sem's mind with stories of dangerous forest creatures, so I answered her, "Yes, my child. But there are no šdón-ályášna. And we will watch over you. See, I am not afraid. The only sound is the soft voice of the wind. Listen. You will hear it."

The children fell asleep as we talked. My watchful, inquiring son dreamed, no doubt, of sailing a big ship, and perhaps even of paddling his kayak and fixing his way by the stars. Sem was probably hoping to see hummingbirds and run with the tree spirits.

While I had been busy with the children, Jabila had walked away; I assumed he had found a place for himself for the night. Restless by the dying fire, my eyes seeing him again at the edge of the grove, waiting, I stood up. I leaned back against the cliff wall, staring into the darkness, desire for my lover rising in me, my heart calling to his. Beyond the dimming circle of light, silhouetted against the moon on a small knoll, an image of tiqun took shape. Had Jabila joined his brothers? My question answered itself as I felt his arms reaching around me, turning me to him.

"No, Ashana." He read me well. "I have not left you." He covered my mouth with kisses, his hands holding me close, his voice soft in my ear. "I made our bed for the night. We can hear the children. But Denedi Belik'a will not have his eye on us."

"Do not worry. He is asleep."

"You son is growing up. He should soon have his young manhood rites."

"But he never will. Baranov and the monks draw him away from me. Teach him everything Russian." My voice could not conceal my hurt. "I fear for Sem. Kadyak is so bad. I am desperate. We need to go home."

"The qeshqa of our clan know of your desperation. I keep insisting we have to bring you home, and we will—"

"Stop, Jabila, stop! If I escape, who will die?"

"There is no answer for that, Ashana." Jabila's despair showed.

"I am so afraid Denedi Belik'a will soon begin to ask questions about us. I think we must tell—"

"Not yet. Later. For now, we must never let him know anything lies between us except friendship. *Uncle* I have been, and that is the way it must stay."

"I need to tell him so much. Tell both of them. Remember when you brought your bride-price?"

His laugh sounded young again. "I was scared, never more scared in my life."

"You looked so brave. Tall. Handsome. I wondered if you shivered like I did."

"I think your mother was testing me. She let me suffer."

"I will never forget that summer. Remember, Jabila? We were young, and for a short time we had each other. Nothing else in the world counted."

"You are my summer. Always." He took me in his arms, did not hear me whisper to myself, "And Aleksandr my winter."

The many seasons since that long-ago summer had added age to both of us; the continual separations had worn us far beyond the effect of time. That night, in the freedom of being able to touch, the tightness that had kept our emotions in check earlier in the day melted; we came alive in each other's arms, as young in feeling as we were those first nights in our japoon on Yaghenen.

"Shani Jabila, my summer rainbow." I settled myself more closely against him, delighting in his warmth and strength.

"When you call me 'Shani Jabila,' all time disappears, and we are young again, so young." He breathed the words into my hair, gently unraveling my braids until they fell loose about my shoulders.

The long twilight of early autumn still lingered, wreaths of mist drifting across the pond and reaching out to us. The air was fragrant with the scent of the evergreen boughs and sweet grasses crushed under our entwined bodies. The only sound that disturbed the silence was the occasional call of a distant nightbird.

"Qanilch'ey Ashana, my windflower. Never have you been more beautiful than you are now." Jabila cupped my face in his long hands, his eyes darkening with passion, liquid in the deepening light.

Gently, with my fingertips, I traced his high cheekbones, moving down from the broad forehead to caress that one raised, questioning eyebrow.

"Shani Jabila, you always come to me at the right time, at the moment I need you most."

That night belonged to us, to our love. We wasted no moments in sleep. Slowly our hands explored each other's bodies with soft, lingering touches, longing and hunger making our pulses race, our blood run faster. I reveled in the sweetness of my Jabila's mouth, the taste of one who walked in The Great Country's freedom, Aláyeksa's freedom, the man who knew nothing of vodka, or the stinking tobacco and rank sweat of an alien life. His tongue delighted mine; and I took him within me. Always before this we had known it would be dangerous were his seed to stay in me, but that night was different. We burned with a special need to belong, to create. I lay quietly in my lover's arms as the early morning light glowed around us, protecting that seed, that precious burden, my Jabila had given me.

The spirits of distant, long-ago lovers shared our wonder, their heartbeats ours. Time after time, we came passionately together; in that calm, still place where there is nothing but a gentle peace—a peace swept suddenly away, and when the throbbing faded we rested again as the storm of our kisses fused the rhythm of our bodies into the rushing mountain streams of springtime. Qanilch'ey Ashana . . . Shani Jabila. Windflower wrapped in rainbow.

⬡ ⬡ ⬡

27

On the command of the *baidarshchik* who served as fleet leader, several hundred double-bladed paddles struck the water; the fleet of Ulchena hunting boats moved away from Kadyak into the channel for the last hunt before winter settled in.

I stood on the shore watching the fleet leave, Denedi Belik'a beside me, when Siga-yak, an Ulchena hunter worn out and no longer fit for the hunt, came up to us. He wore a hat of bent driftwood as gray and weathered as his face. It was decorated on both sides with slender pieces of carved ivory, whiskers from the many sea lions he had killed trailing back from it. The Tahtna no longer levied him, but whenever a fleet pushed away from Kadyak he was there to bid the men a safe journey. That day his third son was in the kayak behind that of the *baidarshchik*. His two elder sons had been lost at sea, and my hope joined his for the safety of the fleet and of his youngest son. As the men vanished out of sight in the distant haze where the sky meets the sea, the air was filled with the wails of the women who watched the departure, troubled that it might be the last time they would see those beloved faces.

"Your son wore a fine new seal decoy helmet," I said to Siga-yak.

"I carved it from weathered driftwood. Painted it red and white and black. I made the chinstrap from the toughest strip of walrus hide I could find. It will not blow off," said the old hunter, pride in his voice.

"Your son looked handsome."

"The helmet will protect him and draw the seal to him."

On the way back to the house, my logically minded son asked, "How can the helmet draw a seal to the hunter?"

"Denedi Belik'a, the helmet shaped like a seal head will bring the animal to him. That will make his hunt easier."

"A hat cannot do that."

We walked on a few moments, then Denedi Belik'a brightened. "Anyway, Mama, don't worry about me. I am going to learn the right way to sail a big ship. Father says he will send me to the naval school. To learn navigation. How to sail a ship anywhere. I will not go out in those little boats. So you will never have to worry about me."

"Denedi Belik'a, you have lived all your life around the best navigators. Ulchena hunters can paddle their kayaks where no Russian dares sail. They begin learning when they are little boys. They watch the birds. Listen to the winds. Read the currents. They know, and what they know saves them from storms."

"But Papa said there are better ways to sail. The Ulchenas do not know navigation. I will."

Every day, my son showed more of the Tahtna influence. Even with his father absent, the monks wove thick layers of alien ideas through his thoughts. Every day, the gap between Denedi Belik'a and me widened, as the trough between waves widens and deepens, even though I kept telling him of our Athabaskan ways, teaching him our lach'u.

We were just finishing our evening meal when Siga-yak came to see us. As I opened the door, he said, "I would like to talk to your son."

Denedi Belik'a pushed in front of me.

"Here. I have carved this arrow case to lash on your kayak when you go to sea. The arrows, too, are for you." Siga-yak smiled as he thrust the gifts into Denedi Belik'a's hands.

For once, I had no words to describe how I felt about the gift. Of cedar driftwood, highly polished, the case was bound at four joints with woven seal-gut string, the design painted on with red and black.

"I carved these for you, son. No one else has a case like this." Siga-yak's fingers traced the lines cut into the wood. "When you strike a sea lion or an otter with one of your arrows, no man can dispute your catch, for it bears your own mark."

Unbelieving, Denedi Belik'a turned the case in his hands, ran his fingers along the designs.

"This is like the men tie onto their kayaks. Mama—" In his excitement, the little boy in him came out and he hurried off to show his sister the gifts.

"Thank you, Siga-yak. I am sorry my son is short of manners this evening."

"You need not be. I know boys." Tears flooding his eyes, the old man turned away and left the house.

The icy sleet pelting their faces, Denedi Belik'a headed to the church for the teaching by the monks, Sem to Mrs. Banner's house. I cut a small qenich'eni for my daughter and commenced sewing the pieces together. Again the question hammered through my mind: How could I balance the monks' teachings with my own? I saw at least part of the answer in dressing the children in Kahtnuht'ana clothing.

A smile crept over my face; one of the ironies of life on Pavlovsk lay in the few choices my children had of what they could wear. Aleksandr Baranov insisted on Tahtna clothing, but, as the years had passed, he had conceded that the Aláyeksan styles were far more practical.

Without goods from his homeland, he and his men had often been forced to dress as we did. We Athabaskans, who hunted the forests and mountains of the huge land around us, fashioned our clothing differently from that of the Uĺchena, who had only sea mammals—no caribou, no lynx, no wolverine. Land furs have always been precious to me. The pelts have that sweet-strong smell, the smell of home. That day, I cut soft, graceful pieces for the cuffs and neck of Sem's qenich'eni; they were not of the best fur, for Baranov had never lifted his ban on Aláyeksans using fine furs for themselves. Copying my old qenich'-eni, I arranged fringe around the shoulders and the hem, fur around the neck for softness, then sewed on embroidered strips of porcupine quills, seeds, and small shells—but no trade beads adorned my daughter's dress.

The evening after our berry picking, Jabila and I had walked through tusheĺ. The foggy woman had walked ahead of us, wrapped herself in our fear and despair and took them far away with her, leaving us in a bright meadow where love bloomed.

Warmth crept over me at thoughts of the night Jabila and I had created the new life within me. We had lived far too long in the shadow of tusheĺ, and we could find no way out. We had lived too long with fears for each other, our people, the young growing up in Kahtnuht'ana villages, despair so heavy we could see no way through or around them.

I would never give up the new one for the Tahtna to change into an alien as they were changing Denedi Belik'a and Sem.

Baranov, far away on Sitka Sound, must never know of a child not his; I must plan carefully to hide it from the prying eyes of the monks and Banner, from his entire crew. Jabila said Watnaw could always be trusted; the time would come when I would need her help more than ever.

There was an insistent knocking on the door at first light one morning. Puzzled at who had come to the house so early, I loosened the latch.

Siga-yak faced me. "I am sorry to disturb you, Ashana. Banner has ordered me to pick a crew. A short hunt off the islands just north of us. We won't be gone long. Shouldn't be any danger."

I remember thinking, crews come and go all the time, yet no one has made a special point of telling me about it. Mothers with strong young boys yielded them to the alien levies all too often; I realized Siga-yak had come for Denedi Belik'a.

Hunters now old and useless on the dangerous sea journeys, along with boys scarcely old enough to start training, were pressed by my captor's company into service for hunts to nearby bays and islands. Not many sea mammals still bred in the waters close to the shore, but the aliens did not tolerate even the elderly or the young failing to produce for them; the least useful men, those who had finished the puffin hunts, were forced to search the most depleted waters for whatever otters might remain.

Siga-yak's words came hesitantly. "I have been ordered to take several boys out for training. I have already picked some. I want to include your son."

"Did Banner tell you to come here?" I played for time, choosing my words carefully in order not to insult the old man, who had sacrificed two sons to the hunts, his third now rowing far away on the ocean waters. My mind raced. Had I become so much of a "Russian princess" that I had the right to count my son above the other niⱮdulchinen, who had no choice to say "I will" or "I won't" to the levies? In no way could I imply to that Aláyeksan father that Baranov's son must be favored.

"Not an order for your son, no, but I want to be the first to teach him the hunting skills."

"When do you go?"

"In three days."

Old Half-Man of the Yaghenen mountains, at last I know how you feel! My thoughts raced ahead as I watched Siga-yak walk away. For years I had sought comfort behind that mask, and my

divided mind had served me well many times. That day, facing
the Aláyeksan father, I argued with myself for my son's life: I,
too, am split down the middle. Half of me says: Other sons go,
and he can learn more of our ways with Siga-yak; mine should
not be protected more than they, he must risk the heavy seas as
other hostage sons do. My other half says: No, he is different, I
cannot let him go, you know the governor would never allow
his son to risk his life in the sea hunt.

These arguments fought inside my head, took sleep from me.

Early the third morning, watching from the shore as Denedi
Belik'a secured the gutskin covering onto his kayak, I felt the
dread of generations of UIchena and other Aláyeksan parents
who for the first time have been forced to yield a son to the
spirits of the sea. Oh, the agony, watching that little kayak move
into the channel and disappear in the distance!

Sem clutched my hand. We were both trembling. "Denedi
Belik'a will become a great hunter," she whispered.

"No, my child. That takes many, many seasons of hard training."

A sudden storm hit Pavlovsk: Aleksandr Baranov returned
unexpectedly. When he heard why Denedi Belik'a was not
home, the wrath of a father broke loose. "Why did you send
my son on that sea hunt?"

"Your company levied him."

"No one levies my son." Fury swept the man, and he
knocked me to the floor. "I sent you back here to Kadyak for
the safety of my children. You are not fit to be their mother. You
have risked Antipatr's life. You have failed me. Get out of my
house."

At first, I could not move; his cane beat down on me before
I managed to escape. Halfway down the path to the workers'
quarters I stumbled into Watnaw's arms. No questions were
asked; our trust was open and accepting. Too many had known
the sudden wrath of Baranov.

I sent for Sem. My captor refused to let her come to me; she
could cry, but her father and the serving women would look
after her. The next day, word passed that Baranov had drunk
himself into a stupor. Two days later, when Denedi Belik'a
walked in safe, he was suddenly sober.

He sent for me, and his first words came as no surprise.
"Take Antipatr and Irina to the storehouse. Get anything you
want for them. For yourself."

I looked the man straight in the eyes. "Remember, Governor

Baranov, the *ukaz* of your Tzar named me 'The Princess of Kenai.' I am not to be abused''—my eyes held his, saw the flicker that passed across them as his face tensed—''nor bought as you bargain for a stack of furs. I do not want your gift.''

The morning of his next departure for Sitka Sound, Baranov lingered again with the children, ignored me until the last minute. ''Those troublemakers at Novo-Arkhangelsk have been shipped out. Conditions have much improved. Trade is good, and I have more supplies. I will send for all of you. Get ready to stay in the new house for good.''

I remained silent.

Lashing rains drenched Kadyak earlier than usual that fall, with winds so strong our little house shook with every gust. Sleet thickened to slush and turned from slush to snow. Clouds hid the mountains and the island was blanketed in thick fog. The aliens hated the gloom, but to us *savages*, the spirits had again brought respite. No one could be forced to the hunt during such tempestuous weather. It was a time for families to recover from heavy labor, from the anguish over men lost at sea. But with the good came the bad—for women like K'atl' or Sutina, abuse was more frequent when the men were cooped up.

Finally the sky brightened, a warmer wind blew across the island, and a lighter mood touched us. Watnaw walked with me a great distance on one of the paths we used to know so well. It was the furthest we had ventured from Pavlovsk since my return. We stood watching the waves rising lazily into small crests and gently lapping the rocky coast. Then, without warning, the earth under our feet trembled.

''Watnaw!''

I began running, then stopped and listened. There was more shaking of the earth—sometimes a soft roll, followed by jerking. The quiet waters in the cove were coming alive. My first fright gave way to concern about my children back at Pavlovsk. Watnaw and I ran all the way to the house for them, and before the waves began surging wildly up onto the shore, we had climbed with other mothers and their children high on the headland.

Oh, we were frightened. But I calmed down when I remembered my father's explanation: ''When the earth rumbles and shakes, do not fear. The qegh nutnughel'an dance and shout.'' We Aláyeksans know earthquakes. They have long had much to do with the formation of the shorelines and the island stretching along The Great Country.

Whenever the spirits shake our land, or ash drifts eastward from volcanoes west of us on the mainland, spreading a coating over this island, or giant tidal waves sweep inland and swamp everything in their paths, I have seen fright on the faces of the aliens and agitation in the monks as they cross themselves. The Tahtna lack an understanding of Aláyeksa's natural forces. At these times we Aláyeksans extract a measure of revenge, and we make certain that the Tahtna shriek in fright. We tell the aliens old horror stories and invent new ones of the earth ripping open and swallowing entire villages, people's screams rending the night. We Kahtnuht'ana know that those who have died before us have gone to dwell in the interior of the earth; their spirits work and play while we sleep, sleep while we work. It is in the nature of things that sometimes their activities cause the land to rumble and quake, or to spew rocks and ash high in the air. I felt certain of the truth about the quaking earth, for the time I had thought Jabila killed in our failed escape, the earth neither rumbled nor moved; I could not understand, and I said to myself, ''My husband is not a quiet man.'' For a fact, the earth did not shake because Jabila still lived.

When the seas had calmed, the children ran ahead of us back to the house. Watnaw and I walked slowly toward Pavlovsk. I had chosen that afternoon to tell her of the new baby, so that she could help me plan for its coming and concealment. We had to concern ourselves with the Tahtna traders, the alien visitors, the monks, Baranov's sudden returns, the eyes of Banner—and, in my own house, with two bright, inquisitive children. But my tall, slender figure gave me an advantage over many women, who became ungainly in pregnancy.

Excited for me, Watnaw asked, ''Jabila's?''

I laughed at her question. ''The raven dropped spruce needles into the water that I drank, and I started to swell.''

''How can you be sure it is Jabila's?''

''Because Baranov has not touched me within the time.''

''How will you explain it to him?''

''I do not intend to tell him anything.'' I looked straight into Watnaw's eyes. ''He must never know.''

She took my hand. Peace spread through me as we planned together.

''You know, on Sitka I learned to wear big Russian skirts.''

She smiled, read me well. "Yes. I see what you have in mind."

"Aleksandr has often joked that the royal Catherine wore wide skirts to conceal the pregnancies that were not of her husband's making."

"The governor will not be back before spring, I hear. But prying eyes are all around us. The monks and traders would delight in carrying word of this to him."

"I will see that a proper dress gets made." She giggled, then went on, "You will be the best-dressed *Russian* woman in The Great Country. All we need tell anyone is that we are preparing for life in Novo-Arkhangelsk." She eyed me sideways. "You are the governor's woman."

"Yes. And I do need *Russian* clothes."

"To throw off any suspicion, we will make new outfits for Sem and Denedi Belik'a, too."

"Oh, Watnaw!" I felt heartened as I had not in weeks. "Can we do all this without anyone knowing?"

"We will have to take extra caution. Most important, do not change your way of doing things—just do as you always have. Never a word to another soul from either of us. You and I know tongues wag too easily."

"The days right after the baby comes will be the hardest. I am not sure how to handle it."

Watnaw paused, puzzled a moment, for she knew what a serious problem this could be. "We must find a woman who is newly pregnant. One we can trust. Maybe a woman who lives some distance from Pavlovsk—and does not have a young child of talking age."

"Aa', that is how I think of it. She could simply have two babies."

"I would bring your little one to her. But you would need to help her nurse it."

I thought with joy to the days of holding a small one in my arms, but mixing with that joy was the fear of being discovered. I knew the baby would not be safe on Kadyak; its only sure protection would be with Jabila on Yaghenen: He could take our child far away into the mountains.

Our walk home led us past the kashim, into which now, in the late afternoon, people were busy carrying ferns, grasses, and feathers, decorating it for another ceremony honoring hunters and their success, a festival in preparation for the coming winter season.

"Come with me tonight," Watnaw urged.

"No, I should not. You know the governor has forbidden me to attend such things since that other night."

"But that was so long ago, and he is not here. Bring the children—let them see our beautiful dances. You know everyone is welcome."

I longed to see the dances and hear the songs once more. We will all go, I thought. A man I knew to be from one of the northernmost villages was walking slowly toward the kashim, cradling in his hands a carved bird: It looked like a snowbird, but I was too far away to see it closely. I had often seen this man around Pavlovsk, but had never spoken with him. I turned to Watnaw.

"I will come, Watnaw. Let me run to the house and fetch Denedi Belik'a and Sem." A sense of strength quickened in me, a quiet rebellion nudged me. Was it my joncha?

"Yes! We will have a happy evening." Watnaw hugged me in a bear's warm clasp and dashed off.

"Pffft." Antipatr wrinkled his nose as we walked into the kashim.

Quickly, I stepped on his foot to quiet him. How deeply my boy had been drawn into the Tahtna thinking, more unwilling recently to accept the nanutset I tried to teach my children! That night he eyed me in a way that said he did not want to stay, for he knew nothing of the dances, the songs, the ceremonies we Aláyeksans treasured.

The dances brought back to mind that long-ago performance when Jabila, having come to take me home, had danced so near me. I looked for Jabila, but I knew he was far away. As the singing and dancing came to an end and I left with my children, I felt old, so old. That failed escape, how many seasons past?

The next morning I opened the door to loud banging. Ivan Banner pushed inside without allowing me even a moment to give him the usual greeting expected by the Tahtna.

"I must talk to you, Anna."

I motioned him to a bench, but he ignored me.

"Father Herman just left me. Angry. Demanded that I do something about you."

"Father Herman? Concerned about me? What have I done wrong now?" I was surprised, for the monk seldom failed to speak a kind word to me when I passed him. He seemed less certain of my "sinful" state than his brother monks; and, although strict with Antipatr in the school, he was fair—unusual for a monk.

"You should know. Taking the governor's children to that heathen performance last night. I did not believe you were so stupid. The governor has forbidden you and the children to see such *savage* doings." His words cut into me, his voice stern, reproving. "You know the monks are doing all they can to make Christians out of you."

"But I wanted—"

"Wanted! Anna, I must remind you that you are the governor's woman. What you do sets an example for the others." Although the man did not shout, his words, his manner were sneering. "Instead, you disobey orders. You are impudent, Anna."

"My children need to know Aláyeksan ways. Last night we went to the ceremony honoring hunters. The performance was proper for anyone to see. You could have come."

"I would never think of it. The savages wear hideous masks. Wild outfits. Some men dance naked. Devilish." He paused a moment, the red creeping from his throat up to his forehead, "My God, Anna, did you watch those men? Your children, too?"

"You do not understand our traditional dances."

"Traditional! Those crazy performances do not have any meaning."

Banner's attack made me angry. I wanted to blast him, tell him he should shed his ignorance; but I held my tongue so as not to aggravate him further.

"I must report your indiscretion in my next message to Governor Baranov."

Indiscretion? The word frightened me. What did he suspect?

"As manager, I am doing my best to rid the settlement of backward, savage ways. Anna, you disgraced yourself before Nikolai Rezanov. You make trouble. I will not tolerate any more foolishness. I am responsible for the governor's children. And for you."

Foolishness. Tolerate. Insulting to me. My anger boiled, but I pulled the mask tighter over my face and fixed my eyes beyond him, divided my mind, controlled the sharpness of my tongue.

"I have spent hours calming the monks." Banner paced the room, his agitation quite unusual for him. He stared out of the window. Turning back, he continued in a calmer mood. "Anna, your people must give up their primitive ways. They are uncivilized. The governor expects better conduct from you. You are privileged. You could lead your people away from their darkness. They are so damned ignorant. Help civilize them.''

''I tell you, Ivan Banner, my people have a heritage more ancient—''

''Don't you dare brag about your ways to me!''

''I have a right to defend—''

''Not in this colony you don't. All these years you have used''—jutting out his chin, he changed his words—''enjoyed the beneficence of Governor Baranov.''

''Beneficence? Enjoyed?'' My mask almost slipped as I struggled to keep from slapping that chin of his.

''I tell you, woman, I will get an order from the governor to ship you back to Novo-Arkhangelsk as soon as possible.''

Panic rippled through me. I must stall him from carrying out his threat. Buy time. I dared not go to Sitka till summer. Raising both hands to silence him, I said as meekly as I could, ''Mr. Banner, I need to tell you the reason—''

''Reason? What reason?''

''I am trying to tell you. This afternoon Watnaw talked with me about clothes. The children and I need to get ready to live at Sitka. We must look right for the governor's mansion.''

My abrupt change of subject surprised him. He eyed me sharply.

My divided mind was serving me well!

''Mr. Banner, we do not have any of the Russian cloth I need in Pavlovsk. I would like to ask your help.''

I pushed aside his attack on my people's culture. For the first time, a brief smile flickered across his face. I had nudged him off center, and I knew he was thinking that perhaps he had handled this *savage* in the proper way.

''Help? That's what I am doing.''

''About the clothes. Please send word to Aleksandr to ship over suitable cloth from Novo-Arkhangelsk. Then we can sew the garments we need. I know he bought a cargo of Yankee goods. Some from the English. Maybe, by now, he has silk from China.'' Banner's mood seemed to soften as I talked. ''Ask him to send along pictures of the Russian ladies and their children. They are in Rezanov's books. Then Watnaw and the others can see how my dresses must look.''

Perhaps thinking he had shamed me into acceptable behavior, he said, ''That should keep you busy for some time.''

''Yes. The right clothes. For the children, too.''

He ran his eyes over me, started to speak, paused, must have decided not to criticize my qenich'eni. I knew from his past jabs that he had no use for any clothes made in the native style, believed as strongly as Baranov that the *civilizing* influence of the Tahtna among us had as much to do with the coverings for our bodies as it did with what the monks tried to push into our heads.

"Umiaks will soon leave for Sitka, and your message for the governor will be included."

Winter turned suddenly vicious—bitter, freezing weather, more sleet and ice than most people could remember settled over the island. The wind burned our faces when we ventured out, and lashing seas surged high into the bays and coves. The harsh storms drove us indoors—it seemed to me that the spirits of Aláyeksa had intervened, were shielding me from prying eyes.

⊙ ⊙ ⊙

28

I stood under the sunless sky watching the snowbirds from the Arctic tundra as they circled the gray sky like flurries of blizzard-driven snow before alighting on the frozen marshland in front of me. Sweeping low, the birds searched the stiffened plants for seeds to sustain them on their southern journey. Protected from the harsh wind by my long gutskin cape, feet dry in salmon-skin moccasins, I moved closer to them as silently as I could: They were unafraid, not easily disturbed at their task. As yet no aliens had intruded into their country to the far north, bringing destruction. A light gust of wind dusted snowflakes over the new arrivals as, twittering, they stabbed their beaks into the hard-crusted snow to loosen any stray seed pods. Their movements followed a curious pattern: The front line of birds fed first, then the line at the very back fluttered up and replaced them. Line followed line, and the movement repeated continually—it was nature's way of making certain the food was shared equally among these passing visitors.

Lost in wonder, peace filling my heart, I pushed my worries about Baranov and Novo-Arkhangelsk to the back of my mind. Watnaw had been visiting the house less frequently: We had agreed that one of the best ways to hide my condition would be for me to isolate myself more than I had done in the past. The idea—cutting off friends and company—was not pleasant for me, but Watnaw told the other women Baranov had forbidden me to visit them. Banner saw that I now held myself aloof, that my only contact was with Watnaw, and he knew she was helping me to prepare for my return to Sitka Island. No doubt it made him feel very smug.

For a long time I stood watching the northern birds. They were the survivors, the untouched. Slowly I came to sense another presence beside me, quiet and waiting. I knew it was no one who could hurt me, and had no fear as I turned to meet the smiling face of the Eskimo from the far north. He stepped closer, cradling in his arms the ivory snowbird I had glimpsed the day of the ceremony at the kashim. The carving was a creation of pure beauty, a treasure from the harshest regions of The Great Country.

"They are the birds from our home," he whispered, motioning toward the flocks scattered on the marshland.

Immobile, we watched, our spirits linked by the beauty of the scene. Stronger gusts of wind whistled around us and, as if at some silent command, the snowbirds whirled upward and vanished.

"Ashana." The man held out his carving, motioning to me that I should take it. "I want you to have this."

The last of the birds had disappeared, mingling with the snow on the wind, flying into a white stillness beyond my imagining.

"Ashana," he whispered again, "it is for you. For you to keep."

"Oh, no, I cannot." I ran my hand over the head, along the beautifully carved feathers. "You have spent many days making this. You must keep it."

"My children have been taken from me. I am alone. I have watched you with your two, know the grief you bear for your home in Yaghenen."

"But you should not give this to me . . ."

"The snowbirds. Let me tell you of the snowbirds, Ashana. Before the coming of man, there was only the land and the sea and the ice." His voice was old and hoarse, yet it had a strength and a tenderness that moved me. "The world was empty. Except for the snowbirds. Birds like those we saw. They lived in the far north. Where my people come from." He stood silent, looking down at the marshland as if still seeing those small, snow-covered birds shaking their feathers free of their white blankets. The smile deepened on his weathered face. A strange sense of awe filled me, and I did not interrupt him.

"One day the snowbirds molded a man from the soil and ice of the Arctic. Time passed, and the snowbirds realized that the man could not continue through the world by himself. The world was too big. So they molded four new men, and named them East, South, West, and North. They sent these men out into the four directions of the world. It is this way that we were created."

We were silent for a moment; again, he held out the carving to me.

Did he know of my worry? I could not turn him away. I said nothing, took his gift, and held it to my cheek for a moment. My tears froze on the carved ivory.

"You saw the snowbirds, Ashana. They have no fear of humans. When you are afraid, take my snowbird. Hold it to you. As you do now. Remember how close the snowbirds kept together today, remember how they trusted each other." He smiled. "We must trust each other. That is the way for us Aláyeksans. Let my snowbird be the symbol. You will survive, Ashana, as they do."

Trust. Agagasik's spirit had spoken to me of trust that night on the snowfield.

The Eskimo's eyes searched deeply into mine as if he knew my secret. A swirl of wind lifted the soft, powdered snow; and a drifting, misty light spread over the marshes. With a wave of his hand, my new friend turned and, graceful on his long snowshoes, headed in the opposite direction from Pavlovsk. Suspicious minds could breed no tales that day.

The carved snowbird, the man who created it—each spoke a lesson of survival: Count on friends. Stay close together. Trust one another.

Blistering winds swept Kadyak. The ivory snowbird watched me from a shelf, while across hundreds of yi*l* covered with fog banks so dense that days were no different from nights, its spirit flew to me from the north.

Long-awaited sails finally slipped into our harbor under a low overcast; they brought me heavy wool, damask, linen, nankeen from China, spools of thread—more cloth than I had hoped for. In the books that came with the supplies were pictures of ladies preening in dresses and capes and coats and puffed-out skirts, looking ready to walk across my room. Watnaw held the pictures first at one angle then another, unable to put into words what she saw, unable even to laugh at some that I thought looked like fat ptarmigans, cumbersome in their drapes and flounces.

We studied the cloth several times during the next week. Each roll of goods left my friend speechless, as had the pictures: the linen heavy, the damask lustrous, both firm to our touch; the silk iridescent and soft in the glow of the firelight; the wool scratchy but warm to our hands. It was hard for me to admit there was beauty in Tahtna materials, yet I had to be fair: Each fabric was, in its way, beautiful.

We managed to select five pictures of ladies' gowns from which Watnaw thought she could make a design for me. Many hours went into planning what we would cut from the different kinds of cloth, but we did not push actually sewing them. Watnaw's work took up most of her daytime hours; this was good, for I needed to keep the dressmaking as long drawn out as possible.

I always carried with me the dread that when Baranov's order came for the children and me to join him, I would be in danger again. One day, Banner began asking why the sewing went so slowly. I told Watnaw of his questioning, and we decided it would look better if we had a woman or two working with us. Knowing we could trust K'atl' and Sutina, Watnaw brought them to the house. I explained how the goods must be cut and sewn, and pointed out ways to avoid miscutting the cloth so strange to them. And thinking back to the awful night of the orgy, I took heart: They both looked well; even K'atl' could laugh again. The four of us enjoyed plotting and planning ways to slow down the sewing; their coming to the house might satisfy Banner, but it would not necessarily speed up the work.

My easy arrangements for the children's lessons with Abram Jones ended abruptly when he decided he would no longer put up with Pavlovsk, packed his belongings, and sailed on a passing ship to Sitka Island.

After he left, my children had me for their teacher; and we spent much time on Kahtnuht'ana lach'u and nanutset. But that extra time was lost, for the monks intruded and took over even more hours of the day than had Abram Jones, insisting that they were responsible for the instruction of the governor's son and daughter. The monks, who had once denied Antipatr and Irina entry into the church school, now changed face and accepted them, all because the *ukaz* of the faraway Tzar had proclaimed my son and daughter "legitimate" and officially named me "princess." The monks seemed to listen more to their Tzar than to their God.

Reminding me of his orders from Baranov, Ivan Banner made certain that Sem took daily lessons with Mrs. Banner, a Tahtna newcomer to Kadyak and Pavlovsk who had arrived while we were in Novo-Arkhangelsk. I had yet to meet the woman or speak to her, for she stayed indoors, fearful, perhaps, of us *savages.* She taught Sem how to make tea, something every Tahtna lady must know; how to sew the alien stitches, embroider only with her Russian thread, and the rest of housekeeping—all the things Baranov had wanted me to do. It was a matter of civilizing my child so she would not sit cross-legged on the floor, or pretend not to understand when Mrs. Banner knew she did, or pull the blank look over her face (I had not realized until then that my Sem had learned how to cover her face with the mask from deep in her mind). Many mornings she sat close or hugged me, whispering that she would rather stay home.

During the winter, the Russian church beliefs raised even deeper conflict within my son.

"Mama," Antipatr shouted to me as he burst in the door from an afternoon at the church school, "how long did it take raven to make the world?"

"I do not know, Antipatr. The world was here, and the animals—"

"But Mama, God did it in six days."

"Antipatr, as I have told you, chulyin—"

"No, Mama. Chulyin is only a bird. Not a god. Father Herman told me. He said his God created the world."

"But all your life you have watched the raven. Good, sometimes. Bad, other times."

"Father Herman took us walking along the shore. He waved his arms at a raven in the tree. The bird got scared and flew away. What kind of god is that?"

"Remember the lach'u of our people. I have taught you, Antipatr, that long, long ago, before human beings walked the earth, the animals and birds were like us. They talked with one another, helped one another, built villages, hunted. In time, the raven became the first person of our clan. In Watnaw's clan it was the eagle. The wolf in Jabila's. And that is why the spirits of animals and birds and people will belong to one another forever. I am sure it all took far, far longer than six days."

"No, Mama. I think Father Herman told it right. His God made the world. And it took just six days." Antipatr looked distressed; for the first time, he was openly denying what I had told him about the ancient beliefs of my people.

Irina leaned her head against my shoulder. "I like the way you said it, Mama. It must have taken a very long time to make all the water in the ocean. The big, big whales. No one could make a whale in only six days."

I needed to be more subtle in my teaching, so that my son

would weave what I had told him in with whatever talk the monks had with him. Long ago, he had accepted my beliefs easily: The small boy who gave his father a shesh for safety believed the words I had taught him.

"The foggy woman must be back on Kadyak," Antipatr said, banging the door and dropping his school slate on a bench. His words surprised me. They showed that he did hear and remember what I said.

"Yes. She must be. I went out this morning, and the fog was so thick I could hardly see an arm's length away."

"Mama, Antipatr kept calling me 'Foggy Woman.' " Irina, hands on hips, grimaced at her brother. "What did he mean? I did not bring the fog."

"Sit here, and I will tell you the story." I set out a plate of smoked salmon for us before I began.

As I told the ancient "Foggy Woman" story, I again saw four young people on Dilah Vena Tustes, heard Jabila's and Seltan's voices urging us on when weary feet dragged, and remembered K'i'un's easy tone trying to lighten our fears as we fled westward. "Follow me. I will be the foggy woman."

For whatever reason, Antipatr paid as much attention to the story as Irina, and expressed an interest in what I was saying that he did not often show.

"So there. You see: She was a *good* woman. She saved the village." Irina pushed the pieces of salmon around the edge of her plate. "She brought the caribou back so the hunter could catch them for food. Then she took the fog away."

Before I could respond, Antipatr swallowed the last bite of fish, and began practicing on his slate. "Mama, I remember when Jabila told me about the eagles. Where they live. How they hunt. He said they are very important birds." He leaned back on the bench, looked straight at me. "My father's very important. So he is like the big eagle."

What could have happened at Father Herman's to draw my son closer to me? I sensed he reached out, but no reason came through. He had to speak Russian at school, read and write it; but when his father left Kadyak, we spoke Kahtnuht'ana. That day, more than difficulty with the Russian language must have prompted his talk.

I waited.

Irina stirred from my side, skipped to the window, her doll in her arms. I started on a band of embroidery that would take hours to finish, and had done only a few stitches when Irina's teasing voice asked her brother, ''Why did you get a licking this morning?''

Antipatr picked up his slate, jabbed it at her, and stamped out of the room.

''I felt like running in and punching that old monk.'' Her eyes blazed. ''He caned Antipatr.''

''What happened?''

She crossed one foot, then the other. ''The boys said they had story time at school. And Antipatr started to tell the one about the foggy woman. They said the monk told him to stop. Then, he grabbed Antipatr and whacked him a lot.''

''Irina. Irina. Do you think it fair to your brother for you to tell me? I am sure Antipatr will talk to me about it when he wants to.''

''But, Mama, I just—'' She burst into tears and rushed off to her bed.

Outside, the fog hung heavier than ever. For a long time, I stood by the window, staring into the gray blankness. My children were growing up in two worlds, and nothing was simple for them; every day their lives became more complicated, as they tried to fit together my teachings and those of the monks and Mrs. Banner.

The tug between the two beliefs was starting to pull Denedi Belik'a apart.

''Why do you make me sit listening to your stories?'' my son asked defiantly later that evening. ''Father Herman says Aláyeksan tales about monsters and animals and spirits are nonsense. He forbids me to waste my time on them.''

''Forbids? He has no right.''

''But he did.''

''Denedi Belik'a, I have heard the monks talk of a devil that—''

''Do not call me Denedi Belik'a anymore,'' he shouted at me. ''I am Antipatr.''

I needed Seltan.

He should have been training my son, not the monks. Among my people, by custom, at Denedi Belik'a's age, he would have learned from his mother's oldest brother. It was known that the uncle would lead the boy along a sterner path to manhood than his own father. Seltan had been lost to me for years; any teachings my son learned about the Kahtnuht'ana must come from me. Denedi Belik'a needed to know our lach'u. How best to give him the strength to face the monks, their whippings and canings? It would take great wisdom.

My son would always be Denedi Belik'a to me, but as his interest in Tahtna ways grew, my teachings were pushed aside. As the weeks passed, more of Antipatr's time at home was filled with talk of his studies. He marked lines on his slate, said they had to do with directions for sailing a ship; at the top of his work he drew the stars by which he said he would be able to navigate. From the sureness of his talk I knew he understood what the monks were teaching him. As Aleksandr had told me, the subjects he learned were technical; they must be well understood before one could navigate a ship.

Lieutenant Davydov, an officer on one of the Russian navy ships that called on Kadyak, had early on been an inspiration to Denedi Belik'a in his studies. A good-looking officer—for a Russian—he talked to my son about his naval service and Russia's around-the-earth voyage. He treated my son as an equal, spent much time explaining how he used the stars to set his course, and brought Denedi Belik'a's lessons to life.

Young and happy, experience had not hardened Gavriil Davydov; during the winter, when he had more free time, he often came to the house, took a fancy to my children, learned our Kahtnuht'ana names—''Pretty, Ashana. I like 'Sem' and 'Denedi Belik'a.' ''

One afternoon, amidst much banter and joking, he and several men from his ship built an ice mound. ''Back in Russia, we have great fun doing this,'' they said, laughing as my two slid and bounced down the slope. Snowshoeing came naturally to them, for Yaghenen children snowshoe almost as soon as they can walk. During those days spent playing with Gavriil and his friends, they moved across the snow with far more ease than the sailors.

That was the way it came about that my son took the Russian Davydov for his hero. Denedi Belik'a would accept no Kahtnuht'ana hero, no Qishvet'.

Antipatr was all science and mathematics; he had little talent for music. But Irina was different. While still an infant cradled in Aleksandr's arms, she would look up at him and coo. He would turn to me, saying, ''Anna, this child is filled with music. I hear it in her voice, see it in her eyes.'' Often, as he held her, he would dance slowly around the room, sometimes with an almost stately grace for so lumbering a man, singing old Russian ballads to her, teaching her the words and the tunes.

Years earlier, in one of the cargoes from Irkutsk, Aleksandr had found an instrument he called a "balalaika." He had fixed a peg for it high on the wall, and some evenings, Irina on his knee, he would take it down and pluck the strings, teaching her more tunes to sing with him. Quite often, when she grew older, I would hear her strumming those same melodies, their notes weaving in harmony with her soft voice. Later, I noticed a different sound, both familiar and remote. As I listened one afternoon, I recognized it: Irina was putting music to the Gregorian chants of the monks, usually so monotonous and heavy to my ears, sung by the churchmen without instruments, but so beautiful when sung by my Sem, as her slender fingers ran across the strings, following her voice. She learned the Kahtnuht'ana songs as easily as the monks' chants and the Tahtna songs she had picked up from Aleksandr. A few things in life one never forgets: I remember the summer day I raced through patches of glowing flowers trying to catch a hummingbird. It was from the hummingbird I heard my special song, the one that I sang to my children when they were babies: "Hummingbird, small wings, strong wings . . ."

After only a few tries, Sem could pick out the melody of my song on the balalaika: One frigid winter day her playing brought a brief summer moment back to my mind, fragile as the beating wings of the hummingbird. Aa', aa', who can hold a hummingbird in her hand?

As I worked and worried about my children, the new life within me grew. My friends and I had said nothing about the baby to anyone. But one day our Ułchena cook, her face stern, put bowls of boiled beluga blubber and cabbage on the table before us. We Aláyeksans despise the cabbage, fit, we think, only for the long-tusked Tahtna pigs. One spoonful and sickness hit me, wave after wave. I barely managed to reach the door before my stomach rebelled and all the food for the past two days poured out of me. The knowing eyes of the cook followed me as I returned to the room; she nodded to herself as she went back to the kitchen.

The children minded their manners: They had been taught not to fuss over their food when the cooks were present. In their own dislike of cabbage and blubber they were busy trying to find a way to avoid eating it, and mercifully ignored my undignified behavior.

I was glad for the trust of Aláyeksans that held me in a silence as solid as our mountains. My pregnancy had not been talked about, but some were beginning to sense it. I read the knowledge of my condition in their eyes of the Arctic Eskimo who had given me the snowbird; I saw it again that day in the knowing eyes of the Uĺchena cook. But I had no fear of word passing to the Tahtna.

Anakhta-yan. Word came from Sitka Sound that he had learned through Banner's messages to Baranov of Lingen-Aka's death. For several days my friend stayed apart from everyone, sat without eating, brooded.

Anakhta-yan laced himself into a kayak; although he had not had food for many days, he paddled into the waters off the shore of Novo-Arkhangelsk and rowed away. Governor Baranov watched, his expression closed and unyielding. He issued no orders to shoot as "my Attu" disappeared into the heavy gray fog blanketing the open sea. In absolute silence, Aláyeksans followed the wake of the little boat as Anakhta-yan slipped away, a lone kayakman searching for his Lingen-Aka in the depths of the sea, seeking to share her love in the arms of the nutin'at dnayi.

My hands played over the nankeen and woolens that Baranov had sent to Kadyak; the alien silk against my cheek was as soft as flower petals. I looked through the "fashion drawings"—incredible, the weight of a woman's gown, with its huge bulges from waist to floor, with layer upon layer of side aprons, sashes, ruffles, underskirts. How many hours would it take for Watnaw and me to construct a gown, for *construct* it would be? All that work for only one gown, and I would need two or three. Each time Watnaw came, we pored over the pictures and planned how to cut and shape the material, how to sew all the pieces together. To keep my secret safe, no one but Sutina and K'atl' worked with us.

Watnaw ran her ulu in a straight line across the length of material spread on the floor, cutting a piece for my skirt. She held it up. It looked huge.

Watnaw smiled. "We'll turn it over at the top, around your waist. Then we'll run a drawstring through it. That way, as time goes on and you get larger, you can let out the string and make your skirt bigger around the waist."

Sutina put her hand on mine. "This baby? Kahtnuht'ana?"

"All Kahtnuht'ana."

She grinned. "You will be safe, Ashana, under all this puffed-out cloth. The Tahtna will think you have learned to be a fine lady.''

Watnaw pulled the woven string tightly around my waist, and laughed. ''This is how you are now. Come spring and summer you will need more room. Like this.''

Sutina studied the drawing in her mind. ''The more ruffles and drapes and layers we put on, the more body you can hide.''

''Baranov has laughed about Tzarina Catherine's splendid gowns. 'Designed to hide pregnancies that were not the Tzar's,' he explained.''

''Huh. Smart for Tahtna.'' Watnaw looked at me mischievously.

''For them, not bad!'' Sutina spread the cloth flat on the floor, laid another piece over it, then pulled it aside, forming a drape like the one in the picture.

''We have to cut the cloth and allow enough so that all the layers can be sewn together at the waist.''

''Let's be sure before we cut. We cannot allow a mistake.''

Sutina looked up from the floor. ''It will be fun to make a smaller one for Irina.''

''Good-looking Tahtna you two will be.'' Watnaw poked me.

''Antipatr's grown out of his old coat. We will stitch a new one from the heavy blue wool. He will look like a real little sailor.''

The season of short days gave us only a few hours of good light, and we had to hurry because the fine sewing could not be done by the light of our flickering grease lamps. Stitching carefully with bird-bone, Ulchena-style needles, in a few weeks we had finished the many layers of underskirts. Irina and Antipatr wondered why we had turned the place into a storehouse as full of garments and cloth as a building stacked with bundles of furs.

''We are getting ready for the trip to Novo-Arkhangelsk,'' I told my children, my eyes meeting those of my friends.

Late one afternoon I held the new gown up to the light and examined it: strong cloth, well stitched. The night before leaving Novo-Arkhangelsk I had despised the idea of Tahtna covering for my body, but on Kadyak I would use it to protect myself, not for my captor's pleasure, though he would see my wearing it as a giving-in.

The ruffles were supposed to hide my swelling body, make people think the pouching-out was not me but the cloth around my waist. I could not know how Russian court ladies felt, but the bigness of the dress made me feel hugely pregnant. And I only hoped that every Tahtna, seeing the change in me, would believe I had become a "Russian lady" in fine clothes.

Once I had put on my new dress, Watnaw picked up a couple of the drawings, eyed them, then me. "Now you will fool them, Ashana." She stood back, looking me over, stepped close and pulled at the side of my dress, then the front. "Needs to be a bit more fancy. Put a ruffle on this side and one on the other. Another drape here will make this one fuller. It can be your number one dress. But what about your hair?"

"Aleksandr says my Kahtnuht'ana braids hanging down my back will never do. 'Most unsuitable,' he called them." I remembered that long ago my captor had helped fasten my braids across the top of my head, "Russian-lady style," he described it. Sutina rummaged in her sewing basket for her ivory case and shook out a couple of slender bird-bone needles. Twisting my braids around the crown of my head, she secured them with the needles. "Here, this way."

Making the second and third gowns took far less time than the first one; Sutina and Watnaw copied the design of the original, reversing a drape here and there, and using different colors and materials.

Then came the great surprise: During the weeks my friends had sewed for me, my hostage family had not been idle. That day, several of them came to visit, one of them carrying a large bundle that she at once pushed behind the table, hoping, I suppose, to hide it from me. Mysterious glances and laughter surrounded me. I had worn one of the new gowns, and Sutina and Watnaw trailed behind me, straightening it here, twitching and pulling at it as I moved around the room. Chattering in four or five different languages, everyone seemed to be telling me something at the same time. Then K'atl' pulled the half-hidden bundle from behind the table and untied the cord around it. Eager hands held up a long fur cape.

One of the men stepped to my side, a twinkle in his eye. "Qanilch'ey Ashana, you are the governor's woman. You need a warm cape. We wanted to use fine, fresh pelts, but you know the orders. So all of us dug into our old garments, cut out the best pieces of fur. Sewed up they look very nice, don't they?"

Ehu! Magnificent! Words were not big enough to thank my friends, but I tried to say how much they had touched my heart. My fingers played over the soft old furs, traced the fine stitching. I would wear the cape with pride.

They were all laborers for the company, and none had the

right to linger, but they stayed long enough for Sutina to drape the fur around my shoulders, covering the Tahtna dress completely.

Another expression of the trust between us Aláyeksans had drawn us together that day, an unspoken message to me that I could count on them through the next months. All of us who were captive on the island of Kadyak survived because of the links of trust we had woven together, tangible and strong, whenever the need arose. For those moments at least, Kadyak seemed less bleak.

"One thing you have to do, Ashana: As soon as we finish the children's clothes, you must all dress up and call on Ivan Banner." Watnaw's mood appeared serious, yet her voice was mischievous.

"Oh, no!" Sutina could not hold back her fright.

"The risk is too great," I said, reacting to the same thought that must have struck Sutina. "He almost slapped me for bothering him the night of the orgy. Give him an excuse, and most likely he will do it."

"But maybe you *should* go." K'atl' spoke slowly. "It might be the best way to show him you have done what you said you would. You have made new clothes for going back to live at Novo-Arkhangelsk."

"He dare not slap you," said Watnaw, "not in these clothes. He will see how Russian you look, and think—"

"—how much work we have done to get you ready. Clothes for the children, too," interrupted Sutina, catching on to the plot. "They are right. You must go, Ashana."

The next night, late, there was a tapping on the window— Jabila's signal. I came alive; gladness that my husband had returned filled the night around me. Quickly making sure the children were sound asleep, I opened the side door. There had been so many times that I had said over and over in my head the words I wanted to remember to say to Jabila when next I saw him, but that night the need lay in feelings, not in words. We clung to each other, his lips on mine; his hands held me tightly against him; my fingers slipped through his hair, over his face. We sat a long time in the darkness, our first need satisfied by touching.

"I have worried about you, Qaniłch'ey Ashana. The time is coming to take you home."

"Jabila! You cannot. Governor Baranov will kill you. I will not—"

He silenced me, his hand over my mouth. "I have come to tell you to be ready soon."

"Jabila, they killed the first time we escaped. They took hostages. I am one of them paying the price. They have killed again, and they will kill if I go."

"Minya and Seltan and I are the new qeshqa on Yaghenen. We have talked long with the other men around the fires. We are making plans to take you back. You have given enough of your life to save us." He took my shaking hands in his. "Try as they might, the Tahtna have not taken our clans over. We—"

My heart pounded. Take me home? How many seasons had I waited to hear him say that? I eased away from the fear of Tahtna killings. "I know the great danger. But, Jabila, I will be ready."

"Ashana, an end is coming to our troubles. At first, before our clans had figured ways to resist, our old qeshqa gave hostages. Like the Ulchena did. Out on their islands, they lived scattered far apart. They could not defend themselves, had no place to escape to. We have the vast lands stretching north and east of us. We will move deep into the mainland. The aliens will never find us."

He paused, and his next words sent shivers through me. "If Tahtna do kill some hostages, then that is the awful price we must pay. The raven and the wolf will rest no more until we are free." He rested his hand on the slight bulge of my stomach. "Ashana, this child must be born free. It is mine, too."

I had never forgotten what *free* meant.

"I have told you little of our resistance to the aliens. It was safer for you not to know." His voice lightened, and his face bore the trace of a smile. "You should be proud of Seltan. Nowhere among all the clans is there another slocin like him."

"Yes. I know."

"We became slocin when we were young. Now we have a trust stronger than ever." His thoughts shifted. "I know you hear of Tahtna hunters disappearing—one here, another in a different place, a small band. A few days before I came, men from one of our clans killed an entire camp of them. We waited for a night when they were carousing, rapped the Tahtna on the back of the necks by hurling sinew thongs with rocks tied to the ends. We wiped out every sign of what we had done. No arrow wounds. Nothing Tahtna can trace. The place looks as if waves driven by storm winds had washed over it, leaving a few bits of driftwood and bodies on the beach."

"And the Gulushutna on Sitka Sound?" I asked.

He chuckled. "Yes. The Gulushutna."

"Baranov stormed around this house for months. Angry at all the *savage* clans who joined Kotlean."

"*If* there were any of *us* Kahtnuht'ana there. Those aliens"—his eyes twinkled—"think we put on masks and headpieces and paint just for show. You and I know we hide who we truly are behind the paint and masks. That is how we keep on fighting in Aláyeksa. But I came to talk about you."

A whistling in the fireplace. Wind? Spirit?

"QaniІch'ey Ashana, listen to me carefully. I know of the church time the Tahtna call Christmas. In the coldest days, all of them—hunters, monks, visitors, everyone—spend long hours in the church. The Aláyeksans the monks have persuaded to their beliefs will go. And you must go, you and the children, dressed in all those Tahtna clothes you have. Be sure Banner and the whole village see you."

"You do not realize the risk. Remember. You could be killed." Fear seized me again when I thought of what Jabila had in mind. Much blood might be shed.

"I know, too, that long hours of drinking follow. They will be drunk for a couple of days." He laughed. "All in celebration of a baby born long ago. I do not know when or where. And most of those *promyshlenniki* do not either."

He stopped; sensing he had more to say, I waited.

"That is when I will come with my men to take you home. Then, QaniІch'ey Ashana, you and I will know where our baby will be born."

For a few hours we rested, neither of us sleeping, the time together brief, but a time to be lived. We touched gently, our hungers stirred; we tasted again the love we knew during the night in which we had created the new life in me.

In the mist before daylight, I told my husband of my plan to conceal my pregnancy.

"Good. But say nothing of my plans for you. Watch your time. Be ready when I come. Watnaw knows, and she can help you. Trust her."

He left me before first light.

29

Escape! The word rang in my head day and night. In my dreams, the three of us—Sem, Denedi Belik'a, and me—were always running, endlessly running; the Arctic cold closed around us, and we never reached our trail's end. Sometimes I would wake sweating and shivering; at other times I cried out in my sleep, awakened by Antipatr or Irina shaking me, crying, "What's wrong, Mama?"

Had we waited too long? Were the children too old? Dared we take them across the seas and into the mountains? Were we always to be fugitives from the Tahtna? We could not ignore that Aleksandr Baranov loved both his children fiercely; he would stop at nothing to take them back, and I dared not think of my fate in the event of recapture. But, even more important, who would the Tahtna choose to die with me, for I knew killings would come?

When the sleet and snow stopped falling and the mists and fog lifted for a day, I walked to the headland. As I looked toward Yaghenen, a feeling came to me that escape might perhaps not be so difficult. We could cross the waters in darkness. Jabila and his men needed no lessons in navigation; they knew every rock and current that marked their course; fresh rowers would be placed along the way to relieve his men and speed us on. None of them would risk our lives in a foolish venture; they had planned and practiced for years. Our qeshqa had made the decision: I must trust them.

The struggle racked me: Should I go? Should I stay? Finally, I made my decision. I stopped trying to balance the arguments, pushed aside my fears. The time had come for me to leave everything Tahtna behind me. Jabila harbored no doubt that we would succeed; he, too, believed that we could wait no longer,

345

would not listen to talk about what might lie ahead, and assured me that he and Seltan could teach my son to take on Kahtnuht-'ana ways. Jabila's skills, his self-confidence, and my longing to live with him among my own people, bred in me a lightness that overcame the questions and doubts and dread.

There were treasures I longed to take with me, but they would slow us down; I must leave them. I could take only our warm clothes. Never once did I hint of the plans to my children, not wanting to put a burden on them and afraid that chance words might warn the Tahtna of our flight.

A few days before the Russian Christmas festivities, Watnaw and Sutina came to the house and helped me dress in one of the new gowns. I reserved the finest for the special celebration at the church. The children looked strange, alien, in the Tahtna garments.

Irina laughed at me. "Mama, your skirts look big as a cloud."

"Ssssh, chickadee. Mother is dressed the way a Russian lady should be. Father will be proud of her." Antipatr swaggered about in his sailor-style coat and trousers.

"These things scratch me," Irina said, squirming. "The skins feel softer and nicer."

"You know this is how Papa wants us to look. No more of the old skin stuff," her brother persisted, strutting toward me. "This suit is as good as the one I had in Novo-Arkhangelsk."

"Now, children, that is why your father sent all these things to us." I smoothed Irina's hair, pulling the long black strands behind her ears, holding her close a moment. "We will see what Ivan Banner has to say about our new clothes."

The Pavlovsk manager opened the door, surprise written all over his face. "Well . . . I wondered what you would make of the cloth. Very fine, I must say. Come in."

He watched me closely as I slipped off the cape and laid it on the bench beside me. He stared at the furs, but said nothing. We talked of the school, of the latest storms, of when the next ship might drop anchor—all with a stiff pretense at pleasantry that pointed up our lack of common interests. A samovar steamed at one end of the room, slices of bread filled a platter. Tahtna boast of their hospitality, but in that season of celebration, Banner shared nothing with us. His wife, busy in another room, kept her distance, clearly avoiding me. The fact that she had to teach Irina was perhaps enough contact for her. The Banners did not drink tea with a *savage* woman.

"I have another message for you from Governor Baranov."
Ivan leaned forward. "His house will be ready by this summer.
Irina"—he turned to my daughter—"a German governess is
coming to Novo-Arkhangelsk to teach you. She has lived in
Russia for many years. You must learn to be a lady. And you,
Antipatr, must continue to work hard at your studies. Your father
plans to send you to the Naval Academy in Russia."

Banner stood up abruptly, and I knew it was time to go. A
coldness surrounded us, as if an Arctic wind had swept down
from the far north and across Kadyak. The children and I left
without another word.

At the celebration of the Russian Christmas Mass, I stood with
Sem on the women's side of the church, and Denedi Belik'a stood
with the men. Candles lighted the front and glittered brightly in
the windows. Aleksandr Andreevich Baranov had paid fifteen
hundred rubles of his own money to lay the foundations of that
building in which the Christian rituals were being held.

Anyone watching would have thought me intent on the services, but though my eyes kept track of the monks—watched the
signing of chests with small brass crosses, the kneeling down
and standing up at certain times, the singing of the chants my
two niłdulchinen had learned to understand—my thoughts were
far away. In my mind I saw only Jabila and his men beaching a
small umiak, then stealing silently toward Pavlovsk.

I watched my son, lost in the alien fantasy, worship with the
men, murmur the liturgy in response to the monks. That night
the little space separating us might as well have been an ocean.

My mind and spirit sought refuge in my ancient joncha;
through it I heard a Kahtnuht'ana voice speaking as clearly as
if I stood alone deep in the Yaghenen mountains:

Qanilch'ey Ashana, walk with care. Grave dangers lie ahead.
The voice faded to a whisper. *You have become a woman of
wisdom, Qanilch'ey Ashana. For your safety, for the future of
your children, use that wisdom.*

A sob rose from within me, and I could not hold it back. Sem
gripped my hand, looked up at me, a question on her face.
Though they dared not move to shield us, my Aláyeksan friends
sent their spirits to give me strength for what lay ahead. In a
moment I had control of myself, swallowed the lump in my
throat. It was then that I caught Denedi Belik'a's glowering stare
as he turned back to the liturgy. His cold eyes and stern face
were those of a young Baranov.

BOOK FIVE

◇ ◇ ◇

30

The celebration following the Christmas services lasted throughout the night, one of the longest of the season. Busy preparing the small packs for our escape, I permitted myself no worry at the passage of time. The calls of tiqun sounded faintly from a distance, then closer. Hope shut out fear, and my spirits sang as my hands flew: I was leaving Pavlovsk forever.

Silently, the room filled with Jabila and four of his men; a quick nod to me, and two of them slipped into Denedi Belik'a's room. There was a sleepy exclamation, then all was quiet. I shut my eyes as they carried my son to the back door, his hands and feet tied, mouth gagged. Jabila wrapped Sem in the fur covering her bed while I slipped moccasins on her feet.

She opened her eyes. "Mama, I don't want to get up yet."

"Sssssh, my child. We are going with Jabila. He has come for us."

Sem smiled, put her arms around his neck, closed her eyes; they left, followed by his men, who carried out our few bundles.

The Tahtna garments lay piled on the floor, alien, out of place in Aláyeksa; I stepped over them into a world of clean midnight snow that swirled around me in the rising wind, thankful that it would quickly hide our tracks and give us extra protection. At the beach, Seltan grasped my hands for a moment; I could not see him in the darkness; touching him almost paralyzed me, then my tears fell as I whispered, "Seltan . . . Seltan . . . Seltan," the wind covering the sound of his name as my brother stood beside me on the shores of Kadyak.

By the time faint light penetrated the snow-filled air, the umiak had covered a great distance from Pavlovsk, and the men ungagged Antipatr. My son's protests frightened me—he threatened to kill whoever had carried him out of the house. There was the muffled sound of a struggle, then silence.

Why couldn't I have trusted Denedi Belik'a not to spread word of our escape? But there had been no choice; it was not safe to tell him ahead of time. Close to his father, an admiring son, there was an openness between them that had not existed between Aleksandr and me. I feared that Denedi Belik'a would send word of my plan to Baranov; I could not risk this—it could cause many deaths among my Kahtnuht'ana people.

The snow did not abate until late afternoon; the only sounds were the sluicing of the sea against the umiak and the rhythmic bite of the paddles cutting the water. I felt the drive of the boat as it raced through the rolling sea; and with distance falling behind us, hopes began rising. The men had chosen the day well: The raging storms rested, snowfall covered our tracks on Kadyak, and the village lay torpid from its Christmas indulgences.

On islands where we had fought the Tahtna years ago, strong men waited to take over the paddles and speed the rowing northward. Fatigue would not be our enemy this time. A second umiak trailed us to guard and help if need be. Jabila and Seltan talked often as the boats moved on, slocin never closer than in the flight with me to freedom. The planning of that escape, the strength of the men on the paddles, the daring in their eyes, could only come from the trust between Seltan and Jabila, a trust that had been tested and proven.

But Denedi Belik'a was a problem they had not foreseen. His surly, accusing words struck at the men, his voice strident. I slipped to his side, almost cried out at seeing the thongs tying him so he could not jump from the boat.

"Antipatr, listen to me." My hand rested on his shoulder. "The men will untie you, but you must control yourself. No argument. No fighting." My voice was low, the words spoken to him in Tahtna.

His muscles were tense, fright and defiance in his face; agitated, unable to move, he could easily gulp in too much freezing air and be in danger. I spoke a few words in Kahtnuht'ana to my brother, who had been keeping a close watch over Antipatr, telling him I would explain to my son exactly what had happened. We faced a difficult task: how to establish trust between us and a young man who must think he had been taken captive by raiders.

Gripping my son's shoulder firmly, I leaned toward him and

said, "You *must* listen, Antipatr. The man beside you is your Uncle Seltan. Sit still, now." Antipatr fought back a sob, it would have been unmanly to cry; he bore enough Kahtnuht'ana in him to hide what he considered a weakness. He struggled for control, and then his words whipped at me. "My uncle? Why did he tie me up?"

"Antipatr. We are going home to our people on Yaghenen. I—"

"*Nyet!* Not my people. I am going to Novo-Arkhangelsk to live with my father."

Seltan tried to calm him. "You are safe with us. I *am* your uncle. Your mother is here. These men are friends. Hold still, and I will untie your wrists."

Antipatr glared, rubbing the flesh where he had strained against the thongs. Defiant, he twisted toward me; his eyes bored into mine with a force not yet quite the strength of his father's.

"Did you know?" he said, his voice an echo of Aleksandr Baranov's.

Was escape a terrible mistake? It may have come many seasons too late for my son. None of us could turn back to a younger season, nor would we turn back to Pavlovsk.

During the long hours that followed, the broken talk between the three of us strung no bows. Seltan's patience never frayed, even though Antipatr's anger flared at every word of explanation. From the front of the umiak, Irina's soft laughter and Jabila's easy words assured me those two had no problem. The men at the paddles wasted no breath on talk, using every ounce of energy to carry us as far and as fast as possible from Kadyak before we changed rowers. What went through the minds of those men who had risked their lives for us, trapped there on the sea with a boy spewing hateful words? They said nothing as we beached twice to change men at the paddles, but their eyes questioned why that angry young one was going home to Yaghenen with them.

As we approached Yaghenen, and the pace of the umiak finally slowed, I sat unmoving, drinking in the sight: the long narrow strip of land bordering Tikahtnu, the forest that swept upslope, the sparkle of snow shining on a far ridge high in the sky. Happiness, tears, a sense of freedom, awe at the daring of the men, mixed in me.

"Why don't we stop at home?" I cried, as the umiak picked up speed again without even heading in to the shore where our villagers had always beached their boats.

"Ashana, we dare not. The Tahtna will think we stopped there, and it would be too easy to track us from the village. We have cached supplies at a cove a good distance up the ocean river," Seltan answered.

"But our parents—?"

"Our families have moved far away. No one lives there. Our village is dead."

Jabila had said on Kadyak that our people were moving far inland, but not until the shoreline of home slipped away did the lach'u of his words sink into my heart.

We reached the cache as dusk was slipping over us; Seltan and the men had to drag Antipatr from the umiak, his defiance a raw wound on my happiness. Respect was owed the men for our safe passage, and, once on shore, I told them, "You have given me back my freedom, my life. I will never forget."

No greetings, no familiar faces except those of my loved ones and the men who had rowed with us, left me a stranger returning to her own land after a long absence. On the trail late in the day, when I tried to speak with my son as we warmed ourselves at a fire behind a ledge, he said nothing, even though his eyes pleaded. To put my arms around him, to hold him close—but it was not the time. Jabila tried to speak to him, but he turned away. When his uncle promised, "Antipatr, we will not tie you again if you stay close to me. I warn you, do not run off into the forest. Many a lone man has lost his way and died out there," my son turned aside with an angry shrug. He bristled at his sister, resentful that she fitted in, her talk easy, friendly. Some of my pain over her brother eased at seeing her light-heartedness, her acceptance.

Antipatr refused to help when the men pounded spruce branches into the ground for our night camp, stood back when they turned over the umiak and lifted it upside down onto poles to give us shelter. Only with difficulty did Seltan persuade him to eat, and he rebuffed any attempt to speak to him, rolling up tighter in his fur wraps.

During the night, when Seltan took his turn to watch the camp, I slipped to his side; I saw the lines of care that etched his face. Many seasons had worn our trails wide apart; how could I talk of the past to my brother? Where to begin? "I have longed for you, for our family. What of Father? Mother?"

"They try to keep up their spirits. They have roamed so long. The exile began the season after Baranov took you. Many fled into the interior."

"K'i'un. How is she?"

For a moment, he did not answer. "Qani𝘭ch'ey Ashana, it took her so long to recover from the ravage by the Tahtna. She seldom leaves our house. For the moment, we are living in a canyon far to the north, and we keep moving inland."

"How far do we have to go?"

"Many yi𝘭. We have cached food and snowshoes where we will need them."

There was a slight stirring at the edge of camp; Seltan rushed to grab Antipatr before he could disappear into the darkness.

"Leave me alone!" my son demanded. "I need to go to the brush."

"Then we will go together."

Side by side, they headed away from camp. A firm, strong uncle, that brother of mine. No longer the easy, yielding boy whom a sister could sometimes coax to take her on an early-morning secret trip in his kayak.

Before sleep claimed Denedi Belik'a, the three of us sat late into the night, watching, listening. Two of us hoped no one would pounce on us with guns. The other, I was certain, expected the Tahtna to come for him so that he could go back to his father.

Unused to day-long walking and climbing, muscles aching and breath sometimes short, my body forced to the limit, I held us back for badly needed rest, my pregnancy adding to my weariness. My husband, my brother, pushed us hard, in part driven by fear, in part by their Athabaskan blood, which allowed them to walk, walk almost forever. Antipatr carried his own pack, silently conceding that otherwise he might have neither shelter nor food. The men never stopped watching him; had he nurtured any plan to run away, he would have found it short-lived. To Sem's delight, Jabila sometimes hoisted her up to ride on his shoulder.

What a double-edged knife life is: Qani𝘭ch'ey Ashana leaves Yaghenen hostage and under protest; her son returns with her unwillingly and under the threat of being bound.

Days later, deep in the interior, the men lifted a sled and snowshoes from a cache. They did not stop to rest, pausing only long enough for Irina and me to climb onto the sled. From there on, the men wore snowshoes with bear claws attached to them as an aid in gripping the white, icy crust. Antipatr was able to keep pace with the men; I had taught him the Yaghenen way of

snowshoeing while we were on Kadyak. Only occasionally did
he and Seltan manage a few curt words. Jabila, Antipatr ignored; it was as if he did not exist. My son had made up his
own mind as to whom he should blame for his situation.

As the sled carried us in and out of groves of young birches,
along a cliff, and beside a frozen stream, questions about the
wisdom of having accepted Jabila's plan beat in my head. My
fourteen-year-old son might stay on the trail at full pace, determined not to show more fatigue than the men; but the fracture
between us lay deep. I knew there would be problems, could
not keep from thinking that he would no doubt reject my people,
at least at first; but I lived in the belief that Seltan would be able
to draw Antipatr into our Kahtnuht'ana way of life. I had allowed him to plan, to dream, sometimes even encouraged his
efforts to please his father and then, without warning, he had
been torn loose from all he knew. How cruel we must have
looked to him! Many times the cry, "Turn back! Turn back!"
nearly broke from me, but I knew that our safety lay in speeding
ahead, putting more distance between us and the aliens.

One night, around the fire, the men asked questions. "What
of the Tahtna? What will they do?"

They looked to me for an answer.

"I cannot be sure. Banner, the head man at Pavlovsk, may
order boats and men after us. I know he will send word to
Governor Baranov on Sitka Sound. The children's father will
come looking for them."

Seltan figured the distances, the days, as he had done in planning our flight. "We are putting a lot of space behind us. The
snow favors you, Ashana. The Tahtna will have no idea where
to track us this far inland."

"Chort' s/neem!" For the first time in my presence, Antipatr
swore the Russian oath he had heard since the day he was born.
"My father will find us wherever you try to hide."

Our small band trudged on, along slopes rather than over
ridges, the sled easing the trip for me. We crossed unfamiliar
country far from the old home on Yaghenen.

Finally, after many days, we arrived at a small village, and
Jabila settled us in a dwelling shared by several families.
Strangers would pass without seeing the carefully hidden houses
in the narrow valley between two high, heavily forested ridges.
Only thin spirals of smoke from snow-covered mounds signaled
human life. A new japoon had been attached to the house for
me. I crawled into it exhausted, able to relax for the first time

since leaving Kadyak, yet wondering if the Tahtna had indeed tracked us. Later, I awakened with a start, uncertain how much time had passed. The sound of Kahtnuht'ana voices, the feeling of strange surroundings, pulled me out of weariness. For a few moments, all was confusion; my japoon seemed a part of my father's large dwelling, yet yesterday we had come to Jabila's house.

Without waking Sem, I slipped into my qenich'eni and walked into the main room. A hush settled over everyone, all eyes on me. Across the fire, between Seltan and Jabila, sat Denedi Belik'a, hunched, his face drawn; his clamped mouth showed that he despised the place, his narrowed eyes held anger against everyone.

"Please, Antipatr"—the effort must be made to ease the strain between us, and perhaps using his Tahtna name would reach him—"you can speak Kahtnuht'ana well enough. And here it will be used so that all may understand." I had begun in Tahtna, but changed to my own language. "Before your father came with his men to Yaghenen, Jabila had paid his bride-price to my family. My father pledged me to be Jabila's wife; and by Atha-baskan custom I was his wife. Then, Aleksandr Baranov took me away as his hostage. I never agreed to that. Neither did Seltan nor Jabila."

Antipatr flinched. Hostage to him must have meant *kayuri*, women and men pressed into alien service at the level of slaves who eked out a bare existence in the hovels on Kadyak. He knew that no one in Baranov's house suffered that kind of life. He said nothing.

Seltan took over when words failed me. "Denedi Belik'a, your mother's bondage to Aleksandr Baranov made sure, we understood, the freedom of our people from Tahtna attacks. That pledge has been broken many times by the aliens. So it is our right to bring the hostage home with her children. Even the Tahtna recognize that an Aláyeksan mother's children belong to her."

"Pledge broken! *Nyet!* You people broke the promises. Many times. You have killed my father's hunters." Antipatr flung the words at Seltan. "My father told me."

"Our people have been patient." Jabila kept his voice even, spoke slowly. "The Tahtna have taken many more hostages, more than they first demanded. Then they levied men for the sea hunts. The Tahtna have abused our girls and women. Our only choice was to defend ourselves. Many fled into the mountains. Men have died on both sides. There has been killing, suffering.''

''When I was a girl growing up, Denedi Belik'a, my family lived far south of here above the shore of Tikahtnu,'' I said. ''The land, the sea, the streams were filled with all we needed for food and clothing. We had a comfortable life. Yaghenen was a good place to live. Now, our people have been forced into this frozen region, a harsh land compared to the home they have known. They struggle to keep ahead of starvation and from freezing.'' The words seemed almost to form themselves. ''I have to tell you, son, we must face the cause of these hardships: It is your father, his *promyshlenniki*, his guns.''

''Your father's trading company has made slaves of Aláyeksans. I know firsthand the cruelty of the Tahtna,'' said Seltan. ''One week, when I was away hunting, they broke into my house. Dragged your aunt K'i'un into the brush. First one, then another, used her body. They beat her when she tried to run. Cut her face. Left her for dead. It has taken her years to recover. She will always suffer the scars. Inside and out.''

For the first time, Denedi Belik'a seemed shaken, and he looked down at his feet, avoiding my eyes.

Sounding less stern, Jabila added, ''Denedi Belik'a, I have always feared for your mother's life. I want only safety for her. For you. For your sister.''

One of the men threw fresh logs onto the fire. In a few moments, the blaze sent warmth into every corner of the room. We talked, we reasoned, far into the night. But my son held aloof, unbending, unbelieving.

''I am not Kahtnuht'ana. I am Russian. I do not belong here. You have nothing for me to learn. I will go back to my father.''

And then it came to me: Denedi Belik'a truly believed that my people were savages; he wanted no part of us. At the same time, I sensed that the men understood him.

''The winter and spring will pass quickly. I will make this understanding with you, my nephew, and both of us will honor it. By Kahtnuht'ana ways, the uncle trains his sister's oldest son for manhood. While you are here, you are my responsibility. We will answer to each other. I will teach you everything you can learn about hunting caribou, trapping salmon in the river, making a kayak for yourself, building shelters—everything you need to know to be a leader among us. Your grandfather is wise, and our people respect him. If you learn well and walk in the clans with wisdom, you could become like him. You must consider the loss you will suffer if you deny your Kahtnuht'ana blood.''

As Seltan reasoned with Denedi Belik'a, I wondered if my son grasped the fact that my ''noble lineage''—his father's words—recognized in the *ukaz*, the directive of the Russian Tzar, was what opened the way for his right to become a student at the Naval Academy in St. Petersburg.

''Our people must find the right place to build their village. As soon as we are settled, I will begin your training; after that if you still do not want to stay with us,'' Seltan continued, unruffled, ''I give you my word that in the summer season, the time of our longest days, I will see you back to your father safely. We will lay no more claim on you.''

''You would take me back to my father?''

For the first time, my brother's patience frayed; a trace of anger flashed through his fatigue. ''Once Seltan gives his word, a man can rely on it as surely as human beings rely on the coming of yuyqush.''

Denedi Belik'a stood up, stretched, his eyes on mine a moment before he faced his uncle. ''I don't have a choice. If I did, I would go back now,'' he lashed out defiantly. ''Let's try what you say. It's dark. Teach me your Kahtnuht'ana ways. Show me how you track a caribou at night.''

Seltan drew a quick breath. He had not anticipated such an immediate challenge, but he ignored the insolent tone. ''We will go. First, we will get arrows and bows at my house. And a spear.''

A mother knows that certain things need be said to a son, but when the uncle has taken charge, she must hold back. Whatever they do lies solely between the two of them. Only days later did word come out that in Seltan's house, as he was explaining to his nephew how to use a spear in a caribou hunt, Denedi Belik'a, warmed by the heat from the fire pit, gave way to fatigue and sank into deep sleep. Seltan covered him with a caribou robe and the next morning ordered quiet in the house. My son slept through the night and most of the next day.

Exhausted, I slept almost as long as Denedi Belik'a. In the nightmare that broke my rest, a woman's voice shouted of my pollution by an alien, condemned me to banishment, and I felt myself running, running, running. Always behind me the shouting, and there was no escape from it. Again, the screaming without words, without sound. Then strong arms grasped me.

Jabila's voice came from far away, "Ashana. Ashana! Wake up. You are having a bad dream."

"I'm running . . . A frightening woman . . ."

"No more of that. You are home. You can stop running."

I hid my face on his shoulder, clung to him. "Jabila. I am so afraid when I wake up. On Kadyak I called to you so many times, but you were not there."

"Do not think of the sad times. Think ahead. We will know the better times again."

"It is good to be here. With you. Yet I can't find the words to tell you the way I feel." There was so much I needed to say to my husband.

His hands massaged my neck muscles, my tight shoulders and back, came to rest on my swollen stomach. He looked deeply into my eyes. "To have you in my house again, to know you carry my child—nothing has greater meaning."

"We have lived a difficult life, we have known little happiness, my husband. Being with you, that is happiness.

Sem peered over Jabila's shoulder. "You've slept so long. It's time to get up." She giggled and pushed another child her own size toward me. "I have a new friend. She says I can sleep with her and the other girls. They have a special place all their own."

Beautiful black eyes smiled down at me. As tall as my Sem, the child still retained some of her baby roundness; her skin was a shade or two darker than my daughter's and her whole appearance marked her unmistakably . . . Jabila's.

Jabila stood up, put his arm around both girls. "My daughter, Kat-oon. She came with the new leaves of spring, so we named her 'Kat-oon'—leaf."

"A beautiful name for a beautiful child."

The girls beamed at me.

"I will take Sem and Kat-oon with me; join us as soon as you can—everyone wants to talk with you again." Jabila's voice was filled with the warmth of my never-forgotten Yaghenen homeland.

Several women were busy cooking in waterproof spruce-root baskets when I pushed aside the reed mat separating the japoon from the rest of the room. Red-hot rocks had been dropped into the water in the baskets to make it steam, cooking the wild rice and edible roots steeped with dried berries. One woman's basket suddenly started leaking, and I ran to help her, dragging another basket with me. But the woman gave me an impudent bump—

not hard, just enough to show contempt, hissing something I did not understand. Shocked, I stood still a moment, uncertain; then, ignoring her, I went to look for Sem, but she was off somewhere playing with Kat-oon.

The woman's voice came at me harshly, insulting: "You come to us with your mixed-breed bastards. Expect us to take you in. We've no food for you." It was the same voice I had heard in my nightmare: That dream had not been a dream. A dark cloud passed over the sun of my homecoming.

I was grateful that the other women in the room paid no attention to the outburst. Their movements, as they went about their cooking, were quick and sure, their words to one another few but friendly—very different from in Pavlovsk, where the Ulchena women who had slaved over the Tahtna cooking often did not understand what they were supposed to do and were too frightened to ask for help. "They're stupid; they don't care," the Tahtna would grumble when the food turned out to be less than edible.

One of the women came forward and placed a cooked moose head in the center of a long, scooped-out log that was used as a main serving dish. Much care had been taken in preparing this delicacy: It had been steamed and allowed to sit in its own broth until cooled. Another cook was piling tasty brown-bear feet on the other side of the moose head, and setting nuts, dried berries, and salmon at the end of the dish. The cooks had also poured in the contents of their steaming baskets—roots laced with seal oil. Using carved goat-horn spoons, the fine carving of which made me want to laugh aloud at my own miserable efforts, the servants of each family prepared to ladle out the helpings to the guests.

Still troubled over the insults but not really wanting to talk about them, I said in a low voice to Jabila, when he came to sit beside me, "Where is Denedi Belik'a? Seltan's here without him."

His eyes hardened. "The boy refused to come."

"But he might run away."

"He can't. Seltan left two men to watch him."

My son posed a serious problem for me in the midst of my homecoming, but I warmed to the many greetings and good wishes, not in a babble of different tongues, but all pure Athabaskan. Then the people near the door parted, and my father and mother entered the room.

They had come from Seltan's house farther back in the mountains. The years had worn them. The fear, the running, the privation showed on their faces, in their stooped shoulders, but my father walked without a stick and their steps appeared unfaltering. They started toward a seat beside Jabila, then stopped. In the middle of the room stood little Sem, her face white. I read her thoughts: My fabled grandmother and grandfather? That wrinkled old man and woman?

"You must be Ashana's child." My mother held out her arms, but Sem hesitated.

My daughter must not turn defiant, like her brother.

My father stepped toward her, the lines of his face rounding into smiles. "Come, child."

Sem ran to her grandparents, hugged them; arms of love encircled her. A few whispers, and the strangeness between them melted as ice under the summer sun. My worry passed.

By Kahtnuht'ana custom, guests received the first bowls of food. My father, the eldest, and his wife were served, then little Sem and me. After us, all the men; finally, their women and children. Jabila had provided well for the homecoming feast, and I hoped that we would not thin his stores too much for the cold weeks ahead.

Jabila's family had not known the exact day of my return and so had no time to make a little celebration. It mattered not. The meal had brought me together with my people again. Many in the room told me of their families; a few, those who had children taken hostage, questioned me about my life among the aliens on Kadyak. Words had to be chosen carefully so as not to deepen their hurt. As the evening drew on, the guests left, knowing that my parents and I had much to say to each other.

Hurt mingled with love and longing had walked my mind for those many seasons of separation from my family; Ni'i, now an enfeebled elder of the clan, had yielded his authority to Minya. I remembered Father as a robust, decisive, powerful qeshqa with a voice that expected and received obedience and cooperation. Part of my pain lay in the belief that, with his wisdom and power among our clans, he, too, could have found safety, as Jabila and Seltan had done, by leading our people into the interior of The Great Country long before the aliens came to Yaghenen. It was his duty in the face of the Tahtna threat. Why had Father and other qeshqa not wanted to leave the coast? Was it because our villages there knew an easier climate and had a more plentiful food supply than could be found in the northern region? Had the men seen themselves as wily traders, as partners of the Tahtna in a venture that could make them even greater leaders than they were? Such questions had tormented me through the many seasons of my captivity. Whatever their reasons, what did father and the other leaders achieve? Loss of authority and power . . . trinkets and beads of no value in exchange for Aláyeksa's prime furs . . . endless fighting, bloodshed, and hostage-taking.

Looking at the aged man and woman, I felt reverence and pity—and a deep sense of loss. Love for my parents had survived; but interwoven with that love was resentment at the hostage state into which my father had sold me, even though it had been at gunpoint. One act of submission by a people opens the way to the spread of submission, just as one small rent in a kayak will send it to the bottom of the sea. There is no turning back.

"And how are you, Father? Mother?"

"We are fine, Ashana. Your brother provides well for us."

"How is it with you, Daughter?" my mother asked. Though she was standing beside me, she seemed fragile and far away. Her qenich'eni, once a lush garment trimmed with red fox and embroidered with dentalium shells, hung worn and tattered on her emaciated frame.

Our talk, stilted and formal, did not touch the depth of our feelings, did not speak of the past. We were together again. Let it be, daq'u.

"We are home, Mother. Look at your granddaughter. I have named her Sem."

"She is you, Ashana, when you were that age. She is very Kahtnuht'ana."

"She has found a friend in Kat-oon."

"Yes, Kat-oon. Jabila's child. A leaf like those along the bright streams in the mountains."

"He named her well, Mother."

Ni'i straightened his shoulders, motioned toward Sem. "Our young one will grow up to be a fine Kahtnuht'ana woman."

His lined face bore regret. He had enjoyed no voice in naming his grandchild, and he had little time left to be with her. He struggled to bridge the seasons that had flowed between us. "Your japoon. Did you find it comfortable?"

"Yes, Father. I slept quite well." No need to mention the nightmares.

"The same day the men left to get you, we began to cut trees and added the japoon to Jabila's house. I wanted it warm and comfortable for you.''

"You built well, Father. I thank you for it.''

Slowly, the long evening drew to a close. Nothing was said about Aleksandr Baranov, nothing about Denedi Belik'a. I sensed my parents' relief when we finally said good-night. As they left, I stared after them for some moments, my longing of the past years unsatisfied.

That night we met. We talked. We did not touch. We patched no kayaks.

Kahtnuht'ana sounds: hiss of steam escaping from green logs. Clamshells scraping clean the wooden food bowl. Scratch of tree limbs on the roof. Distant howl of the wolf pack. Wind whistling across the fire hole. Athabaskan voices and laughter. Sounds, the sounds that made that place home. Yaghenen.

Kahtnuht'ana smells: blend of meat, fish, and oil wafting from meals. Old furs. Fresh pelts. Stale steam from the sweat-house. Deerskins wet and not yet changed. Breath and feet and bodies. But no stench of over-cooked cabbage and tobacco and vodka. Smells, the smells that made that place home. Yaghenen.

But sounds and smells alone are not a home.

Early next morning I slipped from Jabila's side in our japoon, where my arm had cradled his shoulder and his breath had warmed my hair. His life, my life, at last. I knew that my future lay with that man, to love him and want him, to know his strong hands reached out and held and fought for me, whatever happened, and the full meaning of *home* began to take shape.

In the center of the large room of the winter house, the fire was low. All around people still slept; at one end, the young boys; at the other, the girls, among them Sem. Several japoons extended out from the main walls, and in one the shaman sat, repairing his rattles and dolls. From the japoon next to his, Nidoc stepped out and spoke to another woman. I hesitated; we had met, but I had not yet talked to Jabila's second wife, for she had seemed reserved. Had she resented my coming back, taking my rightful place as Jabila's first wife? Doubts began dissolving when she smiled and motioned me to follow her into the japoon, where her new baby slept. We kept our voices low. The baby whimpered, and she lifted him to her full breasts.

In Nidoc's eyes stirred the warmth that Watnaw's eyes always held for me. I caught my breath, held it a moment; a sense of being in the same room with Watnaw surrounded me. Over the baby's head, Nidoc's smile reached me.

"Sit with me, Ashana. I need to know you."

On her bed of stretched-out furs, we sat side by side.

"Kadyak is so far from here. They took you so long ago."

I started to speak, but Nidoc motioned me to wait.

"I want you to know, Ashana, that when Jabila and I first became friends, he told me of his love for you. To us, and to all the clan, you have always been his first wife. We respect your right here." She shifted the baby to her other breast. "You are welcome among us. This is your home."

"I feel it already. This morning I thought of all that it means. I see how much you have done to make this home."

"It was hard moving here. Many old ones hung back. Gathering food is difficult in these forests. Much harder than along the shore of Tikahtnu and in the mountains we knew."

The accent in Nidoc's voice sounded different from that of my family. She was Dena'ina, as we Kahtnuht'ana are, but her roots must have been in another place.

"Your words carry a softness mine do not, traces of song. Where did you come from, Nidoc?"

Her smile broadened. "Jabila likes to tease me. Says I sound like the lapping waves of Lake Iliamna."

"Oh, that is across Tikahtnu, isn't it?"

"Yes, that is where I lived as a child. But we are all Athabaskans."

Her infant satisfied, his head tilted to one side, he lay sound asleep against her shoulder. Nidoc wrapped him in squirrel skins and laid him in his birch-bark basket, tucking clean moss under and around his bottom.

"Nidoc, this is home. But I have forgotten so many things. It will not be easy to adjust to all the changes." Worry about Denedi Belik'a lay heavily on my mind. "What about my children here? They have lived in two worlds. These have been difficult times for them."

"Seltan is a wise man. He will guide Denedi Belik'a. Your son is fortunate to have him for uncle." She laughed. "Sem will have no trouble. Kat-oon tells me they are already sisters."

"Yes, I saw them dressing Kat-oon's doll yesterday."

"She has two or three that Jabila's father carved for her before he died. I had some scraps of squirrel skins, and his mother sewed them into blankets for the dolls. Kat-oon will share them with Sem."

The morning passed quickly. We talked a little of our own interests, but more of our concern with feeding our families, of finding safety for us all. I learned to know Nidoc, warmed to her open manner; like Watnaw or Sutina or my lost Lingen-Aka, she was another woman who could be trusted. Her bright mind cut through to the heart of my problems: the difficulty of returning with two children, pregnant with another. She explained how the food would be divided, how I would be provided with an equal part of whatever the day's supply would allow.

"Jabila and I began to plan for your coming home as far back as the summer," she assured me. "We put food aside."

Nidoc did not pry into my life among the aliens. It would be easy, I knew, in the seasons ahead, to confide in her, share the best and also the worst parts of that life. As Nidoc sat beside me, free, I thought of all the others back on Kadyak, still captive. Distance separated us, but they seemed very close to me that morning, even though I was saddened that my sisters could not have fled with me. We had walked the paths of Kadyak together so many times, shared its burdens and fears and its small happiness.

As the passage of time drew me further and further from the Tahtna, the Kahtnuht'ana ways took hold and refreshed me; this taste of freedom filled me with the hope that never again would I be in the hostage state, never again be claimed by the aliens. My past on Kadyak could never be wiped out, but the keen, painful memories of those seasons dimmed with each changing of the moon.

K'i'un, scarred and sad, warned of the evil presence of aliens in Aláyeksa. The livid hole through her lip where they had torn loose the labret, the scar from a knife slash that stretched from forehead down over cheek to neck, her limp and crooked arm, spoke more loudly than words of the abuse of the *promyshlenniki*.

Denedi Belik'a watched K'i'un closely across the evening fires, but never questioned why his gentle aunt bore these terrible scars. He sat silent, struggling with the thought that his father could be the cause of such cruelty, the father who had said to him, "Do not be a brute."

Seltan met me the next day on the path from his house, the snow nearly shoulder high.

"Do you see any change in my son?" I asked him.

"Change in attitude, no. Progress in the hunt, yes. Your son is an intelligent young man. Strong. He keeps up with the best of the beginners.''

''Do you think you can train him to be Kahtnuht'ana?''

For some moments my brother's eyes searched the woods as if reading each sign, every movement. ''Ashana . . . I do a little work with him every day. He should start the manhood rites, but that would drive him deeper into himself. I am not sure about him. Given time, perhaps.''

''Where is he this morning?''

''He went on ahead with the hunters. The shaman delayed me, but I will catch them soon.'' His face broke into a rare smile. ''It is good to have you home, Little Sister.''

''I am so glad to be here, Big Brother.''

His strong arms held me close a moment before he snow-shoed up the trail toward the distant ridge. ''Little Sister'' . . . the words brought back happy memories from those days far-off on Yaghenen.

Later, as Nidoc and I watched the children, she took both my hands in hers. Her face sobered. Her eyes searched mine. ''Most of the people here welcome you, they are glad you have come home. But I must tell you, Ashana, one woman here will probably never accept you.''

Nidoc paused, seeming for a moment uncertain how best to tell me what she was thinking. Through my mind flashed the hostile voice of the woman who had shouted at me before I went to sleep and again in my nightmare, and I told Nidoc of the woman who had insulted me when I had tried to help her.

''Yes. Too bad. It was Tash'i—she's a jealous young woman who wants a husband. She takes every chance possible to be near Jabila. He's told her to look elsewhere, but she keeps demanding that he pay attention to her. She thinks he ought to take her for her beauty, so she schemes to be a wife to him. She has caused much ill feeling in our village.''

No doubt we will have to come to terms. But how does one handle a woman whose nature must have caused parents to name her after tash'i, the sourdock, a bitter stalk of rhubarb? Was she born a sour, complaining baby? Did her mother bear her in a patch of rhubarb? Or did her nature as she grew up leave no other choice for a name, however beautiful she might be?

''She is unhappy most of the time. Quarrelsome. Difficult for all of us.'' Again Nidoc paused. ''She is pretty, and it has made her vain and selfish. I mention her to warn you.''

Nidoc rubbed my back, sensed the tension in me. "Many times her words will cut you. They have me, but I've learned to shrug them off. There is no use getting angry over what she says. Do not be shocked by her. In time, you will find your own way of handling her."

Did I hear a note of contention in Nidoc's soft voice? Would I find myself in the middle of two feuding women?

The next week most of my time was spent cutting and sewing a new qenich'eni for me, another for Sem, and starting trousers for Denedi Belik'a. Nidoc helped, and we worked together, talking pleasantly. I told her of the pleasure her moccasins had given me the day I met with Nikolai Rezanov. Once or twice Tash'i swished by, glaring. We ignored her.

One evening Seltan and I walked together, talking of our family, of Yaghenen, of the seasons ahead. Suddenly he changed the subject. "Nidoc says she has told you about Tash'i. I must warn you of her brother, Kazhna. Both bear watching. I want you to guard against them causing you trouble."

"Yes, Seltan, Tash'i makes it very clear she does not want me here. It has been no use trying to talk to her, so I'm already on guard."

"Kazhna is a sly one. A man always on the edge of trouble. Yet we cannot order him before the elders because we never learn quite enough to hold against him. I think someday he will do something terrible. Then we can banish him. The man is mean."

"Kazhna. The lynx."

"A good name for him." Seltan's voice showed the scorn he felt for Tash'i's brother. "A loner. Doesn't even have a wife. I'll point him out to you next time he's around."

"I may have already seen him, Seltan."

My brother grimaced. "I had better tell you. Kazhna started tormenting Denedi Belik'a, made fun of his little mistakes in the hunting. Jabila caught him one day, cuffed him up a bit. Then he got nasty, and Minya ran him out of our hunting party. None of us have seen him since."

I recalled the lynx eyes and grating voice of a sullen man who had strode past me the first night I returned home; I had seen him several days later as he was hurrying away from camp.

As Seltan walked toward a trail in the woods, I noticed that Tash'i was cutting across the camp toward Jabila, but he hurried to join Seltan and they slipped quickly in among the birches.

Tash'i jerked her head around, stared at me a moment, then turned away.

Our food supply had dwindled even before the mountain snows had melted, but by carefully parceling out what little remained we had enough to keep us alive. My baby drew more energy from me than I remembered with Denedi Belik'a or Sem. Nidoc and Jabila watched me every day, and shared their food with me.

Spring. Its welcome signs: wet snow dropping from the tree limbs. Ice cracking. Snow drifting down the streams. Honking of the first geese returning to their northland homes. The lighter wind whistling. All the sounds of the coming of the Kahtnuht-'ana spring.

The spirits of our people lifted, especially when our hunters found meat; around our evening fires we talked of building warm homes to shelter us from the severe winters of the interior, but for a while the temporary camp was home. We avoided any mention of the long walk ahead of us in our eastward flight from the Tahtna, keeping buried the fear that at any time, if the hunters saw or sensed alien men, a quick move would have to be made.

Then, at an evening meeting of our leaders, Minya said, "Spring is passing. We have rested here. Our lives depend on moving farther inland."

With Sem at my side, Denedi Belik'a with Seltan, packs on our backs, some of the men pulling loaded sleds, the entire village moved east and then north while the land was still wet with the last of winter snows. Blue skies looked down on us more frequently than they did on Kadyak. On distant slopes, herds of caribou, deer, or moose, unaware of us, offered easy targets for our hunters. The weather was so clear that I knew the foggy woman must have passed that way, taking tushe*l* with her.

The Athabaskans believe there is a reason for every happening, natural or human or animal. My father, who by myth or legend could give meaning to everything in our world, struggled to weave into our traditions the lach'u of the flight into the interior forced upon us by the aliens. His way of explaining life depended on tales: "A man without stories is like a man without a head," he would say.

My father tried to talk with Denedi Belik'a—"As soon as the winter snows turn to running water, we will move toward the rising sun. We will turn our backs on"—but my son stayed silent, his face as blank as the distant glacier on the mountain to the north.

Then, at an evening campfire, waiting for the caribou meat to finish steaming in the cooking baskets, my father passed by Denedi Belik'a and said to Sem, "Come, little one, sit by me. Do you know, if it had not been for chulyin, for the raven, those caribou would never have been able to smell us?"

"How did that happen, Grandfather?" Sem warmed to Father.

"In the long, long-ago time, my child, the caribou had no sense of smell. He was the prey of wolves and bears. Even of the lynx. He couldn't smell them coming. Then one day raven walked up to him and said, 'Why don't you run away? Why do you allow everyone to kill you so easily? I came downwind. You should have smelled me.'

"The caribou looked at the hunter with great sad eyes. 'I have no way of smelling you.'

" 'That gives every hunter unfair advantage over you.' The caribou shook his great antlers in sorrow. 'Many of my brothers and sisters have been killed because they could not smell enemies coming and run away.'

"The mighty raven hunter sat down and thought for a long, long time. He kept looking, kept watching; but he could not bring himself to kill the caribou because he knew he had an unfair advantage. Then he saw a birch tree. 'Ah,' he said to himself, 'I have the solution.' He took out his hunting knife, skinned off some birch bark. He split it and made two pipes. 'Come,' he said to the caribou. 'I can solve your problem.' Raven put the birch-bark pipes up the nostrils of the caribou. 'Now,' he said, 'forever after, you caribou can smell us through the pipes. No one can take unfair advantage because you will be able to smell hunters when they creep up on you.' "

Sem laughed with her grandfather, hugged him. "Tell another one."

As he smiled and began the next story, I recalled the sounds, the colors that he had brought to life in the long-ago years when his voice held everyone's attention, tales told during my childhood that often continued from one day to the next. I realized that for little Sem each tale was only a short, intriguing fragment of the ones people of our clan had often gathered to hear, but they were all that his energy could sustain.

Listening, I felt the bond of strength with my people, the

Athabaskan bond that made endurance possible, had made the clan qeshqa—Minya, Seltan, and Jabila—strong enough to say, "Now is the time to bring Qanilch'ey Ashana home."

On the trail, my daughter usually beside me, I saw each day the tortured steps by which Father and Mother kept pace. Refusing to ride the sleds, never wanting to be a burden, my mother's bent head and shoulders sagged lower as we slogged eastward through melting patches of snow, stretches of mud. Walking. Walking. Walking. Not one, not even the leaders, knew our final destination, only that somewhere in the distance lay safety. At night, resting my weary body, feeling the life move within me, active but heavy, I wondered where that walk might finally end.

Step by step, our band crossed the unfamiliar terrain. We forded streams, trudged along animal trails, over hills, through gullies. We fought our way through dense forests, sometimes guided only by sounds. Limbs moving, food easing hunger, whispers of a loved one close at night—these were the only sensations that carried true meaning. During the times of rest we talked of the vast region and began to believe its very size gave protection from the Tahtna. One evening at the fire, I told of the sisters who had followed the butterfly, not knowing where it led them. We needed a spider to spin shining thread to guide us to the end of our journey.

We knew that our walk was life itself.

One morning my mother did not rise with us. Wrapped in her blanket, a small bundle of bones, she lay still. Father called the shaman. First he danced three times around her. Then he placed his doll against her breast, but could find no flutter of life. He bent down beside the doll and listened.

Rising, he straightened up to his full height. "Her spirit has left to join the Kahtnuht'ana ancient ones." He faced Father. "No ceremony can cure her now. I will call the clan of Jabila to attend her."

In deep grief, a clan in mourning, we blackened our faces with ashes of burnt bark and loosened our hair until it fell around our shoulders. With my mother gone, no time could be wasted at that spot, so we moved out of camp. Looking back, I saw the flames engulfing my mother's body and her possessions, which we had sent to be with her. People said a few words of consolation as we took to the ancient animal trail. Without a word to me, Father tried to appear that he had known the loss was coming and had prepared for it, but the deepened lines of his weathered face and the grief his eyes could not conceal told me otherwise. As if she understood the need to sustain him by her young strength, my Sem slipped her hand into his and walked beside him. The loss touched Denedi Belik'a also, and for several days he too walked beside my father, talked with him, and carried his pack. My son even spared a few words to ease my own grief for my mother, the mother lost to me during all my years as hostage.

Even in the face of death, Tash'i threw her sourdock shadow. "One less of your family to feed," she snarled. I wanted to lash back at her, but angry words would have dishonored the memory of my mother.

That night, sleep did not come. The stars that had given Mother the name *Sem* the day she had been born still burned bright, reminding me of the fire of life that had burned deep in my mother's eyes. Knowing that her fire had dimmed to embers, then to ashes, I could no longer hold back tears of sorrow.

On our walk, ever north and east, the children of the clans had no difficulty keeping up; they would run ahead, dash into a grove close by to hide from one another, rush out to surprise a friend. Mothers kept an endless watch, fearful of their being lost, hurt, attacked by an animal. Seltan's small ones obeyed best of all—a mark of K'i'un's special place in his home. The Tahtna rapes had left her barren, and the two children she had borne to Seltan were old enough to fend for themselves, so she watched over the other wives' babies when their mothers had to leave on squirrel-snaring trips.

As my time drew near, K'i'un brought her furs and stayed close to me, her presence quiet and reassuring. Late one night, when I felt the pains begin, I called out to her. She and Nidoc took me to a small cave hidden from the camp by a thicket. They quickly built a fire and heated rocks to warm water in a spruce-root basket.

The baby started its way downward. Violent crampings jerked my whole body, eased, and for a few minutes stopped completely. Nidoc and K'i'un supported me as I walked up and down until a sudden gush of water told me a baby would soon lie in my arms. I felt the closeness of the Athabaskan spirits, those spirits who had always accompanied me through the many travails of the hostage world.

As dawn broke over the far ridge, our child greeted the new

day, and with the baby safe in Nidoc's arms I lay back to rest on the vines spread on the floor of the cave. Another rush of pain seized me as the placenta separated itself from my body.

Nidoc took the bloody, squalling mass that was my new child, wrapped him in a soft squirrel-skin robe she had sewn for him. She tucked tufts of dried moss around his bottom to keep him clean and dry. In a haze, I heard K'i'un scraping away the placenta and burying it in a far corner of the cave, where it would remain dry; Kahtnuht'ana know that if the afterbirth should become wet, the baby will die. Washing me, binding my belly with a soft skin to help speed recovery, K'i'un bent over me. "A sturdy one, this son of you and Jabila."

During the day, I slipped in and out of a half sleep, sometimes aware of the sun shining into the entrance of the cave, the new one feeding at my breast. My faithful sisters watched, one on each side. By tradition, neither the father nor any other man could enter the birthing cave, a place solely the province of women.

In the hours of my waking the three of us talked, drew closer than we had thought possible in my first weeks there. A question from K'i'un surprised me. "Who are Lingen-Aka? Watnaw? Sutina? You cried out for them in your pain."

A flood of memories warmed me at hearing those names. "My true friends on Kadyak. Like you two here. They dreamed with me. Sutina from the Copper River, bright and shining like the copper bracelet she gave me and as daring a hostage as the rest of us. Watnaw, so different from anyone I have ever known, was a Gulushutna from Sitka Sound, with an indestructible spirit. Her home was destroyed before her eyes when the aliens took her hostage.

"Watnaw suffered so much, but she gained freedom of the spirit and that gave her freedom from fear. 'Life is a matter of survival,' she often said. 'You have to create an inner strength, then nourish it and never let it die. Men may use your body, but once you have walked through the fog of fear, you know freedom of the spirit. No man can take that from you.' "

"Lingen-Aka. Who was she?" K'i'un asked quietly.

"She reminded me of you, K'i'un, when we were young. As sparkling as a spray of spindrift racing across the sea. Lingen-Aka, an Ulchena woman. A remnant of her island people. Killed one night in an orgy by the *promyshlenniki*." Tears filled my eyes, I choked.

Nidoc clasped my right hand, K'i'un my left. "Do not go on, if it sorrows you," K'i'un whispered.

"No. Let me tell you, Sisters. K'i'un, you are here with us. You survived. But my Ulchena friend, Lingen-Aka"—my voice caught—"abused all night by the drunken beasts. They dumped her out where the tide could wash her away. Our hunters found her in the morning. Dead. Her friends hardly recognized her, the Tahtna had hurt her so brutally. From the abuse I saw on Kadyak, I know what you went through, K'i'un, how you suffered."

K'i'un grasped my hand, tears slid down her face, and for a moment she leaned her head against my shoulder.

"We are thankful Seltan found you in time." Nidoc spoke the thought that had been growing in my mind, turned to me. "K'i'un has the strength you talk about in Watnaw."

"Yes, I sensed K'i'un has walked through the fog that is fear. No man can ever take away her freedom of spirit." I held my sister close.

"Forget your past," Akoota had cried out many times on Kadyak. The tragedies of mind and body inflicted by the aliens had happened in the past, but they could never be forgotten. Deep within me hid the dread that the long arm of Baranov might reach out to drag us back to Pavlovsk, but I said nothing of that fear to my sisters.

A whimper. My child demanded to be fed again. His black eyes opened wide, peering into mine as if he wanted to say urgent words to me. As he sucked, a thought troubled me, one that my sisters must know.

"Nidoc. K'i'un. Listen to me. If ever I should be taken away—"

They both attempted to speak at once. I waved them to silence.

"—if ever I should be taken away, promise me, each one of you, that you will mother this child as your own. Teach him to grow up a strong Kahtnuht'ana. Train him in all the traditions of our people."

"Ashana, nothing will happen to you. You will always be with us," Nidoc said.

"We will never leave you." K'i'un brushed the hair back from my face. "You have returned to us. Jabila and Seltan will protect you."

A need to hear their spoken promise could not be pushed aside. I insisted.

"Yes, Ashana. I give you my promise. Your child is my child," K'i'un offered first.

"And my child, too," Nidoc assured me. "Remember, these breasts of mine can provide enough for my baby and yours for many months to come." The brightness of her face faded for a moment. "Say no more of such worry. You and your children are safe with us."

One day's rest was all I needed before our walk resumed.

A sudden cool breeze fanned around me, seemed to isolate me from the others for a moment before we started on the trail again. I told our shaman about it.

"So, Ashana, you have borne the child of Jabila. That cool wind brought the touch of Naq'eltani to you."

The shaman walked away a few steps. From his pack, he drew out the wise man mask that signified his rank, pushed his head into it, held the strap between his teeth. He slipped bands adorned with feathers onto his arms, and around his neck tied a necklace of brown-bear teeth and claws. He danced toward me, shaking two of his red-painted bird rattles carved from spruce wood.

"Now I can tell you who your child is." He shook a rattle in each hand, chanted a sacred Kahtnuht'ana song.

A hand grasped mine. Jabila stood beside me.

"Your child . . . I hear it in the voice of Naq'eltani, carried by the wind." The shaman straightened up, listened to the rustle of the new birch leaves. "He is your brother reborn, your brother you lost long ago, when the bear took him." He danced in time to the music of his rattles, finally stopping before us. "I see a stalwart, brave, wise one. A qeshqa of our people. A new Qishvet'."

My father took the baby, held him high, and said, "This child, born with the dawn, shall be called after the dawn— Q'ut'en Gheli, early in the morning."

Many of our clan had gathered around during the ceremony, willing their strength into me for my baby. Sem ran to me as the shaman finished, stood close, grasping my free hand. In the shadows, far back from the circle of people, my firstborn stood, arms akimbo, a brown-haired, brown-eyed image of Aleksandr Andreevich Baranov.

○ ○ ○

31

The warmth of early summer spilled over the hills and into the valleys as we walked north and eastward. The vast region, endless though it might seem, began turning a hospitable face to us: streams flashed with fish; meadows offered roots and greens; the hunters flushed birds from the thickets, a relief from our diet of heavier meat.

One day Denedi Belik'a brought a fat gander into camp, his arrow still through its throat, and handed it to me. His growing skills of the hunt needed to be recognized. Little talk had passed between us through the months, for it seemed that cliffs towered between us. Our hands touched across the goose, our eyes met. The question that had plagued me since the move began could no longer be held back.

"Denedi Belik'a, I must know. Will you stay with us?"

"Mother, I cannot stay. This life holds nothing for me." His answers came without hesitation. "I must go back. I have already missed months at the school. Better that—"

"What of Seltan? Hasn't he made you welcome with him?"

"He has, Mother. I respect my uncle. He keeps his word. He has taught me many things. But Aleksandr Baranov is my father. I must go back to him."

"I had hoped you would see the good in the Kahtnuht'ana life. Stay to become a qeshqa among us." My voice grew firmer. "We need you, Denedi Belik'a."

"My life is not to be in following trails of animals, fishing streams in places I know nothing about." He shook his head, a frown crossing his face. "No books. No figuring. No charts to study navigation. I cannot go on this way. Soon I will—"

"Does Seltan know?"

"Yes, Mother. We have talked of it many times. He will take

me back this summer. We agreed in the beginning. That's the way I want it. My uncle will keep his word.''

I reached out to touch my son, wanting to hold him close; but he turned from me and strode away.

A decision had to be made. Even though the summer sun shone on us during those long days, the clans must prepare for the cold winds and the snows of winter. The elders and leaders had contended, argued, debated for weeks both the good and the bad points of establishing our winter village in that protected, remote basin tucked between ridges on the slopes of the great mountains north of the coastal ranges.

''We have not moved far enough from Yaghenen,'' my father insisted. ''We cannot assume that we will be safe here.''

An elder countered, ''This valley will be far more secure than where we lived last winter. From the ridge to the south, we can see great distances in all directions. Post guards, and they can warn us in time of any intruders.''

One of the qeshqa reasoned in support of my father: ''We have seen signs in these woods of hunters other than our own more than once. This is a sure warning that we can be tracked. I believe we have no choice but to move eastward and join the Athabaskan clans far beyond the great mountains.''

''Remember, we have old people and small ones. We have never before moved during winter. The snows in these mountains will bury us. Stopping here during the summer gives us time to build our shelters for winter. To gather fish and meat and berries. I say our choice lies here.'' Another man spoke, pounding his knee for emphasis.

So the talk went on, night after night.

Sitting on the bank of a stream, its cool water playing over my feet, relieving the ache in my muscles, I, too, found the choice a difficult one. The towering, glaciered slopes, shimmering in the summer light, did not look so difficult to walk across; but I knew from the slowness of our pace over the lower reaches what a forbidding, inhospitable barrier those high ridges could prove. My father's fear of remaining through the winter had been born of the days long ago when the Tahtna first invaded our lives, a fear that we had not set enough distance between us and the aliens.

Minya called us all together for a final decision. By a close count, the voices favored moving through the pass and into the safe country beyond the great mountains, where we would join Athabaskan clans too distant for the aliens to reach.

During the long walk our people had to be fed. Hunting parties took up the trail of a large herd of caribou. Others scaled the ridges for goats. The older men made fish traps for the streams, while women gathered berries and set snares for squirrels and rabbits. Life settled into a routine. As we traveled, we did our best to meet each day's demands for survival, all sharing according to ancient custom, dividing whatever we had with every family in the village, the best pieces to the elderly and those unable to join the hunts.

As the chilly nights of fall warned us of the cold time ahead, we hurried our steps. Seltan not only brought down his share of the game but also led groups of hunters who asked his help in the search for food. Since their early understanding, little had been said between Seltan and Denedi Belik'a about my son's return to his father. I held back from questioning him because the responsibility rested with my brother, and I honored his right. Some bond had developed between my brother and my son, growing stronger as the months passed; and hope began to rise that Denedi Belik'a would change his mind.

Each day's climb brought us nearer the high pass. One afternoon a hunting party under Jabila returned with the hides and meat of many mountain goats. The men were satisfied, for the hunt had been more successful than was expected; the women in camp at once set about scraping the new skins.

"This will make a fine, soft blanket for our son," Jabila said, handing me a shining white goat-hair pelt, softer than any skin I had felt for many seasons. Carrying it to the creek bed to scrape off the bits of fat and meat remaining on it, and wash away the blood, I asked for the goat horns, telling Jabila how I had tried so hard to be a carver, to make a Kahtnuht'ana spoon out of a goat horn; we laughed together as I mimicked Watnaw's voice: "Get a sharper stone."

By the stream, as I prepared the pelt, my fingers touching its softness, I listened to the birds calling to their mates and closed my eyes. The warmth of the sun reached down to me through the leafy branches of the trees, and I knew the feeling of home that I had longed for during my many seasons on Kadyak. Jabila took me in his arms, and in the closeness of those moments we lived again our summer's love on Yaghenen.

Then they came.

"Grab Anna! That's her over there!"

Our camp filled with men. Tahtna. Heavy boots. Cursing voices. Drawn guns.

Confusion. Panic. Shouts. Running. Our people scattered in all directions, dragged screaming children with them.

"Jabila! Here! Run with Sem! I will—" A hand grabbed me from behind, forcing my mouth shut.

"Mama! Ma—" Sem's shriek cut off.

Wrenching loose, running toward her as the *promyshlennik* dragged my struggling child toward the woods, I cried out, "Sem! Sem! Sem!"

Violent hands seized me, clamped over my mouth.

Along the slope by the stream where Denedi Belik'a had been helping with the canoe, three men pushed me forward at gunpoint. I bit the hand covering my mouth, screamed "No! No! No!"

Out of the corner of my eye, I saw Jabila running toward me, knife in his hand. He leaped, plunging the blade deep into the Tahtna attacking me. My captor's hand dropped, and I struggled free. A shot whistled, thudded close by. Jabila pitched forward clutching at his chest, his hand covered with blood.

A wrenching, anguished cry broke from me. I struggled, tore loose from the hands of the *promyshlennik* pulling me away from the camp.

"Ashana, run—" Jabila's voice died as he sank to the ground. I threw myself on top of him, his blood pumping onto the green grass of the mountain valley. "Qan . . . Ashana . . ."

Half sitting, half lying on the ground, I drew Jabila's body to mine, held his head against my face, my anguish mingling with the coarse alien voices and the cries of the women in our camp, a keening that sounded loud above the stamping and running.

The gush of Jabila's blood slowed to a trickle; the grass was wet with his life. I covered his wounded chest with the goatskin he had given me only a short time before, crushing myself to him, the agony on his face slowly easing as, still alive, he opened his eyes.

Naq'eltani, give me strength, I must take Jabila to safety. I tried to gather him in my arms, praying I could run into the hills with him; but a Tahtna pulled me from my husband as another shot ripped away half his face, smashing his head.

My screams turned to keening. Scanning the camp searching for Seltan, for *anyone* to help, I saw an eerie shaft of light stretch through the trees, high into the sky; it hovered a moment, then broke. Jabila's life.

A Tahtna voice in a twisted Kahtnuht'ana accent ordered, "Stay where you are, or we shoot all." Everyone froze in their places. "We come only for Anna and her children."

My spirit fled that time and place. Once before Baranov's men had shot Jabila, but he lived. There, in the faraway mountain basin, I knew the aliens had at last destroyed him, for I had seen the shaft of life break.

Seeming to come from a distance, the sound of voices sifted slowly through the air, Kazhna's words mingling with those of the Tahtna. Guns ready, four men strode toward me. Rough hands jerked me from Jabila, tearing my arms from around him as a booted foot kicked his body aside. Ice filled my veins. My last sight of him has stayed with me to this day: his bloodied, torn head and his hand grasping the dirt of that land across which he could never again take up the walk that is life.

Torn from all that had restored hope to me, dragged to the edge of the clearing where our men had built camp and cut trees to make homes for the winter, I twisted in the alien hands. Suddenly, Q'ut'en Gheli's cry reached out to me, gently at first, then swelling into an infant's demand for a mother lost, a wail that would hang on the air for my eternity.

Suddenly, the wailing stopped. Silence. Nidoc's promise. I knew she had taken my baby to her breast.

The streaks of blood that stained my qenich'eni were all I had left of Jabila: blood from my shattered summer rainbow, Shani Jabila. All yesterdays had been torn from me, my tomorrows stripped of meaning.

We tramped southward and westward, my body and mind numb, ears unhearing, eyes unseeing. At night, Sem clung to me, tossed in her sleep. How she held back her tears after the first days on the trail I did not know; her small hand in mine, her few words offered the comfort only a child can give a parent. My son, too, seemed shadowed by the tragedy. We had no chance to talk, he and I, for the Tahtna kept us separated during the day as well as at night. Since those coarse hands had dragged me from Jabila's body, no one had touched me. Men eyed both me and Sem, but they kept away, knowing they would pay with their lives if they molested either of us.

Ironic: Aleksandr Andreevich Baranov, my protector as well as my curse.

My exhaustion on the trail meant nothing to the aliens as they pushed west, then south to a branch of the Susitna River. There was no chance to escape from their guns, no survival in the forests, even if we could slip away. The coarse food sickened me, and several days I retched until I was almost too weak to stumble farther, thankful that no life stirred inside me. The *pro-myshlenniki* reached one of their caches and pulled out kayaks; the struggle of tramping across the land yielded to relentless bumping on the rapids and white water as the river coursed on a winding route toward Tikahtnu.

Beyond the point where the fresh river waters met the salty tides of Tikahtnu a ship waited, bearing the flag of Imperial Russia and the ensign of Baranov's Russian-American Company. Once we had climbed on board, the captain tacked rapidly to port. We cleared the headlands, and as the wind filled the sails, the vessel scudded southeast toward the harbor of Pavlovsk.

Denedi Belik'a sensed my need to keep him and Sem close to me, and made no effort to join the sailors on deck. The three of us shared our grief in silence. My son might not have approved of my relationship to Jabila, schooled as he had been by the monks that the ways of Aláyeksans were sinful; yet, even if he could not understand Jabila's place as husband, he did see Jabila shot down trying to protect me. At that moment, Denedi Belik'a knew firsthand the terror the Tahtna inflicted on Aláyeksa.

My children had faced death and bloodshed they should not have seen; they must be healed. I was their mother, but could I fully grasp the conflict that must have torn them? My niłdulchinen, children of two worlds, had no easy trail. Love and respect for their father pulled them one way, love for me suddenly mixed with sorrow for Jabila pulled them another.

For the first hours of the voyage we lay exhausted on our bunks, barely touching the food brought to our cramped cabin. Later, whispering seeped into my haziness. When I awakened, Sem and Denedi Belik'a stood close by, watching.

"Mama, we were worried about you." Sem reached her hand out to me. "You cried while you were sleeping."

I raised up on my elbow, pushed her hair back. "We need to talk. I want to ask—"

"I am sorry about Jabila. I didn't want it to end that way." The words rushed out of Denedi Belik'a as if held back too long. "He was good to me. Made me laugh with his stories. They should not have shot him."

Sem burst into tears. "What will we do without him?" She put her head in my lap and sobbed.

Never again the tap on my window, the trips into the mountains with the children. No more of Jabila's laughter, his tenderness, his love. Behind us in those distant mountains, with my people and his, lived our child, Sem's and Denedi Belik'a's half brother. My mind warned me: The Tahtna must not know.

I sat up, took their hands between mine. "Children, we must agree between us about your little brother." I stared into their eyes. "No one on Kadyak must know about him."

"But, Mama, I'm worried for him. Jabila's dead. You're gone." Tears streamed down Sem's face. "Who will take care of him?"

"I tried to get away from the men to pick him up for you. But I had no chance." Denedi Belik'a's concern surprised me; he had always ignored the baby.

Fright flashed through me. "You didn't tell the Tahtna about him?"

"No, Mother. I said nothing."

"Who will care for him now?" Sem repeated.

"The morning he was born Nidoc and K'i'un and I agreed on what to do if I should ever be taken away. Nidoc will nurse him with her own, and K'i'un will always look after him."

As the boat moved toward Kadyak, another concern had to be talked over with my children, so I said, "We must make a promise to each other. Now. A promise never to be broken: Say nothing to your father about the baby. Never, never to a Tahtna. Q'ut'en Gheli belongs with my Kahtnuht'ana people. Forever."

Looking me straight in the eyes, Denedi Belik'a said, "Father has taught me to be honest. So did Seltan. Mother, I promise you, Father will never hear about Q'ut'en Gheli from me."

"I promise, too. Forever," Sem whispered.

Pulling each child into my arms, I felt I must also talk to them about what lay ahead with their father. Before the escape from Kadyak, thoughts of my fate if I were recaptured had haunted me: banishment, being sent to the shacks, even death.

"Children, you have seen how uncertain life is. The day may come when we could be separated from each other. But I want you to know—"

"No, Mama!" Sem cried.

"Listen to me. Whatever happens, even if something takes me away, remember, I am always with you."

Sem and Denedi Belik'a both clutched me, sobbing; my arms

tightened around them, and we cried for a long time. Then we sat in silence, the only sounds the lapping of the sea against the planking, the crack of the sails in the wind as the ship took a different tack. Grief bound the three of us, and I had never felt closer to my children.

Kadyak Island. A few hours of midafternoon sunshine as we approached Pavlovsk harbor offered the only welcome. No friend waited to cheer us home. A strange quiet hung in the air as we stepped from the umiak that took us from the ship to the beach, and I wondered what friend had died because of our escape. Aleksandr Andreevich Baranov paced the path in front of our house, stoop-shouldered, his body sagging; he moved as if every joint pained him.

Many seasons had passed since Richard had begun teaching me the Tahtna words for "I am glad to be here." That day I could not say them, they would have borne no honesty; nor did my captor say, "Welcome home."

"Irina." Her father hugged her closely as she sobbed on his shoulder. "It's all right."

"You are safe, Antipatr." In the Tahtna style, Aleksandr embraced his son and kissed him on both cheeks.

Without a word for me, his attention still on the children, Aleksandr said, "You stink. Get to the sweathouse and wash. Strip off those filthy clothes. I'll send a servant with clean things." Leaning heavily on his cane, he started toward the house, turned and looked at me. "For all three of you."

Our bodies sweated, washed, clad again in the Tahtna garments we had left behind, we stood before Governor Baranov in our old house. Age and struggle showed in him; his face bore the scars of the years of labor, danger, and hardship fate had thrown in his path: And, more, beneath those scars, I saw his stubbornness, his cunning, the belief in his right to power. A chik'dghesh roaming at will, taking what he wanted.

The ticking of Aleksandr's old wooden clock, the hissing of steam from the samovar, the odor of cabbage and beluga from the kitchen, the stink of his tobacco—the familiar sounds and smells of Tahtna Kadyak. He let us feel his presence while his pen scratched out the lines of his report before he wiped the pen and put it down.

Sitting back, his eyes raked me. "You look better." He picked up one of the papers from his desk. "I have drawn an order for supplies from the warehouse here. The ship will be loaded and ready to sail for Novo-Arkhangelsk the morning after tomorrow.''

His voice calm, his tone breathed not an iota of warmth even toward Antipatr and Irina; his presence weighed on us.

''I have ordered the servants to pack your belongings, Anna. And for both of you, Irina and Antipatr. We will all be on board ahead of time. I will not have the sailing delayed.''

''Aleksandr, the children did not—''

He cut me off. ''Anna, go to the sleeping room. I will talk to you later. Now, I speak with the children here. Alone.''

His eyes stared me down; it was useless to argue with him. Too much had happened. It was better there be no open dissension in front of our children; they had seen enough of the cruel and bitter side of human beings.

As I turned away, Denedi Belik'a's eyes held mine, an unspoken message reassuring me of his promise. And from Sem's steady eyes a message of trust and hope fluttered to me as if on wings. The strength of that girl!

''Stand up, woman. I am not through with you yet.'' Aleksandr strode to the bed, yanked me to my feet, pinned me against the wall. ''Anna, Princess Anna, why did you do it? Why did you run away?'' He waited, then shouted, ''They stole you. That's the excuse, isn't it?''

I answered slowly and clearly, ''No. I helped with the plan. I knew.''

He roared, ''I should throw you to the ravens you prattle so much about! Don't think you have made a fool of me all these years—your Kenai savage sneaking in when I have been gone. I've known about him.'' His fingers dug into my flesh, shaking me.

Limp, through half-open eyes, I watched Baranov, a great tiredness sliding over me. Many times, I had scratched, shoved him away, kicked, screamed; these were actions he understood. To hold myself still and silent maddened him, tripped something inside him, and he flung me onto the bed.

''That savage is dead.'' Baranov glared at me with bloodshot eyes, and I shuddered at what he would do. ''Your savage surprised us and stole you. But my trackers knew who he was. They killed him. We made sure of it this time. He can no longer sneak in here to use you behind my back.''

The spirit of Jabila suddenly walked between us, and tiqun's mask dropped over me. Still without emotion, withdrawn, I watched Aleksandr Baranov from behind the mask in the way the wolf has always waited and watched—from a high hilltop.

"Did you hear me? He's *dead*, I tell you. That savage is dead." His face purple, he beat me with his cane, threw it down, then wheeled around and strode across the room.

"You have been nothing but trouble! You broke your father's word to me. There is no honor in any of you. You Kenai, you are traitors even to one another. Kazhna thought he slipped in here without anyone seeing him. Told me he had information about you and the children he would trade for food and clothes. Crafty sneak. Showed me the true side of all you Kenai savages."

If Aleksandr Baranov intended to shock me, he did not. Betrayal was part of Kazhna's very nature. "A man always on the edge of trouble. I think some day he will be banished," Seltan had told me. But the elders of our villages had failed to banish Kazhna soon enough. Kazhna, the traitor. Baranov, the alien who used him. Who was the worse?

"You disgraced me, woman. Put me to great expense. Forced me to take men away from company work to bring you back." Standing by the window, seething, he let me wait.

He turned toward me, eyes blazing. "Your Kenai lover will never set foot on Kadyak again. Listen to me! He stole my children. I ordered him killed. Do you hear? *Ordered!*"

The door slammed behind Aleksandr Baranov. I was alone.

Icy fingers gripped me, a coldness that has never left. Sliding to the floor, I lay at the threshold of death.

An endless time later, the door creaked and as if from a great distance, I heard Sem. "Mama! *Mama!* What's wrong? Antipatr! Bring our furs. She's shaking to pieces. Hurry!"

My children covered me, and their nearness lessened the terrible cold. The shivering receded; shock and grief and exhaustion bore me into a deep sleep. In the distance, a song. Far away on Yaghenen. Children again. Seltan and I, at dawn, sitting neck deep in water, singing our grandmother back to health. The song she had taught us. The same song we sang those mornings when she lay near death. Much later, reaching out, I felt my children, one on each side of me. I had not been on Yaghenen. I had not heard Seltan's and my song from long ago; Sem and Denedi Belik'a had crawled next to me, given me warmth, sung me back to life with the old song. Half awake, half asleep, they lay beside me.

Oh, those weeks after I had returned to my mother and we

walked the escape trail together! The days had been so filled with work, hunting, worry, we had found no time to sit and talk as in the days when I was a child. And her death took away forever my hope of knowing her again. In this Kadyak house, the breathing of my children flowed around me; and I felt the touch of my mother's shadow-spirit—still wandering, for it was not yet time for it to seek the center of the earth, there to join the other dead. Her shadow-spirit spoke: *Ashana, remember, you are the child of raven. We have borne raven's trickster side for so long, but now I see the strength of raven coming to you, its wisdom. Listen to the bird of our clan.*

We Kahtnuht'ana know that danger walks with the shadow-spirit in its wanderings—danger to the person who hears it. Danger faced me that day, for Baranov had said, "I am not through with you yet."

Death or life: Death, my fate if rage controlled his reason. Life, if he so chose. At that point I am not certain I cared.

Early on the day we were to sail, I watched from the window as the servants carried the last bundles for Irina and Antipatr to the ship. The governor's notes, reports, and gear had been stowed on board, leaving behind only the few furnishings that would be needed when he came back to Kadyak on company business.

Baranov started down the path, stopped suddenly, stood still. After a moment, he turned and came back to the house. A less angry captor than the day we had returned, he closed the door, stepped close to me, and held out his hands. Keeping his voice low, he said, "Anna, please listen. We must get on with the move. You will go to Sitka with me. You are the mother of my children, so you must live with us in my new house. Then the men in the company can see that we are a family according to the Russian style.

"You will behave. Never disgrace me again. I warn you, I will not allow it. It could destroy Antipatr's chance to enter the Imperial Naval Academy at St. Petersburg."

He still does not know me: Words will never change my feeling about Denedi Belik'a's training.

"I have a tutor for my son, and a governess for Irina, a German woman who has lived in Russia many years, knows civilized customs. I have a piano for my daughter, and she must learn music. It is time she becomes a lady, associates with Europeans. I will never allow Irina Baranov to consort with a savage man."

But you allow yourself *savage* women—me, every other *Anna*.

"The house in Novo-Arkhangelsk has been ready for you for months. We must forget the past, forget what has happened. We will start over again." As he had pleaded once before, that day he repeated, "Princess Anna, I need you."

Forget the past, Aleksandr Andreevich Baranov? Forget, because you order me to?

As the man who was master of all Aláyeksa tried to placate me, the change in his tactics became clear. "The four of us have much to look forward to in the times ahead. My capital on Sitka Island is safe. The Kolosh have made peace. The Russians who tried to kill us have been shipped off to Siberia. You will like Novo-Arkhangelsk. We shall be a family. Together."

A family? Us? The Princess of Kenai by the Tzar's decree! But, Aleksandr Baranov, you did not consider me in your plans. I would be only a fixture in your house. Part of the furniture. A woman who would grow old sitting hidden away, embroidering with your worthless trade beads. Wanting to say that and more to his face, I held my tongue, for my words would only cause new and bitter arguments.

Uncaring that I said nothing, he pressed on. "The ship is ready to sail. Hurry, Princess Anna. I will come back for you as soon as I finish my orders to the men." Then his voice turned to iron. "You will give up all your heathen ways. There will be no more of your foolish superstitions. You will follow the Russian way."

As he walked along the path leaning on his cane, his limp seemed more noticeable; but he still moved with purpose, and his servants hustled to keep up with him.

On the ship's deck, Sem and Denedi Belik'a waited.

Above the fireplace, in all its terrible splendor, the raven seemed to spread its wings and speak to me, as he had my first night in this house, when I was young, scared, just torn from my Yaghenen home. *Wear my mask today, Ashana, not the invisible ones you have pulled on when you needed courage through the years. The Russian has never understood that your power comes from the spirits of Aláyeksa. You know the way of the spirits. Let the alien know the truth. So, today, put on my visible raven mask, the one that he can truly see. QaniIch'ey Ashana, have courage and strength, for I see heartbreak in the choice that lies ahead for you.*

The awful fear that had long accompanied me disappeared;

and as the raven vanished, the snowfield message of the qegh nutnughel'an swam through my head, reminding me of the purpose of my survival on Kadyak.

In the sleeping room, pushing Baranov's bed aside, I pulled up the boards covering the cache where Watnaw and I had stowed the few guns we had managed to steal from our captors. But I sought no gun. There lay the huge raven mask that a Tahtna had stolen from somewhere in Yakutat or Chugach country. Watnaw "disappeared it" from his shack one day, and we had hidden it in my house before the escape. "We might need it," Watnaw had said, "and besides, I do not want filthy alien hands touching it."

I tore off my Tahtna dress, shook out my quenich'eni, and placed the moccasins on the floor near me. My hand rested for a moment on the deep red stains dulling the white deerskin on my lap, all that remained of the man I loved. A sob rose to my throat, but I choked it back. Dressing hurriedly, before Baranov could return, I pulled the raven mask over my face. Danger could walk through the door at any time, but fear no longer lived in my heart. I stood by the fireplace, waiting, as I had so often waited, for my captor.

"We must sail now, Princess Anna. Hurry." Aleksandr called, rushing into the room. And then the Russian governor of Aláyeksa came face to face with the powerful, full-faced mask of chulyin, raven feathers cascading down its back. The long, sharp beak curved slightly at the tip. The lower bill could be pulled open or shut by a sinew cord attached at the jawline; as the bill snapped open, there inside the mouth was perched a smaller raven, the spirit of chulyin. Under the heavy brows on the low forehead of its black-blue head, unblinking, slanted eyes stared back at Aleksandr Baranov with the full power of the raven.

My captor stopped, glared, no recognition in his eyes. "Who the hell are you? Get out of my house!" he roared as he hurried past, calling, "Anna! Where are you? We must leave."

"No. I am not going."

"What? Who said that? Get out!"

Behind him, two Koniag servants watched. One nudged the other as they waited in the doorway to see what would happen. I did not know their names, but felt their support.

"I said I must stay on Kadyak." The raven mask spoke.

"Anna? That you, Anna? What did you say?" He stepped closer.

"I said, I am not going to Novo-Arkhangelsk."

"What are you doing with that savage . . . thing over your face? I told you, get rid of your heathen ways. Put your clothes on. We're sailing."

Baranov raised his cane. I braced myself as he struck the long beak, but the blow did not even crack it.

"I am not going with you." I held myself steady. "I have told you, I will not go. It is too late for us." Then, for the first time, I spoke my husband's name to him. "You killed Shani Jabila, and you bragged about it. I will never forgive you. I cannot live with you. Never again."

"You have to. *I order you.*"

"You go. Leave the children here."

"The children? Leave them with you? Never."

"Yes. Leave them. They are mine."

"This is foolishness, Anna. Behave yourself. You waste time."

"Take my children off the ship."

"No!"

Courage, Ashana, courage. A power greater than I had ever known took hold.

"I order you to come. Now."

With one hand, Aleksandr raised his stick to strike me again, his other hand jerking up to his face as if to ward off evil. Over its sharp, long beak, the raven's unblinking eyes challenged him. Years ago on Yaghenen, when Baranov claimed me hostage, my father had cried out, "The raven turns his evil side on us." By the fireplace on Kadyak that day, the raven's good side stood with me, and the blows fell without harm. His bravery was my bravery. The spirits of Aláyeksa encouraged me: *Ashana, stay on Kadyak. Prepare to tell the truth to the four winds.*

"I am not going. You must leave the children with me."

"Never."

As if he could no longer stand the sight of me, Baranov turned his back, pointed to the ship. "Look out there, Anna. Your children. Take that heathen thing off. One last time, Princess Anna, I say *come.* Antipatr and Irina need you."

The children: That argument alone could make me change my decision. Crafty, my captor.

Danger walks wherever a Tahtna walks, and as long as one of them remained in my land, no ni*l*dulchinen was safe. Without Aleksandr Baranov's arm shielding them on Kadyak, clutching hands could levy Denedi Belik'a for sea hunts, seize Sem for hostage. There was so much jealousy and mistrust of the governor that if his children were here and he was absent, away on Sitka Sound, unable to protect them, they could lose their freedom.

The grief of separation might kill me, but better that Baranov and I did not pull the children apart—tugging them my way, yanking them his way, killing their spirits because our differences collided. Baranov considered me a savage, a heathen: he would never yield.

"I stay here." Again the raven mask spoke.

The heartbreaking choice became my fate: I lost my children to my captor, but I saved them from the levies.

Aleksandr Baranov picked up the last of the furs. The old Dĕduška Domovoy fell to the floor, and he kicked it aside. "You have deserted this house, Old Man. You have not been of any use to me for a long time." Without another glance, the governor of Aláyeksa strode through the door, his heavy steps pounding angrily down the path.

From the small, smoke-streaked window, I watched the ship weigh anchor. The sails filled with wind and the vessel pointed its course toward the open sea and Sitka Island; I saw the three of them on deck, staring back at me. Aleksandr's arm was around his children, claiming them. Their heads were bowed to hide their tears. I watched for a moment longer as the great fog that hangs over the water swirled around Sem and Denedi Belik'a and hid them from me.

As I saw my two children disappear, anguish made its home in me, an anguish for the choice I had made. I had shed many, many tears in the past: tears for Jabila, for our baby, Q'ut'en Gheli, for my mother and father. For my brother and for my lost Yaghenen.

Now, alone and empty, I cried endlessly, but the tears were inner tears, and unshed.

32

Yuyqush! Yuyqush! Northern lights. Great curtains of color stream across the skies far to the north. An unseen hand paints slashes of yellow, bands of orange and violet, misty veils of red and green; flashing white flames merge into evanescent flares. Yuyqush: colors no human artist can paint. Yuyqush: movements no dancer can copy. In the faint hiss of Yuyqush, I hear other sounds: sounds of all those who walked with me long ago and are gone. The gunfire that spilled Jabila's life. The agonized cries of hostages all across Aláyeksa. The laughter of my children, lost to me forever. And always, always, the icy voice of Aleksandr Andreevich Baranov.

"Come, Ashana." Watnaw touched my arm. "Tushe*l* will soon blot out the light."

We walked down from the headland together, as we had done so many times since Aleksandr Baranov had taken Sem and Denedi Belik'a from me to live in the Tahtna settlement on Sitka Sound. A cold and lonely walk lay before me, but my life had warmed when Watnaw came to live with me. As we aged, drawing closer to the day when the ceremonial fires would consume us, we were still sustained by our mutual love and trust.

For many seasons Watnaw had fought the curse the aliens had brought to our shores, a disease that eventually destroyed her sight. Before the Tahtna came, Aláyeksans knew no such word as "syphillis." The curse had scourged her body, covered her with unspeakable sores. She survived the most terrible ravages, only for the disease to come to rest in her eyes. Those flashing black eyes that had blazed so fiercely when we plotted the poisoning and the gun stealing now stared out blindly into the world. When we walked, I led her; though scarred, she held her head high, her Gulushutna spirit alive, the strands of our friendship still tightly woven.

The summer after my children sailed away with their father, I learned the depths of Watnaw's strength. A fever brought by a sailor on a Yankee ship spread through Pavlovsk like fire in dry timber. More than a hundred people, too weak and racked with pain to help themselves, lay dying in one of the large shacks. Little children, babies crawling over their dead mothers, cried to be fed. We were all helpless before that strange, unheard-of fever, a fever that began with a terrible cough, followed by a shortness of breath, and then no breath at all. And in three days, death.

The shaman stayed with the sufferers day and night, until Ivan Banner saw him and forbid him to go among us on his healing visits. "A savage. He does not know the first thing about medicine," he said, himself ignorant of how to cure that fever.

I called the shaman back. "Stay," I told him, "stay. Do what healing you can."

Banner must have seen from my face that I had gone beyond fear of him, and he backed away from my defiance. I remained with the sick, Watnaw helping me. We talked to them, gave them what comfort we could. Day and night Watnaw, who had never known the joy of holding a child of her own, rocked the sick little ones, sang softly to them, and eased the dying of many small ones whose mothers were too sick to help them.

It was during these awful days that we learned of a different side to the monks. They came to aid the ill and the dying. Father Herman had moved, years past, to a small island where he hoped he could find the peace and quiet that had not come to him on Kadyak. He named his mission "New Valaam," after the distant monastery where he had been trained and had lived before being called to serve the Russian church in Aláyeksa.

When Father Herman heard of the sickness, he at once ordered his men to row him to Pavlovsk. Ceaselessly he performed his church rites over the dying, spread his words of comfort among the fevered. I watched the man carefully as I moved from one sufferer to another. His actions, the tone of his voice, his humble attitude, the look in his eyes told me that he did indeed care for those human beings in their misery; his every action and word was filled with compassion. He treated us with respect, never ordering us around, never insulting us, never scorning anyone or calling them "heathen."

Father Herman: a quiet monk growing old in the work of his

church in Aláyeksa. A man of books. Teacher of my lost son. I could understand more clearly in those days of the dread fever why Denedi Balik'a had listened to him. If only the monk had not forced his beliefs on my child, perhaps we could have found ways earlier to accept each other, to talk about our different lach'u.

After the dreadful illness had passed, Watnaw and I rested in our house. Father Herman called on us before he left Pavlovsk for the quiet of his New Valaam and said, "Thank God that Antipatr and Irina are with their father. I have not heard of an outbreak of the fever on Sitka Sound. They are safe."

"Better that my children had been left high in Yaghenen's mountains. Away from those ships that bring diseases." I felt Watnaw's hand close over mine with a squeeze that said *Be careful, Ashana,* but I needed to make the monk hear me.

Sem and Denedi Belik'a with Aleksandr Baranov. As if they stood close enough for me to reach for their hands, I saw them clearly, remembered the last time I had touched them, heard them laugh and tease each other, heard their chatter in the many tongues of Kadyak, saw them again on that last day, when I forced myself to watch them sail out of Pavlovsk harbor, the arms of my captor clasping them to him.

My past held too many tears, too many partings, too much sorrow. My crying had been within myself: In old age, the deep waters of our feelings are kept within us. And the images of my loved ones never dimmed; the imagination that bore me back to the bright flowers of Yaghenen's meadows never faltered.

"Anna, what are you thinking?" Father Herman's eyes were questioning me. "The ships will come. We cannot prevent them. That is the way of progress."

"Progress—the curse of Aláyeksa since the first Tahtna ship came to our shores."

"Curse?"

"Can't you see? If the hunters had not come to steal our furs, none of this sickness could have crawled among us. The ships brought them all."

"The hunters have been cruel. I know how cruel. But they did not plan to bring the fever. It struck them hard, too. The company has done wrong, thinking only of profits for its owners. We are monks: We see the injustice to Aláyeksa. We have written reports about the wrongs and sent them home. Anna, you know how much we have written against the injustice."

Ah, yes. Those reports. The Tahtna always wrote reports.

"Then why haven't all the hunters, the navy men, the company men, the monks, been ordered back to Russia? They do not belong here." No alien would ever understand the loathing I felt for them.

He studied me, opened his Bible, then closed it. "Anna, everything takes time."

"Yes. I remember Count Rezanov saying, 'Be patient, civilizing takes time.' " My words cut more deeply than I had intended, but I did not stop myself.

Many of our people had died of a *civilized* disease. But a measure of my respect never extended to another Tahtna went to Father Herman; after he left us he sent back umiaks loaded with food and supplies from his personal stores. "Give them to the weakest ones," he ordered his men.

Father Herman visited me regularly during the years after the disease had passed. We talked many times, and he tried to narrow the distance between us, but one afternoon he nearly caused a shutting-down of all talk. He had noticed my caribou-hide painting, and was staring at it. "A mural. Remarkable. A true artist painted that piece. A lifetime of work." He stroked his chin, then said, "Such fine art should be sent home to Russia. Our people should see what is being done in Aláyeksa."

Tiqun's mask slipped over my face. The wolf's spirit warned: *Watch him.* I watched and waited until Father Herman left. Then I took my painting and hid it in the cache.

He continued to visit, never asking about the painting. In wanting to draw me into his beliefs, he would read from his Bible, try to explain why he and the other monks had been sent to The Great Country. " 'Go ye therefore, and teach all nations,' " the book said, " 'baptizing them in the name of the Father, and of the Son, and of the Holy Ghost; Teaching them to observe all things whatsoever I have commanded you.' "

Father Herman talked at length one day about his Bible, the truths of his Christian religion, why I must learn them and help him teach other Aláyeksans the truth about his powerful God who knew all.

"Father Herman, we must make a truce," I said, looking at him across the Tahtna samovar, drawing on the strength and wisdom of raven. "I will not insist that you learn the lach'u of Aláyeksa, if you do not insist I learn your truth as written in your book."

"But Princess Anna," he said, "I wish to know about your

people of Aláyeksa. I am studying your languages. I speak Koniag words whenever they are needed. I am learning.''

I sat on my bench in thought a while, I remember, trying to understand the difference between ''word'' and ''truth.'' Then it struck me what the monks sought to do. My blood ran cold. ''But it pains me. You learn the words of Aláyeksans so you can speak to us in our tongues. But you do not use our words to teach Aláyeksan truths. You ignore our truth about Naq'eltani, our animal spirits, the birds and the sea people, the lach'u that speaks all around us, in every blade of grass, in a snowflake, in the spindrift on the crest of a wave. Everywhere in the open air, we can hear a truth. You confuse our people. You use our words, but you fill them with your Bible teachings; you refuse to speak our lach'u, our truth. Dress a baby eagle in lynx skin, and it cannot grow.'' The voices, the laughter and sobs, of two children who had played at my feet flooded into my head, and I could not go on.

Father Herman sat a long time, chin on hand, but did not open his Bible. ''Princess Anna, one day you will learn the truth of this book. I will wait. To Christianize takes a long time. Till then, let us meet as friends.''

As he rose to leave, he said, ''You are a wise woman. Very wise. I have watched you through the years. I saw your tenderness in the sick house. Your courage has grown. Your love for your people is your power. You may live hostage here, but you are free, Anna, free in the way very few people are.''

From the aliens sailing the Tahtna trading vessels that dropped anchor in Pavlovsk harbor many months apart, we were able to patch together the fates of those no longer among us. The years passed. It took him a long time, but the colonial governor for Russia in Aláyeksa built his new capital as he had dreamed; he gained a trader-ruler's reputation, our callers told us, whose skills at bargaining had become legendary in nations far away.

When finally relieved of his duties in Aláyeksa, Baranov boarded ship for St. Petersburg without returning to Kadyak. He intended to serve out his years as adviser on Aláyeksan affairs to the Russian-American Company from his home in Russia. But the life voyage of Aleksandr Andreevich Baranov ended in the South Seas when fever struck him. After a brief ceremony, sailors dropped the governor's body into the Java Sea. So, fate denied him the service he yearned to give in his homeland.

I endured beyond the life of my captor.

The heart may resolve that it will always stay true to its beginnings; but outside voices crowd in, and the mind and the tongue slip. So it was with my son Denedi Belik'a's name—how many times I have slipped and called him by his Tahtna name, Antipatr! My son studied and graduated from the Imperial Naval Academy in the alien city on the River Neva. I never saw him again, for he was not permitted a visit to Kadyak before he left Aláyeksa. From the first moment I set eyes on his tiny body, I knew my son for Russian; yet in spite of the Baranov blood marking him and the loss of trust between us, brought on in part by the alien teachings, in part by me, I know in my heart that my son, if allowed a choice, would have come to say farewell.

Denedi Belik'a. A handsome, bright boy. I can see him in his first uniform on board ship after that miserable trip to Sitka Island. Strong, healthy, intelligent, he absorbed all things Russian in order to draw closer to the father whom he admired. How proud he must have been of his assignment to duty on a vessel in the service of his father's homeland. But Denedi Belik'a did not transplant well into alien soil; he died in St. Petersburg shortly after he became an officer in the Russian Imperial Navy. Word never reached me as to where my son lies.

Sem. Word of the governor's beautiful, talented daughter carried back to me in Pavlovsk. My Sem polished her Tahtna with the governess and learned German. She lived as easily in Baranov's house as a Russian as she had lived easily with me as an Athabaskan. Her father guarded her closely; no rough Igor would ever put his hands on Sem. At home, I was told, she wore the alien dresses that pleased her father; and she delighted him by playing the piano and singing the songs of Russia. My daughter spoke several Aláyeksan languages fluently and moved freely among the Gulushutna around Novo-Arkhangelsk. When she went among our people, she wore her Kahtnuht'ana garments and talked with them in their own tongues; they warmed to her for her friendly spirit and the traces of themselves they saw in her.

A few months before Aleksandr had sailed for his homeland, a young Tahtna naval officer arrived in Novo-Arkhangelsk. A man of high birth, he loved my Sem; and they were "married properly" in the Russian church. Simeon Ivanovich Yanovskii became the second governor of Aláyeksa. They visited me once. My daughter stepped off the ship wearing a beautiful fringed Athabaskan deerskin quenich'eni. The young man she introduced as her husband walked proudly at her side. Had I not known Simeon was an alien, I would have thought him Athabaskan. His gentle manner with Sem and their small son, his respect toward me, marked him with the high bearing of a Kahtnuht'ana leader. I do not know what Baranov told Simeon Yanovskii about Sem's mother, but I could see that Simeon respected my daughter, loved her well. I cuddled their baby boy in my arms; and the last evening Sem spent with me, I gave her the carved snowbird from the north, the bird of survival. If only I could have kept them with me forever! But Simeon had duties in Novo-Arkhangelsk, and he had requested return to Russia within a couple of years: His family had large holdings in the Ukraine regions of Baranov's Russia. His mother had written that, as a favored son, Simeon was needed at home.

While they were with me, Simeon sought to soften my attitude toward Aleksandr Baranov's memory. "He is dead now. We must forgive him his sins. He was an honest man, Qanil-ch'ey Ashana." (Simeon always used my Kahtnuht'ana name; my Sem had taught him well.) "The company sent an accountant from Russia to go over every line of his accounts and records. Men had written mean reports through the years accusing Baranov of cheating the company, lining his own pockets. But you should know, Mother, the accountant found each of Baranov's business deals in order. Nothing missing. Not a kopek misused." Simeon's young face moved me with its sincerity as he finished. "He sacrificed himself to the company, even paid out his own funds when the company was short."

"Mother," Sem continued, trying to close the rift between me and the memory of her father, "remember the small deerskin? The one you embroidered with father's trade beads and hid in the rafters of the Sitka house? He found it. He kept it on the table by his bed. When he left, he folded it and kept it in the pocket close to his heart. Father has it with him still. At the bottom of the Java Sea."

We took the baby and walked outside. I stood with Sem on the headland as I had done so many times long ago. For a moment Sem turned away, then, her eyes solemn brown pools, she put her arms around me. "I can't ask that you forget the hurt," she said. "But be gentle with yourself, Mother. Try to ease away the anger."

Hearing the Athabaskan kindness in your voice, I loved you the more for your words, my dear one, and, to my surprise, an easing of the anger began to pass through me, easing, too, the pain of the years. My lost Sem, who knows what forgiveness I might have felt had your father left you with me on Kadyak?

Many times, facing Baranov, I had drawn strength from the spirit of the mask that I pulled down over my face. But I would wear no mask with my daughter. That day on the shore, as the wind buffeted the drifting tushe*l*, we watched a lone sea gull glide down toward the coast on the waves—it rose, hovered, seeming to ride the spindrift a moment.

Then it was gone.

Does the passage of time lessen the sting of loss? With Sem and Simeon in this house, the years faded away; I walked with them in the present, but as we waved good-bye, I knew nothing could erode my belief in the wrongs done to The Great Country. *Stay angry*, Agagasik's spirit had directed me long ago: *Stay angry until you find a way to tell the four winds the lach'u of Aláyeksa.* Not even my daughter's gentle words could lessen that charge. But who knew if time's weathering might again bring the easing of anger and pain, the easing that had passed through me when Sem and I talked?

While Sem and her husband visited Kadyak, Father Herman came often. He and Sem's husband became close friends, and soon were talking about their homeland like longtime acquaintances, about Simeon's plans for the future, the state of affairs in Novo-Arkhangelsk, and, of course, Father Herman's religious beliefs.

One afternoon, the monk said something that frightened me: A chill seemed to sweep through the room when he said to Simeon, "You are going to Russia, to St. Petersburg. Do not take your wife to the city with you. She was born here. She knows nothing of the outside world, its temptations, its devious ways, its captivating luxuries. It would be better to leave her in the Ukraine with your mother while you go about your business in St. Petersburg."

Simeon promised.

Simeon Ivanovich Yanovskii did not keep his word. "She did not want to be without me," he said later. He took her to St. Petersburg. In a year she was dead.

Denedi Belik'a. Sem. Pick a flower and it dies.

Aliens in The Great Country seem to believe that the Tzar's *ukaz* decreeing better treatment for Aláyeksans has resulted in improved conditions. We who know see no change. Part of the clans of my villages still live far inland, farther than the place to which we fled the summer the Tahtna killed Jabila. Kadyak remains guarded, a hostage island. The *promyshlenniki* with their guns, the armed Tahtna who have walked within sight of me anywhere in the village all those years, even after Baranov left Aláyeksa, do not come from my imagination. "Keep Anna on Kadyak," Baranov had ordered. Our men and women still slave, despite the kind words the faraway Tzar had written: Do not molest them. Be more humane. Do not take them from their islands. But now, as always, the Company still seizes its levies of men for the sea hunts, ignores the cries of women and children.

Many of our people continue to die, more numbers to be added to the reports shipped to men in St. Petersburg. The pages written by our alien captors and sent home to Russia try to explain us, and in doing so they damn their own acts.

The monks think they make order out of the chaos that is Aláyeksa by writing "criticism of injustice." One of the head monks wrote about the low birth rate among Aláyeksans, comparing us with Russian women, who bore ten to fifteen babies while we often bore only two or three, sometimes none. No skilled midwives; "poor understanding" as to how to treat pregnant women; many seasons of hunger; syphilis; the "great affability" of the native married women toward Tahtna men—all these were said to be the fault of the *victims* and the cause of the low number of births. More: He accused our women of practicing adultery. *Adultery*, when one Tahtna after another forced a woman? "Lascivious," he said, but what Aláyeksan woman has the right to say "I will" or "I won't"? This churchman actually wrote that the Tahtna hunters had led our women to believe that virginity was injurious to health and ought to be ended as early as possible—by a Tahtna man.

The fact was that very few Aláyeksan women birthed live children—usually only one out of nine. The monk did not understand the reason for the numbers he reported, did not listen to the cries of the abused women of Aláyeksa.

Perhaps all the talk, the worry, the reports by the aliens about our low birth rate, came from their concern that we did not produce enough babies to grow up and fill their levies for the sea hunts.

I will never tell, nor will any other woman ever tell, the dark secrets behind the dwindling number of babies across The Great Country. What mother in her right mind will bring a baby into this evil if she can prevent it? "Better that my child die than slave for the Tahtna,'' the whispers continue among our clans, brave words no one screams aloud. Are they less mothers than I, who let my children go?

Those tragedies were so plain to see that even my son's Russian hero, the friendly Lieutenant Gavriil Davydov, knew of them and made notes to take home. A savage, he wrote, had a son that he wished to kill; when asked why, ''Better it should die than become a kaiur [slave],'' the Koniag had answered.

Through the seasons Seltan has visited me, has led the Kahtnuht'ana boats with supplies. Our men must row greater distances because my people had not yet returned to the shores of Tikahtnu, but the *bargain* was kept to ensure that we hostages were not killed. He has brought me a few keepsakes: the Old Half-Man masks, another raven mask, Jabila's tiqun headpiece and mask, clothes from Nidoc. He brings news: Ni'i died. Minya's wisdom guides the clans. Kazhna has been banished as a traitor—the worst punishment, for no man can survive alone in the frozen wilds, and no clan will take in a banished man.

When my brother comes, we find a way to talk alone. Always, we speak of our people going home to Yaghenen: That is our dream.

Because we have always fought against the Tahtna, my homeland is an unsafe place for families. Guns are few; but each time one can be ''disappeared'' to send home with Seltan, the feeling grows that the Kahtnuht'ana struggle is still *my* struggle and that here on Kadyak I do have purpose.

Once in a while, my brother would bring a Kahtnuht'ana youngster to visit me, one skillfully trained by his uncle to use the paddle. We never admitted his identity to any Tahtna. If Aláyeksans wondered about my son, they kept it to themselves; no one would risk his life by speaking about him. Q'ut'en Gheli, a young and handsome Jabila, will pass our blood into future generations of Kahtnuht'ana. Seltan and I would whisper, ''Our next Qishvet'.''

I had one gift for Q'ut'en Gheli. My caribou-hide painting of Aláyeksa's nanutset, which had hung on my wall ever since I finished it, except during the time I hid it from the grasping hand of the monk. It needed a home with the son of Jabila and me, so that he could learn the lach'u of his mother's life and could pass it on to those who would come after. But before I gave it to him, I painted in two children lost to me, two children who should have known the streams and mountains of Yaghenen.

Q'ut'en Gheli walks beyond the Tahtna, free. He is my victory over Governor Aleksandr Andreevich Baranov.

Long ago, I had told High Chamberlain Nikolai Rezanov, "Mother Russia has forced herself onto our land, saying she brings us civilization and better conditions for our bodies. Her monks drone that they bring salvation for our spirits. The fact is, Your Excellency, that Mother Russia *kills* our bodies. Her monks *destroy* our spirits. Be that as it may, Nikolazi Rezanov, I tell you that long after you Russians have gone from these shores our people will still be here. We will endure, and we will prevail."

Watnaw and I endure. We survive like the two brown bears of ancient Yaghenen: *Long ago, when birds and animals changed into humans and back again, two brown bears—women—lived with one man bear. He died. Then, he went to live with a strange brown-bear-woman. That made his first two bear-women very angry. After a long walk, the two women found him. They destroyed him. Then they knew peace. They went to live on the slope of a high mountain. They ate well. Walking. Talking. Working. The bears can still be seen on Yaghenen. No one can destroy them. Two old brown bears. They endure. Survivors.*

A rap on the door.

Before me stood a young man in monk's garb, cleaner, newer, and finer than anyone on Kadyak wears. He had quick brown eyes in a lean, smooth face, high cheekbones for a Tahtna, straight black hair. I had never seen the man before, had not heard that a new monk had arrived on the trading ship anchored in Pavlovsk harbor.

"May I come in?"

I hesitated, but saw no reason to treat the stranger rudely. "Yes. Come in."

I had a strange feeling about him. The face . . . the person . . . I had seen . . . known . . . felt that presence before. No. My imagination. I was growing old. I knew few of the monks. Except for Father Herman, I had avoided the black-robed men of the Tahtna church.

"I am the Monk Kristofor. From Valaam Monastery on Lake Ladoga. I will be in Pavlovsk only a short time, until the ship loads and sails back to Russia."

If he wanted to try to teach me the Christian way, let him. I would listen, for he had a pleasant voice, but he could never convert me in a few days; the monks tried with me over all the years they have been here, and failed. I smiled to myself, poured him a cup of tea, wondered why he had called on me.

He sipped, looked up at me, took a long breath. "Thank you for the tea, Qaniɫch'ey Ashana."

Qaniɫch'ey Ashana! Qaniɫch'ey Ashana? No Tahtna calls me by that name. I started to speak, but could not.

He put the cup down beside the samovar. Again, the feeling came over me as I watched his movements that I had known that presence all my life.

"Your name. I heard it many times when I was a small boy. Yes, I knew it well. Qaniɫch'ey Ashana."

His voice bore a remembered rhythm.

"At Valaam Monastery near St. Petersburg, where I studied to be a monk, I took the name Kristofor." He stopped, his voice lowering almost to a whisper. He watched me carefully. "In my home, I was Aleksandr. My last name, Yanovskii. The Aleksandr for my grandfather Baranov. The Yanovskii for my father."

I held up my hands, as if to push away any mention of names that have haunted me through all the years of separation from my loved ones. "No! No! They left me a long time ago. They are gone."

His voice gentle, he took both my trembling hands in his, looked deeply into my eyes. "Irina was my mother."

I jerked my hands away from him, sank into the chair near the table, and rocked my body back and forth. Tears for my lost children, long shed inside me, washed my wrinkled face.

"No. Not Sem. She has been lost from me a long time. A long, long time."

He stood quietly, his hands stretched toward me, but not touching mine. "Grandmother Ashana, I am Irina's son."

It was impossible after all those years that someone should come back to me from Russia. Someone with my blood. Impossible that the young monk was Sem's baby, the tiny boy I had held in my arms before she and Simeon sailed for Russia when he had finished his service as governor of Russian Aláyeksa. A flood of memories stretched my grief into a low keening for my lost Denedi Belik'a and Sem, for Yaghenen, for my beloved Jabila.

The Monk Kristofor took the balalaika from the wall where

it had hung untouched since the days Sem had sung to it in this room. He picked the strings, turned the pegs to bring the ancient instrument into tune, strummed and sang. The words? The tune? He sang our morning song.

I was once again a small child sitting with Seltan on the bank of a mountain stream, our feet stinging in the cold water, our grandmother teaching us the words and tune of her secret song, the one we later sang in the days of her illness and brought her back to health. The same song my children sang to me when I lay near death from the shock of Jabila's murder and our recapture.

The young monk's hands lightly strummed the old balalaika. Other hands like his, smaller hands but with the same long, tapering fingers, had picked those strings long ago. My Sem's hands. His deep brown eyes, Sem's eyes, never left my face. The melody, the words. He kept repeating them. The song that is mine. The song my grandmother had taught me long ago. I had taught Sem, told her never to forget. She had taught it to her son.

Sem birthed him in Aláyeksa. I held him when he was a baby. I knew that young monk for my grandson.

"What can I do for you, Grandmother, before I leave?" My grandson had visited every day, asking the same question.

"Nothing, Kristofor. There is so little I need anymore."

Without warning, a voice whispered, a spirit heard long ago from the snowfield, the qegh nutnughel'an: *Tell it to the four winds.* (I had tried with Nikolai Rezanov, trusting he would spread my words abroad. But, riding home through Siberia, he died. My message was lost.)

I must have whispered the words to myself, for he asked, "What did you say, Grandmother? I could not hear you."

"Tell it to the winds. Can you write?"

"Yes. I have had many years of training." His words came quickly, his tone reassuring. "The monks who taught me said I had a good hand."

"Tell it to the four winds."

"What? I do not understand."

"Grandson, the truth of the history of Aláyeksa—or, as we say, the lach'u of the nanutset—needs to be told. I have lived it. Can you write it as I tell you? Not change a word?"

"Yes. Yes, of course."

"Some of our nanutset will not be pretty. It may pain you to hear its lach'u.'' I paused a moment, needing his assurance. "Will you write the words as I tell them to you? I must know. Will you?''

His face thoughtful, he gave me a long, piercing look, then said, "Yes, Grandmother. I will write exactly as you tell me. You have my word.''

"Then write. Tell the four winds. So all people will know what was done in Aláyeksa.''

"I have to bring parchment and pen from the ship.''

"I must tell you again, write exactly as I say. If you do not, the šdónályášna, the monsters of our mountains, will stay your hand.''

A quizzical look played over his features, but Sem had taught him well, for he did not question me and said as he left the house, "I will come back this afternoon.''

To ready myself, I changed into my old qenich'eni. Jabila's bloodstains had aged to a dark red-brown. I thought to put on the chulyin mask, then decided that it would be too much for the young man. I turned my mind back into the past.

With Kristofor settled at his grandfather Aleksandr Baranov's old desk, I began my story. The nanutset took many days, but my memory opened wider as the telling went on, one part often leading to another stored deep inside me. Many happenings and names and sorrows and people crowded against one another, insisting they be heard. My grandson's hand flew over the sheets of parchment. He asked several questions—some to clarify the meaning of a word or phrase, others to help him relate an earlier thought to one set down later, a few to assure the accurate telling of the lach'u unfamiliar to him.

The day we finished, dusk had begun to settle over Pavlovsk. For a covering to protect the pages, I gave him a deerskin, one I had embroidered with dentalium shells, tiny bird claws, porcupine quills, and seeds, all stitched together with fine sinew.

The telling of the nanutset had drawn me close to him, given me a feeling of someone belonging to me that had not filled my heart since Sem had visited here. Those weeks were happy on Kadyak, for Kristofor was the presence of Sem sitting at the desk or playing the balalaika, her voice soünding through his.

Handwritten sheets of parchment covered the desk, lay piled around the room. My grandson dried his pen, checked the papers to make certain they would not smudge, placed all in order, tied the parchment in my embroidered deerskin, and placed my story in a waterproof box for the long journey to the Monastery of Valaam on Lake Ladoga near St. Petersburg.

We walked to the headlands of Kadyak one last time. Waves lapped in the shadows below; we heard them breaking against the rocky cliffs and felt the spray on our faces.

"Grandmother Ashana, I sail tomorrow."

I gripped my grandson's arm, said nothing. Too often partings leave sorrow in their wake. I wanted there to be no sorrow with my grandson.

Then, softly, we sang together the words of our old and secret Kahtnuht'ana song, words not known to any other. As we sang, I felt Kristofor slip something hard and cold into my hand. A shimmer of white northern light shone on the carved ivory, on the treasure given me long ago by the Eskimo hunter when I had stood, scared and frozen and alone, on those same headlands. I had given it to Sem when she had left with her husband for Russia.

Her son had brought it back to me. Aláyeksa's snowbird.

Yuyqush! Yuyqush!

Pulsating shafts of light and streamers of reds and yellows and whites cascaded high above us, an unseen hand adding great slashes of orange and violet. Yuyqush. My grandson and I were bathed in its brilliance, a brilliance that was more the absence of darkness than the presence of light.

As the glowing, flickering curtains of color unfolded against the northern sky, I heard in the soft voice of yuyqush the echoes of my Aláyeksan people.

And then I heard the qegh nutghel'an from long ago on the snowfield, telling through Agagasik's voice the way of survival: *Stay angry at your captors. Create a family of friends. Build trust. Tell your story to the four winds.*

I, Qanilch'ey Ashana of Yaghenen, have done as the spirit directed. Inscribed on the parchment pages in Monk Kristofor's hand rests the lach'u of the nanutset of Aláyeksa.

AUTHOR'S NOTE

The questions are always asked of us, Why this story? Why did you spend years of your lives recreating this person and culture?

Our answers rest in our early beginnings. We grew up along the great rivers of the American Midwest, the rivers of the French voyageurs whose romantic songs—"Who is it cries in the mist, in the mist where the rivers run?"—meant to us not the love left far behind in France but the cry of the Native American woman abused by the European invader. As children, we know the Sioux, the Ojibwa; as adults living on the far Northwest coast we heard in Alaska the same cry from the Athabaskan. And the young woman Ashana became part of our lives, demanding a settlement of accounts, demanding a telling of the story of greed, exploitation, degradation that became the fate of America's natives from the day the European first stepped ashore in the Western Hemisphere. The story of Ashana's people is the story of Native Americans anywhere on these continents.

Challenged by that demand, we undertook extensive research focused on recreating Ashana's life and times in order to present with accuracy the factual elements of her life—food, clothing, houses, love, family, the Athabaskan law ways, the hunt, the customs, the arts, the beliefs. To do justice to the rich culture and heritage of Ashana and to set a tone that could not otherwise be achieved for the story, we used Athabaskan names and a few selected words from her ancient language—not to prove erudition but out of respect for the people.

Drawing upon the knowledge we gained and exercising the privilege of the novelist, we created fictional events and characters to flesh out Ashana's full story.

Much has been written by and about Aleksandr Baranov, manager of the Russian-American Company and Russia's Colonial Governor of Alaska, and his fur hunters and traders; and through those writings the story of the rape of Alaska comes clear. During that exploitation, navigators, traders, adventurers, and churchmen set down copious records of their lives and times in the Great Country that is Alaska. Minute details were reported, but native peoples were stripped of their names, their identities, their human essence.

Ashana was a true-to-life person almost lost to history. Baranov wrote, "I have for a long time now been keeping a girl . . ." Stripping her of her rightful name, he called her "Anna." From meager strands, we began weaving the story of a life that knew the cruel side of the occupation of Alaska in the 1790s.

Our challenge carried responsibility for establishing identities so that people might be written back into history. We named individuals according to ancient Athabaskan traditions which require that a new child be given a name related to whatever the mother first sees after the birth: thus, Qaniłch'ey Ashana, the windflower that grows wild on the Kenai peninsula . . . Shani Jabila, the summer rainbow . . . Sem, a star . . . Denedi Belik'a, the sundog of Alaska's morning sky. Ashana's father, known in history as a leader of his people, was one of the few Kenai Athabaskans identified by Baranov who labeled him with the Russian "Raskashikov." He was a man entitled to a name true to his culture, so we called him Ni'i, sun. Kotlean, the Gulushutna (Tlingit) leader, still holds a place in the hearts of northwesterners for his steadfast opposition to the encroaching "discoverers." Agagasik, Anakhta-yan, and Siga-yak are historic Ułchena (Aleut) men; and we found their names on an obscure list of hunters forced in 1792 to pay tribute in furs to the Geographic, Astronomic, and Naval secret expedition of her Imperial Majesty, Empress Catherine.

As for the Russians and others alien to Alaska, with two exceptions, they are historic personages: Aleksandr Baranov, Ivan Kuskov, High Chamberlain Nikolai Rezanov, Captain Urey Lisianskii, Lieutenant Gavriil Davydov, Midshipman Talin, Archimandrite Ioasaf, Father Herman, Agent and Mrs. Ivan Banner, Agent Larionov, Captain Podgasch, and the like. Fictional Russian characters are Maximilien Solnikov and Father Emelian. All the visiting ships' captains and personnel from countries such as the United States and England are historic. Not the least, the man from Bengal, Richard.

From our research we learned that the young woman Ashana and her people knew a good life in a closely knit society respecting the forces of the natural world. Growing up in the majesty of Alaska's mountains and seas, nurtured by caring parents, looking toward the time of raising her own family, Ashana lived in her village enjoying the pleasures of that life and meeting its demands, for the environment was as harsh at times as it was bountiful with game and fish.

Before the coming of the white man, Ashana's people took part in trade across Alaska, their way of life revealing that the crafts and creations of one clan were exchanged for those of another. From the Aleutian Islander—the Ulchena in our novel—her people learned the skills of the kayak and the sea hunt. From the Tlingit—the Gulushutna—the awe-inspiring carvings. From the Eskimo, the way to survival in the far north. In turn, the Athabaskan gave of his way of life and his creations.

The history of the evolution of the clans shows that Ashana's people believed in animistic origins; they recited no tradition of entry into Alaska across the land bridge from Asia. Long before humans walked the earth, they believed, creation began with the raven, the wolf, the eagle, the bear—and each clan rose from a particular bird or animal and was endowed with its special spirit. In order to understand the natural world around them, people heeded the voices of the spirits: spirits of the wind, the trees, the land, the mountains, the grass, the sky were reality to them. Spirits guided them to the right way of living and supported them in their deeds and thoughts or punished those who exploited nature and allowed greed to take over their lives. They knew sea spirits, for the Cook Inlet and Kenai peoples were perhaps the sole Athabaskans adapting to a marine environment.

The Athabaskan peoples two hundred years ago lived as partners with nature. The people were as one with the land, the sea, the wind, the sun, the birds, the animals. They believed that the essence of life lay in sharing the earth and its bounty, living in harmony with nature, accepting from the land and the sea only enough to provide for life. They knew that nature required care if her bounty provender were to replenish and maintain itself for all generations to come. What the Athabaskan of two hundred years ago believed and practiced, the environmentalist of today is beginning to understand.

The lore of the Athabaskan carries themes similar to that of the Christian. Immaculate conception, the revered story of the birth of Jesus who brought light to the world, had its mystical counterpart in the raven who flew over and dropped spruce needles into the maiden raven's water basket; and soon a raven was born who brought light to the four corners of the world. And the hero stories: Fearless Qishvet's deeds rival any dragon slayer in world literature.

Alien intrusion shattered the rich Athabaskan culture, and the fate of Ashana became a primary example of the destruction of an indigenous people, of a particular individual, of an environment. Ashana, taken hostage at fifteen or sixteen years of age by Aleksandr Baranov, struggled through captivity for the balance of her lifetime. She died on Kodiak Island and lies in an unknown grave.

In creating a historical novel, the facts of history must never be changed—their integrity must always be maintained. If a person lived at a particular period in history, if an event occurred at a specific point in time, if a natural phenomenon swept the land and the sea, those the writer must accept as facts. Likewise, in our novel, the belief system, the stories, the symbols, the customs are those of Ashana's people, not a single one a fictional creation by us. Ashana and her people could not be brought to life without respect for those core elements of her culture.

In pursuing our research and study to gain insight, we spent countless hours in many archives, libraries, and historical repositories throughout the country from Washington, D.C., to Berkeley, California, to Anchorage, Alaska; studied a vast range of materials; and listened at seminars and conferences in Alaska and elsewhere. As we focused our studies, there came a turning point when we gained the insight enabling us to write Ashana's story.

We had marshalled the facts. We knew the parameters of the events that took place, the characteristics of the people, the motivations for their actions. But those facts lacked essence, essence we found only in the oral history recited from generation to generation by the Alaskan storytellers. "The man without a story is a man without a head." And residing in that oral history are the beliefs that guided and sustained the people, the vital forces that were their souls.

Ashana and the many other Alaskan captives of the Russian traders and hunters suffered their hostage fate for entire lifetimes. To gain insight into that awesome experience, we made in-depth study of the hostage accounts of Holocaust victims. We interviewed prisoners of war and internees. In our own experience, we knew intimately a person who had suffered long-term incarceration in a wartime prison camp. Coming to grips with those harrowing experiences opened the door to a glimpse of the way of hostage survival, the struggle that was Ashana's most of her adult life.

We believed that as long as one human being holds another in bondage—whatever the form or degree—within that dimension every human being suffers loss of freedom and of the dispensation of justice, and society is the less. The words of Ashana—her *lach'u*, her truth—are replete with warnings of the dangers that enslave, humiliate, and destroy.

E. P. Roesch
Washington State
July 12, 1991

❋ ❋ ❋

FOR FURTHER READING

In writing *Ashana*, the authors consulted a broad range of source materials—books, documents, maps. Some are difficult to locate. From those most accessible, the following are recommended to readers everywhere.

Collins, Henry B., Frederica de Laguna, Edmund Carpenter, and Peter Stone. *The Far North: 2000 Years of American Eskimo and Indian Art.* Bloomington, Indiana: Indiana University Press, 1977.

Davydov, Gavriil Ivanovich. *Two Voyages to Russian America, 1802-1807.* Translated by Colin Bearne. Edited by Richard A. Pierce. Kingston, Ontario: Limestone Press, 1977.

Documents on the History of the Russian-American Company. Translated by Marina Ramsay. Edited by Richard A. Pierce. Translated from the Russian edition of 1957. Materials for Study of Alaska History, No. 7. Kingston, Ontario: Limestone Press, 1976.

Kalifornsky, Peter. *Kahtnuht'ana Qenaga: The Kenai People's Language.* [Tanaina Athabaskan]. Edited by James Kari. Photographs courtesy of Mary Nissen. Fairbanks, Alaska: Alaska Native Language Center, University of Alaska, 1977.

Kari, James. *Dena'ina Noun Dictionary.* Fairbanks, Alaska: Alaska Native Language Center, University of Alaska, 1977. First printing.

Kari, James, and Priscilla Russell Kari. *Dena'ina Elhena = Tanaina Country.* Fairbanks, Alaska: Alaska Native Language Center, University of Alaska. First printing 1982.

Khlebnikov, Kyrill. *Colonial Russian America: Kyrill T. Khlebnikov's Reports, 1817-1832.* Translated with introduction and notes by Basil Dmytryshyn and E. A. P. Crownhart-Vaughan. Portland, Oregon: Oregon Historical Society, 1976.

Lisiansky, Urey. *A Voyage Round the World, in the Years 1803, 4, 5, & 6 . . . in the ship Neva.* London: Printed for John Booth and Others, 1814. Amsterdam: N. Israel; New York: Da Capo Press, 1968.

Osgood, Cornelius. *The Ethnography of the Tanaina.* New Haven: Yale

University Press, 1937. New Haven: Human Relations Area Files, 1976; reprinted from the 1937 edition.

Shem Pete's Alaska: The Territory of the Upper Cook Inlet Dena'ina. Compiled and edited by James Kari and James A. Fall. Principal contributor, Shem Pete. Fairbanks, Alaska: Alaska Native Language Center, University of Alaska, The CIRI Foundation, 1987.

Siebert, Erna, and Werner Forman. *North Anerican Indian Art: Masks, Amulets, Wood Carvings, and Ceremonial Dress from the North-West Coast.* London: Paul Hamlyn, 1967.

Tenenbaum, Joan M., editor, translator, transcriber. [Tanaina Stories] *Dena'ina Sukdu'a.* Volume I, stories called *sukdu.* Volume II, raven stories. Volume III, mountain stories. Volume IV, wars they had before our time. Fairbanks, Alaska: Alaska Native Language Center, University of Alaska, 1976.

Tikhmenev, Petr Aleksandrovich. *A History of the Russian-American Company,* Volume 2: Documents. Translated and edited by Richard A. Pierce and Alton S. Donnelly. A classic account. Translated from the Russian edition of 1861–1863 published in St. Petersburg in two volumes. (Volume One is a publication of the University of Washington Press, Seattle, Washington, 1978). Materials for Study of Alaska History, No. 13. Kingston, Ontario: Limestone Press, 1979.

Tillion, Germaine. *Ravensbrück.* Translation by Gerald Satterwhite from *Editions du Seuil,* Paris, France. New York: Doubleday, 1975.

VanStone, James W. *Athapaskan Adaptations: Hunters and Fishermen of the Subarctic Forests.* Chicago: Aldine Publishing, 1974.

About the Authors

"E. P. ROESCH" is the husband-and-wife team of Ethel and Paul Roesch; they live in Washington State and travel widely. Ethel Roesch was formerly a teacher and YWCA director and has published short stories and articles. Paul Roesch is a lawyer and poet. They are both active in the field of human rights. The Roesches are currently working on a new historical novel.